知 識 無 疆 界

英文商業書信&電子郵件寫作技巧與範例

Model Business
Letters, E-mails &
Other Business Documents
6th Edition

雪麗·泰勒（Shirley Taylor）**著**　　劉秋枝、羅明珠 **譯**

PEARSON

Longman 朗文

雪麗・泰勒（Shirley Taylor）是許多暢銷書的作者。她的第一本書 *Communication for Business* 於 1991 年出版，現已是第三版，廣被全球各地的學院所採用。自那時起，雪麗寫了許多成功的作品，除本書外，還包括 *Essential Communication Skills, Pocket Business Communicator, The Secretary in Training, Guide to Effective E-mail.* 等。

雪麗在英國受過專業教師訓練，1983 年在新加坡謀得第一份教職，並擔任多年的教育訓練顧問及祕書暨商業課程講師，也先後在巴林、英國及加拿大做過系主任及資深講師。

雪麗現居新加坡，成立了 Shirley Taylor 訓練顧問公司，爲自己的事業而努力。她喜歡在亞洲各處親自規畫教育訓練課程、研討會及講座，也經常應邀出席國際性會議發表演說。讀者可在其發行的電子報 *Shirley Says* 上找到風格新穎的商業寫作、小祕訣，以及各式提問。歡迎到雪麗個人網頁 www.shirleytaylor.com，在登入欄鍵入姓名後，即可成爲電子報的會員。

請利用以下網址聯絡雪麗： shirley@shirleytaylor.com

作者序

'With reference to your letter'（關於您的來信）
'Enclosed herewith please find'（隨函附上）
'I am writing to inform you'（我寫信通知您）
'Please be advised'（在此通知您）

你還在用上述制式、無趣的陳腔濫調來寫信或電子郵件嗎？身處今日變化迅速、重視有效溝通的商業社會，乏味呆板、拘泥俗套的遣詞用字，只會讓你的書信變得累贅又欠缺個人特色。無奈辦公室內仍不乏陶醉於這類冗長贅言的寫信者，一再重複 'We have received your letter', 'Kindly be advised', 'Please find enclosed herewith' 等曾祖父時代留下的老掉牙措詞。在一分鐘可以敲擊電腦兩千次的商業社會中使用如此迂迴的語言，根本就是悖離現實！

我們應該做的是隨著科技的發展，不斷學習最新的設備與軟體。遇有普及且好用的版本，要趕快學會，有新的科技產品也要適時引進。與科技發展一致，商業交易模式在過去幾十年來已有很大的改變，不再那麼講究繁文縟節，大家開會或參與研討會，使用的是自然、輕鬆的語言。但反觀商業書信寫作，仍有許多人沿用適合古早時期更甚於 21 世紀商業潮流的文體。

現在寫信的頻率似乎比以前更高，大部分的經理人擁有專屬的書面溝通範本，包括信件、備忘錄、傳真、報告、文章、行銷素材，尤其是電子郵件。在這全球化的時代，速度常是談判、協商成功的關鍵，人人都應該具備有效的書信溝通能力。

電子郵件讓我們能夠用最少的努力達到最大的溝通效果。以前，文字是傳遞想法的符號；現在，文字已逐漸被符號所取代如： ;-)。儘管如此，還是經常可以見到違反這股狂潮及高效率的奇怪現象。有人無視於電子郵件的成長以及電子郵件用語，對類似下面的傳統寫作「情有獨鍾」：

'As spoken in our telecom...'（如同我們在電話中所言……）、'Please revert to me on this matter...'（請向我重提這件事……）、'Kindly furnish us with this information...'（敬請提供我們這項資訊……）、'The above-mentioned goods...'（以上所提及的商品……）、'at your soonest convenience...'（以您最方便的時間……）、'for your reference and perusal'（作為您的參考資料）……。

這類拖泥帶水的措詞只會模糊真正的意思，讀信者常被迫要在一堆修辭中摸索寫信者真正的意思。

現在不是1903年！人們講求的是思考的速度。如果你仍堅持使用這些老舊標準的無趣用語來撰寫書信，既不能幫自己，也對公司無所助益，甚至給讀信者帶來負擔。現在就把這些陳腔濫調丟進垃圾桶！

在《英文商業書信&電子郵件寫作技巧與範例》（*Model Business Letters, E-mails & Other Business Documents*）一書中，你看不到保守、乏味、老掉牙的寫作風格。這本資料豐富的參考書收錄了現代商業書信寫作的範例、有用的指導方針、提示與技巧，能幫助你做更有效的溝通。

有效的溝通可為你及公司塑造專業形象，讓事情順利推展。其中，高效率的書寫技巧也許是我們最想學習的。訊息要能有效傳遞並獲致預期結果，書寫時必須結合想像力、創造力、組織力、企畫力等諸多要素。瞬息萬變的商業社會沒有多餘空間容納過時、冗長的用語。

今日的商業語言要求的是主動、正面、激勵、有趣，且多半要能反映個性。與其重彈過去數十年以來的老調，不如使用像談話一般自然的寫作風格。請記住本書一再提及的溝通黃金準則：如果你不會這樣說，就不要這樣寫。

拜網際網路之賜，我們得以便利地與全球人士溝通。而唯一能引起對方反應的方法，當然是引人入勝的內容。希望這本書能夠幫助你在書信寫作上更上層樓。

雪麗・泰勒（*Shirley Taylor*）

目 錄

Unit 2　例行性商業文件
（Routine business documents）　　85

Unit 4　分類商業書信
（**Classified business letters**）　429

引 言

本書是為有以下需求的讀者而撰寫的：

◆ 想拋開老掉牙的英文書面溝通方式，不再使用Please be advised ...（在此通知您……）、for your reference and perusal ...（作為您的參考資料……）、I would like to inform you ...（我想要通知您……）等俗套措詞。

◆ 讓讀信的人對你及公司留下良好印象。

◆ 學習如口語般順暢、自然的寫作風格，並呈現積極、正面與風趣的一面。

◆ 展現個人風格，而不是沿襲曾祖父時代的陳腔濫調。

本書就像一間可以一次購足的商業溝通專賣店，不只提供你撰寫各類書信的指南，還列舉許多實用的範例，對於寫出一封清楚又具說服力的書信有著極高的參考價值。

適讀對象

本書對很多人都十分實用，包括：

◆ 經常撰寫書信的主管與經理們。很多經理在他們的電腦中建立一些隨時可啟用的文件，每次使用時只需複製並做些適當的修改，就能將訊息傳遞出去。如此一來，不但省去費心思索該如何下筆及編排的時間，又能把工作做得更好，更有效率。

◆ 海外使用者。本書的前幾個版本廣泛銷及印度、印尼、馬來西亞、馬爾地夫、新加坡、斯里蘭卡、香港、哈洛加特、上海、雪菲爾、多倫多以及泰國等地。海外使用者對這本包羅萬象的參考書給予高度的評價。在運用現代商業語言的國際貿易上，尤其有用。

◆ 學生及老師。在商業、專業領域、祕書或行政等課程中，學生經常需要撰寫商業書信或其他商業文件。書中的指導方針、理論、文件範例、四點計畫，以及檢查清單等，在訓練書面溝通效率上特別有用。

本書編排

本書已依主題做好編排，讀者們可直接跳到感興趣的部分閱讀。在遇到留白時，可稍做沉澱，或許能找到一些開始的靈感或完成工作的提示。

全書包含四大單元、三十章，概述如下：

◆ 第一單元的「書面溝通概論」是必讀部分。主要是探討商業文件呈現格式的重要性，包括「完全齊頭式的版面設計及開放式標點」（一種已有三十多年歷史的現代標點形式）的編排方式。同時也歸納用來組織訊息的「四點計畫」、「使用電子郵件的七大原罪」、「寫好商業書信的十個步驟」，以及「檢查清單」等，目的在教導讀者撰寫符合時代潮流的有效書面溝通。最後是本版新增的「使用電子郵件的十個需改善項目」、「如何讓電子郵件成為工作利器？」，以及「網路禮節」等實用資訊。

◆ 第二單元的「例行性商業文件」，內容包含：詢問、報價、估價、下訂、開立發票、請求付款、商業徵信等的寫作規則及範本，每則都是以標準的商業交易寫成。

◆ 第三單元的「富創造力與說服力的文件」，有鑑於現代的書面溝通十分著重創造力與想像力，因而收錄了許多前面幾個版本沒有的新題材，像是需要特殊寫作技巧的抱怨信、報告、通知函、廣告、促銷信、新聞稿、營運計畫書、求職信、推薦函、預訂機票與飯店的信函等。

◆ 第四單元的「分類商業書信」，內容包含會議記錄、人事、祕書及行政類的書信，以及國際貿易與銀行業務等。

光碟內容

為了讓學習效果放到最大，我們將所有商業書信範例的中譯，編成電子書。建議先閱讀英文範例，遇有不懂處再翻閱電子書查詢。各冊的書信右上角均標有中英文互相參照的頁碼，以利讀者使用。

本書特色

◆ 在介紹每一類書信、文件的同時，會搭配範例做說明，並提示重點。
◆ 每一章均包含完整的說明、討論，以及與各種文件的相關解說。
◆ 全書信件範例都以色塊與內文做區隔，並適時於邊欄加註說明，以指出信件的重要特徵。
◆ 「四點計畫」幫助你有效地規畫及組織足以反映個人特色的溝通訊息。
◆ 特殊專有名詞或用語的定義置於相關頁面下方的註腳處。

書中另設計了以下代表不同意思的標記：

 提示：可有效促進溝通的小祕訣。

 實用網站：挑選一些特別有用的網站。

 檢查清單：附於每章的最後，以提醒讀者牢記重點。

 錯誤用法：指粗劣的商業書信範例。

 正確用法：緊接在「錯誤用法」之後，以說明應當如何做修正。

我希望這本在版面、架構、遣詞用字及語氣上都具備優秀品質的實用工具書能夠協助你適當及有效地傳遞訊息。請牢記，這樣做不只可以幫助你建立及提升公司的企業形象，且能賦予你個人更高的價值，在職場上扮演重要角色。

你會購買本書，表示有心要學習更多現代商業書信的寫作技巧。本書擁有完整的建議及實用的指導方針，並收錄數百篇書信範例，定能協助你發展出一套高效率的書面溝通技巧。

祝好運！

請注意：為了內容的一致性及避免混淆，本書一律使用以 **-ise** 結尾的英式拼法，有別於以 **-ize** 結尾的相對應美式拼法。另外，單引號、 **Mr/Mrs** 的縮寫，以及日期標示也都採英式英語的用法。

Unit 1

書面溝通概論
Written communication — an overview

儘管現代溝通的方式日趨多樣化，但傳統的商業書信在訊息傳遞上仍具有舉足輕重的地位。商業書信就像企業大使，能讓外界留下良好的第一印象是相當重要的。針對這一點，企業有必要確認其所使用的信紙在紙張和印刷上具備良好品質。此外，商業書信也傳遞出一個企業的文化，茲概述如下。

外觀、結構、語言和語氣

科技的發展使我們得以與全球人士進行即時溝通，速度於是成為今日商業能否成功的關鍵，書信因而逐漸被速度較快的傳真和電子郵件所取代。公司內部常用的備忘錄也因電子郵件而日漸式微，儘管有些公司還是喜歡用備忘錄。但不管如何，本單元將就所有的書面溝通做探討。

不論你的溝通工具是信件、傳真、電子郵件或備忘錄，都必須在外觀、結構，以及語言和語氣這三點上樹立一個高標準，請牢記「第一印象」的重要性，而優質的書面溝通正可以塑造與提升公司的企業形象。

現在有愈來愈多的雇主，不再由祕書代勞，而是自己鍵入書信內容並直接傳送給對方。雖然這麼做從時間與效率上來說是合理的，可

是讓祕書再做個整理，會是更妥當的做法。老闆也許是某個領域的專家，但祕書在版面編排及結構上通常更勝一籌。

身處競爭激烈的商業世界，高規格的書面溝通是必要的，我們非但不能為了速度而降低溝通品質，反而還要善用不斷進步的科技來改善與提升溝通效率，並將商業潛力發揮到極致。

本單元將針對版面呈現、結構、語言和語氣這三方面，逐一就書信、傳真、備忘錄及電子郵件進行深入剖析。

 優秀的寫作技巧如同其他的努力，下的功夫愈深，收穫愈大。

商業文件的版面呈現
Presentation of business documents

印製好的信紙

如果要給人良好印象，商業文件的版面呈現必須既引人注意，又有一致性，這點很重要。

事先印製好的公司信紙（通常配有信封）必須具備一定的品質，尤其是用來寄給外部人士的書信更是馬虎不得，至於公司內部使用的則不需要如此講究。

企業用的信紙象徵公司的門面，在信頭上會顯示以下資訊：

◆ 代表公司的標誌或圖案。
◆ 公司名稱。
◆ 完整的郵寄地址。
◆ 聯絡方式：電話、傳眞、電子郵件。
◆ 公司的網站。
◆ 註冊編號或註冊辦事處。當註冊辦事處和信頭上的辦公處不同地點時，通常會將註冊辦事處連同註冊編號印在信紙的底部。

公司一般會請專家設計信頭，尤其是醒目的企業識別商標。

底下是兩個信頭的範例。

【範例 1】

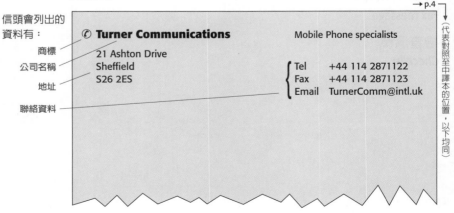

信頭會列出的
資料有：

商標
公司名稱
地址

聯絡資料

Turner Communications　　Mobile Phone specialists

21 Ashton Drive
Sheffield
S26 2ES

Tel　　+44 114 2871122
Fax　　+44 114 2871123
Email　TurnerComm@intl.uk

→ p.4

（代表對照至中譯本的位置，以下均同）

【範例 2】

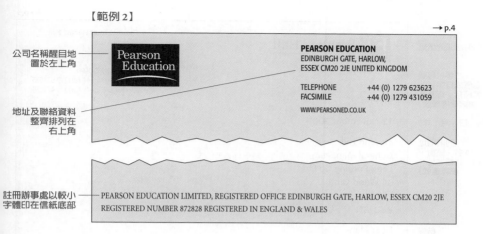

公司名稱醒目地
置於左上角

地址及聯絡資料
整齊排列在
右上角

註冊辦事處以較小
字體印在信紙底部

→ p.4

完全齊頭式搭配開放式標點

完全齊頭式（fully blocked style，一律向左對齊）爲現行商業文件中使用最廣泛的編排方式，它省去了每一個新起段落或信尾的結束區塊首行縮排的打字時間，被視爲較具商業風格。

常與完全齊頭式搭配使用的是開放式標點（open punctuation），它將所有非必要的句點和逗點均加以省略，同樣可以減少打字的時間。

完全齊頭式雖然被許多機構採用，但有些機構仍舊有自己偏好的編排方式。不論你使用的是哪一種，最重要的原則是「一致性」，也就是確保所有的文件都以相同的格式呈現。

本書收錄的所有範例均採用完全齊頭式，再搭配開放式標點，且信文的每個段落之間均間隔一行。

 中國人會說，好的外觀就是好的風水。

→ p.5

印有信頭的信紙 —

FT Prentice Hall
FINANCIAL TIMES

Financial Times Prentice Hall
Edinburgh Gate
Harlow, Essex
CM20 2JE
UNITED KINGDOM
Telephone:　+44 (0)1279 623623
Facsimile:　+44 (0)1279 431059

參考編號
（寫信或打字者的
姓名縮寫，有時是
檔案參考編號）

ST/PJ

日期（日、月、年） — 12 November 200—

封內地址
（姓名、頭銜、
公司、詳細地址、
郵遞區號）

Mr Alan Hill
General Manager
Long Printing Co Ltd
34 Wood Lane
London
WC1 8TJ

稱呼 — Dear Alan

標題
（快速掌握主旨）

FULLY BLOCKED LETTER LAYOUT

This layout has become firmly established as the most popular way of setting out letters, fax messages, memos, reports – in fact all business communications. The main feature of fully blocked style is that all lines begin at the left-hand margin.

正文
（段落之間空一行）

Open punctuation is usually used with the fully blocked layout. This means that no punctuation marks are necessary in the reference, date, inside address, salutation and closing section. Of course essential punctuation must still be used in the text of the message itself. However, remember to use commas minimally today; they should be used only when their omission would make the sense of the message unclear.

Consistency is important in layout and spacing of all documents. It is usual to leave just one clear line space between each section.

I enclose some other examples of fully blocked layout as used in fax messages and memoranda.

Most people agree that this layout is very attractive and easy to produce as well as businesslike.

結尾敬辭 — Yours sincerely

Shirley Taylor

寄件人姓名 — SHIRLEY TAYLOR (Miss)
寄件人職稱或部門 — Training Specialist

附件 — Enc

副本
（兩人以上依英文
字母順序排列）

Copy　Pradeep Jethi, Publisher
　　　Amelia Lakin, Acquisitions Executive

續頁的處理

有些公司備有印上「續頁」字樣的信紙（continuation sheet），作爲書信的第二頁或之後的頁面使用。這些續頁的紙張上通常只印有公司的名稱和商標，如果手邊沒有這類信紙，就得自行在品質相近的空白紙張鍵入信頭資料。

當書信內容超過兩張信紙，必須在第二張及之後的信紙上方標註如下的固定細節，以防萬一書信的第一頁與後面的頁面分開時作爲辨識之用：

◆ 頁碼。
◆ 日期。
◆ 收件人姓名。

有必要續頁時，要牢記以下原則：

◆ 不必在首頁的底部說明內容尙未結束，因爲沒有結尾段落或簽名，就表示還有下一頁。
◆ 續頁中的內容必須包含至少三至四行文字，以及平常的結尾段落。
◆ 不要留下段落的第一行在前一頁的頁尾，而前頁最後一段文字也不要掉一行到次頁，新的頁面儘量保持爲新起段落。

→ p.6

這是該公司的
續頁信紙

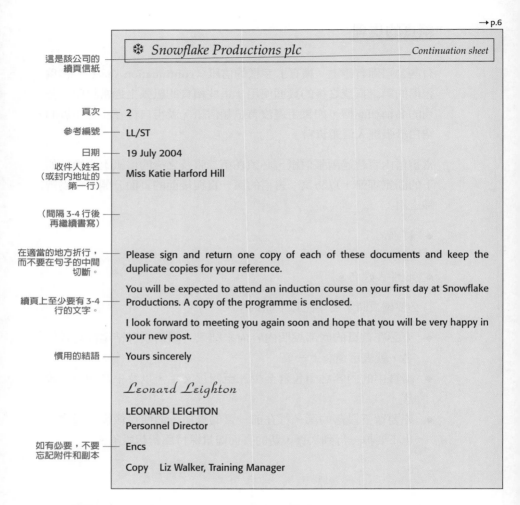

❋ *Snowflake Productions plc*　　　　　　　　　_Continuation sheet_

頁次 —— 2

參考編號 —— LL/ST

日期 —— 19 July 2004

收件人姓名
（或封內地址的
第一行） —— Miss Katie Harford Hill

（間隔 3-4 行後
再繼續書寫）

在適當的地方折行，
而不要在句子的中間
切斷。 —— Please sign and return one copy of each of these documents and keep the duplicate copies for your reference.

續頁上至少要有 3-4
行的文字。 —— You will be expected to attend an induction course on your first day at Snowflake Productions. A copy of the programme is enclosed.

I look forward to meeting you again soon and hope that you will be very happy in your new post.

慣用的結語 —— Yours sincerely

Leonard Leighton

LEONARD LEIGHTON
Personnel Director

如有必要，不要
忘記附件和副本 —— Encs

Copy　Liz Walker, Training Manager

 提示　你不需要畫出一條簽名用的線，那是給五歲小孩用的。

商業書信的組成要素

1.1 參考編號（Reference）

過去的信頭習慣印上 Our ref 或 Your ref 的字樣。但現在的文書處理機和印表機較難在這種印製好的信紙上去對齊，所以這種作法已經不多見了，多半改由打字者自行插入一行參考編號，如寫信人姓名（通常全部用大寫）及打字員姓名（可全部大寫或小寫）的縮寫，或是再加上檔案編號或部門代號等。

【範例】

GBD/ST　　　　　GBD/st/Per1　　　　GBD/ST/134

1.2 日期（Date）

日期應完整書寫。在英國，習慣使用「日／月／年」的順序，且不必加逗點。

【範例】

12 July 2004

有些國家習慣以「月／日／年」的順序來表示日期，而且會在年份之前加上逗號。

【範例】

July 12, 2004

1.3 封內地址（Inside address）

封內地址是指列於信封上的收件人的地址。收件人的姓名和地址必須分行排列，就跟信封上的姓名和地址一樣，且特別留意必須和收件人在文件上的簽名同款，例如，若收件人簽的是 Douglas Cowles，那麼信封和信紙上就必須用 Douglas Cowles，並且在前面加上 Mr 的尊稱。寫成 Mr D Cowles（用縮寫）是不適當的。

【範例】

Mr Dougles Cowles
General Manager
Cowles Engineering Co Ltd
12 Bracken Hill
Manchester
M60 8AS

寄至國外的信函，國家名稱要列在地址欄的最後一行。如寄航空，則在封內地址（inside address，即置於信紙上的收件人地址）上方空一行後加註 AIRMAIL。同時別忘了加上適當的尊稱，例如 Mr/Mrs/Miss/Ms（先生／太太／小姐／女士）等。

【範例】

AIRMAIL

Mr Doug Allen
Eagle Press Inc
24 South Bank
Toronto
Ontario
Canada M4J 7LK

1.4 特殊標記（Special markings）

如果是機密文件，通常會在封內地址欄上方空出一行，寫上全部大寫的 CONFIDENTIAL（機密）或是以開頭字母大寫再加底線的方式註明。

【範例】

CONFIDENTIAL

Miss Iria Tan
Personnel Director
Soft Toys plc
21 Windsor Road
Birmingham
B2 5JT

幾十年前，寄件者為了確保該信件能送達某位人士桌上，會加上一行提示句（attention line），即使信上寫著公司地址，而且以「敬啓者」為開頭。

【範例】

FOR THE ATTENTION OF MR JOHN TAYLER, SALES MANAGER
業務部經理，約翰・泰勒先生親啓

Garden Supplies Ltd
24 Amber Street
Sheffield
S44 9DJ
Dear Sirs

現今的商業書信，很少使用這種提示句。當你知道收件人的姓名時，就把它列在信紙的封內地址欄上，並使用個人化的稱呼。

1.5　稱呼（Salutation）

如果收件人的姓名已經列在封內地址欄中，接下來通常會使用個人化的稱呼。

【範例】

Dear Mr Leighton　Dear Douglas　Dear Miss Tan　Dear Rosehannah

如果收件人是公司行號，而不是特定人士，應該使用較正式的稱呼，如底下的範例。

【範例】

Dear Sirs

如果收件人為部門或公司的主管，且不知道對方姓名時，可採用以下表達方式：

【範例】

Dear Sir or Madam

1.6　標題（Heading）

標題（或主旨）的目的在於簡短說明信件的內容，常置於稱呼下方間隔一行處。雖然可使用開頭字母大寫加底線的方式，但通常用全部大寫來表示。

【範例】

Dear Mrs Marshall

INTERNATIONAL CONFERENCE — 24 AUGUST 2003
（2003 年 8 月 24 日國際研討會）

1.7　結尾敬辭（Complimentary close）

在結束正文時，會習慣性地禮貌問候，而最常見的兩種結尾敬辭是 Yours faithfully（謹啓、敬啓，只用在稱呼爲 Dear Sir/Sirs 或 Madam 時）及 Yours sincerely（敬上、眞誠地，在知道收件人是誰時使用）。

【範例】

1.8　寄件人姓名及頭銜（Name of sender and designation）

在結尾敬辭下方應該空出四至五行作爲簽名之用。寄件人的姓名可以全部大寫，或者是只有開頭字母大寫，頭銜則直接置於姓名下方。下列範例中，讀者可以注意到如果寫信的人是男性，則不必寫上 Mr。如果是女性，通常會在名字旁邊用括弧來加註 Mrs 等。

【範例】

Yours faithfully　　　　　　　　　　Yours sincerely

PATRICK ASHE　　　　　　　　　　LESLEY BOLAN (Mrs)
Chairman　　　　　　　　　　　　　General Manager

如果是代替寄件人簽名，通常會在寄件人姓名前方寫上 for 或 pp，
其中的 pp 為「委任、授權」之意，是 per procurationem 的縮寫。

【範例】

Yours faithfully

Shirley Johnson

for EDWARD NATHAN
Chairman

1.9　附件（Enclosures）

要說明資料是隨函寄出的方式有很多種：

◆　在信件左下角貼上印有 enclosure 字樣的有色標籤。

◆　在信件正文提到附件的該行文字左邊，鍵入三個小點。

◆　最常使用的方式是在寄件人頭銜下方間隔一行處鍵入 Enc 或
　　Encs。

【範例】

Yours sincerely

LINDA PATERSON (Mrs)
Marketing Manager

Enc

1.10　副本（Copies）

如果信件副本必須交付第三者（通常是寄件人公司的某位人士），可
以鍵入 cc 或 Copy 的字樣，之後加上副本收件人的姓名和頭銜。如
果同一封信的副本收件人超過兩位，通常按姓的字母順序排列。

【範例】

> Copy　Ravi Gopal, General Manager
> Ashley Ow Yong, Company Secretary
> Candice Reeves, Accountant

如果不希望收件人知道有第三者收到副本，可以使用 bcc（blind courtesy copy，密件副本）。bcc 不能出現在信件的上方，只有要歸檔的文件副本與密件副本才有。

【範例】

> bcc　　Mr Gordon Clark, Chief Executive

 不要將副本寄給所有人，只寄給需要知道的人。

開放式標點

通常，開放式標點是用在完全齊頭式的書信中。正文內只有為確保合乎文法的基本標點。除此之外，所有的逗點及句點都省略掉，尤其是在日期、封內地址欄等。

 逗點的使用規則現在已少了很多。

1.11　日期（Dates）

使用	不使用
25 September 2005	25th September, 2005
14 July 2004	July 14th, 2004

1.12　姓名及地址（Names and addresses）

> Mr G P Ashe → 不必用句點
> Chief Executiue
> Ashe Publications Pte Ltd → 文字列最後不加逗點
> #03-45 Ashe Towers
> 212 Holland Avenue
> Singapore 2535

1.13　稱呼（Salutation）

Dear Patrick→ 不加逗點

1.14　結尾敬辭（Complimentary close）

Yours sincerely → 不加逗點

1.15　縮寫（Abbreviations）

使用		不使用	
Mr	eg	Mr.	e.g.
Dr	ie	Dr.	i.e.
BA	pm	B.A.	p.m.
IBM	am	I.B.M.	a.m.
MRT		M.R.T.	
NB		N.B.	
PS		P.S.	

1.16　時間和數字（Time and numbers）

使用		不使用	
9.30 am		9.30 a.m.	
0950		09.50 am	
1400		14:00	
1	8	1.	8)
2	9	2.	9)
3	10	3.	10)

 提示　使用開放式標點，並移除雜亂無章的文字。

備忘錄

備忘錄（memos or memoranda）是用來將訊息傳達給同公司的一位或多位人士。備忘錄有幾個使用目的：

◆ 提供資訊。
◆ 詢問資訊。
◆ 告知行動或決定。
◆ 要求行動或決定。

有些公司會事先印製備忘錄用紙供員工使用，但常見的情況是將範本儲存於電腦中，要用時只需在印好的標題旁輸入相關細節即可。

1.17 格式 (Format)

以下範例是一種簡單、清楚的公司內部備忘錄格式。

→ p.7

強調是「備忘錄」

收件人姓名及頭銜

寄件人姓名及頭銜

參考編號（寄件人／打字者的姓名縮寫）

日期

不必加稱呼

標題（清楚陳述訊息主旨）

備忘錄正文必須分段，並且導引出切題的結論與結尾

不必加結尾敬辭

留空間來簽名（寄件人姓名及頭銜已標示在上方，此處不必重複細節）

附件（如果需要）

副本（如果需要）

MEMORANDUM

To   Christine Winters, Administrative Assistant

From   Sally Yap, PA to Chairman

Ref   SY/JJ

Date   14 August 200—

INHOUSE DOCUMENT FORMATS

Many congratulations on recently joining the staff in the Chairman's office. I hope you will be very happy here.

I am enclosing a booklet explaining the company's general rules regarding document formats. However, I thought it would be helpful if I summarised the rules for ease of reference.

1   DOCUMENT FORMATS

All documents should be presented in the fully blocked format using open punctuation. Specimen letters, fax messages, memoranda and other documents are included in the booklet. These examples should guide you in our requirements.

2   SIGNATURE BLOCK (LETTERS)

In outgoing letters it is usual practice to display the sender's name in capitals and the title directly underneath in lower case with initial capitals.

3   NUMBERED ITEMS

In reports and other documents it is often necessary to number items. In such cases the numbers should be displayed alone with no full stops or brackets. Subsequent numbering should be decimal, ie 3.1, 3.2, etc.

I hope these guidelines will be useful and that you will study the layouts shown in your booklet. If you have any questions please do not hesitate to ask me.

Sally Yap

Enc

Copy   Personnel Department

 提示　將所有的信件書寫都設定一個高標準。一般來說，高水準的信件可激發出高品質的商業交易。

傳真

對任何企業而言，傳真機是一種花費不高的基本配備。傳真的訊息可以在同一家公司的分行間傳遞，或者是對外溝通。事實上現在許多透過信件所做的溝通也可改用傳真方式。本書收錄的書信範例就可以應用在傳真或電子郵件上。

1.18 印製好的表格或範本

許多公司將傳真的格式標準化，事先印好或存於電腦中，使用者只需輸入相關資訊。以下是傳真表格的範例。

→ p.8

Fax

To	From	
Company	Date	
Fax No	No of Pages	(including this page)

1.19 完全齊頭式

如果沒有事先印製好的表格，也可以使用完全齊頭式來編排傳真的
內容，如下例所示。

→ p.9

信頭 —

© **Turner Communications**　　　Mobile Phone specialists

21 Ashton Drive
Sheffield
S26 2ES

Tel　　+44 114 2871122
Fax　　+44 114 2871123
Email　TurnerComm@intl.uk

包含『傳真』字樣
的主標頭 —

FAX MESSAGE

這些標頭很重要，
所有的基本細節
均並列呈現 —

To	Susan Gingell, General Manager
Company	Asia Communication (Singapore) Pte Ltd
Fax Number	65 6767677
From	Low Chwee Leong, Managing Director
Ref	LCL/DA
Date	6 June 200—

請註明傳真的頁數
這點很重要 —

Number of Pages
(including this page)　1

如果需要，
可以加入稱呼 —

標題應該陳述傳真
內容的主旨 —

VISIT TO SINGAPORE

Thank you for calling this morning regarding my trip to Singapore next month. I am very grateful to you for offering to meet me at the airport and drive me to my hotel.

傳真的正文應該
和商業書信相似 —

I will be arriving on flight SQ101 on Monday 8 July at 1830 hours. Accommodation has been arranged for me at the Supreme International Hotel, Scotts Road.

I will be travelling up to Kuala Lumpur on Sunday 14 July on MH989 which departs from Singapore Changi Airport Terminal 2 at 1545 hours.

不需要結尾敬辭 —

I look forward to meeting you.

Low Chwee Leong

提示　傳真或信件寫得好不好，會被拿來做評估——所以請用心學習。

檢查清單

☐ 為公司的信紙設計一個富吸引力的信頭，並放上獨特的商標。

☐ 所有的商業文件都使用統一的格式，其中完全齊頭式搭配開放式標點的編排是最常見的。

☐ 文件的段落之間要間隔一行，維持一致性。

☐ 地址欄要包含寄件人的姓名及頭銜，但不需要加上「提示句」。

☐ 如果有適當的標題，就加上去。如果沒有，可空下來。

☐ 若有隨函附件，記得要指出，可於信尾加註 Enc 來表示。

☐ 要傳副本給其他人時，用 Copy 或 cc 來表示。

☐ 當信件、備忘錄或傳真的內容延續到第二頁時，不必在第一頁的底部輸入任何說明文字。

☐ 在續頁的頂端註明頁次、日期和收件人的姓名（完全齊頭式，即靠左對齊）。

☐ 你寄發的商業文件代表著你與公司的形象，務必要確保能讓他人留下好印象。

組織你的訊息
Structuring your communications

四點計畫
4 point plan

檢查清單
Checklist

不論是撰寫商業書信、傳眞、備忘錄或電子郵件，組織、架構訊息的基本原則都是相同的。一篇結構完善，並使用適當商業語言的訊息，正是有效溝通的核心。本單元將協助讀者們建立這方面的技巧，以達成既定目標。

四點計畫

許多函件都是例行且簡短的，不必特別構思或準備就能下筆寫成或口述出來。但對於不是那麼例行性的文件，就需要更多的思考與謹愼的規畫。我第一次提出「四點計畫」是在《商業溝通》（*Communication for Business*）這本書中，這「四點計畫」如下圖所示，提供了簡單卻實用的訊息組織準則：

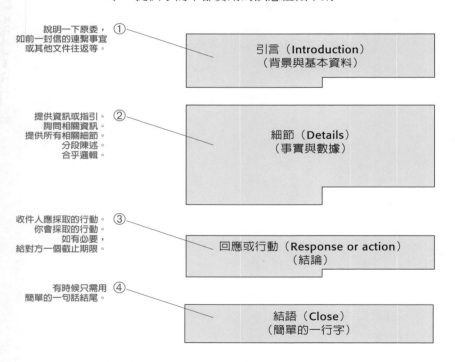

接著，讓我們更深入地探討這「四點計畫」。

1. 開場或引言

首段是闡述此次溝通的理由，基本上是在敘述背景。內容可以是：

◆　告知收到先前的書信。
◆　提及某次的會面或聯繫事宜。
◆　簡介欲討論的事項。

【範例】

> Thank you for your letter of ...
> 謝謝您……的信
>
> It was good to meet you again at last week's conference.
> 非常高興能夠在上週的研討會再次與您見面。
>
> We wish to hold our annual conference at a London hotel In September.
> 我們希望於九月份在倫敦的飯店舉行年度研討會。

 提示　若以 **Further to your letter of...** 開頭，其後面的說法將會是：

> Further to your letter of 12 July, I am sorry for the delay in attending to this matter.
> 關於您 7 月 12 日的來信，我很抱歉沒有即時注意到此事。

2. 中間段落（細節）

此部分所提供的不是收件人必須知道的所有資訊，就是你要求對方提供的資訊，或是以上兩者都是。細節的陳述一樣要簡潔，並分段說明。另外，必須合乎邏輯，自然導出結論。

3. 結論（行動或回應）

此部分是將細節的內容做個合理的結論。它可以是：

◆　指出希望收件人採取的行動。
◆　根據已提供的細節，說明自己可能採取的行動。

【範例】

Please let me have full details of the costs involved together with some sample menus.
請提供詳細的相關費用和樣品清單。

If payment is not received within seven days this matter will be placed in the hands of our solicitor.
如果我們七天內未收到款項，此事將交由我們的律師處理。

4. 結語

結語通常是簡單的一句話，用來為某一訊息做總結，它應當與訊息的內容相關。

【範例】

I look forward to meeting you soon.
期待早日跟您見面。

I look forward to seeing you at next month's conference.
期待在下個月的研討會中與您見面。

A prompt reply would be appreciated.
感激您的立即回覆。

Please let me know if you need any further information.
如果您需要進一步的資訊，請讓我知道。

 以下的結語是不完整的，應避免使用：

Hope to hear from you soon.
Looking forward to hearing from you.

下面這封信是運用「四點計畫」來架構書面訊息的良好範例。

→ p.12

Institute of Secretaries
Wilson House, West Street, London SW1 2AR

Telephone 020 8987 2432
Fax 020 8987 2556

LD/ST

12 May 2004

Miss Ong Lee Fong
15 Windsor Road
Manchester
M2 9GJ

Dear Lee Fong

2004 SECRETARIES CONFERENCE, 8/9 OCTOBER 2004

開場
（簡短的介紹）— As a valued member of the Institute of Secretaries, I have pleasure in inviting you to attend our special conference to be held at the Clifton Hotel, London on Tuesday/Wednesday 8/9 October 2004.

This intensive, practical conference for professional secretaries aims to:

細節
（分段、邏輯流暢）
- increase your managerial and office productivity
- improve your communication skills
- bring you up to date with the latest technology and techniques
- enable networking with other secretaries

除了簽名處外，
各段落均間隔一行 — The seminar is power-packed with a distinguished panel of professional speakers who will give expert advice on many useful topics. A programme is enclosed giving full details of this seminar which I know you will not want to miss.

結論
（期望收件人
採取的行動）— If you would like to join us please complete the enclosed registration form and return it to me before 30 June with your fee of £50 per person.

結語
（簡短的一句話）— I look forward to seeing you again at this exciting conference.

Yours sincerely

Louise Dunscombe

LOUISE DUNSCOMBE (Mrs)
Conference Secretary

Encs

這封電子郵件是應用「四點計畫」的另一個範例。

→ p.13

From	johnwang@stelectronics.co.sg
Date	14 October 2003　12:30:45
To	suzieliu@videoworks.com
CC	
Subject	25th anniversary video

Dear Suzie

引言 —— Thank you for inviting me to visit your studios last week. I was most impressed by your new facilities.

細節 —— I am delighted that you can accept our invitation to produce a video to celebrate the company's 25th anniversary. This is a very special landmark in our history, and it is important that this video portrays both past, present and future.

行動 —— You promised to let me have a draft outlining your thoughts for this special video. I look forward to receiving this before 30 October together with your approximate costings.

If you need any further information please give me a call on 2757272.

結語 —— Best wishes

John Wang
Marketing Manager
ST Electronics
www.stelectronics.co.sg

 提示　研讀本書所收錄的書信及文件，它們都是應用「四點計畫」撰寫的好例子。

檢查清單

☐ 記住，結構完善的商業文件是有效溝通的核心。

☐ 使用主題式的標題來說明訊息的主旨。

☐ 在引言中（第一段）提及先前往來的信件、聯繫或文件。

☐ 撰寫中間段落（細節），讓各項重點以合理順序呈現，並確認各重點資訊間保有一定的邏輯。

☐ 將訊息區分為數個段落，各段落間以一行空白區隔。

☐ 說明你希望收件人在讀完信後採取何種行動來做總結。

☐ 如果適當，可針對回應事項給收件人一個截止日期。

☐ 結語可以是任何有關該事項的一個簡單句子。

☐ 仔細校對訊息內容，花點時間來思考在組織上是否恰當，以及合乎邏輯與否。

☐ 把自己當成收件人，將最後寫好的訊息從頭到尾讀一遍，想像對方讀信後的感受。如果有任何不對勁，就做些必要的調整。

語言和語氣
Language and tone

商業書信中最弱的環節
The weakest link in your business writing

寫好商業書信的十個步驟
10 steps to good business writing

檢查清單
Checklist

良好的商業溝通祕訣在於使用簡單清楚的語言，就像是將一般會話「寫下來」一樣。簡單的說，就是將你想傳達的訊息以有禮、自然的方式呈現。一般的商業書信可以採用非正式的寫作風格而不必太過拘謹。

所有的書面溝通都必須確保文法、拼字和標點符號的用法正確無誤，然而，你需要的不只是正確組成句子的能力而已。溝通的目的在於將想法和意見傳達給他人，所以必須牢記你所對應的不只是事情本身，還包括人。所選擇的文件格式、方法、語氣都將視收件人是誰來決定。

設身處地想像，當對方讀到使用這樣語氣的信件時，會作何感想。事先評估收件人的需求、希望、興趣和問題，思索在特定情況下選擇什麼樣的語氣才是最恰當的。

無論你選擇用書信、傳眞、備忘錄或電子郵件做溝通，切記遵守以下重點：

◆　愼選溝通方式。
◆　認眞書寫文件。

- 用心編排，給人有效率、可靠的印象。
- 使用整齊、易讀，且具邏輯架構的格式。
- 考量環境、狀況，以及收件人本身，選用合適的語氣。
- 確保文法、拼字和標點符號正確無誤。

 牢記 **3R** 定律：引導閱讀者（**Reader**）朝你所期望的做出回應（**Respone**），以達到正面的結果（**Results**）。

商業書信中最弱的環節

我的母親是一個頗受歡迎同時爲國際所肯定的遊戲節目「智者生存」（The Weakest Link）的忠實觀眾。那是一個很棒的遊戲節目，在節目中，參賽者必須找出同伴中「最弱的競爭者」，並儘快將之淘汰出局。

多棒的遊戲規則！我們可以引用這樣的規則來改善商業寫作技巧，以提升企業形象。現在的商業環境趨向口語化、通俗化，大家在會議及研討會中使用的是自然、輕鬆的語言，不像幾十年前那般咬文嚼字。但令人不解的是，爲什麼還有許多人在商業寫作上仍沿用曾祖父時代的老套文體，而不改用符合二十一世紀潮流的風格呢？在這裡，我舉出七個二十一世紀商業寫作的「最弱環節」，並比照「智者生存」的遊戲規則將其一一剔除。

1. 有太多的年輕人用太多的老套用語

人們何時才會理解到商業語言已經改變？像 Please be informed（在此告知您）、Kindly be advised（仁慈地通知）、I would like to bring to your attention（我要請您注意）和 I am writing to advise you（我寫信來通知您）這一類的詞句，早該在新世紀來臨時就把它們全部扔進垃圾桶。但很遺憾，現在的寫作仍舊充斥著這一類的陳腔濫調，更別提那些更糟的用語，如 Enclosed herewith please find our catalogue for your reference and perusal（隨函附上我們的產品目錄作

為參考或閱讀之用）、With reference to your above-mentioned order（關於您上述提及的訂單）和 Further to the telecon today between your goodself and the undersigned（進一步關於閣下您與署名者的電話會議）等，這些用語簡直乏味透頂。大家會用這些老掉牙措詞，理由很簡單，因為每個人都這樣用，而且已沿用了數世紀之久。拜託！請在寫作中注入個人的想法、個性和感情。

使用	不使用
Thank you for your letter of 21 Oct. 謝謝您 10 月 21 日的來信。	We refer to your letter of 21st October 2004. 我們提及您 2004 年 10 月 21 日的來信。
Thank you for calling me this morning. 謝謝您今早的來電。	As spoken in our telecon today. 如我們今天在電話會議中所談的。
I hope to hear from you soon. 我希望能早日聽到您的回音。	Please revert to me soonest possible. 請儘快回覆我。
Please give me a call on 2874722 if you have any questions. 如果您有任何問題，請打電話給我，電話是 2874722。	Should you require any further clarification please do not hesitate to contact the undersigned. 如果您想獲得更進一步的說明，請不要猶豫地與本人聯繫。

2. 文句冗長

冗長的字詞、句子和段落，無法讓人留下好印象，只會造成困惑。稍後，我會在這個單元談到「**KISS** 原則」，也就是 **K**eep **I**t **S**hort and **S**imple（保持簡短）。與其說 I should be very grateful（我會非常感激），不如簡單說 Please（請、拜託），但切莫用 Kindly（親切地、仁慈地）。用字儘量簡潔，如用 buy（買）、try（試）、start（開始）和 end（結束）來取代 purchase（購買）、endeavour（竭力）、commence（開始）和 terminate（終止）。記得在商業寫作中導入 **KISS** 原則——清楚簡潔的詞彙、句子和段落。

3. 愛用被動

曾祖父那一輩的人之所以在寫作上使用被動語態，是因為他們不想表明誰該負責。他們偏好拐彎抹角的長句子，卻從不洩露事情的真相及責任者。今天的商業寫作應當改用主動口吻，這樣才是更生動、更集中焦點、更個人化，也更有趣及清楚的作法。

使用	不使用
I have arranged for a repeat order to be sent to you today. 我已安排妥追加訂單，今天會寄給您。	Arrangements have been made for a repeat order to be despatched to you immediately. 追加訂單已安排妥當，會馬上出貨給您。
I have looked into this matter. 我已調查此事。	The cause of your complaint has been investigated. 您抱怨的原因已在調查中。
Adrian Chan will conduct the seminar. 安卓‧詹會主持這個專題研討會。	The seminar will be conducted by Adrian Chan. 這個專題研討會將由安卓‧詹主持。
X101 sales have gone sky high. X101 的銷量達到高峰。	Sales of the X101 have exceeded all expectations. X101 的銷量已超過預期。

 提示　在你的寫作中注入一些想法、個性及感情。

4. 冒號充斥

為什麼許多人一定要在列舉項目中加上冒號？這樣看起來很雜亂無章。就讓我們一同刪除商業寫作中這些雜亂的部分，使它看起來簡潔、清楚、有組織。

Date	Thursday 29 November 2005		Date:	29 November 2005 (Thursday)
Time	9.00 am to 5.00 pm		Time:	9.00am to 5.00pm
Venue	Sheraton Towers Hotel		lVenue:	Sheraton Towers Hotel

5. 使用提示句

以前的人發明了「提示句」(attention line)，且勤快地完整寫上 For the attention of...（某某人親啓），目的只是想讓信件送至一個實際的收件人桌上，並非寫信給特定的個人。在那個時代，即使用「提示句」，信件內容仍是以 Dear Sirs（敬啓者）開頭，加上用字正式及使用被動語態，彷彿是在跟整個公司說話，而不是個人。這些年來，這種提示句已被誤用，而偷懶的人把它簡化成 Attention，甚至 Attn。提示句被誤用在私人信件中，與個人化稱呼，如 Dear John（親愛的約翰）、Dear Mr Tan（親愛的譚先生）等併用。讓我們將這個上個世紀的用語丟入垃圾桶吧，現在已很少會用到。如果你知道收件人是誰，如果你想要使用個人化稱呼，那就直接將對方的姓名及頭銜放入地址欄中。

Mr Leslie Lim Boon Hup
Product and Sales Manager
STP Distributors Pet Ltd (Books)
30 Old Toh Tuck Road #05-02
Singapore 597654

Attn: Leslie Lim Boon Hup

STP Distributors Pet Ltd (Books)
30 Old Toh Tuck Road #05-02
Singapore 597654

6. 畫一條線讓對方簽名

我認爲只有小孩子才需要畫條線告訴他在此寫上名字。如果沒有這條線指名簽名處，難道經理們就會勃然大怒？還是他們眞的會坐在那裡思考要將名字簽在哪裡才好？我眞的很懷疑介於 Yours sincerely 與寫信者名字 / 頭銜間的空白處不就是簽名的地方嗎？請將那條用來簽名的橫線刪去，以剔除寫作上過多的雜亂部分。

【範例】

Yours sincerely

Tan Lee Hong
Managing Director

7. 頻頻道謝

爲什麼有這麼多的人需要在信件結尾處寫上 Thank you（謝謝您）？謝什麼呢？謝謝您讀我的信嗎？拜託！不要浪費時間與印表機的墨水。如果你的信件自始至終都很有禮貌（讓我們面對現實，不論在何種情況下，你都應該有禮貌），就沒必要因爲有人讀你的信或電子郵件而不斷說 Thank you。

今日快節奏的商業世界，應該沒有多餘的空間容納昨日舊式且冗長的術語。請丟掉乏味的陳腔濫調，在商業寫作中注入一些活力，使用自然、輕鬆、友善的口吻，以更爲主動、鼓舞、有趣個人的風格來呈現，現在已經是二十一世紀了。

 不要用那些行之數十年的無趣、枯燥措詞，採用自然風格，就好像在與人對話一般，這才是重點。

寫好商業書信的十個步驟

我們已經討論了在寫作中不應該出現的問題，接著來看我所提出的「寫好商業書信的十個步驟」。如果你能確實遵循，必定能在商業寫作上有所精進。

1. 牢記 ABC 法則

好的書面溝通在於將你的想法以適當的語氣表達出來。你所傳遞的訊息必須符合以下基本法則：

正確（**Accurate**）	仔細檢查事實 涵蓋所有相關細節 徹底校對
簡短（**Brief**）	句子保持簡短 使用簡單措詞 使用非技術性語言
清楚（**Clear**）	使用平易、簡單的英文 以簡單、自然的風格寫作 避免過分正式或太過親密

2. 有禮、體貼

措詞有禮並不代表要用諸如 your kind consideration（您善意的關心）或 your esteemed order（您那令人敬重的訂單）等老套說法。而是指表現關心和同理心，也就是尊重對方的感覺。行文有禮，即使請求被拒，也不會破壞了未來合作的機會。正所謂「買賣不成，仁義在」。有禮貌指的是：

◆ 迅速回覆所有的信件——儘量在同一天內回覆。

◆ 如果無法立即回覆，寫封短箋說明原因，以建立友好關係。

◆ 了解並尊重對方的觀點。

◆ 回信不能寫得好像過錯都在對方。

◆ 如果你覺得對方的說法不公正，要婉轉地處理，切勿引起對方的反感。

◆ 先忍住怒氣，不要使用相同的語氣反擊對方，選擇有禮但不失尊嚴的口吻。

 為何要在信尾說「謝謝您」？你要做的是行文有禮，並省略這類贅詞。

3. 使用適當的語氣

要讓訊息達到溝通的目的，語氣就必須適當。語氣反應出寫信者投注在訊息上的情緒。即使書寫或回覆抗議信，行文仍可避免粗暴或觸怒對方。若忽略了使用恰當語氣的重要性，容易讓訊息流露挑釁、笨拙、草率、無禮、諷刺或使人不悅，失去了溝通的用意。

使用	不使用
Unfortunately we are unable to help you on this occasion. 很遺憾，關於這件事我們無法幫上忙。	We cannot do anything about your problem. 您的問題，我們沒辦法處理。
The problem may be resolved by connecting the wires as shown in the handbook. 如果依照手冊連接線路，問題應該可以解決。	This problem would not have happened if you had connected the wires properly. 如果當初您能適當連接線路，就不會發生今天的問題了。
Your television's guarantee has ended, so unfortunately you must bear the cost of any repairs. 電視保固期間已過。很遺憾您必須承擔修理費。	Your television's guarantee is up, so you will have to pay for it to be fixed. 您的電視保固期已經過了，所以必須支付修理費。
I was most unhappy with the standard of service I received in your store today. 對於今天貴店的服務，我感到十分的不悅。	I am writing to complain because I was very unhappy with the way I was treated in your store today. 我之所以寫這封抱怨信，是因為我對於今天在貴店受到的對待相當不悅。

改變說話的音調可以傳遞出不同的訊息。一些非口頭的暗示，例如眼神、手勢及聲調等，也會影響他人如何去詮釋你所說的話。但書面溝通無法有這樣的效果，所以慎選用字變得格外重要。你的語氣是要堅定、友善、勸誘或是溫和，完全取決於你想要傳達給對方的印象。最重要的是，選對語氣，語氣使用不當可能會引起收件人的反感。

以下是一些**避免**在商業寫作中使用的措詞：

◆ Your failure to reply ...	您未能回覆……
◆ You did not see ...	您沒有看到……
◆ We must insist ...	我們必須堅持……
◆ You should not expect to ...	您不應該期望……
◆ Your refusal to co-operate ...	您拒絕合作……
◆ You have ignored ...	您忽視了……
◆ This is not our fault ...	這不是我們的過失……
◆ I can assure you ...	我可以向您保證……
◆ You failed to ...	您沒有……
◆ I have received your complaint ...	我已收到您的抱怨……

在「簡易英語運動」（The Plain English Campaign）中有一個有趣的單元叫作「A 到 Z 的替代字」（The A–Z of Alternative Words），它提供了數百個字詞來取代那些擾亂正式寫作的浮誇字彙與片語。網址為：
www.plainenglish.co.uk/A-Z.html

4. 自然、真誠的表達

試著對收件人的問題展現真正的關心，那麼你在用自己的風格書寫訊息時，就會真誠流露。自然地表達，就像你在跟對方說話一般。

使用	不使用
I am pleased to tell you 我很高興告訴您……	I have pleasure in informing you 我很高興地通知您……
We do not expect prices to rise 我們未預期價格會調漲	We do not anticipate any increase in prices 我們並未預估價格會上漲
Please let me know 請讓我知道……	I should be grateful if you would be good enough to advise us 如果您能慷慨提供建議，我將非常感激
I hope to receive a prompt reply 希望儘快收到回覆	Please favour us with a prompt reply 請儘速回覆
I hope to hear from you soon 希望很快有回音	Please revert to us soonest 請儘速告知

5. 謹記 KISS 原則

現在的商業人士有許多的文件要讀，一份行文有禮、直指重點的訊息才是令人賞識的。在努力累積寫作能力的同時，你也應當不斷磨練 KISS 技巧(Keep It Short and Simple)，也就是避開冗長或複雜的字詞，改以簡短的字詞代替，如下列所示：

	使用	不使用
開始	start	commence
關於	about	regarding
買	buy	purchase
使用	use	utilise
需要	need	require
嘗試	try	endeavour, attempt
結束	end	terminate
說	say	state
加快	hurry, speed up	expedite
告訴	tell	advise, inform

	使用	不使用
看	see	visualise
送	send	despatch
協助	help	assist
足夠	enough	sufficient
請	please	kindly

KISS 原則也指出，不要使用長片語，能用一個字來代替的就儘量這麼做。

	使用	不使用
請您	please	I should be glad if you would
儘管	despite	in spite of the fact that
關於	about	with regard to
現在	now	at the present moment in time
調查	investigate	conduct an investigation
因為	as ... because	in view of the fact that
如果	if	in the event that
不久	soon	in the very near future
之後	later	at a later date
請您	please	we would like to ask you to

有人針對一般人對不同長度句子的理解程度做了相關的研究調查。請看看下列數字：

句子的字數	第一次閱讀就能理解者的百分比
7-10 個字	95%
15-20 個字	75%
27 個字以上	4%

你可以使用包含 7-20 個字的句子來符合 KISS 原則。

如果要找一個提供單字、標點符號、文法、用法、字典、同義字等相關資訊的絕佳網站，請至 Merriam-Webster Online。網址為 **www.m-w.com**

避免使用以下的措詞：

I have noticed that	我已注意到
It has come to my attention that	我已留意到
I am pleased to inform you that	很高興通知您
I am writing to let you know that	我寫信來讓您知道
I must inform you that	我必須要通知您
Please be informed(advised) that	在此通知您
Thanking you in anticipation	先謝謝您
Thank you and regards	謝謝並且問候您
Kindest regards	最親切的問候

 提示 如果你太拘泥於形式，容易讓句子拖泥帶水，模糊了原先要表達的意思。收件人到頭來還得在你那誇張華麗的修辭中摸索你真正的含義。

6. 使用現代的術語

老式的慣用語並不能為你的訊息加分。這種不必要和冗長的措詞只會讓收件人留下不好印象，甚至引起困惑。一封好的商業書信需要的是訊息清楚、正確，而非多餘的修飾語。

使用	不使用
Thank you for your letter of 12 June 謝謝您 6 月 12 日的來信	We are in receipt of your letter of 12 June 我們收到您 6 月 12 日的來信
Thank you for your letter of 12 June 謝謝您 6 月 12 日的來信	We have received your letter of 12 Jun 我們已經收到您 6 月 12 日的來信
I enclose ... 我隨函附上……	Enclosed herewith you will find ... Please find enclosed ... 隨函附上……
Please let me know ... 請讓我知道……	Please be good enough to advise me ... 請您給我建議……
Please remember ... 請記得……	Please be reminded ... 在此提醒您……
... these goods ……這些商品	... the above-mentioned goods ……以上所提的商品

 提示 現代術語應當是主動、鼓舞、有趣的，最重要的是能反映你的個性。

7. 涵蓋必要的細節

如果收件人必須發問或者有不清楚的地方，表示你的訊息有所遺漏。不要做冒險的事，將所有必要的資訊都納入信中。

使用	不使用
My flight BA 121 from London Heathrow should arrive at Singapore Changi Airport at 1530 on Wednesday 12 June. 我的班機號碼是 BA 121，從倫敦希斯洛機場起飛，預計 6 月 12 日星期三下午 3 點 30 分抵達新加坡樟宜機場。	My flight arrives at 3.30 on Wednesday. 我的班機在週三 3 點 30 分抵達。
I thoroughly enjoyed your article on *feng shui* in last month's company newsletter. 我非常欣賞您上個月在公司通訊中那篇討論風水的文章。	I thoroughly enjoyed your article in last month's newsletter. 我非常欣賞您在上個月的公司通訊中所發表的文章。
Mr John Matthews, our Sales Manager, will contact you soon. 我們的業務經理約翰‧馬修先生會很快與您聯絡。	Our Sales Manager will contact you soon. 我們的業務經理會很快與您聯繫。

8. 保持一致性

一致性不僅攸關訊息的呈現，對訊息本身來說也很重要。

使用	不使用
The people attending the next committee meeting will be John Wilson, Gloria Turner, Mandy Harrison and Bob Turner. 參加下次委員會會議的人員是約翰‧威爾森、葛洛麗亞‧透納、曼蒂‧哈理遜，以及鮑伯‧透納。	The people attending will be John Wilson, G Turner, Mandy Harrison and Bob from Sales. 參加者為約翰‧威爾森、G. 透納、曼蒂‧哈理遜，以及業務部的鮑伯。

I confirm my reservation of a single room on 16 July and a double room on 17 October.	I confirm my reservation of a single room on 16/7 and a double room on 17 Oct.
我確認 7 月 16 日預約一間單人房，10 月 17 日一間雙人房。	我確認我 7 月 16 日預約一間單人房，10 月 17 日一間雙人房。

9. 使用主動語態取代被動語態

「語態」（voice）是文法上的一個術語，它指出句子的主詞是做動作者，還是接收動作者。主動語態能有效改善你的寫作風格，讓你的寫作更有趣、生動，以及更主動。

下列兩個範例所傳達的訊息是類似的，你可以做個比較：

主動語態：Tim played the violin.（提姆拉小提琴）
在這裡，主詞是提姆。你幾乎可以看到提姆在拉小提琴，而且完全投入音樂中。這個句子顯得主動、活潑且有趣。

被動語態：The violin was played by Tim.（小提琴被提姆拉）
在這裡，主詞是小提琴。動作已結束，而重點也由做動作的主詞移至接收動作的主詞。我們很難看出發生了什麼事，句子顯得枯燥、乏味。

這裡有些小祕訣來幫你分辨該句子是屬於被動語態：

◆ 注意那些以動作而不是以主角開始的句子。以動作開始的句子通常為被動語態。

◆ 注意動詞 to be 的各種不同形式，如 is, are, was, were, will be, have been, should be 等。使用這些動詞的句子不代表都是被動語態，但通常能給你一些暗示。

曾祖父那一輩的人較喜歡用被動語態，因為他們不想就所寫的內容負任何責任。而這種方式也在寄件人及收件人之間築起一段距離。是的，被動語態對我們的曾祖父來說是完美的。

反觀今日的寫作，應當要表現出責任感，並且更個人化、更自然，以及更集中焦點。請記住我的黃金法則：「如果你不會這樣說，那就不要這樣寫」。

使用	不使用
The use of hydraulics simplified the design of our new systems. 運用水力學來簡化我們新系統的設計。	The design of our new systems was simplified by the use of hydraulics. 我們新系統的設計，是由水力學來予以簡化的。
Our staff developed the new system. 我們的員工發展了這個新系統。	The new system was developed by our staff. 這個新系統是由我們的員工所發展出來的。
Our client has concluded the investigation and signed the paperwork. 我們的客戶已就該項調查做出結論並簽妥書面報告。	The investigation has been concluded by our client, and the paperwork has been signed. 該項調查已由我們的客戶做出結論，而書面報告也已簽妥。
The Prince of Wales presented the cheque to the charity. 查爾斯王子將支票交給了慈善機構。	The cheque was presented to the charity by the Prince of Wales. 這張支票是由查爾斯王子交予該慈善機構。

 寫作時請使用主動語態，它能讓內容顯得更生動、更聚焦、更具個人化，也更加有趣及清楚。

不過在某些場合，使用被動語態會比主動語態更適當，例如：

◆ 句子的主詞是一個特別重要的名詞時，使用被動語態會比較好，可特別強調該主詞。

Our restaurant has been recommended by all the leading hotels in Singapore.
我們的餐廳是由新加坡具領導地位的飯店所推薦的。

這句話強調「我們的餐廳」（our restaurant），比下面的句子好：

All the leading hotels in Singapore recommend our service.
所有在新加坡具領導地位的飯店都推薦我們的服務。

◆ 當你要將焦點放在動作上，而非做動作者時。

The noise was heard all over the island.
全島到處都能聽到這個噪音。

本句要強調的是噪音本身，而非製造噪音的人。

◆ 當你要隱藏某事，或者當表現圓滑很重要時。

An unfortunate mistake was made.
一個不幸的錯誤已造成。

10. 寫一份清楚（CLEAR）的溝通文件

最後，在撰寫訊息時，問問自己是否能符合 CLEAR 的原則，你的訊息應當要：

清楚（Clear）：不要讓讀信者有任何疑問。表達方式明確，避免模糊，並選用熟悉的文字及簡易的英語。記得要用對方能理解的直率語言，並呈現友善、自然，以及會話式的風格。

合乎邏輯（Logical）：用「四點計畫」有邏輯地架構訊息。由「引言」開始寫起，於中間段落合理地延伸重點，最後自然導出結論，結論中詳述你需要讀信者採取的行動。最後用一行文字來作結尾。

同理心（Empathetic）：站在讀者的立場問自己一個問題：「閱讀訊息的人感覺如何？」如果有任何不清楚，或用字不當處，在寄出訊息前先加以改正。

準確（Accurate）：要確保所有相關細節都包含在訊息中，包括時間、日期、姓名、事實以及數字。

正確（Right）：小心謹慎地校對（不只是檢查拼字），在寄出訊息前確定每一個部分都是百分之百正確。

 一個小失誤都不允許。

下面這封信充滿了舊式的專用術語、陳腔濫調、被動語態以及冗長的字詞。你能將它們一一揪出來嗎？

→ p.16

> Dear Sirs,
>
> We have received your letter dated 27 March 200–.
>
> We are extremely distressed to learn that an error was made pertaining to your esteemed order. Please be informed that the cause of your complaint has been investigated and it actually appears that the error occurred in our packing section and it was not discerned before this order was despatched to your goodself.
>
> Arrangements have been made for a repeat order to be despatched to you immediately and this should leave our warehouse later today. It is our sincere hope that you will have no cause for further complaint with this replacement order.
>
> Once again we offer our humblest apologies for the unnecessary inconvenience that you have been caused in this instance.
>
> Please find enclosed herewith a copy of our new catalogue for your reference and perusal.
>
> Kindly contact the undersigned if you require any further clarifications.
>
> Very truly yours,
>
> Zachariah Creep & Partners

上封信是以現代用語改寫的結果如下：

→ p.16

> Dear Mr Tan
>
> YOUR ORDER NUMBER TH 2457
>
> Thank you for your letter of 27 March.
>
> I am very sorry to hear about the mistake made with your order. I have looked into this and found that the mistake happened in the packing section. Unfortunately it was not discovered before the goods were sent to you.
>
> I have arranged for a repeat order to be sent to you today, and I hope this meets your requirements.
>
> Once again, please accept my apologies for the inconvenience caused.
>
> I enclose a copy of our new catalogue and I hope you find it interesting.
>
> Please give me a call soon on 2358272 if you have any questions.
>
> Yours sincerely

提示　好的商業寫作，關鍵在於風格自然，就好像在跟人對話一般。

 想知道更多有關昨日與今日的商業寫作差異，請參考筆者個人網站上的學習區。網址為 **www.shirleytaylor.com/index.html**

 ## 檢查清單

在簽名、寄出任何書面文件前，試著問自己下列問題：

☐ 你相信你自己所寫的嗎？讀信者會了解嗎？

☐ 你使用了簡單的文字及表達方式嗎？

☐ 當你要表現禮貌時，是否避開了文字冗贅這個問題？

☐ 你的語氣是否像對話般自然？

☐ 對於你所提及的議題或人物，你使用了合適的語氣嗎？

☐ 你是否使用了那些應當被淘汰的陳腐措詞及術語？

☐ 你是否依據「四點計畫」，有邏輯地架構內容？

☐ 全文具一致性嗎？這裡是指風格（人稱 I, We 等）及版面設計（完全齊頭式搭配開放式標點）。它是否吸引人並完美呈現？

☐ 拼字、標點符號及文法正確嗎？

☐ 納入所有必要資訊了嗎？有再次確認事實與數字是否正確無誤嗎？是否每一部分都清楚、明確，不會模稜兩可呢？

 一個有關如何使用簡易英語，而不用許多術語及浮誇、冗長、費解字眼來撰寫訊息的絕佳網站的網址為 **www.plainenglish.co.uk**

電子郵件
E-mail

快速成長的電子郵件

電子郵件是生活上的一項偉大發明，對於我們的溝通方式有著驚人的影響。它不只是一個與家人及朋友保持聯繫的快速、簡單，以及相對便宜的方式，更進一步成為不可或缺的商業利器，在日常工作中扮演重要的角色。

然而，電子郵件的爆炸性成長也帶來了某些問題，主要原因是從來沒有嚴格的標準或方針來規範電子郵件的使用方式。每天有數百人登記成為網路新用戶，但他們並沒有接受發展多年的網路文化的洗禮。對於網路族共同的標準與期望，也一直沒有一個明確的指南可循，結果導致網路系統超載；錯誤的溝通猖獗；聲譽遭破壞；情感受傷；時間也被浪費掉了。

另一個原因是，由於電子郵件很明顯地不拘禮節，以往不會出現在商業書信中的內容如今紛紛在電子郵件中現身，使得某些企業可能嚴重受牽累，他們可能察覺到自己正面臨法律問題。

企業界因而體認到保護自己、遠離電子郵件危險的重要性。然而，這樣做還不夠，必須進一步確保電子郵件能有效地運用在工作上。本單元將帶你透視電子郵件的優缺點，協助你善用電子郵件。你將學會如何增強線上溝通技巧，與客戶和同事建立和諧的線上關係。

使用電子郵件的七大原罪

在開始說明之前，請先閱讀下列敘述，並在符合的項目上打勾。勾選的項目愈多，表示你在電子郵件的使用上愈需要協助。

1. 電子郵件常因為地址錯誤而被退回。　　　　　　　　　　☐

2. 有時郵件寄出後就想追回，但為時已晚。　　　　　　　☐

3. 一整天下來時常被不斷湧入的電子郵件打斷工作。　　　☐

4. 有時明知道打電話會更好，但還是寫了電子郵件。　　　☐

5. 有很長一段時間未曾去整理、刪除郵件。　　☐

6. 以電子郵件寄送私人或機密訊息，但事後又感到後悔。　　☐

7. 因急著要將訊息寄出，既沒招呼語，也不簽名做結尾，更沒
有檢查文法、拼字與標點符號的正確性。　　☐

 提示　如果是在盛怒之下撰寫的信，請將它存放在寄件匣中至少一個小時，然後再
回頭檢視。如果感受不變，還是想寄出去，那就寄吧。

電子郵件的優缺點

我們喜歡（或討厭）電子郵件的理由很多。

喜歡的理由	不喜歡的理由
它是非正式的。	太通俗、隨便了。
按一個鍵就能將訊息寄給許多人。	因為太容易傳送，所以訊息排山倒海而來。
可以輕易地將檔案附上並寄出去。	稍有不慎，可能會下載一個夾帶病毒的檔案，而大型檔案的下載時間又太久。
它是即時的，訊息數秒後就傳至對方手上。	太過即時了（你曾經在寄出訊息後就想立刻將它追回嗎？）
費用相對便宜。	收到很多垃圾郵件。
可隨時傳給全球各地的人士。	許多人寄送副本（cc）或密件副本（bcc）的原因只因為有這項功能，而不是收件人真的需要閱讀那些郵件。
可以將郵件排出優先順序，決定先閱讀哪一封。	面對需快速回覆的電子郵件，會有壓力。
	上班時會不斷被郵件干擾，間接影響已規劃好的工作。
	毫無機密可言。
	增加緊張度。及時處理電子郵件是工作壓力的來源之一。
	對話已死。員工寄電子郵件給鄰近的同事，而不願走過去跟他們說話。

 提示　訊息一旦寄出，收件人可能在數秒後就在閱讀，無法再把它追回來。所以，
在按下「傳送」鍵之前，務必謹慎地校對訊息內容。

使用電子郵件的十個需改善項目

當我跟專題研討會的與會者聊天時，我常會問他們，電子郵件最令他們感覺困擾的是什麼。以下是我蒐集到的十個電子郵件寫作上最需要改進的項目。

1. 時間與日期不正確

如果你的電腦沒有設定正確的時間與日期，會衍生諸多困擾。藉著設定正確的時間與日期，可同時協助自己及他人追蹤訊息的來源。

2. 主旨模糊不清

收件匣內有許多郵件的人不會去開啟你在主旨欄上標示「緊急」（Urgent）或「詢問」（Enquiry）的郵件。你應該試著撰寫一個「聰明」（SMART）的主旨：

Specific	具體的
Meaningful	有意義的
Appropriate	適當的
Relevant	切題的
Thoughtful	體貼的

提示　主旨欄上的文字，將左右你的訊息會於現在、今天、明天、下星期被閱讀或永不見天日。

3. 既不打招呼也不簽名做結尾

許多人不喜歡收到這些沒有招呼語的不禮貌郵件。加上招呼語（Hello Sally, Hi Sally, Dear Mr Lim）的主要理由有兩個：第一是表示禮貌；其次是讓收件人確認該訊息是寫給他們的，而不只是副本或密件副本的收件者。而加上簽名做結尾的兩個好理由則是禮貌及用來確認該訊息已經結束，就是這麼簡單！

4. 格式拙劣

一個很長且沒有分段的訊息會造成收件人閱讀上的困惑。如果你行文不加思索，也不將內容分段呈現，郵件內容將變得混亂不清。把訊息編排得富吸引力，並用空白來區隔各段落，這樣不但是幫助讀郵件的人，也幫了自己。

5. 語意不清

這也許跟第 4 點有關，人們抱怨他們收到的訊息有很多是語意不清的，弄不懂來信者的目的或是他們請託何事。請花點時間，謹慎撰寫你的訊息，然後徹底檢查，以確保該訊息是容易閱讀的，然後在點選「傳送」鍵之前，再檢查一次。

6. 收件人不知如何回應

這又跟第 4 、 5 點有關聯。如果訊息含糊而且缺乏組織，收件人即使反覆閱讀後還是可能不知道該如何回應。謹記 3R 原則（Reader, Response, Result），引導收件人找到你所期待的回應，否則你無法保證能獲得正確的結果。

7. 語氣不友善

電子郵件不易精確傳達情緒。有些人只是將要說的話一字不漏地打字出來，卻未考慮到語氣是會顯示出情緒的。而使用電子郵件，我們唯一能掌握的又只有語彙，若使用了不當的語氣，很可能會引起誤會，或者激怒對方，失去一個重要的商業夥伴或朋友。一位好的寫作者會學習謹慎用字及使用適當的語氣。

8. 將副本寄給全世界

要將副本寄給其他人真是太容易了，所以很多人都隨意寄送副本，塞爆他人的收件匣，浪費大家的時間。請將副本寄給需要知道的人，而不是你認識的人。

9. 拙劣的文法、拼字及標點符號

隨著愈來愈多的人使用電子郵件，內容粗糙的郵件也愈來愈讓人頭疼，像是版面設計拙劣的一長段文字、未針對要求提出具體答覆且結構雜亂的訊息、全部用大寫或小寫等，當然還有那些充斥拙劣文法、拼字及標點符號的訊息。

10. 內容草率

當我做了一些有關於電子郵件的調查時發現，大部分的人會抱怨電子郵件給人一種因為是電子郵件所以需要馬上回信的急迫感。為急著回信，往往未能謹慎思索，訊息變得混亂不清、拼字錯誤、欠缺組織，導致收件人不解其意或被激怒。簡單地說，這些訊息草率而未能發揮效用。有一位朋友告訴我：「當我收到一封錯誤百出、拼字差勁、格式拙劣的訊息時，我會認為寫信的人不尊重我，因為他們不願意在點選「傳送」鍵之前，花一分鐘的時間檢查全文。」以後，請多尊重你的收件人，而它只需花你一分鐘的時間。

網際網路使我們能夠與全世界的人進行溝通。電子郵件的內容因而成為評斷彼此的依據。個人的可靠度可能因為匆促點選「傳送」鍵而毀於一旦。

如何讓電子郵件成為工作利器？

4.1 關掉即時傳送系統

有人告訴我，他們每一次收到新郵件，即時傳送系統就會大叫「亞巴答巴杜！」不管你使用哪一種即時傳送系統，請看在老天爺的份上，偶爾關掉它，例如遇有重要的專案在進行時。不要讓電子郵件控制了你的生活。

4.2 不要覺得有義務立即給對方詳細答覆

當對方要求你限時回覆，但你無法立即辦理時，不必覺得有負擔，否則只會寫出草率、錯誤、也許不夠詳盡或沒有效力的訊息。取而

代之的，你可以先寄一個通知，說明你稍後將會詳細回覆。如此一來，對方就知道你已收到該訊息並正在處理中。

4.3　將副本寄給有必要知道的而不是認識的人

如果我們正為自己收件匣內氾濫的郵件所苦，想想這其中有多少是咎由自取呢？是不是只因為寄送方便，所以你就濫送信件呢？我們必須學習更小心謹慎地使用電子郵件，分辨何時該用、何時不該用。想想你真的需要將那些副本、密件副本或信件轉寄出去嗎？如果你收到大批其實不需要的訊息，請直接告訴寄件人，以阻止同樣的情形再度發生。

4.4　設定篩選功能

「篩選功能」（filters）可以讓你依據寄件人及主旨將信件分至不同的群組，另外也可擋掉不必要的郵件。有些篩選功能是用表示優先的代碼或顏色來強調訊息的重要性。

4.5　不要驚慌，你永遠都可以拿起電話

你曾經耗在歷時達數日之久的電子郵件往返中嗎？拿起電話不會更快一些嗎？電子郵件的超載降低了口頭溝通技巧的使用機會，人們寧可寄電子郵件給隔壁辦公室的人，而不願走幾步路過去交談！請記住，談話是很好的方式，不要讓電子郵件「終結」了會話。

 如果你長時間陷在電子郵件的往返中，改用電話會不會更好呢？

客服與電子郵件

今日的商業是在為客戶提供服務。如果你一點都不重視客服，你的客戶肯定會跑去跟別人交易。而這裡說的客服，當然也包括了電子郵件。

　　研究指出，當你第一次跟客戶見面問候時，對方會花十五秒鐘做評估，然後決定是否要聽從你、相信你和信賴你。更重要的是，這十五秒決定了他們是否會跟你交易。

　　客戶對你的第一印象取決於三個要素：肢體語言、語氣和言辭。你會驚訝於初次與客戶見面或談話時，這三要素的影響力有多大。圖表 4.1 清楚地說明了肢體語言是吸引他人注意的最重要因素。但是電子郵件無法呈現肢體語言，你只有言辭和語氣，所以必須學習如何運用這兩個要素來創造你自己的電子郵件肢體語言。學會這麼做，才能建立一個真正的聯繫，好的客服指的就是這個。

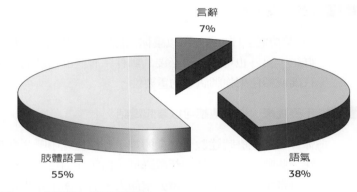

圖表 4.1　影響第一印象的要素

 試著不但與所有客戶，也要與同事建立親密的關係。

 若要找一個跟電子郵件有關的網站，請查看 **www.everythingemail.net**

比較下列兩封電子郵件，並指出哪一封郵件會給人更好的印象、建立起更好的關係。

Dear John
Thanks for your e-mail. I'm glad your complaint has been sorted out. Please let me know if you need further assistance.
Regards
Mary Tan

親愛的約翰
謝謝您的電子郵件。我很高興您的抱怨已獲解決。如果您需要更進一步的協助，請讓我知道。
瑪莉‧譚

Hi John

Thanks for your e-mail.

I'm really pleased that we have been able to find a solution to this problem. Good luck with future progress.

I'll be here when you decide on how we can help you again.

Mary

嗨　約翰

謝謝您的電子郵件。

對於我們能夠針對這個問題找出一個解決的辦法，我真的感到很高興。也祝您未來的發展順利。

當您需要再次協助時，我隨時候教。

瑪莉

建立和諧的線上關係

要將客服的原則付諸實踐，面對面的方式會比用電話來得容易，因為你面對的是可以看見及聽見的真實人物。但跟電子郵件相比，電話又顯得較容易，因為即使無法看到對方，起碼還能聽到聲音，知道他的口氣如何，而且，沒錯，從聲音你也可以聽出微笑。電子郵件就沒有這些優勢，所以你必須採取其他方法來跟你的客戶和同事建立一個和諧的線上關係。接著說明一些你可以使用的技巧。

4.6　引導讀者進入訊息

不要盲目地一頭栽進訊息裡，藉著提供或回顧一些基本的背景資料，使收件人能輕易理解你的訊息內容。適當的話，可用如下列的溫馨友善方式開場：

◆ Thanks for lunch last week. It gave us a good opportunity to learn more about your new project, which sounds very interesting.
謝謝您上個星期的午餐，它給了我一個很好的機會去了解您的新專案，聽起來很有趣。

◆ I am glad we were able to speak on the telephone this morning. It was good to clarify this issue.
很高興今天早上能跟您通電話，能夠釐清這個議題真好。

◆ Thanks for calling me today. It made a nice change to speak to a real person for once instead of always using e-mail.
謝謝您今天的來電。能夠偶爾不用電子郵件而與一個真實的人談話真好。

◆ Your news today is interesting – it sounds like you've been working really hard to ensure the success of this project.
您今天的訊息很有趣，看起來您為了確保專案成功而十分努力。

4.7　注入感情

有些人只陳述事實，沒有任何問候語之類的。因為急著要切入重點而忘了放入情感，記住：情緒或感性的文字能為一般性的訊息添加質感與空間感。請將那些可以幫你建立友好關係的語言運用在寫給客戶及同事的郵件中，展現出你的情感。例如：

◆ I'll be pleased to help you sort out this problem.
我很高興幫您解決這個問題。

◆ I appreciate your understanding in trying to resolve this issue.
感謝您體諒我們正在處理這個問題。

◆ I hope I can shed some light on this problem very soon.
　我希望我能很快地將這問題解釋清楚。

◆ I see what you mean and can appreciate your concern.
　我知道您的意思，也感謝您的關心。

◆ This has shown me a clearer perspective and I can see a true picture now.
　它給了我一個更清楚的想法，我現在能真正釐清這件事。

◆ I am happy to offer you an extra discount of 5% in the circumstances.
　在這樣的情況下，我很樂意給您額外 5% 的優惠折扣。

 只需要在訊息中額外加上幾個字以示溫馨之意即可，不要放入太多感情，否則會流於濫情。

4.8　使用視覺化語言

試著將你所溝通的內容勾勒成畫面，讓讀者看見你想要傳達的情境，像是：

◆ I can see what you mean.
　我理解您的意思。

◆ This is all quite clear to me now.
　現在，我都很清楚了。

◆ This will now enable us to focus on our mutal goals.
　這能讓我們將重點放在共同的目標上。

◆ Your suggestions look good.
　您的建議看起來還不錯。

 認同你的讀者、重視他們的感覺、使用他們能夠理解的文字，並用合適的語氣來撰寫郵件內容。

電子郵件在工作上的運用

我們來看一些電子郵件的實例，並找出其優點及缺點。

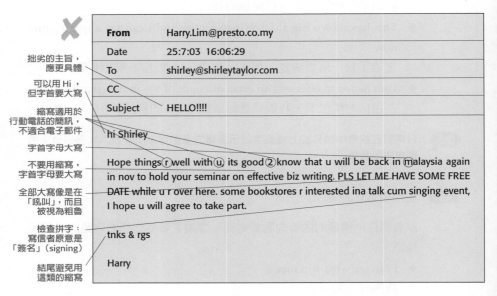

拙劣的主旨，
應更具體

可以用 Hi，
但字首要大寫

縮寫適用於
行動電話的簡訊，
不適合電子郵件

字首字母大寫

不要用縮寫，
字首字母要大寫

全部大寫像是在
「吼叫」，而且
被視為粗魯

檢查拼字：
寫信者原意是
「簽名」（signing）

結尾避免用
這類的縮寫

From	Harry.Lim@presto.co.my
Date	25:7:03　16:06:29
To	shirley@shirleytaylor.com
CC	
Subject	HELLO!!!!

hi Shirley

Hope things r well with u. its good 2 know that u will be back in malaysia again in nov to hold your seminar on effective biz writing. PLS LET ME HAVE SOME FREE DATE while u r over here. some bookstores r interested ina talk cum singing event, I hope u will agree to take part.

tnks & rgs

Harry

 提示　不要在電子郵件中任意使用全部大寫的單字，因為它們帶有「吼叫」（**SHOUTING**）及「挑釁」（**AGGRESSION**）的意味，而且不禮貌。

→ p.18

From	Harry.Lim@presto.co.my
Date	25 July 2003　16:06:29
To	shirley@shirleytaylor.com
CC	
Subject	Book signing in Malaysia

一個「聰明」（SMART）的主旨

一個很好的開頭段落，而且段落間留有清楚的間距

沒有縮寫，也沒有代號

依據「四點計畫」來組織訊息

結語將訊息做了一個很好的結束

Hello Shirley

I hope things are well with you.

I was pleased to hear that you will be back in Malaysia again in November to hold your seminar on Effective Business Writing.

Some bookstores are interested in asking you to do a talk and signing event. I hope you will agree to take part. If so, please let me have some free dates while you are over here.

See you soon.

Harry

提示　有效的溝通讓你及公司樹立良好的專業形象，且能順利處理好事情。

想學會更多如何使用電子郵件的技巧，請參考：
www.shirleytaylor.com/learninglinks.html

4.9　一封簡單、非正式的電子郵件

→ p.19

To	SueGingell@GlobalComms.co.uk
From	shirley@shirleytaylor.com (Shirley Taylor)
Date	22 October 2003　9:55

「聰明」的主旨

非正式的招呼語

適用於電子郵件中的縮寫

在適當的地方用非正式的會話文體

沒有正式的結尾，沒有 Regards

Subject　Lunch 28 October

Hi Sue

This is just a reminder that I'm looking forward to seeing you for lunch next Friday 28th. I am glad you've arranged for Jenny Chew to join us too. Can I suggest 12.30 at Hemingways on Orchard Road? I hear this new restaurant is fabulous. My treat of course. Please confirm.

Shirley

4.10 一封稍微正式的電子郵件

→ p.19

To	RosehannahWethern@Pioneer.co.sg
From	shirley@shirleytaylor.com (Shirley Taylor)
Date	14 August 2004 14:30
Subject	Customer Services Training

這種文體稍微正式 ── Dear Rosehannah

句子簡潔，
沒有廢話 ── We are considering sending some of our staff on a training course on Customer Services. Do you have a suitable course available within the next few months? If so please let me have the dates and times plus costs.

段落簡短，
且留有間距 ── If there isn't a regular Pioneer course scheduled, can you tailor-make a course specially for our staff? We could hold it in our conference room.

用非正式的
文體，就像
在說話一樣 ── Perhaps we can arrange to meet to discuss this – are you free next Friday 20 August at 11 am? I could come over to you, or you could come over to my office. Please let me know.

Shirley Taylor
Project Manager
標準的「簽名」欄 ── Shirley Taylor Training and Consultancy
Tel: +65 64726076 Fax: +65 63392710
Mobile: +65 96355907
http://www.shirleytaylor.com

4.11 會議後的電子郵件

看看底下這封電子郵件如何符合下列的要求：

◆ 「聰明」的主旨。

◆ 「四點計畫」。

→ p.20

「聰明」的主旨 ———

From	georgiathomas@aurorasuperstores.co.uk
Date	10 July 2004　11:35:14
To	lilymcbeal@healthylife.com
CC	richardcage@aurorasuperstores.co.uk
Subject	Eating for Health Campaign

Dear Lily

引言 ——— It was good to meet you again last week. As discussed, I would like to invite you to give the opening speech at the launch of our Healthy Eating Campaign. This will be held at our Leeds superstore on Monday 8 August.

細節 ——— Richard and I are very excited about this campaign. We are hoping it will make the public more aware of the importance of choosing a variety of fresh fruit and vegetables as part of their daily diet.

行動 ——— I am attaching a provisional programme, from which you will see that 10 minutes has been allocated for the opening speech at 9.30 am. We will be happy to arrange your transport to and from our superstore on launch day.

結尾 ——— I know that your high profile in this industry would bring the crowds flocking to this launch. We hope you will decide to join us.

Best wishes

Georgia Thomas
Marketing Manager
Aurora Superstores Ltd
Telephone +44 114 2888724
Mobile +44 7770 2342342
www.aurora.com

 提示　當你送出一封電子郵件時，你的責任是確保該郵件會被開啓、閱讀，並付諸行動。一個明確、具體的主旨可以幫你達成這個目的。

4.12　撰寫電子郵件語氣很重要

電子郵件經常是快快寫好、快快寄出，未能用心思索該如何選用適當的語氣。下面是一封會計部的行政人員寄給業務經理的電子郵件。讀一讀這封電子郵件，並想想看如果你是收件人，將作何感受？

→ p.21

From	sallyturner@rightway.com
Date	25 July 2003　16:06:29
To	johnwong@rightway.com
Subject	REMINDER!!!

John

Appreciate if you would consider and bear in mind that I am no longer responsible for dealing with petty cash. Some of your staffs keep bringing their vouchers to me, but this responsibility has been taken over by Martin in Accounts, he is the one who should be contacted henceforth for all petty cash matters.

Your co-operation is appreciated in making sure all your staffs know about this.

BRgs/Sally

這樣的主旨肯定會激怒收件人

這種用字十分惡劣且刺耳

當用句點，而非逗點

henceforth 這個字是老掉牙的用法

這種說法當然會引起憤怒

結尾的語氣非常惡劣，而且 staffs 字尾不需加 s

不要懶於完整寫出結尾敬辭

底下是使用更適當語氣的同一封郵件。

→ p.21

From	sallyturner@rightway.com
Date	25 July 2003　16:06:29
To	johnwong@rightway.com
Subject	Petty Cash Vouchers

Hi John

Some of the staff from your department are still bringing their petty cash vouchers to me. However this responsibility was taken over by Martin in Accounts last month.

Please inform your staff that they should deal with Martin in future.

Thanks for your help John.

Sally

網路禮節

就像人際關係的互動有一定的禮節（etiquette），在電子郵件的世界也有所謂的網路禮節（netiquette），它們是從經驗中發展出來的一套電子郵件使用禮節。接著列出一些我認為可以表現出較好禮節的重要祕訣。

- **絕對不要認為自己是在跟電腦說話**（**N**ever think you're talking to a computer!）

  當你在考慮用字、文體及語氣時，要記住在另一端有一個真實的人物存在。

- **確保你遵循了良好的寫作規則**（**E**nsure you follow the rules of good writing.）

  商業書信就像是企業的外交官，而電子郵件也扮演了同樣的角色。所以請不要濫用電子郵件的速度及簡便性，以免淪為草率魯莽、隨意使用縮寫，以及錯誤百出的郵件作者。小心謹慎地撰寫你的訊息，並仔細想想現代商業寫作的規則。

- **解開大寫字母鍵，不要吼叫！**（**T**ake off the caps lock. DO'NT SHOUT!）

  即使你想引人注意，也別在電子郵件中使用全部大寫的字彙：感覺像在「吼叫」，沒有禮貌，且通常會有反效果。另外，永遠不要仰賴過量的標點符號（像是 *@!!**?!!!!等）。

◆ **在電子郵件中，非正式的寫作是可行的**（Informality is OK in e-mails.）
用 Hi Leslie（嗨！雷斯里）或只用 Leslie（雷斯里）來代替較正式的稱呼── Dear Leslie（親愛的雷斯里）。也可用 Best wishes 或其他一些非正式的結尾敬辭來代替 Yours sincerely。

◆ **善用主旨**（Question your subject heading.）
人們最喜歡閱讀看來重要的電子郵件，請提供一個清楚具體的主旨。

◆ **句子和段落保持簡潔**（Use short sentences and short paragraphs.）
你的訊息愈短，就愈有機會被閱讀、理解。但也不宜過分簡短，以免流於唐突或意思不明。使用完整的句子明確表達意思，分段方式則跟商業文件一樣。

◆ **用數字或圓點來做列舉**（Enumerate with numbers or bullets.）
用引人注意的方式來呈現訊息，可能的話，加上數字、圓點或副標題來提升訊息的明確度。

◆ **整理長句子**（Tidy up long sentences.）
把你所想的逐字打在鍵盤上，句子很容易變長。小心謹慎地將你的訊息讀一遍，提高訊息的明確度與理解度。

◆ **令人自豪的訊息內容**（Take a pride in your finished message.）
確保你的訊息準確、簡短、清楚並編排生動，這樣就能被閱讀、理解，達到預期結果。

◆ **在按「傳送」鍵之前，確定一切都是正確無誤的**（Ensure everything is right before you hit 'send'.）
即使後悔，也無法將訊息追回。所以，一開始就要做對。

 如果你想增進與客戶及同事之間的線上關係，或想提高可靠度、聲譽及創造力。請記住，你不是在跟電腦說話，而是跟一個真實存在的人物做溝通。

 **檢查清單**

- [ ] 寫完訊息之後，請提供一個聰明的主旨。

- [ ] 加入適當的開頭問候語及結尾敬辭。

- [ ] 使用現代商業語言及簡單的句子來代替老式、冗長的措詞。

- [ ] 內文的任何部分絕不全部大寫。

- [ ] 學習合乎邏輯地架構訊息是很重要的。

- [ ] 如同與收件人說話一般的寫作。

- [ ] 重視對方的感覺，並確保語氣適當。

- [ ] 富吸引力的版面編排；使用完整的單字與句子；段落間留有空隔。

- [ ] 將電子郵件視為促進溝通而非代替所有溝通工具的一項利器。

- [ ] 如果透過電子郵件溝通的時間變得愈來愈長、愈複雜，也許改用電話會更有效率。

Unit 2

例行性商業文件
Routine business documents

詢問與相關回覆
Enquiries and replies

詢問商品或服務等資訊是商業上常見的例行性書信，在書寫時可以遵循以下原則：

1. 清楚扼要地陳述需求，包括：一般資訊、產品目錄、價目表、樣品或報價等。
2. 如果採購預算有上限，不要在信中提及，以免供應商將報價提高到你的採購上限。
3. 除非你希望取得特別的折扣，否則不需要特別詢問交易條件，因為大部分的供應商會在回覆時主動告知。
4. 詢問內容宜扼要、簡潔。

詢問信代表潛在的交易，因此必須儘快回覆。如果對方為固定客戶，可致上感激之意；如果對方是新客戶，回覆時可以指出非常高興收到來信，並表達出期望未來可以維繫良好的業務關係。

索取產品目錄和價目表

5.1　不必正式回覆的例行性詢價

供應商會收到許多有關產品目錄或價目表的例行性請求。除非對方要求其他特定資訊，否則不需寫信回覆，可以「敬贈」（With the compliments）便條代替。下列就是只需將所要求的資料，附在印有公司名稱、地址、聯絡電話，以及加註 With the compliments 字樣的便條一同寄出的詢問範例。

【範例 1】

→ p.24

> Dear Sir/Madam
>
> Please send me a copy of your catalogue and price list of fax machines, together with copies of any descriptive leaflets that I could pass to <u>prospective customers</u>[1].
>
> Yours faithfully

---

1. prospective customers：潛在客戶，指可能會購買的客戶。

【範例 2】

→ p.24

> Dear Sir/Madam
>
> I have seen one of your safes in the office of a local firm and they passed on your address to me.
>
> Please send me a copy of your current catalogue. I am particularly interested in safes suitable for a small office.
>
> Yours faithfully

5.2　潛藏大筆生意的詢問信

當詢問信可能帶來大筆訂單或是固定的訂單時，只回以「敬贈便條」是不夠的，應該寫信回覆，並趁此機會大力推銷公司產品。

(a) 詢價

→ p.24

> Dear Sir/Madam
>
> I have a large hardware store in Southampton and am interested in the electric heaters you are advertising in the *West Country Gazette*.
>
> Please send me your illustrated catalogue and a price list.
>
> Yours faithfully

(b) 回覆

→ p.25

> Dear Mrs Johnson
>
> 感謝 —— Thank you for your letter enquiring about electric heaters. I am pleased to enclose a copy of our latest illustrated catalogue.
>
> 提供特定產品的進一步資訊及目錄內容 —— You may be particularly interested in our newest heater, the FX21 model. Without any increase in fuel consumption, it gives out 15% more heat than earlier models. You will find details of our terms in the price list printed on the inside front cover of the catalogue.
>
> 建議對方採取的行動 —— Perhaps you would consider placing a trial order to provide you with an opportunity to test its efficiency. At the same time this would enable you to see for yourself the high quality of material and finish put into this model.
>
> 合適的結尾 —— If you have any questions please contact me on 6234917.
>
> Yours sincerely

5.3 請求提供建議

在收到希望取得建議及指導的詢問信時，應該要給對方一個書面的回覆。

(a) 詢問

→ p.25

> Dear Sir/Madam
>
> Please send me a copy of your current typewriter catalogue and price list. I am particularly interested in purchasing an electronic typewriter with a memory and single-line display.
>
> Yours faithfully

(b) 回覆

→ p.25

> Dear Mr Freeman
>
> 感謝 —— Thank you for your enquiry dated 8 February.
>
> 附上對方要求的目錄 —— I have pleasure in enclosing the catalogue of typewriters as you requested. This includes details of a number of electronic typewriters by various manufacturers.
>
> 提供有關特定詢問商品的進一步細節 —— As you mention your requirement for a memory, have you considered a dedicated word processor? You will find details on pages 15–25, and will see from the price list that prices of the smaller models compare very reasonably with electronic typewriters.
>
> 以提供示範來結尾 —— If you would like demonstrations of any of the models in the catalogue, I would be happy to arrange for our representative to call on you whenever convenient.
>
> Yours sincerely

 提示　清晰的文體給人效率良好的印象，所以遣詞用字宜謹慎小心。

5.4　透過推薦前來詢問

如果供應商是他人推薦給你的，那麼在寫信給供應商時提及此事對你或許會有一些幫助。

(a) 詢問

→ p.26

> Dear Sir/Madam
>
> My neighbour, Mr W Stevens of 29 High Street, Derby, recently bought an electric lawnmower from you. He is delighted with the machine and has recommended that I contact you.
>
> I need a similar machine, but smaller, and should be glad if you would send me a copy of your catalogue and any other information that will help me to make the best choice for my purpose.
>
> Yours faithfully

(b) 回覆

→ p.26

> Dear Mrs Garson
>
> I enclose a catalogue and price list of our lawnmowers, as requested in your letter of 18 May.
>
> The machine bought by your friend was a 38 cm RANSOME' which is an excellent machine. You will find details of the smaller size of 30 cm shown on page 15 of the catalogue. Alternatively, smaller than this is the PANTHER JUNIOR shown on page 17.
>
> We have both these models in stock and should be glad to show them to you if you would care to call at our showroom.
>
> Please contact me on 2314679 if I can provide any further help.
>
> Yours sincerely

5.5　索取樣品

客戶來信索取樣品提供了供應商一個展示產品優越性能的絕佳機會。回函必須具說服力，並展現出對該項產品的信心。

(a) 詢問

→ p.26

> Dear Sirs
>
> We have received a number of enquiries for floor coverings suitable for use on the rough floors which seem to be a feature of much of the new building taking place in this region.
>
> It would be helpful if you could send us samples showing your range of suitable coverings. A pattern-card of the designs in which they are supplied would also be very useful.
>
> Yours faithfully

(b) 回覆

→ p.27

> Dear Mrs King
>
> 感謝 ── Thank you for your enquiry for samples and a pattern-card of our floor coverings.
>
> 回應詢問信中的請求 ── We have today sent to you separately <u>a range</u>[2] of samples specially selected for their hard-wearing qualities. A pattern-card is enclosed.
>
> 建議特定的樣品及後續相關事宜 ── For the purpose you mention we recommend sample number 5 which is specially suitable for rough and uneven surfaces.
>
> We encourage you to test the samples provided. When you have done this if you feel it would help to discuss the matter we will arrange for our technical representative to arrange to come and see you.
>
> 附上價目表 ── Meanwhile, our price list is enclosed which also shows details of our conditions and terms of trading.
>
> 給予聯絡電話 ── Please contact me on 3456891 if I can be of further help.
>
> 合適的結尾敬辭 ── Yours sincerely

---

2. **a range**：代表性產品。

一般的詢問和回覆

在寫一般的詢問信時，務必在所要求的事項上做具體的說明，如價格、交貨細節、付款條件等。而在回覆詢問信時，也要確認每項詢問均已逐一答覆。

5.6　詢問辦公室設備

(a) 詢問

→ p.27

Dear Sir/Madam

Please send me details of fax machines which you supply, together with prices.

We need a model suitable for sending complex diagrams and printed messages, mostly within the UK.

Yours faithfully

(b) 回覆

→ p.27

Dear Mrs Rawson

In reply to your enquiry I have pleasure in enclosing a leaflet showing our latest fax machines.

All the models illustrated can be supplied from stock at competitive prices as shown on the price list inside the catalogue.

May I suggest a visit to our showrooms where you could see demonstrations of the various machines and at the same time view our wide range of office equipment.

Yours sincerely

(c) 要求產品示範

→ p.28

Dear Mr Jenkinson

I have studied with interest the literature you sent me with your letter of 28 April.

Our Administration Manager, Mr Gordon Tan, would like to visit your showrooms to see a demonstration and report on which machine would be most suitable for our purposes. Can we arrange this for next Friday 6 May at 3.30 pm? If this is inconvenient please call me on 2916347.

Yours sincerely

5.7　條列詢問事項

如果需要同時詢問好幾件事情，最好分項說明。

(a) 詢問

→ p.28

Dear Sir/Madam

略提有關詢問事項
的背景

During a recent visit to the Ideal Home Exhibition I saw a sample of your plastic tile flooring. I think this type of flooring would be suitable for the ground floor of my house, but I have not been able to find anyone who is familiar with such tiling.

Would you please give me the following information:

1 What special preparation would be necessary for the underflooring?

以數字標示
特定問題

2 In what colours and designs can the tiles be supplied?

3 Are the tiles likely to be affected by rising damp?

4 Would it be necessary to employ a specialist to lay the floor? If so, can you recommend one in my area?

以要求提供建議
來做結尾

I should appreciate your advice on these matters.

Yours faithfully

(b) 回覆

→ p.29

個人化稱呼

Dear Mr Wilson

感謝來信並說明
已附上產品小冊子

Thank you for your enquiry of 18 August regarding our plastic tile flooring. A copy of our brochure is enclosed showing the designs and range of colours in which the tiles are supplied.

有關當地專家
的詳細資訊

Bottomline, 22 The Square, Rugby, is a very reliable firm which carries out all our work in your area. I have asked the company to get in touch with you to inspect your floors. Their consultant will be able to advise you on what preparation is necessary and whether dampness is likely to cause a problem.

對產品品質
提出保證

Our plastic tile flooring is hard-wearing and if the tiles are <u>laid professionally</u>,[3] I am sure the work will give you lasting satisfaction.

Please let me know if I can provide any further help.

Yours sincerely

---

3. laid professionally：由專家負責鋪設。

5.8　首次詢問

如果過去和對方沒有任何接觸，那麼應該在詢問信中說明你如何取得對方的資料，並提供你公司的一些資料。

而收信的一方為了建立友好的關係，也應該要小心回覆首次詢問的信函。

(a) 詢問

→ p.29

Dear Sir/Madam

背景資料 —

Dekkers of Sheffield inform us that you are manufacturers of polyester cotton bedsheets and pillow cases.

We are dealers in textiles and believe there is a promising market in our area for moderately priced goods of this kind.

要求提供詳細資料 —

Please let me have details of your various ranges including sizes, colours and prices, together with samples of the different qualities of material used.

進一步詢問採購
具體數量的價格 —

Please state your terms of payment and discounts allowed on purchases of quantities of not less than 500 of specific items. Prices quoted should include delivery to our address shown above.

Your prompt reply would be appreciated.

Yours faithfully

(b) 回覆

→ p.30

個人化稱呼 —— Dear Mrs Harrison

感謝來函並附上
目錄及價目表 —— I was very pleased to receive your enquiry of 15 January and enclose our illustrated catalogue and price list giving the details requested.

關於樣品的
詳細資料 —— A full range of samples has also been sent by separate post. When you have had an opportunity to examine them, I feel confident you will agree that the goods are excellent in quality and very reasonably priced.

回覆特定
採購數量一事 —— On regular purchases of quantities of not less than 500 individual items, we would allow a trade discount of 33%. For payment within 10 days from receipt of invoice, an extra discount of 5% of net price would be allowed.

確認品質、需求
與運送事宜 —— Polyester cotton products are rapidly becoming popular because they are strong, warm and light. After studying our prices you will not be surprised to learn that we are finding it difficult to meet the demand. However, if you place your order not later than the end of this month, we guarantee delivery within 14 days of receipt.

提及其他產品 —— I am sure you will also be interested to see information on our other products which are shown in our catalogue; if you need further details on any of these please contact me.

I look forward to hearing from you.

Yours sincerely

5.9　外國進口商的首次詢問

以下範例是一家外國進口商的詢問信。此時，一封友善且提供協助的回信，可以讓對方留下好印象。

(a) 詢問

→ p.30

Dear Sir/Madam

We learn from Spett, Mancienne of Rome that you are producing for export handmade gloves in a variety of natural leathers. There is a steady demand in this country for gloves of high quality, and although sales are not particularly high, good prices are obtained.

Please send me a copy of your catalogue with details of your prices and payment terms. It would also be helpful if you could supply samples of the various skins in which the gloves are supplied.

I look forward to hearing from you soon.

Yours faithfully

(b) 回覆

→ p.31

Dear Mr Fratelli

Thank you for the interest shown in our products in your letter of 22 August.

A copy of our illustrated catalogue is enclosed, together with samples of some of the skins we regularly use in our manufactures. Unfortunately we cannot send you immediately a full range of samples, but you may rest assured that such leathers as chamois and doeskin, which are not represented in the parcel, are of the same high quality.

Mr Frank North, our Overseas Director, will be visiting Rome early next month. He will be pleased to visit you and bring with him a wide range of our goods. When you see them I think you will agree that the quality of materials used and the high standard of the craftsmanship[4] will appeal to the most selective buyer.

We also manufacture a wide range of handmade leather handbags in which you may be interested. They are fully illustrated in the catalogue and are of the same high quality as our gloves. Mr North will be able to show you samples when he calls.

Please let me know if you have any further questions.

Yours sincerely

索取含鑑賞期之試用品

客戶常會要求寄上含鑑賞期之試用品（on approval）。這類商品必須在雙方約定的鑑賞期間內歸還，否則將視同已經購買，不能再予以退還。

---

4. craftsmanship：以專業技術製作。

5.10 客戶索取含鑑賞期之試用品

(a) 請求

→ p.31

Dear Sir/Madam

Several of my customers have recently expressed an interest in your waterproof garments, and have enquired about their quality.

If quality and price are satisfactory there are prospects of good sales here. However before placing a firm order I should be glad if you would send me on 14 days' approval a selection of men's and children's waterproof raincoats and leggings. Any of the items unsold at the end of this period and which I decide not to keep as stock would be returned at my expense.

I hope to hear from you soon.

Yours faithfully

(b) 回覆

→ p.32

Dear Mrs Turner

I was very pleased to receive your request of 12 March for waterproof garments on approval.

As we have not previously done business together, you will appreciate that I must request either the usual trade references, or the name of a bank to which we may refer. As soon as these enquiries are satisfactorily settled we shall be happy to send you a good selection of the items mentioned in your letter.

I sincerely hope that our first transaction together will be the beginning of a long and pleasant business association.

Yours sincerely

在上封信中，供應商藉由要求對方提供備詢商號（trade reference，指可以用來做信用調查的往來公司）來保護自己。另外，有些供應商會要求一筆可退還的保證金或第三者做擔保。但在保護自己的同時，注意不要做出不信任的暗示，以免激怒了客戶。

(c) 寄送產品

在收到來自備詢商號的滿意答覆後，供應商回覆客戶一封自信、直接且提供協助的信函。信中並就售價低廉一事提出解釋，以消除客戶對品質不佳的可能疑慮。

→ p.32

Dear Mrs Turner

I have now received satisfactory references and am pleased to be able to send you a generous selection of our waterproof garments as requested in your letter of 12 March.

This selection includes several new and attractive models in which the water-resistant qualities have been improved by a special process. Due to economies in our methods of manufacture, it has also been possible to reduce our prices which are now lower than those for imported waterproof garments of similar quality.

When you have had an opportunity to inspect the garments, please let us know which you have decided to keep and arrange to return the remainder as early as possible.

I hope this first selection will meet your requirements. If you would like a further selection, please do not hesitate to let me know.

Yours sincerely

(d) 客戶歸還含鑑賞期之試用品

以下這封信是客戶通知供應商要保留哪些商品，並附上貨款。

→ p.32

Dear Mrs Robinson

A few weeks ago you were good enough to send me a selection of waterproof garments on approval.

Quality and prices are both satisfactory and I have arranged to keep the items shown on the attached statement. My cheque for £1209.55 is enclosed in settlement.

Thank you for the prompt and considerate way in which you have handled this transaction.

Yours sincerely

公司代表造訪

客戶通常會將他們對公司代表（representative）的印象，移植到該公司身上。這凸顯了謹慎挑選和適當訓練公司代表的必要性。除了精通說服的藝術外，公司代表還必須符合以下的要求：

◆ 對旗下銷售的商品具備豐富的知識，並知道如何應用。
◆ 能夠預知客戶的需求。
◆ 能夠提供客戶正確的建議和指導。

5.11 要求公司代表到訪

(a) 詢問

→ p.33

Dear Sir/Madam

I read with interest your advertisement for plastic kitchenware in the current issue of the *House Furnishing Review*.

I hope you can arrange for your representative to call when next in this district. It would be helpful if he could bring with him a good selection of items from your product range.

This is a rapidly developing district and if prices are right your goods should find a ready sale.

I look forward to hearing from you soon.

Yours faithfully

(b) 供應商允諾前去拜訪

供應商在回信中使用了親切及會話式的文體。

→ p.33

使用個人化而
非例行性的口吻

從買方的觀點
來舉出案例

藉由提及成功案例
來引起對方興趣

告知為何需要
立刻下單的原因

結尾親切又有幫助

Dear Mr Kennings

Thank you for your enquiry dated 1 November.

Our representative, Ms Jane Whitelaw, will be in your area next week and she will be calling on you. Meanwhile I am enclosing an illustrated catalogue of our plastic goods and details of our terms and conditions of sale.

Plastic kitchenware has long been a popular feature of the modern kitchen. Its bright and attractive colours have strong appeal, and wherever dealers have arranged them in special window displays good sales are reported.

When you have inspected the samples Ms Whitelaw will bring with her, you will understand why we have a large demand for these products. Therefore if you wish to have a stock of these goods before Christmas we advise you to place your order by the end of this month.

We look forward to working with you.

Yours sincerely

要求特許權

當客戶所要求的產品已停止供應，或無法應允特殊的要求時，必須謹慎加以回應，以免激怒對方或喪失交易機會。

5.12　要求獨家代理權

(a) 詢問

→ p.34

Dear Sir/Madam

背景資訊 ── We have recently extended our radio and television department and are thinking
與具體細節　　of adding new ranges to our present stocks. We are particularly interested in your
BELLTONE radio and television models and should be glad if you would send us
your trade catalogue and terms of sale and payment.

要求獨家代理權 ── Your products are not yet offered by any other dealer in this town, and if we decide
to introduce them we should like to request <u>sole distribution rights</u>[5] in this area.

合適的結尾 ── I hope to hear from you soon.

Yours faithfully

(b) 回信婉拒

在這封回信中，供應商技巧地拒絕了獨家代理的要求。雖然沒有多費唇舌解釋拒絕的理由，但在第三段的內容中已做了暗示。

---

5. **sole distribution rights**：獨家代理權，即針對某項產品取得某區域內的唯一銷售權利。

→ p.34

Dear Mr Sanderson

感謝 ── Thank you for your letter of 8 April enquiring about our BELLTONE radio and television products.

附上目錄和
進一步的詳細資料 ── This range has been discontinued and replaced by the CLAIRTONE. You will see from the enclosed catalogue that the new models are attractively designed and include the latest technical improvements. Although rather more expensive than their predecessors, the CLAIRTONE models have already been well received and good sales are being reported regularly from many areas.

針對獨家代理權的
請求予以謹慎的
回應 ── As part of our efforts to keep down manufacturing costs, I am sure you will understand that we must increase sales by distributing through as many outlets as possible. Dealers in other areas appear to be well satisfied with their sales under this arrangement, and it appears to be working very well.

表達未來
合作的期待 ── I hope we can look forward to receiving your orders soon, and will be glad to include your name in our list of approved dealers, with your permission.

I look forward to your early reply.

Yours sincerely

5.13　要求含特別條件的交易

(a) 詢問

請注意，這封信完美地應用了「四點計畫」。

→ p.35

Dear Sir / Madam

引言 ── Please send us your current catalogue and price list for bicycles. We are interested in models for both men and women, and also for children.

提供詳細資料 ── We are the leading bicycle dealers in this city where cycling is popular, and have branches in five neighbouring towns. If the quality of your products is satisfactory and the prices are reasonable, we expect to place regular orders for fairly large numbers.

要求對方的回應 ── In the circumstances please indicate whether you will allow us a special discount. This would enable us to maintain the low selling prices which have been an important reason for the growth of our business. In return we would be prepared to place orders for a guaranteed annual minimum number of bicycles, the figure to be mutually agreed.

結尾
（含聯絡電話） ── If you wish to discuss this please contact me on 6921671.

Yours faithfully

(b) 回覆

在回信中，製造商謹慎地根據滑動比例（sliding scale）來提供折扣。

→ p.35

Dear Ms Denning

I was glad to learn from your letter of 18 July of your interest in our products. As requested our catalogue and price list are enclosed, together with details of our conditions of sale and terms of payment.

We have considered your proposal to place orders for a guaranteed minimum number of machines in return for a special allowance. However after careful consideration we feel it would be better to offer you a special allowance on the following sliding scale basis.

On purchases exceeding an annual total of:

£1,000 but not exceeding £3,000	3%
£3,000 but not exceeding £7,500	4%
£7,500 and above	5%

No special allowance could be given on annual total purchases below £1,000.

I feel that an arrangement on these lines would be more satisfactory to both our companies.

Orders will be subject to the usual trade references.

I look forward to working with you and hope to hear from you soon.

Yours sincerely

5.14　拒絕含特別條件的交易

供應商在回信中藉提出其他建議，技巧地拒絕了客戶的降價要求。

→ p.36

Dear Mr Ellis

We have carefully considered your letter of 18 December.

As our companies have done business with each other for many years, we would like to grant your request to lower the prices of our sportswear. However our own <u>overheads</u>[6] have risen sharply in the past 12 months, and to reduce prices by the 15% you mention could not be done without considerably lowering our standards of quality. This is something we are not prepared to do.

Instead of a 15% reduction on sportswear, we suggest a reduction of 5% on all our products for orders of £800 or more. On orders of this size we could make such a reduction without lowering our standards.

I hope that you will agree to this suggestion and look forward to continuing to receive regular orders from you.

Yours sincerely

實用措詞

詢問、請求

【開頭】

1. We are interested in ... as advertised recently in ...
   我們對於最近廣告上所刊登的⋯⋯感到興趣

2. We have received an enquiry for your ...
   我們收到有關詢問貴公司的⋯⋯

3. I was interested to see your advertisement for ...
   我對於貴公司廣告中刊登的⋯⋯表示興趣

4. I understand you are manufacturers of (dealers in) ... and should like to receive your current catalogue.
   得知貴公司是⋯⋯製造商（經銷商），希望能收到貴公司最新的產品目錄。

6.　overheads：經常性支出，如房租、電費及管理費等。

【主要段落及結尾】

1. When replying please also include delivery details.
   煩請回信時一併附上送貨細節。

2. Please also state whether you can supply the goods from stock as we need them urgently.
   因為急需該產品，請告知是否有存貨。

3. If you can supply suitable goods, we may place regular orders for large quantities.
   如果您能供應適合的產品，我們將考慮定期地大量採購。

回覆

【開頭】

1. Thank you for your letter of ... As requested we enclose ...
   謝謝您……的來信，如您所要求的，隨函附上……

2. I was pleased to learn ... that you are interested in our ...
   很高興得知您對我們的……表示興趣

3. Thank you for your enquiry dated ... regarding ...
   謝謝您（日期）來信詢問有關……

【結尾】

1. We look forward to receiving a trial order from you soon.
   期望儘快收到您的試銷訂單。

2. We shall be pleased to send you any further information you may need.
   如果需要更詳細的資料，我們將樂於為您寄上。

3. Any orders you place with us will have our prompt attention.
   我們將儘快處理您的訂單。

4. Please let me know if you need any further details.
   如需進一步的細節，請與我聯繫。

報價、估價與投標
Quotations, estimates and tenders

所謂的報價是指依據所陳述的條件供應貨物。潛在的買方沒有義務因要求報價就必須購買，而供應商也不會因無法或無意供貨而損及公司聲譽。一項令人滿意的報價應包含以下幾點：

◆ 對來信詢問表示感謝。

◆ 提供價格、折扣和付款條件的細節。

◆ 清楚說明價格是否包含包裝、運費或保險。

◆ 約定交貨日期。

◆ 報價的有效（valid）期。

◆ 希望對方能接受此一報價。

相關術語

在請求報價時，買方務必問清楚價格是否包含運費和保險費等。否則可能會因為供應商的報價不明確而導致嚴重的爭議，尤其是在另外收取的費用很高，如與國外交易的情況下。以下是一些與報價有關的術語：

◆ Carriage paid ：運費付訖。報價包含貨物送至買方所屬地的費用。

◆ Carriage forward ：買方負擔運費。

◆ Loco, ex works, ex factory, ex warehouse ：現場交貨、工廠交貨、倉庫交貨。買方負擔貨物離開工廠或倉庫之後期間的所有費用。

◆ FOR (free on rail)：鐵路交貨價。報價包含了運抵最近火車站的運費，以及將貨物裝上卡車的費用。

◆ FAS (free alongside ship)：船邊交貨。報價包含使用駁船或載貨船將貨物卸至船邊，但不包括運至甲板上的費用。

◆ FOB (free on board)：船上交貨價，或稱離岸價格。報價包含賣方將貨物放至指定的船舶上費用；之後由買方負擔所有的費用。

- CIF (cost, insurance & freight)：到岸價格。報價包含貨物之成本、保險費及運費。
- Ex ship：目的港船上交貨。報價包含運抵對方指定的目的港的載貨船或駁船上，或者假使船就在碼頭附近，就運至碼頭。

例行性報價

6.1 印刷用紙的詢價

(a) 詢價

底下是一封令人滿意的詢價信，它包含了一些要件：

- 清楚、扼要地說明需求。
- 解釋紙張的用途，如此供應商才能提供品質符合的報價。
- 說明所需數量，此點相當重要，因為數量會直接影響價格。
- 說明何時交貨。在任何買賣合約中，都一定要言明此點。
- 陳述報價包含哪些費用。在這個例子中，指的是貨物運抵工廠的費用（delivery at our works）。

→ p.38

Dear Sir,

We will soon be requiring 200 reams of good quality white poster paper suitable for auction bills and poster work generally. We require paper which will retain its white appearance after pasting on walls and hoardings.

Please let us have some samples and a quotation, including delivery at our works within 4 weeks of our order.

Yours faithfully

(b) 報價

供應商必須立刻回覆，並且確保所有詢問重點都已回應完畢。

→ p.38

Dear Mr Keenan

Thank you for your enquiry dated 21 June.

As requested we enclose samples of different qualities of paper suitable for poster work.

We are pleased to quote as follows:

A1 quality Printing Paper white £2.21 per kg
A2 quality Printing Paper white £2.15 per kg
A3 quality Printing Paper white £2.10 per kg

These prices include delivery at your works.

All these papers are of good quality and quite suitable for poster work. We guarantee that they will not discolour when pasted.

We can promise delivery within one week from receiving your order, and hope you will find both samples and prices satisfactory.

Please give me a call on 2634917 if you have any questions.

Yours sincerely

6.2 瓷器的詢價

下例為另一封令人滿意的詢價信，信中明確指出所需商品，以及折扣、包裝、運費及付款條件等重要內容。

(a) 詢價

→ p.39

Dear Sir

You have previously supplied us with crockery and we should be glad if you would now quote for the items named below, manufactured by Ridgeway Pottery Company of Hanley. The pattern we require is 'number 59 Conway Spot (Green)'.

300 Teacups and Saucers
300 Tea Plates
 40 1-litre Teapots

When quoting prices please include packing and delivery to the above address. Please also state discounts allowable, terms of payment and earliest possible date of delivery.

I hope to hear from you soon.

Yours faithfully

(b) 報價

→ p.39

> Dear Mr Clarke
>
> CONWAY SPOT (GREEN) GILT RIMS
>
> Thank you for your enquiry of 18 April for a further supply of our crockery. We are pleased to quote as follows:
>
> | | |
> |---|---|
> | Teacups | £83.75 per hundred |
> | Tea Saucers | £76.00 per hundred |
> | Tea Plates | £76.00 per hundred |
> | Teapots, 1-litre | £4.20 each |
>
> These prices include packing and delivery, but a charge is made for crates, with an allowance for their return in good condition.
>
> Delivery can be made from stock and we will allow you a 5% discount on items ordered in quantities of 100 or more. There would be an additional cash discount of 2% on total cost of payment within one month from date of invoice.
>
> We hope that you will find these terms satisfactory. Please give me a call on 3614917 if you have any questions.
>
> Yours sincerely

含特定條件的報價

依據情況及商業型態的不同，報價中常會包含一些特定的條件限制，包括報價的有效期、限量發行、能追加訂購等。當供應商所供應的商品是限量的，或在收到訂單後需視是否有貨可出時，供應商須如下在報價中清楚說明這些限制條件：

◆ This offer is made subject to the goods being available when the order is received. （此報價以收到訂單後有貨可出爲準。）

◆ This offer is subject to acceptance within 7 days. （此報價有效期爲七天。）

◆ The prices quoted will apply only to orders received on or before 31 March. 〔以上報價僅適用於 3 月 31 日以前（含當日）收到的訂單。〕

◆ Goods ordered from our 2005 catalogue can be supplied only while stocks last. （可以供應您從 2005 年的產品目錄中所訂的產品，但僅限於尚有存貨時。）

◆ For acceptance within 14 days. （此報價有效期爲十四天。）

6.3 國外買主詢價

(a) 詢價

→ p.40

> Dear Sirs
>
> We have recently received a number of requests for your lightweight raincoats and believe that we could place regular orders with you, as long as your prices are competitive.
>
> From the description in your catalogue we feel that your AQUATITE range would be most suitable for this region. Please let me have a quotation for men's and women's coats in both small and medium sizes, delivered CIF Alexandria.
>
> If your prices are right, we will place a first order for 400 raincoats, namely 100 of each of the 4 qualities. Shipment would be required within 4 weeks of order.
>
> I look forward to a prompt reply.
>
> Yours faithfully

(b) 報價

以下是英國製造商回覆的一封相當不錯的現代英文商業書信範例。信件的語氣十分和善，措詞簡單清楚。寫信者表現出對熱帶居民所遭受問題的理解（例如提到水氣凝結的部分），並且提供該產品可帶來銷售佳績的資訊（例如「追加訂購」與「特殊處理」）。

此外，這封信將運費和保險費與產品本身的費用分開列示。除了方便計算商業折扣外，也正確告訴買方他們爲商品所支付的實際價格是多少。注意報價單中提到的「有效期一個月」的條件，這是指供應商承諾產品可在此指定期間內依此報價出售。

供應商還在信中試著推薦其他產品來引起客戶的興趣，這是很好的
商業技巧。

→ p.41

Dear Mrs Barden

AQUATITE RAINWEAR

感謝 —— Thank you for your letter of 15 June. I was pleased to learn about the enquiries you have received for our raincoats.

特別提及熱帶氣候
來凸顯該產品
的受歡迎程度

提及「追加訂購」
來做品質保證

Our AQUATITE range is particularly suitable for warm climates. During the past year we have supplied this range to dealers in several tropical countries. We have already received <u>repeat orders</u>[1] from many of those dealers. This range is popular not only because of its light weight but also because the material used has been specially treated to prevent excessive condensation on the inside surface.

We are pleased to quote as follows:

關於價格的
具體細節

100 AQUATITE coats	men's	medium	£17.50 ea	1750.00
100 AQUATITE coats	men's	small	£16.80 ea	1680.00
100 AQUATITE coats	women's	medium	£16.00 ea	1600.00
100 AQUATITE coats	women's	small	£15.40 ea	1540.00
				6570.00
less 33$\frac{1}{3}$% trade discount				2187.81
Net price				4382.19
Freight (London to Alexandria)				186.00
Insurance				122.50
TOTAL				4690.69

交易條件、裝運及
報價有效期的
相關細節

Terms: 2$\frac{1}{2}$% one month from date of invoice

Shipment: Within 3–4 weeks of receiving order

For acceptance within one month.

提及其他產品
和附件

We feel you may be interested in some of our other products, and enclose descriptive booklets and a supply of sales literature for issue to your customers.

We hope to receive your order soon.

Yours sincerely

---

1. repeat order ：追加訂購。

表列式報價

有些報價單會採用表列式或者備有特別的表格。這種表列示的報價
單優點為：

◆ 清楚，資料以表格呈現，容易理解。
◆ 完整，不會遺漏基本資料。

表列式報價單尤其適合品項較多的報價。在寄送這種特別準備的報
價單時，應附上一封短信（covering letter ，附有其他文件的簡短信
函），內容包括：

◆ 對來函詢價表達謝意。
◆ 針對產品提出有利評論。
◆ 激起買方對其他產品的興趣。
◆ 期待收到訂單。

這樣的做法可以協助企業建立良好的形象及友好關係。

6.4　特殊格式報價單所附的短信

(a) 短信

→ p.42

> Dear Mrs Greenway
>
> Thank you for your enquiry of 15 August. Our quotation for leather shoes and handbags is enclosed. All items can be delivered from stock.
>
> These items are made from very best quality leather and can be supplied in a range of designs and colours wide enough to meet the requirements of a fashionable trade such as yours.
>
> Also enclosed is a copy of our catalogue in which you will find details of our other products. These include leather purses and gloves, described and illustrated on pages 18–25.
>
> The catalogue gives all the essential facts about our goods, but if you have any queries please do not hesitate to give me a call on 9635117.
>
> Yours sincerely

(b) 報價

底下這份報價單的重點如下：

◆ 加註單編號報價，有助於日後參考之用。

◆ 提供產品目錄編號，可精準確認品項，避免誤解。產品的外形和規格也分別加上了編號。

◆ 加註 For acceptance within 21 days（21 天內有效）的目的在保護供應商，告知買方應該在此期間內下單，否則價格可能會有所調漲。

◆ 4% one month 意指買方若同意該報價內容，並於一個月內付款，可享有 4% 的折扣。如果在一至兩個月內付款，折扣將降至 2.5%。

→ p.43

CENTRAL LEATHERCRAFT LTD
85–87 Cheapside, London EC2V 6AA
Telephone 020-7242-2177/8

Quotation no JBS/234   Date 20 August 200—

Smith Jenkins & Co
15 Holme Avenue
SHEFFIELD
S6 2LW

Catalogue Number	Item	Quantity	Unit Price
S 25	Men's Box Calf Shoes (brown)	12 pairs	65.75
	Men's Box Calf Shoes (black)	36 pairs	65.50
S 27	Ladies' Glace Kid Tie Shoes (various colours)	48 pairs	64.80
S 42	Ladies' Calf Colt Court Shoes	24 pairs	64.35
H 212	Ladies' Handbags – Emperor	36	66.50
H 221	Ladies' Handbags – Paladin	36	78.75
H 229	Ladies' Handbags – Aristocrat	12	80.00
	FOR ACCEPTANCE WITHIN 21 DAYS		

Delivery   ex works

Terms   4% one month $2^1/_2$% two months

(signed)

for Central Leathercraft Ltd

圖表 6.1　報價單

6.5　報價單所附的短信

→ p.44

Dear Miss Richardson

Thank you for your interest in StarWay.

I am pleased to enclose our quotation for the StarWay laptop system that you require. This gives details of a standard specification and also outlines the cost of configuring the system to meet your needs.

As one of the world's leading direct marketers of personal computers, we believe our success is primarily due to putting our clients first. We want to custom-build the right personal computer for you as well as ensure that you get the ongoing service and support that you need.

Please call me on 0800 345234 to finalise your purchase. If you have any questions at all, please do not hesitate to give me a call.

Yours sincerely

 好的寫作者會呈現正面而非負面的事項。

估價與規格說明

報價是依設定的條件來提出產品的售價，而估價則是依陳述的價格提供特定的服務，通常是以某一規格說明為依據。和報價一樣，估價也不具法律效力，因此估價者不一定非要接受依估價單所下的任何訂單。

6.6 中央暖氣的安裝估價

(a) 詢問

在以下的詢價信中，寄件人附上一份規格說明（參見下頁）詳述工程內容及欲使用材料的規格，作為承包商估價的參考。規格說明中也包含了草圖（按比例繪製），標示出暖房的安裝位置。

→ p.44

Dear Sirs

Please let me have an estimate for installing central heating in my bungalow at 1 Margate Road, St Annes-on-Sea. A plan of the bungalow is attached showing required positions and sizes of radiators, together with a specification showing further details and materials to be used.

As you will note from the specification, I am interested only in first-class workmanship and in the use of best quality materials. However cost is, of course, a matter of some importance. It is essential that this work is completed by 31 August at the latest.

In your reply please include a firm completion date.

Your prompt reply will be appreciated.

Yours faithfully

(b) 規格說明

→ p.45

SPECIFICATION FOR INSTALLING CENTRAL HEATING at 1 MARGATE ROAD, ST ANNES-ON-SEA

1　Installation of the latest small-bored central heating, to be carried out with best quality copper piping of 15 mm bore, fitted with 'Ryajand' electric pump of fully adequate power and lagged under floor to prevent loss of heat.

2　Existing boiler to be replaced by a Glow-worm No 52 automatic gas-fired boiler, rated at 15.2 kW and complete with gas governor, flame failure safety device and boiler water thermostat.

3　Installation of a Randall No 103 clock controller to give automatic operation of the central heating system at predetermined times.

4　Existing hot-water cylinder to be replaced by a calorifier-type cylinder[2] suitable for supplying domestic hot water separately from the central heating system.

5　Seven 'Dimplex' or similar flat-type radiators to be fitted under windows of five rooms, and in hall and kitchen, according to plan enclosed; also a towel rail in bathroom. Sizes of radiators and towel rail to be as specified in plan attached to my letter dated 5 July 200— addressed to yourselves.

6　Each radiator to be separately controlled, swivelled for cleaning and painted pale cream with red-lead undercoating.

7　The system to be provided with the necessary fall for emptying and to prevent air-locks.

8　All work to be carried out from under floor to avoid cutting or lifting floor boards, which are tongued and grooved.

9　Insulation[3] of roof with 80 mm fibreglass.

J HARRIS

5 July 200—

---

2. calorifier-type cylinder：可以保持水溫的鋼瓶。

3. insulation：一種可隔熱的覆蓋物。

(c) 承包商估價

承包商會根據客戶所提供的資訊估算費用，並且寄上一份估價單及一封短信。信中必須提到以下訊息：

◆ 提及其他成功個案，增加客戶信心。
◆ 承諾一個完工日期。
◆ 為避免增加無法預知的成本，導致利潤下滑，可註明市場價格和工資調整條款作為保護措施。
◆ 期待對方接受此估價。

在下面這封信中，為了強化客戶信心，承包商談到了其他的成功案例，並且允諾如有需要，可以安排客戶實地勘查。

→ p.46

Dear Mr Harris

INSTALLATION OF CENTRAL HEATING AT 1 MARGATE ROAD, ST ANNES-ON-SEA

感謝 ── Thank you for your letter of 5 July enclosing specification and plan for a gas-fired central heating system at the above address.

陳述價格和折扣 ── We should be glad to carry out the work for a total of £2,062.50 with a $2\frac{1}{2}$% discount for settlement within one month of the date of our account. We can

承諾一個完工日期 ── promise to complete all work by 31 August if we receive your instructions by the end of this month. Please note that the price quoted is based on present costs of

此條款保護承包商 免於未來不確定 成本的增加 ── materials and labour. Should these costs rise we should have to add the increased costs to our price.

提及其他個案 以增加對方的信心 ── We have installed many similar heating systems in your area. Our reputation for high class work is well known. If you would like to inspect one of our recent installations before making a firm decision, this can be arranged.

We hope you will be satisfied with the price quoted, and look forward to receiving your instructions soon.

Yours sincerely

投標

參與投標，通常是爲了要爭取公開招標的案子。它依據投標的價格
與條款提供特定產品的供應或工程的履行。投標唯有得標後才具法
律效力，在這之前的投標隨時都可撤回。投標書通常是依公告的表
格填寫，其中包含必要的規格說明及所設定的詳細條件。

6.7　公開招標

→ p.46

> **THE COUNTY COUNCIL OF LANCASHIRE**
> **COUNTY HALL, PRESTON PR1 2RL**
>
> Tenders are invited for the supply to the Council's power station at Bamford, during the year 200—, of approximately 2,000 tonnes of best quality furnace coke, delivered in quantities as required. Tenders must be submitted on the official form obtainable from County Hall to reach the Clerk of the Council not later than 12.00 noon on Friday 30 June.
>
> The Council does not bind itself to accept the lowest, or any, of the tenders submitted.
>
> B BRADEN
>
> Clerk to the Council

6.8　承包商投標函

在取得正式表格並依照規定填寫之後，應該附上一封正式的短信。

→ p.47

> **CONFIDENTIAL**
>
> Clerk to the Council
> County Hall
> PRESTON
> PR1 2RL
>
> Dear Mr Braden
>
> **TENDER FOR FURNACE COKE**
>
> Having read the terms and conditions in the official form supplied by you, I enclose my tender for the supply of coke to the Bamford power station during 200—. I hope to learn that it has been accepted.
>
> Yours sincerely

6.9 封閉式投標

當招標對象僅限於特定組織或團體的成員時，稱爲「封閉式投標」
（closed tender）。以下範例取自於《巴格達觀察員》（*Baghdad Observer*）。

→ p.47

STATE ORGANISATION FOR ENGINEERING INDUSTRIES
P O BOX 3093 BAGHDAD IRAQ

TENDER NO 1977
FOR THE SUPPLY OF 16,145 TONNES
OF
ALUMINIUM AND ALUMINIUM ALLOY INGOTS,
BILLETS AND SLABS

1   The SOEI invites tenderers who are registered in the Chamber of Commerce and hold a Certificate of Income Tax of this year, as well as a certificate issued by the Registrar of Commercial Agencies confirming that he is licensed by the Director General of Registration and Supervision of Companies, to participate in the above tender. General terms and conditions together with specifications and quantities sheets can be obtained from the Planning and Financial Control Department at the 3rd floor of this Organisation against payment of one Iraqi Dinar for each copy.

2   All offers are to be put in the tender box of this Organisation, Commercial Affairs Department, 4th floor, marked with the name and number of the tender at or before 1200 hours on Saturday 31 January 200—.

3   Offers should be accompanied by preliminary guarantee issued by the Rafidain Bank, equal to not less than 5 per cent of the C & F value of the offer.

4   Any offer submitted after the closing date of the tender, or which does not comply with the above terms, will not be accepted.

5   This Organisation does not bind itself to accept the lowest or any other offer.

6   Foreign companies who have no local agents in Iraq shall be exempted from the conditions stated in item number 1 above.

ALI AL-HAMDANI (ENGINEER)
PRESIDENT

報價遭拒或調整報價

當買方要回信拒絕報價者的報價或其他出價時，回函應保持禮貌，一方面謝謝對方的費心費力，一方面解釋拒絕的理由。內容應該要包含：

◆ 感謝供應商的出價。
◆ 表達無法接受的遺憾之意。
◆ 說明拒絕原因。
◆ 如果適當，可提出「還價」（counter-offer，或稱反報價，指任一方對報價內容、條件提出修正或要求增加若干條件）。
◆ 暗示未來仍有合作的機會。

6.10　買方回絕供應商的報價

→ p.48

Dear Mr Walton

Thank you for your quotation dated 19 February for strawboards.

I appreciate your trouble in this matter but as your prices are very much higher than those I have been quoted by other dealers, I regret I cannot give you an immediate order.

I shall bear your company in mind when I require other products in the future.

Yours sincerely

6.11 供應商同意提供更好的條件

(a) 詢價

→ p.48

Dear Ms Hansen

感謝 — Thank you for your letter of 18 August and for the samples of cotton underwear you very kindly sent to me.

談到品質雖佳，但 也表達價格過高導 致利潤減少的考量 — I appreciate the good quality of these garments, but unfortunately your prices appear to be on the high side even for garments of this quality. To accept the prices you quote would leave me with only a small profit on my sales since this is an area in which the principal demand is for articles in the medium price range.

重複對品質的 滿意度，並請求 降價，爭取 合作機會 — I like the quality of your goods and would welcome the opportunity to do business with you. May I suggest that perhaps you could make some allowance on your quoted prices which would help to introduce your goods to my customers. If you cannot do so, then I must regretfully decline your offer as it stands.

I hope to hear from you soon.

Yours sincerely

(b) 回覆

→ p.49

Dear Mr Daniels

已收到來信 — I am sorry to learn from your letter of 23 August that you find our prices too high.

回應關於 價格偏高的疑慮 — We do our best to keep prices as low as possible without sacrificing quality. To this end we are constantly investigating new methods of manufacture.

保證價格合理 — Considering the quality of the goods offered we do not feel that the prices we quoted are at all excessive. However, bearing in mind the special character of your

提供首次下單 的優惠，爭取 新客戶 — trade, we are prepared to offer you a discount of 4% on a first order for £1000. This allowance is made because we should like to do business with you if possible, but I must stress that it is the furthest we can go to help you.

I hope this revised offer will enable you to place an order, and I look forward to hearing from you soon.

Yours sincerely

追蹤信

供應商在提供報價後，未見買方下任何訂單，或未回覆已收到報價時，供應商當然會想了解箇中原因。反應快的供應商會安排公司代表登門拜訪，假如該詢問信是來自較遠處，則會寄一封追蹤信（follow-up letter）給對方。

6.12　供應商的追蹤信

這是一封效果不錯的追蹤信，供應商表達了真誠的協助之意，直接切入重點。為考量買方的方便，信中提供其他選擇，而且用服務保證做結尾。

→ p.49

Dear Mrs Larkin

As we have not heard from you since we sent you our catalogue of filing systems, we wonder whether you require further information before deciding to place an order.

The modern system of lateral filing has important space-saving advantages wherever economy of space is important. However if space is not one of your problems, our flat-top suspended system may suit you better. The neat and tidy appearance it gives to the filing drawers and the ease and speed with which files are located are just two of its features which many users find attractive.

Would you like us to send our representative to call and discuss your needs with you? John Robinson has advised on equipment for many large, modern offices and would be able to recommend the system most suited to your own requirements. There would of course be no obligation of any kind. Perhaps you would prefer to pay a visit to our showroom and see for yourself how the different filing systems work.

You may be sure that whichever of these opportunities you decide to accept, you would receive personal attention and the best possible advice.

If you have any further questions please call me on 2356123.

Yours sincerely

6.13 挽回流失的客戶

沒有哪一家成功的企業禁得起固定客戶的流失。所以供應商應該要定期檢查、確認哪幾位客戶的訂單日漸減少，然後寄一封追蹤信給他們。

→ p.50

Dear Sirs

We notice with regret that it is some considerable time since we last received an order from you. We hope this is in no way due to dissatisfaction with our service or with the quality of goods we have supplied. In either of these situations we should be grateful to hear from you. We are most anxious to ensure that customers obtain maximum satisfaction from their dealings with us. If the lack of orders from you is due to changes in the type of goods you handle, we may still be able to meet your needs if you will let us know in what directions your policy has changed.

As we have not heard otherwise, we assume that you are still selling the same range of sports goods, so a copy of our latest illustrated catalogue is enclosed. We feel this compares favourably in range, quality and price with the catalogues of other manufacturers. At the same time we take the opportunity to mention that our terms are now much easier than previously, following the withdrawal of exchange control[4] and other official measures since we last did business together.

I hope to hear from you soon.

Yours faithfully

---

4. exchange control ：匯率管制，指由政府控制外匯交易市場。

實用措詞

請求報價、估價等

【開頭】

1. Please quote for the supply of ...
   請提供……的報價

2. Please send me a quotation for the supply of ...
   請寄一份……的報價單給我

3. We wish to have the following work carried out and should be glad if you would submit an estimate.
   我們希望進行以下工程，希望您能提供估價單。

【結尾】

1. As the matter is urgent we should like this information by the end of this week.
   事出緊急，我們希望能在本週前取得這些資訊。

2. If you can give us a competitive quotation, we expect to place a large order.
   如果您能提供有競爭力的價格，我們希望大量訂購。

3. If your prices compare favourably with those of other suppliers, we shall send you an early order.
   如果您的價格較其他供應商有利，我們會儘快下單。

回覆報價的請求

【開頭】

1. Thank you for your letter of ...
   感謝您……來信

2. We thank you for your enquiry of ... and are pleased to quote as follows:
   謝謝您……的詢問，我們樂意提供以下的報價：

3. With reference to your enquiry of ... we shall be glad to supply ... at the price of ...
   關於您……的詢價，我們樂意提供……的價格

4. We are sorry to learn that you find our quotation of ... too high.
   對於您認為我們的報價太高，我們感到抱歉。

【結尾】

1. We trust you will find our quotation satisfactory and look forward to receiving your order.
   相信您對我們的報價一定會滿意，期待收到您的訂單。

2. We shall be pleased to receive your order, which will have our prompt and careful attention.
   我們樂意收到您的訂單，並且會快速、謹慎處理。

3. As the prices quoted are exceptionally low and likely to rise, we would advise you to place your order without delay.
   由於報價金額相當低而且近期內可能調漲，建議您儘快下單。

4. As our stocks of these goods are limited, we suggest you place an order immediately.
   因為這些產品庫存有限，建議您立刻下單。

訂單與履行
Orders and their fulfilment

下單

印製好的訂單

大部分的企業都備有印製好的制式訂單（如圖表 7.1），其優點為：

1. 表格事先經過編號，方便參考。
2. 事先印好標題，可確保不會遺漏必要訊息。

此外，有些表格背面印有下訂單的一般條款，訂單的正面通常必須參照這些條款，否則供應商不受法律的約束。

→ p.52

J B SIMPSON & CO LTD
18 Deansgate, Sheffield S11 2BR
Telephone 0114 234234
Fax: 0114 234235

Order no 237   Date 7 July 200—

Nylon Fabrics Ltd
18 Brazenose Street
MANCHESTER
M60 8AS

Please supply:

Quantity	Item(s)	Catalogue Number	Price
25	Bed Sheets (106 cm) blue	75	£10.50 each
25	Bed Sheets (120 cm) primrose	82	£10.00 each
50	Pillow Cases blue	117	£6.90 each
50	Pillow Cases primrose	121	£6.90 each

(signed)

for J B Simpson & Co Ltd

圖表 7.1　訂單

信函式訂單（Letter orders）

有些小公司並沒有制式表格，而以信函代替。在寄送這類信函式訂單時，務必確保它的正確性和清楚性，需包含以下重點：

1. 正確及完整的產品說明。
2. 目錄編號。
3. 數量。
4. 價格。
5. 交貨需求，包括地點、日期、運輸工具。另外註明是運費付訖（carriage paid）或運費到付（carriage forward，即買方負擔運費）等等。
6. 買賣雙方事先協議的付款條件。

交易雙方的法律責任

根據英國法律規定，買方的訂單只是一個有意購買的出價，不具法律效力，直到供應商接受了這買方的出價，之後雙方均受到法律上的約束必須遵守協議。

(a) 買方義務

當協議發生強制力後，買方的法律義務為：

◆ 買方必須接受根據訂單條件出貨的商品。
◆ 在交貨時或供應商指定的特定期間內支付貨款。
◆ 儘早檢查商品（在發現瑕疵後，如果不儘速通知供應商，買方將被認定同意接受該商品）。

(b) 賣方義務

供應商的法律義務為：

◆ 於約定期間內，依照訂單指示出貨。
◆ 擔保商品沒有買方於購買當下察覺不到的瑕疵。

如果商品發生瑕疵，買方可以要求降價、更換商品或取消訂單。有時還可提出損害賠償。

例行性訂單

例行性訂單可以簡短且正式，但仍需明列商品的基本細節，以及交貨和付款條件。如果訂單上的品項有兩種或兩種以上時，應該分開條列，以方便參考。

7.1　電話訂購的確認

→ p.53

Dear

We confirm the order which was placed with you by telephone this morning for the following:

3　'Excelda Studio' electronic typewriters
　　each with 12 pitch daisy wheel

Price: £895 each, less 40% trade discount
　　　　　　　　carriage forward

These machines are urgently required. We understand that you are arranging for immediate delivery from stock.

Yours sincerely

7.2　表列式訂單

→ p.53

Dear

Please accept our order for the following books on our usual discount terms of 25% off published prices:

NUMBER OF COPIES	TITLE	AUTHOR	PUBLISHED PRICE
50	*Communication for Business*	Shirley Taylor	£8.99
40	*Essential Communication Skills*	Shirley Taylor	£7.99

We look forward to prompt delivery.

Yours faithfully

7.3 以報價為基礎的訂單

→ p.53

> Dear
>
> Thank you for your quotation of 4 June. Please supply:
>
> 100 reams of A2 quality Printing Paper, white, at £2.16 per kg, including delivery.
>
> Delivery is required not later than the end of this month.
>
> Yours sincerely

7.4 附短信的訂單

當訂單（參閱圖表 7.1）要連同一封短信寄出時，請將所有的基本細節列於訂單中，額外解釋部分才寫在短信內。

→ p.54

> Dear
>
> Thank you for your quotation of 5 July. Our order number 237 for four of the items is enclosed.
>
> All these items are urgently required by our customer so we hope you will send them immediately.
>
> Yours sincerely

通知收到訂單

收到訂單後如果無法立即處理，應該立刻回信告知對方已收到訂單。對於小筆的例行性訂單，可以用制式信函或電子郵件回覆。但是寫一封短信說明預計何時出貨，則可以促進彼此的關係。如果無法供貨，必須回信解釋原因，適當的話，可建議其他替代品供買方參考。

7.5 例行性訂單的正式回覆──傳真

→ p.54

Thank you for your order number 237 for bed coverings.

As all items were in stock, they will be delivered to you tomorrow by our own transport.

We hope you will find these goods satisfactory and that we may have the pleasure of receiving further orders from you.

7.6 首次訂購的確認通知

對於首次訂購，也就是來自於新客戶的訂單，一定要回信告知已收到訂單。

→ p.54

Dear

感謝 ── We were very pleased to receive your order of 18 June for cotton prints, and welcome you as one of our customers.

確認價格及交貨資訊並保證滿意 ── We confirm supply of the prints at the prices stated in your letter. Delivery should be made by our own vehicles early next week. We feel confident that you will be completely satisfied with these goods and that you will find them of exceptional value for money.

提及其他商品並附上目錄 ── As you may not be aware of the wide range of goods we have available, we are enclosing a copy of our catalogue.

結尾，希望未來繼續合作 ── We hope that our handling of your first order with us will lead to further business between us and mark the beginning of a happy working relationship.

Yours sincerely

7.7 延遲出貨通知

當訂購的貨物無法立刻交貨時，必須寫信道歉並解釋原因。如果可以，請給對方一個交貨日期，同時表達希望這項延遲不會造成客戶太大的不便。

(a) 延遲理由：生產線故障

→ p.55

> Dear
>
> Thank you for your order of 15 March for electric shavers. We regret that we cannot supply them immediately owing to a fire in our factory.
>
> Every effort is being made to resume production and we fully expect to be able to deliver the shavers by the end of this month.
>
> We apologise for the delay and trust it will not cause you serious inconvenience.
>
> Yours sincerely

(b) 延遲理由：無庫存

→ p.55

> Dear
>
> We were pleased to receive your order of 20 January.
>
> Unfortunately we are out of stock of the model you ordered. This is due to the prolonged cold weather which has increased demand considerably. The manufacturers have, however, promised us a further supply by the end of this month and if you can wait until then we will fulfil your order promptly.
>
> We are sorry not to be able to meet your present order immediately, but hope to hear from you soon that delivery at the beginning of next month will not inconvenience you unduly.
>
> Yours sincerely

回絕訂單

有時候，供應商會因為下列的理由而不接受買方的訂單：

◆　不滿意買方的條件。
◆　質疑買方的信用。
◆　沒有庫存。

在撰寫回絕訂單的信函時必須格外小心，才不會影響了友好關係及未來的交易機會。

7.8　供應商拒絕降價

供應商無法答應買方的降價要求時，必須告知原因。

→ p.56

Dear

We have carefully considered your <u>counter-proposal</u>[1] of 15 August to our offer of woollen underwear, but regret that we cannot accept it.

The prices quoted in our letter of 13 August leave us with only the smallest of margins. They are in fact lower than those of our competitors for goods of similar quality.

The wool used in the manufacture of our THERMALINE range undergoes a special patented process which prevents shrinkage and increases durability. The fact that we are the largest suppliers of woollen underwear in this country is in itself evidence of the good value of our products.

We hope you will give further thought to this matter, but if you then still feel you cannot accept our offer we hope it will not prevent you from contacting us on some future occasion.

We will always be happy to consider carefully any proposals likely to lead to business between us.

Yours sincerely

7.9　供應商拒絕買方的交貨條件

如果是交貨條件無法配合，供應商仍應當表現出協助顧客處理困難的誠意。

1.　counter-proposal：針對原先提案的另一替代提案。

→ p.56

Dear Mr Johnson

YOUR ORDER NUMBER R345

感謝並且說明
無法如期交貨 ── We were pleased to receive your order of 2 November for 24 ATLANTIS television sets. However since you state the firm condition of delivery before Christmas, we regret that we cannot supply you on this occasion.

有關訂購商品的進
一步資訊及訂單的
處理 ── The manufacturers of these goods are finding it impossible to meet current demand for this popular television set. We placed an order for 100 sets one month ago but were informed that all orders were being met in strict rotation.[2] Our own order will not be met before the end of January.

建議向其他供應商
訂購，以維繫良好
關係 ── I understand from our telephone conversation this morning that your customers are unwilling to consider other models. In the circumstances I hope you will be able to meet your requirements from some other source. May I suggest that you try Television Services Ltd of Leicester. They usually carry large stocks and may be able to help you.

Yours sincerely

7.10　供應商拒絕擴大信用交易額度

如果買方先前的帳款未結清，供應商打算拒絕其另一筆訂單時，需要運用高度的機智。客戶對於不被信任的感覺最為不悅。在以下範例中，寫信者很有技巧地避開不信任的暗示，改用公司內部有困難為由來拒絕對方擴大信用額度的要求。

→ p.57

Dear Mr Richardson

We were pleased to receive your order of 15 April for a further supply of CD players.

However, owing to current difficult conditions we have had to try to ensure that our many customers keep their accounts within reasonable limits. Only in this way can we meet our own commitments.[3]

At present the balance of your account stands at over £1800. We hope that you will be able to reduce it before we grant credit for further supplies.

In the circumstances we should be grateful if you would send us your cheque for, say, half the amount owed. We could then arrange to supply the goods now requested and charge them to your account.

Yours sincerely

---

2. in strict rotation ：依照收到的先後順序處理。
3. commitments ：應盡的義務。

供應商還價

當供應商因為某些原因而無法接受此筆訂單時，可以提供如下的建議給買方：

1. 寄上替代品（substitute）。替代品總是和實際訂購的產品不符，客戶也許會不高興，因此必須謹慎研議。除非客戶對替代品相當了解，或者迫切需要，才可寄上替代品，且採取「包退包換」的方式，也就是如果買方不接受這個替代品，供應商必須負擔寄出及寄回的運費。
2. 提出還價（counter-offer，編注：或稱反報價，指任一方對報價內容、條件提出修正或要求增加若干條件。）
3. 回絕訂單。

7.11 供應商寄上替代品

→ p.57

Dear

We were pleased to receive your letter of 10 April together with your order for a number of items included in our quotation reference RS980.

All the items ordered are in stock except for the 25 cushion covers in strawberry pink. Stocks of these have been sold out since our quotation, and the manufacturers inform us that it will be another 4 weeks before they can send replacements.

As you state that delivery of all items is a matter of urgency, we have substituted cushion covers in a fuschia pink, identical in design and quality to those ordered. They are attractive and rich-looking, and very popular with our other customers. We hope you will find them satisfactory. If not, please return them at our expense. We shall be glad either to exchange them or to arrange credit.

All items will be on our delivery schedule tomorrow. We hope you will be pleased with them.

Yours sincerely

7.12　供應商還價

供應商若需要提出另一替代品，必須運用相當的技巧，以促成交易。畢竟替代品並非買方原先要求的，因此它的品質至少得和原訂購的商品一樣好。

→ p.58

Dear

感謝

Thank you for your letter of 12 May ordering 800 metres of 100 cm wide watered silk.

回應詢問，並遺憾告知該商品不再供應

We regret to say that we can no longer supply this silk. Fashions constantly change and in recent years the demand for watered silks has fallen to such an extent that we no longer produce them.

建議替代品並就品質與可信度做出保證

In their place we can offer our new GOSSAMER brand of rayon.[4] This is a finely woven, hard-wearing, non-creasable material with a most attractive lustre.[5] The large number of repeat orders we regularly receive from leading distributors and dress manufacturers is clear evidence of the widespread popularity of this brand.

價格資訊

At the low price of only £3.20 per metre, this rayon is much cheaper than silk and its appearance is just as attractive.

提及另外寄出其他產品的樣品並說明交貨細節

We also manufacture other cloths in which you may be interested and are sending a complete range of patterns by separate post. All these cloths are selling very well in many countries and can be supplied from stock. If you decide to place an order we can meet it within one week.

Please contact me if you have any queries.

Yours sincerely

---

4. rayon：人造絲。
5. lustre：閃亮的表面。

包裝與發貨

當商品寄出後，賣方應使用通知書（advice note）或信函來通知買方寄出的貨物內容、寄出時間，以及使用何種方式寄送。如此一來，買方才知道商品已在運送途中並安排收貨作業。

7.13 詢問送貨事宜

→ p.58

> Dear
>
> We are pleased to confirm that the 12 Olivetti KX R193 word processors which you ordered on 15 October are now ready for despatch.
>
> When placing your order you stressed the importance of prompt delivery, and I am glad to say that by making a special effort we have been able to improve by a few days on the delivery date agreed.
>
> We await your shipping instructions, and immediately we hear from you we will send you our advice of despatch.
>
> Yours sincerely

7.14 準備發貨通知

→ p.59

> Dear
>
> We are pleased to confirm that all the books which you ordered on 3 April are packed and ready for despatch.
>
> The consignment awaits collection at our warehouse and consists of two cases, each weighing about 100 kg.
>
> Arrangements for shipment, CIF Singapore, have already been made with W Watson & Co Ltd, our <u>forwarding agents.</u>[6] As soon as we receive their statement of charges, we will arrange for shipping documents to be sent to you through Barclays Bank against our draft for acceptance, as agreed.
>
> We look forward to further business with you.
>
> Yours sincerely

---

6. forwarding agents：攬貨業者或攬貨公司，指負責安排商品運送的代理商。

7.15　已發貨通知

→ p.59

> Dear
>
> ORDER NUMBER S 524
>
> The mohair rugs you ordered on 5 January have been packed in four special waterproof-lined cases. They will be collected tomorrow for consignment by passenger train and should reach you by Friday.
>
> We feel sure you will find the consignment supports our claim to sell the best rugs of their kind and hope we may look forward to further orders from you.
>
> Yours sincerely

7.16　運送途中損毀報告

就法律上而言，買方必須自行從賣方處提取所購買的貨物，除非交易條件中言明由賣方負責運送，否則鐵路公司或其他貨運公司均將認定是為買方的代理，一切從這些承運業者（carrier）接手之後的損失、毀壞或延遲責任均由買方承擔。

→ p.59

> Dear
>
> ORDER NUMBER S 524
>
> We regret to inform you that of the four cases of mohair rugs which were sent on 28 January, one was delivered damaged. The waterproof lining was badly torn and it will be necessary to send seven of the rugs for cleaning before we can offer them for sale.
>
> Will you therefore please arrange to send replacements immediately and charge them to our account.
>
> We realise that the responsibility for damage is ours and have already taken up the matter of compensation[7] with the railway authorities.
>
> Yours sincerely

7.　compensation：損失賠償。

7.17　貨物未送達報告

當貨物無法如期送達時，不一定是供應商的錯，買方應避免一味在信中責備對方，要著重在陳述事實及請求提供相關資訊。

→ p.60

Dear

ORDER NUMBER S 524

You wrote to us on 28 January informing us that the mohair rugs supplied to the above order were being despatched.

We expected these goods a week ago and on the faith of your notification of despatch promised immediate delivery to a number of our customers. As the goods have not yet reached us, we naturally feel our customers have been let down.

Delivery of the rugs is now a matter of urgency. Please find out what has happened to the consignment and let us know when we may expect delivery.

We are of course making our own enquiries at this end.

Yours sincerely

7.18　向承運業者抱怨貨物未運達

在收到買方貨物未運達報告後，供應商應該立即向承運業者詢問此事。信件內容不該含有一般會有的惱怒情緒，而必須清楚陳述事實，並要求立刻查明原因。

→ p.60

Dear

We regret to report that a consignment of mohair rugs addressed to W Hart & Co, 25–27 Gordon Avenue, Warrington, has not yet reached them.

These cases were collected by your carrier on 28 January for consignment by passenger train and should have been delivered by 1 February. We hold your carrier's receipt number 3542.

As our customer is urgently in need of these goods, we must ask you to make enquiries and let us know the cause of the delay and when delivery will be made.

Please treat this matter as one of extreme urgency.

Yours sincerely

實用措詞

下單

【開頭】

1. Thank you for your quotation of ...

   感謝您對……的報價

2. We have received your quotation of ... and enclose our official order form.

   我們已經收到您……的報價，在此附上本公司正式的訂單。

3. Please supply the following items as quickly as possible and charge to our account:

   請儘速提供以下品項，並將帳款記在我們的帳戶：

【結尾】

1. Prompt delivery would be appreciated as the goods are needed urgently.

   因為急需該商品，如能快速交貨，不勝感激。

2. Please acknowledge receipt of this order and confirm that you will be able to deliver by ...

   收到訂單後請函覆通知，並且確定您會於……前送貨

3. We hope to receive your advice of delivery by return of post.

   希望您以回函通知有關送貨事宜。

回覆收到訂單

【開頭】

1. Thank you for your order dated ...

   謝謝您……（日期）的訂單。

2. We thank you for your order number ... and will despatch the goods by ...

   謝謝您……的訂單（訂單編號），此批貨將於（日期）發貨

3. We are sorry to inform you that the goods ordered on ... cannot be supplied.

   很抱歉，您於……所訂購的商品目前無法供貨。

【結尾】

1. We hope the goods reach you safely and that you will be pleased with them.

   希望這批貨能夠安全抵達，並且讓您滿意。

2. We hope you will find the goods satisfactory and look forward to receiving your further orders.

   希望您滿意這些商品，並期待您再次下單。

3. We are pleased to say that these goods have been despatched today (will be despatched in ... / are now awaiting collection at ...).

   很高興通知您，這些商品已於今天發貨（將於……發貨／目前已經在……等待集貨）。

開立發票與結帳
Invoicing and settlement of accounts

付款是產品或服務交易的最後一道程序。零售交易通常是採現金付款，而批發及國際貿易則習慣採取信用交易，即先記帳後付款。

發票與金額調整

如果是信用交易，供應商會寄發票給買方，用來：

◆ 告知買方應付金額。
◆ 讓買方核對已交付的商品是否正確無誤。
◆ 記入買方的進貨日記帳中。

買方收到發票後應該小心核對，除了檢查送來的品項對不對外，還包括價格和結帳金額是否正確無誤。

發票有時候會隨貨寄出，但分開郵寄的情況較常見。任何非定期往來的買主會被要求一次結清帳款，而定期往來的客戶通常可採信用交易，供應商根據發票將帳款記入客戶的帳戶中，再按月或定期將對帳單寄給買方。

發票範例請見圖表 8.1。

預估發票

所謂預估發票（Pro forma invoice，又稱形式發票、估價單或暫定的發票等），是指鑒於形式而開立的發票，目的在於：

◆ 表示所寄的商品是「含鑑賞期之試用品」（on approval）或採「寄售」（on consignment）方式。
◆ 當做正式的報價。
◆ 針對不熟識的客戶或有疑問的付款者，請求對方訂貨後先付款。
◆ 提供出口商品的價值，以備結關。

預估發票金額不記入帳簿中，也不會將帳記入客戶的帳目中。

→ p.62

JOHN G GARTSIDE & CO LTD
Albion Works, Thomas Street
Manchester M60 2QA
Telephone 0161-980-2132

INVOICE

Johnson Tools & Co Ltd
112 Kingsway
LIVERPOOL
L20 6HJ

Your order no: AW 25

Date: 18 August 200—

Invoice no: B 832

Quantity	Item(s)	Unit Price	Total £
10	Polyester shirts, small	25.00	250.00
21	Polyester shirts, medium	26.00	546.00
12	Polyester shirts, large	27.25	327.00
			1123.00
	VAT[1] (@ 17.5%)		196.53
	One case (returnable)		23.25
			1342.78
	Terms 2$\frac{1}{2}$% one month		

E & OE [2]

Registered in England No 523807

圖表 8.1　**發票**（告知買方應付的貨款）

---

1. VAT：Value Added Tax，加值稅，加於商品與服務上的稅金，支付給關稅署（HM Customs and Excise）。
2. E&OE：Error and omission excepted，錯誤及遺漏除外，此項陳述賦予供應商針對文件中可能涵蓋的任何錯誤有修正的權利。

8.1　連同發票寄出的短信

在寄送發票時，通常不需要另附一封短信，尤其當發票是和商品一併寄出時。但如果發票是分開另寄的，則可附上一封簡潔、有禮的短信。

(a) 非固定往來的客戶

→ p.63

> Dear Sir/Madam
>
> YOUR ORDER NUMBER AW25
>
> We are pleased to enclose our invoice number B 832 for the polyester shirts ordered on 13 August.
>
> The goods are available from stock and will be sent to you immediately we receive the amount due, namely £1342.78.
>
> Yours faithfully

(b) 固定往來的客戶

→ p.63

> Dear
>
> YOUR ORDER NUMBER AW 25
>
> Our invoice number B 832 is enclosed covering the polyester shirts ordered on 13 August.
>
> These shirts have been packed ready for despatch and are being sent to you, carriage paid, by rail. They should reach you within a few days.
>
> Yours sincerely

借項單與貸項單

如果供應商向買方少收了錢，有時會針對短少的金額寄發借項單（debit note，或譯借項通知、欠款單）。它是一種追加的發票。

反過來，如果供應商向買方多收了錢，則會寄出貸項單（credit note，或譯貸項通知、付款單等）。此外，當買方退還商品（因為

不合適）或者寄回可以折抵（rebate）的包裝材料時，也會寄出貸
項單。貸項單通常是紅色的，用來和發票及借項單做區隔。圖表
8.2 及 8.3 為借項單和貸項單的範例。

→ p.64

JOHN G GARTSIDE & CO LTD
Albion Works, Thomas Street
Manchester M60 2QA
Telephone 0161-980-2132

DEBIT NOTE

Johnson Tools & Co Ltd
112 Kingsway
LIVERPOOL
L20 6HJ

Date 22 August 200—

Debit Note No. D.75

Date	Details	Price (£)
18.8.200—	To 21 Polyester Shirts, medium charged on invoice number B 832 @ £26.00 each	
	Should be £26.70 each	
	Difference	14.70

Registered in England No 523807

圖表 8.2　借項單（供應商寄發借項單給買方，說明原始發票中的金額有所短缺。）

→ p.64

JOHN G GARTSIDE & CO LTD
Albion Works, Thomas Street
Manchester M60 2QA
Telephone 0161-980-2132

CREDIT NOTE

Johnson Tools & Co Ltd
112 Kingsway
LIVERPOOL
L20 6HJ

Date 25 August 200—

Credit Note No. C.521

Date	Details	Price(£)
18.8.200—	By One case returned charged to you on invoice number B 832	23.25

Registered in England No 523807

圖表 8.3　貸項單
（供應商開貸項單給買方，說明原始發票中多收了錢，或者函覆並針對買方所退回的商品
准予記入貸項中。貸項單通常是紅色的。）

8.2 供應商寄出借項單

→ p.65

Dear Sir/Madam

I regret to inform you that an error was made on our invoice number B 832 of 18 August.

The correct charge for polyester shirts, medium, is £26.70 and not £26.00 as stated. We are therefore enclosing a debit note for the amount undercharged, namely £14.70.

This mistake was due to an input error and we are sorry it was not noticed before the invoice was sent.

Yours faithfully

8.3 買方請求寄回貸項單

有些被多收錢的顧客會寄借項單給供應商。如果供應商同意這項要求，就會回寄貸項單給顧客。

(a) 退還包裝箱子

→ p.65

Dear Sirs

We have today returned to you by rail one empty packing case, charged on your invoice number B 832 of 18 August at £23.25.

A debit note for this amount is enclosed and we shall be glad to receive your credit note in return.

Yours faithfully

(b) 折扣錯誤

→ p.65

Dear Sirs

Your invoice number 2370 dated 10 September allows a trade discount of only $33\frac{1}{3}\%$ instead of the 40% to which you agreed in your letter of 5 August because of the unusually large order.

Calculated on the invoice gross total of £1,500 the difference in discount is exactly £100. If you will please adjust your charge we shall be glad to pass the invoice for immediate payment.

Yours faithfully

8.4　供應商拒絕開立貸項單

(a) 零售商的請求

→ p.66

Dear Sir/Madam

On 1 September we returned to you by parcel post one cassette tape recorder, Model EK76, Serial Number 048617, one of a consignment of 12 delivered on 5 August and charged on your invoice number 5624 dated 2 August.

The customer who bought this recorder complained about its performance. It was for this reason that we returned it to you after satisfying ourselves that the complaint was justified.

We have received no acknowledgement of the returned recorder or of the letter we sent to you on 1 September. It may be that you are trying to obtain a replacement for us. If this is the case and a replacement is not immediately available, please send us a credit note for the invoiced cost of the returned recorder, namely £175.

We hope to hear from you soon.

Yours faithfully

(b) 批發商的回覆

→ p.66

Dear

We are sorry to learn from your letter of 16 September of the need to return one of the recorders supplied to you and charged on our invoice number 5624.

We received your letter of 1 September but regret that we have no trace of the returned recorder. It would help if you could describe the kind of container in which it was packed and state exactly how it was addressed and the method of delivery used. As soon as we receive this information we will make a thorough investigation.

Meanwhile I am sure you will understand that we cannot either provide a free replacement or grant the credit you request. If you could wait for about 10 days, we could replace the tape recorder but would have to charge it to your account if our further enquiries should prove unsuccessful.

Yours sincerely

對帳單

對帳單（statement，見圖表 8.4）是在要求付款時發出的，為買賣雙方在某一段時間內（通常是一個月）的交易摘要，從上期結算餘額開始（如果有的話），接著往下列出每一筆發票的請款金額、借項金額，然後扣掉貸項金額與買方已支付款項，結算出的總額即為至對帳單日期為止的未付款項。

對帳單就像發票一樣，通常不需連同短信寄出。如果需要另附說明，簡短、正式即可。

→ p.67

JOHN G GARTSIDE & CO LTD
Albion Works, Thomas Street
Manchester M60 2QA
Telephone 0161-980-2132

STATEMENT

Johnson Tools & Co Ltd
112 Kingsway
LIVERPOOL
L20 6HJ

Date 31 August 200—

Date	Details	Debit	Credit	Balance
		£	£	£
1.8.200—	Account rendered			115.53
18.8.200—	Invoice B 832	1342.78		1458.31
20.8.200—	Cheque received		500.00	958.31
22.8.200—	Debit Note D 75	35.70		994.01
25.8.200—	Credit Note C 52		23.25	970.76

E & OE   Registered in England No 523807

圖表 8.4　對帳單
（對帳單是付款的請求，由供應商定期寄給買方，它概述了某段期間內的所有交易，可讓買方核對細目。任何發現的錯誤經雙方達成協議後，由借項單或貸項單來調整。）

8.5　對帳單所附的短信

→ p.68

Dear Sirs

We enclose our statement of account for all transactions during August. If payment is made within 14 days you may deduct the customary cash discount of $2\frac{1}{2}$%.

Yours faithfully

8.6　供應商通知付款不足

(a) 供應商來信

→ p.68

Dear Sirs

We are enclosing our September statement totalling £820.57.

The opening balance brought forward is the amount left uncovered by the cheque received from you against our August statement which totalled £560.27. The cheque received from you, however, was drawn for £500.27 only, leaving the unpaid balance of £60 brought forward.

We should appreciate early settlement of the total amount now due.

Yours faithfully

(b) 買方的回覆

→ p.68

Dear Sirs

We have received your letter of 15 October enclosing September's statement.

We apologise for the underpayment of £60 on your August statement. This was due to a misreading of the amount due. The final figure was not very clearly printed and we mistakenly read it as £500.27 instead of £560.27.

Our cheque for £820.57, the total amount on the September statement, is enclosed.

Yours faithfully

8.7　買方通知對帳單有誤

(a) 買方通知

→ p.69

Dear Sirs

On checking your statement for July we notice the following errors:

1　The sum of £14.10 for the return of empty packing cases, covered by your credit note number 621 dated 5 July, has not been entered.

2　Invoice Number W825 for £127.32 has been debited twice – once on 11 July and again on 21 July.

Therefore we are deducting the sum of £141.42 from the balance shown on your statement, and enclose our cheque for £354.50 in full settlement.

Yours faithfully

(b) 賣方回覆收到通知

→ p.69

Dear Sirs

Thank you for your letter of 10 August enclosing your cheque for £354.50 in full settlement of the amount due against our July statement.

We confirm your deduction of £141.42 and apologise for the errors in the statement. Please accept our apologies for the inconvenience caused.

Yours faithfully

變更付款條件

當供應商要求顧客在交貨時或交貨前支付貨款，是指根據發票付款（on invoice）。如果顧客財務健全，值得信任，或許雙方會採用「記帳」（open account，即交貨後付款）方式，也就是說，貨款直接記在買方帳上，結算時就以供應商所寄發的對帳單為基礎。

如果顧客認為有必要延後付款，必須提出強而有力的理由，說服供應商無法付款只是暫時，同時表達將會儘快結清的誠意。

8.8　准許客戶延後付款的要求

(a) 客戶的請求

→ p.70

Dear Sirs

回覆收到供應商的來信 — We have received your letter of 6 August reminding us that payment of the amount owing on your June statement is overdue.

解釋無法付款的原因 — We were under the impression that payment was not due until the end of August when we would have had no difficulty in settling your account. However it seems that we misunderstood your terms of payment.

請求延期付款並提出保證 — In the circumstances we should be grateful if you could allow us to <u>defer payment</u>[4] for a further 3 weeks. Our present difficulty is purely temporary. Before the end of the month payments are due to us from a number of our regular customers who are notably prompt payers.

表達歉意 — We very much regret having to make this request and hope you will be able to grant it.

Yours faithfully

(b) 供應商的回覆

→ p.70

Dear Mr Jensen

回應延期付款的請求 — Having carefully considered your letter of 8 August, we have decided to allow you to defer payment of your account to the end of August.

解釋准許的理由 — This request is granted as an exceptional measure only because of the promptness with which you have settled your accounts in the past. We hope that in future dealings you will be able to keep to our terms of payment. We take this opportunity to remind you that they are as follows:

提醒未來的條件 — $2\frac{1}{2}$% discount for payment within 10 days
Net cash for payment within one month

We look forward to continuing to work with you.

Yours sincerely

---

4. defer payment：延遲付款。

8.9 拒絕客戶延後付款的要求

(a) 客戶的請求

→ p.71

Dear Mr Wilson

Thank you for your letter of 23 July asking for immediate payment of the £687 due on your invoice number AV54.

When we wrote promising to pay you in full by 16 July, we fully expected to be able to do so. However we were unfortunately called upon to meet an unforeseen and unusually heavy demand earlier this month.

We are therefore enclosing a cheque for £200 <u>on account</u>,[5] and ask you to be good enough to allow us a further few weeks in which to settle the balance. We fully expect to be able to settle your account in full by the end of August. If you would grant this deferment, we should be most grateful.

I hope to hear from you soon.

Yours sincerely

(b) 供應商的回覆

供應商在回絕這項請求時，最好強調客戶立即付款可以享有的好處，而非著眼於請求付款時自己所面臨的困境。畢竟客戶在意的是更迫切的問題。

→ p.71

感謝 —

Dear Mrs Billingham

Thank you for your letter of 25 July sending us a cheque for £200 on account and asking for an extension of time in which to pay the balance.

技巧地指出對方付款不足又要延期是不合理的。語氣要堅定，但不激怒人 —

As your account is now more than 2 months overdue we find your present cheque quite insufficient. It is hardly reasonable to expect us to wait a further month for the balance, particularly as we invoiced the goods at a specially low price which was mentioned to you at the time.

表示同情但仍希望立刻付款 —

We sympathise with your difficulties but need hardly remind you that it is in our customers' long-term interests to pay their accounts promptly so as to qualify for discounts and at the same time build a reputation for financial reliability.

要求立即付款的用字要適當 —

In the circumstances we hope that in your own interests you will make arrangements to clear your account without further delay. We look forward to receiving your cheque for the balance on your account within the next few days.

Yours sincerely

---

5. **on account**：部分付款、分批付款、記帳。

8.10　供應商對部分付款提出質疑

在支付對帳單上的帳款時，付款人應當註明這筆錢是要「部分付款」或「全部結清」（in full settlement），否則就會收到以下信件：

→ p.72

Dear

We thank you for your letter of 10 October enclosing your cheque for £58.67. Our official receipt is enclosed as requested.

As you do not say that the cheque is on account, we are wondering whether the amount of £58.67 was intended to be £88.67 – the balance on your account as shown in our September statement.

In any case we look forward to receiving the uncleared balance of £30 within the next few days.

Yours sincerely

8.11　供應商駁回折扣請求

→ p.72

Dear

Thank you for your letter of 15 October enclosing your cheque for £292.50 in full settlement of our May statement.

We regret that we cannot accept this payment as a full discharge of the £300 due on our statement. The terms of payment allow the $2^1/_2$% cash discount only on accounts paid within 10 days of statement whereas your present payment is more than a month overdue.

The balance still owing is £7.50 and to save you the trouble of making a separate payment we will include this amount in your next payment and will prepare our July statement accordingly.

Yours sincerely

付款方式

結清帳款的方式有很多種，究竟要採哪一種，就看雙方的約定。

1. 付現（錢幣和紙幣）。
2. 透過郵局付款。

(a) 郵政匯票（Postal orders）和匯票（Money orders，僅用於國外付款）。英國的郵政匯票和匯票在許多國家皆有發行或作爲付款工具。付款金額按付款地國家的即期匯率兌換成收款地國家的貨幣。郵政匯票用來支付小額的貨款（在英國最高金額爲 20 英鎊）。

除了電報匯票之外，英國一般已經不再發售匯票，除非是支付國外款項，且最高金額是 50 英鎊，提供給沒有銀行或郵局支票帳戶者使用。因爲此方法無付款證明，所以付款人必須要求領款人開立收據。

(b) 劃撥轉帳（Giro transfers）。劃撥一般是透過郵政支票系統來運作，普及於大多數的西歐國家和日本。除了現金交易之外，劃撥轉帳或郵政支票是主要的付款工具。無論是否有開立劃撥帳戶，都可以存提款。

(c) 貨到付現（COD: cash on delivery）。是指買方從承運業者（包含郵政系統）手中接到商品之後就必須付款。供應商在與不認識的顧客交易時，可藉此確保可收到貨款。

3. **透過銀行付款**

(a) 國內交易可透過網路銀行、支票、存款轉帳（銀行轉帳）、銀行匯票及信用狀來付款。

◆ 網路銀行（Online banking）：有愈來愈多的人利用網路銀行付款。在設定好獨一專用的密碼後，就可以利用滑鼠來支付帳單、轉帳等任何與帳戶有關的事項。

◆ 支票（Cheques）：銀行支票見票即付，是銀行支票系統發展良好的國家裡用來結清交易最通用的付款方式，支票也可用於支付國外的款項。收據是最佳但不是唯一的付款證明，當銀行開立的支票轉入顧客手中，即可視同收據，無需另外開立證明，但是付款人依法仍可向收款人索取收據。

◆ 銀行轉帳（Credit transfers）：銀行轉帳在許多層面上如同郵局轉帳。付款人填妥轉帳單或劃撥單，並列出清單，連同支票一併交由銀行處理。銀行將轉帳單轉至受款人的相關銀行，款項就會進入他們的銀行帳戶中，受款人就會收到銀行轉帳單通知。付款人不必再另行開立付款證明，但有時基於實務需要仍會寄發付款證明。

◆ 銀行匯票（Banker's drafts）：銀行匯票指要向銀行購買的文件，該文件指示銀行分行或者往來銀行支付票面金額給指定的受款人。在與國外交易時，受款人收到的是依當地匯率兌換的當地幣別。當付款人不願使用支票支付大筆金額時，就適合使用銀行匯票。就像支票一樣，銀行匯票也應劃線以增加安全性。

(b) 國外貿易會用到銀行轉帳（郵件、電報或電傳）、匯票（bills of exchange）、本票（promissory notes）、銀行商業本票（如果使用跟單匯票，就用跟單信用狀： documentary credits）、銀行匯票，以及信用狀（letters of credit）。

8.12　供應商詢問客戶付款方式

→ p.73

Dear

Thank you for your letter of 3 April, but you do not say whether you wish this transaction to be for cash or on credit.

When we wrote to you on 20 March we explained our willingness to offer easy credit terms to customers who do not wish to pay cash, and also that we allow generous discounts to cash customers.

We may not have made it clear that when placing orders customers should state whether cash or credit terms are required.

Please let me know which you prefer so that we can arrange your account accordingly.

Yours sincerely

8.13　付款或收款的制式信

每一個行業都有許多例行性書信要處理，付款或收款通知便是其中之一。這類信件通常都有適用於各種場合的標準格式，稱為「制式信」（form letter）。信中會留下空白讓寫信者填入各式資訊（參照號碼、名字、地址、日期、總金額等）。

當然，私人往來不會使用這類制式信。但現在許多企業會利用電腦的信件合併功能，將制式信改寫成看起來就像原創般個人化信件。

(a) 付款人的制式信

→ p.73

> Dear Sir/Madam
>
> We have pleasure in enclosing our cheque (bill/draft/etc) for £... in full settlement (part settlement) of your statement (invoice) dated ...
>
> Please send us your official receipt.
>
> Yours faithfully

(b) 表示收到貨款的制式信

→ p.73

> Dear
>
> Thank you for your letter of ... enclosing cheque (bill/draft/etc) for £... in full settlement (part payment) of our statement of account (invoice) dated ...
>
> We enclose our official receipt.
>
> Yours sincerely

8.14 通知供應商會以銀行轉帳付款

→ p.74

> Dear Sirs
>
> A credit transfer has been made to your account at the Barminster Bank, Church Street, Dover, in payment of the amount due for the goods supplied on 2 May and charged on your invoice number 1524.
>
> Yours faithfully

8.15 通知供應商會以銀行匯票付款

→ p.74

> Dear Sirs
>
> Our banker's draft is enclosed, drawn on the Midminster Bank, Benghazi, for £672.72 and crossed 'Account Payee only'.
>
> The draft.is sent in full settlement of your account dated 31 May.
>
> Please acknowledge its safe receipt.
>
> Yours faithfully

8.16　供應商通知已寄出貨到付現商品

→ p.74

Dear Sir/Madam

Thank you for your order for one of our Model X50 cameras. This model is an improved version of our famous Model X40, which has already established itself firmly in public favour. We feel sure you will be delighted with it. At the price of £89.25 we believe it represents the best value on the market for cameras of this type.

Your camera will be sent to you today by compensation-fee parcel post, for delivery against payment of our trade charge of £90. This charge includes packing and postal registration and COD charges.

Under our guarantee you are entitled to a refund of your payment in full if you are not completely satisfied, but you must return the camera by compensation-fee parcel post within 7 days.

Yours faithfully

實用措詞

應付帳款

【開頭】

1. Enclosed is our statement for the quarter ended ...
   隨函附上……季的對帳單

2. We enclose our statement to 31 ... showing a balance of £ ...
   隨函附上……月 31 日的對帳單，餘額爲……英鎊

3. We are sorry it was necessary to return our invoice number ... for correction.
   很抱歉請退回我們所開立的發票（號碼），以便更正。

4. We very much regret having to ask for an extension of credit on your January statement.
   很抱歉不得不要求您讓我們延期支付元月份的帳款。

【結尾】

1. Please let us have your credit note for the amount of this overcharge.
    請寄此項超收金額的貸項單給我們。

2. Please make the necessary adjustment and we will settle the account immediately.
    請做必要的調整，我們將儘快結清帳款。

3. We apologise again for this error and enclose our credit note for the overcharge.
    針對這項錯誤，我們再度向您道歉，並附上超收帳款的貸項單。

付款

【開頭】

1. We enclose our cheque for ... in payment for goods supplied on ...
    隨函附上（金額）的支票，支付……的貨款……

2. We enclose our cheque for ... in payment of your invoice number ...
    隨函附上（金額）的支票以支付……號發票的帳款……

3. We acknowledge with thanks your cheque for ...
    函謝您（金額）的支票……

4. We thank you for your cheque for ... in part payment of your account.
    謝謝您寄上（金額）的支票，支付部分帳款。

【結尾】

1. We hope to receive the amount due by the end of this month.
    希望在本月底前能收到您的貨款。

2. We should be obliged if you would send us your cheque immediately.
    如果您能立刻寄支票給我們，我們將非常感激。

3. As the amount owing is considerably overdue, we must ask you to send us your cheque by return.
    因為貨款已經積欠很長的時間，因此我們必須要求您回覆時連同支票寄出。

請求付款信
Letters requesting payment

語氣

供應商對於無法準時或儘速付款的客戶，總是很傷腦筋。但一般不建議一定要將這些不滿傳達於通信中。如果可能的話，不要寫信，而改以拜訪客戶反而較為妥當，或者在電話中有技巧地說服對方至少支付部分欠款。碰上一些棘手的狀況，接受部分貨款會比耗費時間與金錢訴諸法律要來得好。

有些客戶無法準時付款是情有可原，然而有些則是蓄意拖欠，對於後者應小心提防，依據是非曲直來處理每個案例。

任何催款信的風格和語氣，都應該根據不同因素來呈現，像是積欠時間、是否為習慣性遲付，以及客戶的重要性等。但不論是何者，所有書信往返都要保持一貫的禮貌，甚至包括採取法律途徑的最後通牒，也記得寫上 with regret（為此表示遺憾）。

 更多有關語氣的部分，請參考第 3 章。

延遲付款

當買方需要解釋無法在期限內付款的困難，並請求延後付款時，可以採取以下程序：

1. 提及該筆帳款無法立刻支付。
2. 為無法付款表示歉意並說明理由。
3. 建議延後付款的期間。
4. 希望該建議能被接受。

9.1 客戶解釋無法如期付款

以下信件是來自固定往來且值得信賴的客戶所提出的合理請求，如果供應商予以拒絕，要承擔對方可能會「出走」的風險，亦即，客戶或許在付清積欠的貨款後，就轉而向競爭對手購買，使得供應商喪失日後做生意的機會。

→ p.76

Dear Sirs

Your invoice number 527 dated 20 July for £1516 is due for payment at the end of this month.

Unfortunately a fire broke out in our Despatch Department last week and destroyed a large part of a valuable consignment due for delivery to a cash customer. Our claim is now with the insurance company but it is unlikely to be met for another 3 or 4 weeks. Until then we are faced with a difficult financial problem.

I am therefore writing for permission to defer payment of your invoice until the end of September.

As you are aware, my accounts with you have always been settled promptly, and it is with regret that I am now forced to make this request. I hope that you will find it possible to grant it.

Yours faithfully

9.2 客戶解釋延遲付款的原因

→ p.76

Dear

Further to your letter of 4 July, I enclose a cheque for £1182.57 in full settlement of your invoice number W 563. Many apologies for late payment.

This is due to my absence from the office through illness and my failure to leave instructions for your account to be paid. I did not discover the oversight until I returned to the office yesterday.

I would not like you to think that failure to settle your account on time was in any way intentional. My apologies once again for this delay.

Yours sincerely

催款信

催收帳款的初步步驟如下：

1. 寄發第一封的月底對帳單。
2. 寄發第二封的月底對帳單並加入評語。
3. 寄發第一封措辭正式的信函。
4. 寄發第二及第三封信。
5. 最後一封信通知將採取法律行動，除非對方在約定的期間內結清全部帳款。

如果顧客的帳款只是稍微過期未付，馬上就收到催款信當然會不高興。這也是為什麼前兩封提醒函通常是以寄月底對帳單的方式來提醒對方，即使第二封對帳單也才使用 Second application（第二次催款）、Account overdue — please pay（帳款過期，請付款）、Immediate attention is requested（要求即刻注意）等字眼，目的就是避免引起對方不悅。

第一封催款信

供應商應該先提供機會給顧客結清貨款，若行不通，才另外寫信請求對方付款。請求支付過期帳款的信函稱為「催款信」（collection letter）。其目的是：

(a) 說服顧客結清帳款。
(b) 留住顧客及維持友好關係。

催款信原本就容易引起反感，因此寫作上必須圓融且有所節制。未收到款項也有可能是供應商本身的過失，例如已收到帳款但未記錄，或是寄送的商品或提供的服務顧客不滿意等等。

9.3　制式催款信

第一次的催款信或許可以採用事先印好的「制式信」。如同範例所示，於各欄位輸入詳細資料即可。或者將這些資料儲存於電腦中，以便於寫出個人化的信件。

→ p.77

> Dear Sir/Madam
>
> ACCOUNT NUMBER ...
>
> According to our records the above account dated ... has not been settled.
>
> The enclosed statement shows the amount owing to be £...
>
> We hope to receive an early settlement[1] of this account.
>
> Yours faithfully

9.4　個人化的催款信

有些情況，使用個人化的信函會比制式信函更合適。這類催款信必須致函給具名的資深主管，並且標示 Confidential（機密文件）。

(a) 致固定往來客戶

→ p.77

> Dear
>
> ACCOUNT NUMBER 6251
>
> As you are usually very prompt in settling your accounts, we wonder whether there is any special reason why we have not received payment of this account, which is already a month overdue.
>
> In case you may not have received the statement of account sent on 31 May showing a balance owing of £105.67, a copy is enclosed. We hope this will receive your early attention.
>
> Yours sincerely

---

1. settlement：結算、清帳。

(b) 致新客戶

→ p.77

> Dear Sir/Madam
>
> ACCOUNT NUMBER 5768
>
> We regret having to remind you that we have not received payment of the balance of £105.67 due on our statement for December. This was sent to you on 2 January and a copy is enclosed.
>
> We must remind you that unusually low prices were quoted to you on the understanding of an early settlement.
>
> It may well be that non-payment is due to an oversight, and so we ask you to be good enough to send us your cheque within the next few days.
>
> Yours faithfully

(c) 致已支付部分款項的客戶

→ p.78

> Dear
>
> Thank you for your letter of 8 March enclosing a cheque for £500 in part payment of the balance due on our February statement.
>
> Your payment leaves an unpaid balance of £825.62. As our policy is to work on small profit margins, we regret that we cannot grant long-term credit facilities.
>
> We are sure that you will not think it is unreasonable for us to ask for immediate payment of this balance.
>
> Yours sincerely

9.5　給已付款但誤以為尚未付款客戶的提醒信

處理催款信永遠要小心謹慎，也許錯不在顧客，例如款項在寄送途中遺失，或者供應商已經收到但忘了記錄等。

(a) 請求付款

→ p.78

> Dear Sir/Madam
>
> ACCOUNT NUMBER S542
>
> According to our records our account for cutlery supplied to you on 21 October has not been paid.
>
> We enclose a detailed statement showing the amount owing to be £310.62 and hope you will make an early settlement.
>
> Yours faithfully

(b) 客戶回覆

→ p.78

Dear

YOUR ACCOUNT NUMBER S542

I was surprised to receive your letter of 8 December stating that you had not received payment of the above account.

In fact our cheque (number 065821, drawn on Barclays Bank, Blackpool) for £310.62 was posted to you on 3 November. As this cheque appears to have gone astray, I have instructed the bank not to pay on it. A replacement cheque for the same amount is enclosed.

Yours sincerely

第二封催款信

如果第一次的催款信未收到客戶的回覆，大約可以在十天後寄出第二封。此次的口氣應該更堅定，但仍需客氣，任何引起惱怒或是破壞關係的事項都應避免。此時需要的是合作、協調，激怒對方並不能達到目的。

第二封催款信必須致函資深主管，並且於信封上註明 Confidential，內容則包括：

1.　提及前一封催款信。
2.　假定延遲付款是特殊狀況。
3.　技巧地建議顧客提出一個解釋。
4.　請求付款。

9.6　第二封催款信範例

(a) 第二封催款信，續 9.4 (a)

→ p.79

Dear

ACCOUNT NUMBER 6251

As we have not received a reply to our letter of 5 July requesting settlement of the above account, we are writing again to remind you that the amount still owing is £105.67.

No doubt there is some special reason for the delay in payment, and we should welcome an explanation together with your remittance.

Yours sincerely

(b) 第二封催款信，續 9.4 (b)

→ p.79

Dear Sir/Madam

On 18 February we wrote to remind you that our December statement sent on 2 January showed a balance of £105.67 outstanding and due for payment by 31 January.

Settlement of this account is now more than a month overdue. Therefore we must ask you either to send us your remittance within the next few days or at least to offer an explanation for the delay in payment.

Your prompt reply will be appreciated.

Yours faithfully

(c) 第二封催款信，續 9.4 (c)

→ p.80

Dear

We have not heard from you since we wrote on 10 March about the unpaid balance of £825.62 on your account. In view of your past good record we have not previously pressed for a settlement.

To regular customers such as yourself our terms of payment are 3% one month, and we hope you will not withhold payment any longer, otherwise it will be necessary for us to revise these terms.

In the circumstances we look forward to receiving your cheque for the outstanding amount within the next few days.

Yours sincerely

第三封催款信

如果第二封催款信仍未奏效，也沒收到客戶的任何解釋，就必須寫第三封催款信了。信中應當說明如有必要，將會採取強制付款行動，而相關的步驟則視個別情況而定。第三封催款信的內容包括：

1. 回顧之前對催收帳款所做的努力。
2. 給予一個最後付款的合理期限（deadline date）。
3. 表達希望做到公平、合理。
4. 說明如果對方忽視第三封催款信，將採取行動。
5. 對於必須寄出此信表示遺憾。

9.7　第三封催款信範例

(a) 第三封催款信，續 9.6 (a)

→ p.80

Dear

ACCOUNT NUMBER 6251

We do not appear to have received replies to our two previous requests of 5 and 16 July for payment of the sum of £105.67 still owing on this account.

It is with the utmost regret that we have reached the stage when we must press for immediate payment. We have no wish to be unreasonable, but failing payment by 7 August you will leave us no choice but to place the matter in other hands.

We sincerely hope this will not become necessary.

Yours sincerely

(b) 第三封催款信，續 9.6 (b)

→ p.81

Dear Sir/Madam

即使是第三封信
也要慎用措詞，
避免直接攻擊客戶

It is very difficult to understand why we have not heard from you in reply to our two letters of 18 February and 2 March about the sum of £105.67 due on our December statement. We had hoped that you would at least explain why the account continues to remain unpaid.

採用「每一項
考量」、「別無選擇」
等緩和措詞

I am sure you will agree that we have shown every consideration in the circumstances. Failing any reply to our earlier requests for payment, I am afraid we shall have no choice but to take other steps to recover the amount due.

提供客戶
最後結清機會

We are most anxious to avoid doing anything through which your credit and reputation might suffer. Therefore even at this late stage we are prepared to give you a further opportunity to put matters right.

給予特定期限

In the circumstances, we propose to give you until the end of this month to clear your account.[2]

Yours faithfully

(c) 第三封催款信，續 9.6 (c)

→ p.81

Dear

We are surprised and disappointed not to have heard from you in response to our two letters of 10 and 23 March reminding you of the balance of £825.62 still owing on our February statement.

This failure either to clear your account or even to offer an explanation is all the more disappointing because of our past satisfactory dealings over many years.

In the circumstances we must say that unless we hear from you within 10 days we shall have to consider seriously the further steps we should take to obtain payment.

Yours sincerely

最後一封催款信

如果客戶對三次的催款信仍舊置之不理，可以合理假設對方是沒能力、或者不願意付款。必須再寄出一封告知即將採取行動的短信，當作是最後的警告。

2.　clear your account：結清所有欠款。

9.8　最後一封催款信範例

(a) 最後通牒，續 9.7 (a)

→ p.82

> Dear
>
> We are surprised that we have received no reply to the further letter we sent to you on 28 July regarding the long overdue payment of £105.67 on your account.
>
> Our relations in the past have always been good. Even so we cannot allow the amount to remain unpaid indefinitely. Unless the amount due is paid or a satisfactory explanation received by the end of this month, we shall be reluctantly compelled to put this matter in the hands of our solicitors.
>
> Yours sincerely

(b) 最後通牒，續 9.7 (b)

→ p.82

> Dear Sir/Madam
>
> We are disappointed not to have received any response from you in answer to our letter of 16 March concerning non-payment of the balance of £105.67 outstanding on our December statement.
>
> We are now making a final request for payment in the hope that it will not be necessary to hand the matter over to an agent for collection.
>
> We have decided to defer this step for 7 days to give you the opportunity either to pay or at least to send us an explanation.
>
> Yours faithfully

(c) 最後通牒，續 9.7 (c)

→ p.82

> Dear
>
> We are quite unable to understand why we have received no reply to our letter of 7 April, our third attempt to secure payment of the balance of £825.62 still owing on your account with us.
>
> We feel that we have shown reasonable patience and treated you with every consideration. However we must now regretfully take steps to recover payment at law, and the matter will be placed in the hands of our solicitors.
>
> Yours sincerely

檢查清單

☐ 使用堅定但能諒解的語氣。

☐ 提及最初的付款日。

☐ 指出欠款總額。

☐ 指出可能的損失。

☐ 提供寬限期。

☐ 給予一個新的付款日。

☐ 指明後果。

實用措詞

第一封催款信

【開頭】

1. We notice that your account which was due for payment on ... is still outstanding.
    我們注意到您於（日期）到期的帳款，至今仍未償付。

2. We wish to draw your attention to our invoice number ... for ... which remains unpaid.
    希望您能留意編號……（金額）……的發票，至今仍未償付。

3. We must remind you that we have not yet received the balance of our ... statement amounting to ..., payment of which is now more than a month overdue.
    我們必須提醒您至今仍未收到（時間）對帳單、（金額）……的貨款，如今距付款日期已超過一個月。

【結尾】

1. We hope to receive your cheque by return.
   希望能夠收到您的支票。

2. We look forward to your payment within the next few days.
   期望您能在幾日內付款。

3. As our statement may have gone astray, we enclose a copy and shall
   be glad if you will pass it for payment immediately.
   或許對帳單在中途遺失，附上副本一份，也期望您能立刻付款。

第二封催款信

【開頭】

1. We do not appear to have had any reply to our request of ...for
   settlement of ... due on our invoice ... dated ...
   我們至今仍未收到您回覆我們請求支付發票號碼……、（金額）
   ……的欠款

2. We regret not having received a reply to our letter of ...
   很遺憾未收到您對我方（日期）信函的回覆

3. We are at a loss to understand why we have received no reply to our
   letter of ... requesting settlement of our ... statement in the sum of ...
   我們不明白，為什麼未收到您回覆我們於（日期）去函請求您
   清償（日期）對帳單上總計（金額）……一事

【結尾】

1. We trust you will attend to this matter without further delay.
   我們相信您一定會儘快處理此事。

2. We must ask you to settle this account by return.
   我們必須要求您於回覆時結清帳款。

3. We regret that we must ask for immediate payment of the amount
   outstanding.
   很抱歉，我們必須要求您立刻償付欠款。

第三封催款信

【開頭】

1. We wrote to you on ... and again on ... concerning the amount owing on our invoice number ...
   我們分別於（兩次日期）通知您有關（編號）發票的欠款……

2. We have had no reply to our previous requests for payment of our ... statement ...
   關於先前（日期）對帳單的催款通知，至今仍未收到您的回覆……

3. We note with surprise and disappointment that we have had no replies to our two previous applications for payment of your outstanding account.
   您對先前兩次催款通知未做任何回覆，我們感到驚訝與失望。

【結尾】

1. Unless we receive your cheque in full settlement by ... we shall have no option but to instruct our solicitors to recover the amount due.
   除非我們能於……（日期）前收到您結清欠款的支票，否則我們將別無選擇請求律師協助取回貨款。

2. Unless we receive your cheque in full settlement by the end of this month, we shall be compelled to take further steps to enforce payment.
   除非能在本月底前收到您清償所有帳款的支票，否則我們將被迫採取進一步的強制催款行動。

3. We still hope you will settle this account without further delay and thus save yourself the inconvenience and considerable costs of legal action.
   我們仍希望您能儘快結清帳款，如此可以免除採取法律行動的不便與龐大花費。

信用交易與信用查核
Credit and status enquiries

1
2
3
4
5
6
7
8
9
10
11
12
13
14
15
16
17
18
19
20
21
22
23
24
25
26
27
28
29
30

採行信用交易的理由

買方之所以要求採行信用交易的最主要考量是方便，基本上它可以「現在買，以後付款」：

1. 信用交易讓零售商保有一定庫存，等商品售出後再以實收款項結款。如此可以增加營運資金，有益財務運作。
2. 信用交易讓購買大眾不需存夠錢就可先行擁有，優先享用。
3. 信用交易省去每一次購買就得付款所造成的不便。

另一方面，賣方願意採取信用交易，則是著眼於利潤。它不僅可以吸引新顧客上門，同時還能留住老顧客。擁有信用交易帳戶的人一般仍傾向於在有帳戶之處採購，而以現金交易的人則是四處通行。

信用交易的缺點

當然，對於供應商或顧客而言，信用交易也有它的缺點，像是：

1. 必須另外花心思在記帳及收帳上，增加額外的商業成本。
2. 供應商可能面臨呆帳風險。
3. 供應商會提高售價以彌補墊高的成本，買方可能因此付出較多的錢來購買。

請求信用交易

經常向同一位供應商下單的買方，為了避免每次交易付款的不方便，會要求採「記帳」（open account）方式。在這種交易條件下，買方可在每月、每季或在雙方約定的一定期間內付款。換言之，商品是以信用交易的方式供應。

10.1　客戶請求採信用交易

(a) 請求

→ p.84

Dear

We have been very satisfied with your handling of our past orders, and as our business is growing we expect to place even larger orders with you in the future.

As our dealings have extended over a period of nearly 2 years, we hope you will agree to allow us open-account facilities with, say, quarterly settlements. This arrangement would save us the inconvenience of making separate payments on invoice.

Banker's and trade references can be provided if required.

We hope to receive your favourable reply soon.

Yours sincerely

(b) 回覆

→ p.84

Dear

Thank you for your letter of 18 November requesting the transfer of your business from payment on invoice to open-account terms.

As our business relations with you over the past 2 years have been entirely satisfactory, we are quite willing to make the transfer, based on a 90-day settlement period. In your case it will not be necessary to supply references.

We are pleased that you have been satisfied with our past service and that expansion of your business is likely to lead to increased orders. We can assure you of our continued efforts to give you the same high standard of service as in the past.

Yours sincerely

10.2　客戶要求展延信用帳款

(a) 現金流量問題

→ p.85

Dear

We regret you have had to remind us that we have not settled your account due for payment on 30 October.

We had intended to settle this account before now, but because of the present depressed state of business our own customers have not been meeting their obligations as promptly as usual. This has adversely affected[1] our cash flow.

Investment income due in less than a month's time will enable us to clear your account by the end of next month. We should therefore be grateful if you would accept the enclosed cheque for £200 as a payment on account. The balance will be cleared as soon as possible.

Yours sincerely

(b) 限制借貸與不良交易

→ p.85

Dear

STATEMENT OF ACCOUNT FOR AUGUST 200—

We have just received your letter of 8 October requesting settlement of our outstanding balance of £1686.00.

We are sorry not to have been able to clear this balance with our usual promptness. However, the present depressed state of business and the current restrictions on bank lending have created difficulties for us. These difficulties are purely temporary as payments from customers are due to us early in the New Year on a number of recently completed contracts.

Our resources[2] are quite sufficient to meet all our obligations, but as you will appreciate we have no wish to realise on our assets[3] at the moment. We hope you will therefore grant us a 3-month extension of credit, when we will be able to settle your account in full.

Yours sincerely

---

1. adversely affected ：變得更糟。
2. resources ：財務狀況。
3. realise on our assets ：出售資產以換取現金。

10.3　因顧客破產而請求展延信用帳款

(a) 客戶來信請求

→ p.86

Dear

在引言中提供　We have received and checked your statement for the quarter ended 30 September
背景資料　　and agree with the balance of £785.72 shown to be due.

說明過去準時付款　Until now we have had no difficulty in meeting our commitments and have always
及目前狀況　　settled our accounts with you promptly. We could have done so at this time but for
the bankruptcy of an important customer whose affairs are not likely to be settled
for some time.

技巧性請求　We should be most grateful if you would allow us to defer payment of your present
延後付款　account to the end of next month. This would enable us to meet a temporarily
difficult situation forced upon us by events that could not be foreseen.

最後保證　During the next few weeks we will be receiving payments under a number of large
儘早結清帳款　contracts. If you grant our request we shall have no difficulty in settling with you in
full in due course.

If you wish to discuss this please give me a call on 2468742.

Yours sincerely

(b) 供應商回信答應客戶請求

→ p.86

Dear

提及客戶的來信　Thank you for your letter of 10 October requesting an extension of time for
與請求　payment of the amount due on our 30 September statement.

說明同意　In view of the promptness with which you have always settled with us in the past,
延期付款的理由　we are willing to grant this extension in these special circumstances.

給予結清帳款　Please let us have your cheque in full settlement by 30 November.
的最後期限

Yours sincerely

(c) 供應商拒絕客戶請求

→ p.86

提及客戶
的來信與要求

在拒絕請求時，
必須謹慎用字

對於要求立即付款
表示遺憾

> Dear
>
> I am sorry to learn from your letter of 10 October of the difficulty in which the bankruptcy of an important customer has placed you.
>
> I should like to say at once that we fully understand your wish for an extension of time and would like to be able to help you. Unfortunately this is impossible because of commitments which we must meet by the end of this month.
>
> Your request is not at all unreasonable and if it had been possible we would have been pleased to grant it. In the circumstances, however, we must ask you to settle with us on the terms of payment originally agreed.
>
> Yours sincerely

業務徵詢

如果商品是以現金賣出，供應商當然不必要求買方提出財務證明。但如果是採取信用交易，那麼買方的付款能力就變得很重要了。

供應商在同意採用信用交易之前，會想要知道買方的聲譽及營運狀況與範圍，特別是能否準時支付帳款。供應商再根據這些資訊決定是否讓客戶記帳，如果是，又該給予多少額度。

供應商可以從以下管道進行業務徵詢（或稱同業往來查核），以獲知客戶的信用狀況：

◆ 客戶提供的備詢商號（trade reference）。
◆ 客戶的往來銀行。
◆ 各種商會。
◆ 商業徵信所（credit enquiry agency）。

當客戶向新合作的供應商下單時，通常會提供備詢商號，像是可供供應商查詢打聽的個人或公司行號等，或是往來銀行的名稱和地址。這些備詢人都是由客戶提供的，所以在採用時宜謹慎，畢竟只

有提供有利資料的才會被列為這些備詢人。即使備詢人是銀行也可能會有所誤導，對方或許擁有一個相當令人滿意的銀行帳戶，但實際的營運並不如數字顯示那般亮麗。

10.4　供應商要求提供備詢人

當新客戶下單但未提供備詢人時，供應商當然希望取得一些有關客戶信用度等的證明，尤其是遇上大筆訂單時。供應商請求提供備詢人的書信，必須避免任何不信任對方的暗示。

→ p.87

Dear

We were pleased to receive your first order with us dated 19 May.

When opening new accounts it is our practice to ask customers for trade references. Please be good enough to send us the names and addresses of two other suppliers with whom you have dealings.

We hope to receive this information by return, and meanwhile your order has been put in hand for despatch immediately we hear further from you.

Yours sincerely

10.5　供應商要求填寫信用交易申請表

(a) 供應商來信

→ p.87

Dear

Thank you for your order number 526 of 15 June for polyester bedspreads and pillow cases.

As your name does not appear on our books and as we should like you to take advantage of our usual credit terms, we enclose our credit application form for your completion and return as soon as possible.

We should be able to deliver your present order in about 2 weeks, and look forward to receiving your further orders.

We hope that this first transaction will mark the beginning of a pleasant business connection.

Yours sincerely

(b) 客戶寄回信用交易申請表

Dear

Thank you for your letter of 18 June. As we fully expect to place further orders, we should obviously like to take advantage of your offer of credit facilities.

We quite understand the need for references and have completed your credit application form giving the relevant information. This is enclosed.

We look forward to receiving delivery of our first order by the end of this month and to our future business dealings with you.

Yours sincerely

10.6 客戶提供備詢商號

→ p.88

Dear Sirs

Thank you for the catalogue and price list received earlier this month.

We have pleasure in sending you our first order, number ST6868, for 6 Olivetti portable electronic typewriters, elite type, at your list price of £255 less 25% on your usual monthly terms.

These machines are needed for early delivery to customers and as we understand you have the machines in stock we should be glad if you would arrange for them to reach us by the end of next week. We hope this will leave enough time for you to take up references with the following firms with which we have had dealings over many years:

B Kisby & Co Ltd, 28–30 Lythan Square, Liverpool
The Atlas Manufacturing Co Ltd, Century House, Bristol

We look forward to doing further business with you in the future.

Yours faithfully

10.7　客戶提供備詢銀行

→ p.88

> Dear Sirs
>
> Our cheque for £2513 is enclosed in full settlement of your invoice number 826 for the stereo tape recorders supplied earlier this month.
>
> My directors have good reason to believe that these particular products will be a popular selling line in this part of the country. As we expect to place further orders with you from time to time, we should be glad if you would arrange to provide open-account facilities on a quarterly basis.
>
> For information concerning our credit standing[4] we refer you to Barclays Bank Ltd, 25–27 The Arcade, Southampton.
>
> Yours faithfully

信用查核

在寫信給備詢商號進行信用查核（或稱徵信）時，措詞必須正式、有禮，通常是遵循下列四點原則：

◆ 提供客戶的背景資料。
◆ 請求提供該潛在客戶的身分及聲譽的相關資訊，並就打算給予的信用額度請求備詢人提供睿智的觀點。
◆ 向備詢人保證會對其所提供的資料嚴加保密。
◆ 附上回郵信封，如果對方在國外，應附上國際回郵禮券。

有些大公司備有制式表格，將查詢的問題逐一列出，如此既能簡化作業，又可加快回覆速度。

當供應商收到請求提供的資訊時，應該回信告知並致上謝意。這類信用查核信函應該寫給資深主管，並標示 Confidential 字樣。

---

4. credit standing：信用狀況。

10.8 供應商寫信給備詢商號

(a) 範例 1

→ p.89

Dear Sirs

Watson & Jones of Newcastle wish to open an account with us and have given your name as a reference.

We should be grateful for your view about the firm's general standing and your opinion on whether they are likely to be reliable for credit up to £1000 and to settle their accounts promptly.

Any information provided will of course be treated in strict confidence.

We enclose a stamped, addressed envelope for your reply.

Yours faithfully

(b) 範例 2

→ p.89

Dear Sirs

We have received a request from Shamlan & Shamlan & Co of Bahrain for supplies of our products on open-account terms. They state that they have regularly traded with you over the past 2 years and have given your name as a reference.

We should be obliged if you would tell us in confidence whether you have found this company to be thoroughly reliable in their dealings with you and prompt in settling their accounts.

We understand their requirements with us may amount to approximately £2000 a quarter, and should be glad to know whether you feel they will be able to meet commitments of this size. Any other information you can provide would be very welcome.

Your reply, for which we enclose an international postal reply coupon, will of course be treated in strict confidence.

Yours faithfully

10.9　供應商請其往來銀行協助信用查核

銀行與客戶之間的關係屬於高度機密，因此銀行通常不接受私人詢問有關其客戶的相關資料，但多半樂意提供資訊給同業銀行。所以，供應商要向銀行徵信時，也必須透過本身的往來銀行進行。

→ p.90

Dear Sir/Madam

The Colston Engineering Co Ltd in Mumbai has asked for a standing credit of £5000 but as our knowledge of this company is limited to a few months trading on a cash-on-invoice basis, we should like some information about their financial standing before dealing with their request.

The only reference they give us is that of their bankers – the National Bank of Nigeria, Ibadan. We would appreciate any information you can let us have.

Yours faithfully

10.10　供應商委託商業徵信所進行信用查核

如果供應商希望自行取得客戶商譽的相關資料，可以委託同業公會或一些商業徵信所進行調查。這些徵信所的主要業務就是在提供公司或個人事業上或私人的財務資訊。他們有來自不同管道（包括自己的徵信人員）的龐大資訊庫，並予以更新。如果一時無法從資料庫取得所需資料，他們會立即著手調查，並且在數天內完成。

→ p.90

Dear Sirs

We have been asked by A Griffiths & Co, Cardiff to supply goods to the value of £1750 on open-account terms against their first order.

We have no information about this company but as there are prospects of further large orders from them, we should like to meet the present order on the terms requested if it is safe to do so.

Please let us have a report on the reputation and financial standing of the company and in particular your advice on whether it would be advisable to grant credit for this first order. Your advice on the maximum amount for which it would be safe to grant credit on a quarterly account would also be appreciated.

Yours faithfully

回覆信用查核結果

如果受徵信公司的信用狀況令人滿意，備詢人當然可以直接回覆此一結果。但萬一無法確定對方的信用好壞與否，那麼在回信時需格外小心。一般而言，這樣的回覆都會留待些許空間供委託者去領悟弦外之音，也就是自行推測真正的含意，而不會直率地攤開輕蔑性的事實。

備詢人在回信上需標示 Confidential，並遵循底下四點原則：

◆ 確認收到這次的詢問，並提供背景資訊。
◆ 陳述事實並誠實表達意見。
◆ 希望提供的資訊有所幫助。
◆ 技巧地提醒對方所有的資訊均屬機密，若經採納，並不負任何責任。

10.11 備詢商號對信用查核所做的回覆

(a) 對 10.8 (a) 的徵詢表示贊同

→ p.90

Dear

Thank you for your letter of 25 May.

We are pleased to inform you that this company is a small but well-known and highly respectable firm that has been established in this town for more than 25 years.

We have been doing business with this company for over 7 years on quarterly-account terms. Although they have not usually taken advantage of cash discounts they have always paid their account promptly on the net dates. The credit we have allowed this company has at times been well over the £1000 you mention.

We hope this information will be helpful and that it will be treated as confidential.

Yours sincerely

(b) 不鼓勵提供 10.8 (b) 的信用額度

→ p.91

Dear

The company mentioned in your letter of 25 May has placed regular orders with us for several years. We believe the company to be trustworthy and reliable, but we have to say that they have not always settled their accounts by the due date.

Their account with us is on quarterly settlement terms but we have never allowed it to reach the sum mentioned in your letter. This to us seems to be a case in which caution is necessary.

We are glad to be of help but ask you to ensure that the information provided is treated as strictly confidential.

Yours sincerely

 提示　以寫出有效且富邏輯架構的訊息為傲。

10.12　銀行對信用查核所做的回覆

(a) 贊同 10.9 的信用交易建議

→ p.91

Dear

We have received from the National Bank of Nigeria the information requested in your letter of 18 September.

The company you mention is a private company that was founded 15 years ago and is run as a family concern by three brothers. It enjoys a good reputation. Our information shows that the company punctually meets its commitments and a credit in the sum you mention would seem to be safe.

This information is strictly confidential and is given without any responsibility on our part.

Yours sincerely

(b) 不贊同 10.9 的信用交易建議

→ p.91

> Dear
>
> We have received information from the National Bank of Nigeria concerning the company mentioned in your letter of 18 September.
>
> This is a private company run as a family concern and operating on a small scale.
>
> More detailed information we have received suggests that this is a case in which we would advise caution. You will of course treat this advice as strictly confidential.
>
> Yours sincerely

10.13　商業徵信所回覆信用查核結果

(a) 贊同 10.10 的建議

→ p.92

> Dear
>
> 答謝來信　　— Thank you for your letter of 10 February.
> 並提供細節
>
> We have completed our enquiries relating to A Griffiths & Co and are pleased to report favourably.
>
> 詳述公司狀況　— This is a well-founded and highly reputable firm. There are four partners and their
> 並給予的建議　capital is estimated to be at least £100,000. They do an excellent trade and are regarded as one of the safest accounts in Cardiff.
>
> 就信用額度提出　— From the information we have obtained we believe that you need not hesitate to
> 另一個建議　allow the initial credit of £1750 requested. On a quarterly account you could safely allow at least £5000.
>
> Yours sincerely

(b) 不贊同 10.10 的建議

→ p.92

引言中確認來信 並建議小心處理

Dear

We have completed our enquiries concerning A Griffiths & Co following your letter of 10 February. I am sorry to advise caution in their request for credit.

提供有關這家公司 的詳細資料

About a year ago an action was brought against this company by one of its suppliers for recovery of sums due, though payment was later recovered in full.

陳述事實

Our enquiries reveal nothing to suggest that the firm is not straightforward. On the contrary the firm's difficulties would seem to be due to bad management and in particular to <u>overtrading</u>.[5] Consequently most of the firm's suppliers either give only very short credit for limited sums or make deliveries on a cash basis.

提醒資料保密

This information is of course supplied in the strictest confidence.

Yours sincerely

實用措詞

供應商請求提供備詢人

【開頭】

1. Thank you for your letter of ... Subject to satisfactory references we shall be glad to provide the open account facilities requested.
   謝謝您（日期）的來信。如果公司滿意您所提供的信用查核資料，我們將樂於答應您要求的記帳條件。

2. We were pleased to receive your order dated ... If you will kindly supply the usual trade references, we will be glad to consider open-account terms.
   很高興收到您（日期）的訂單。如果您可以提供您平常的備詢商號，我們將樂意考慮您的記帳條件。

---

5. **overtrading**：超額交易。

【結尾】

1. We will be in touch with you as soon as references are received.
   一收到您提供的備詢人，我們將儘速與您聯繫。

2. It is our usual practice to request references from new customers, and we hope to receive these soon.
   依照慣例，我們會要求新顧客提供備詢人，希望能儘快收到。

顧客提供備詢人

【開頭】

1. Thank you for your letter of ... in reply to our request for open-account terms.
   謝謝您（日期）來信回覆有關我們採記帳條件的請求。

2. We have completed and return your credit application form.
   我們已經將信用交易申請表填妥寄回。

【結尾】

1. The following firms will be pleased to answer your enquiries ...
   下列公司將樂意回應您的詢問……

2. For the information required please refer to our bankers, who are ...
   關於您要求提供備詢人，請洽我們的往來銀行……

供應商聯繫備詢人

【開頭】

1. ... of ... has supplied your name as a reference in connection with his (her, their) application for open-account terms.
   （請求記帳的公司）提供您的名字作為採記帳交易的備詢人。

2. We have received a large order from ... and should be grateful for any information you can provide regarding their reliability.
   我們收到（請求記帳的公司）的一筆大單，若您能提供任何有關他們的可信度資料，我們將由衷感激。

3. We should be grateful if you would obtain reliable information for us concerning ...
如果您能提供我們有關（請求記帳的公司）的可信度資料，我們將由衷感激。

【結尾】

1. Any information you can provide will be appreciated.
我們十分感激您所提供的任何資訊。

2. Any information provided will be treated in strictest confidence.
您所提供的任何資訊均將嚴加保密。

3　Please accept our thanks in advance for any help you can give us.
對於您提供的任何協助，在此先致上謝意。

回覆信用查核結果

【開頭】

1. We welcome the opportunity to report favourably on ...
我們利用此機會向您報告贊同……

2. In reply to your letter of ... we can thoroughly recommend the firm you mention.
回覆您（日期）的來信，我們可以強烈建議您與該公司合作。

3. The firm mentioned in your letter of ... is not well known to us.
您（日期）信中所提到的（請求記帳的公司），我們並不熟悉。

【結尾】

1. This information is given on the clear understanding that it will be treated confidentially.
相信您清楚了解這些提供的資料需要嚴加保密。

2. We would not hesitate granting this company credit up to ...
我們毫不猶豫保證可提供這家公司最多（金額）的信用額度。

3. This information is given to you in confidence and without any responsibility on our part.

   以上資訊請嚴加保密，且我方不負任何責任。

典型的商業交易
（書信與文件）

A typical business transaction
(correspondence and documents)

第二單元討論的是日常的商業往來書信，而本章將舉例說明國內貿易會用到的典型書信。

伍德父子（G Wood & Sons）公司最近在布里斯托市開了家電器行，他們向位於伯明罕的電器供應（Electrical Supplies）有限公司下單訂貨，並採記帳方式。本交易從伍德父子公司寫信請求對方提供報價及記帳條件的資訊揭開序幕。

11.1 請求報價

→ p.94

G WOOD & SONS
36 Castle Street
Bristol BS1 2BQ
Telephone 0117 954967

GW/ST

15 November 200—

Mr Henry Thomas
Electrical Supplies Ltd
29–31 Broad Street
Birmingham
B1 2HE

Dear Mr Thomas

We have recently opened an electrical goods store at the above address and have received a number of enquiries for the following domestic appliances of which at present we do not hold stocks:

Swanson Electric Kettles, 2 litre
Cosiwarm Electric Blankets, single-bed size
Regency Electric Toasters
Marlborough Kitchen Wall Clocks

When I phoned you this morning you informed me that all these items are available in stock for immediate delivery.

Please let me have your prices and terms for payment 2 months from date of invoicing. If prices and terms are satisfactory, we would place with you a first order for 10 of each of these items.

The matter is of some urgency and I would appreciate an early reply.

Yours sincerely

GORDON WOOD

Manager

11.2 供應商報價

→ p.95

ELECTRICAL SUPPLIES LTD
29–31 Broad Street
Birmingham B1 2HE
Tel: 0121–542–6614

HT/JH

17 November 200—

Mr Gordon Wood
G Wood & Sons
36 Castle Street
Bristol
BS1 2BQ

Dear Mr Wood

QUOTATION NUMBER E542

Thank you for your enquiry of 15 November. I am pleased to quote as follows:

	£
Swanson Electric Kettles, 2 litre	25.00 each
Cosiwarm Electric Blankets, single-bed size	24.50 each
Regency Electric Toasters	25.50 each
Marlborough Kitchen Wall Clocks	27.50 each

The above are current catalogue prices from which we would allow you a trade discount of $33\frac{1}{3}$%. Prices include packing and delivery to your premises.

It is our usual practice to ask all new customers for trade references. Please let us have the names and addresses of two suppliers with whom you have had regular dealings. Subject to satisfactory replies, we shall be glad to supply the goods and to allow you the 2 months' credit requested.

As there may be other items in which you are interested, I enclose copies of our current catalogue and price list.

I look forward to the opportunity of doing business with you.

Yours sincerely

HENRY THOMAS
Sales Manager

Enc

11.3 請求列為備詢人

買方在提供其他往來廠商作爲備詢人之前，應該先寫信徵求對方的同意。萬一時間緊迫，可取得口頭同意，但其他情況下，買方應提出書面請求。在此個案中，買方寫信給柯芬里市的威廉森（J Williamson）公司及底下的強生貿易商（Johnson Traders）有限公司，請求將他們列爲備詢人（參考 p.198~200 的信函）。

→ p.96

G Wood & Sons
36 Castle Street
Bristol BS1 2BQ
Telephone 0117 954967

GW/ST

19 November 200—

Mr Robert Johnson
Johnson Traders Ltd
The Hayes
Cardiff
CF1 lJW

Dear Robert

I wish to place an order with Electrical Supplies Ltd, Birmingham, with facilities on credit. As this will be a first order they have asked me to supply trade references.

I have been a regular customer of yours for the past 4 years and should be grateful if you would allow me to submit your company's name as one of my references.

I shall very much appreciate your consent to stand as referee and hope to hear from you soon.

Yours sincerely

GORDON WOOD
Manager

11.4　同意當備詢人

→ p.97

JOHNSON TRADERS LTD
The Hayes
Cardiff CF1 1JW
Telephone 01222 572382

RH/KI

22 November 200—

Mr Gordon Wood
G Wood & Sons
36 Castle Street
Bristol
BS1 2BQ

Dear Mr Wood

Thank you for your letter of 19 November requesting permission to use our name as a reference in your transaction with Electrical Supplies Ltd.

During the time we have done business together you have been a very reliable customer. If your suppliers decide to approach us for a reference we shall be very happy to support your request for credit facilities.

Yours sincerely

ROBERT JOHNSON

Financial Controller

11.5　訂購

(a) 訂單所付的短信

→ p.98

G WOOD & SONS
36 Castle Street
Bristol BS1 2BQ
Telephone 0117 954967

GW/ST

24 November 200—

Mr Henry Thomas
Electrical Supplies Ltd
29–31 Broad Street
Birmingham
B1 2HE

Dear Mr Thomas

ORDER NUMBER 3241

Thank you for your letter of 17 November quoting for domestic appliances and enclosing copies of your current catalogue and price list.

We have had regular dealings with the following suppliers for the past 4 or 5 years. They will be happy to provide the necessary references.

Johnson Traders Ltd, The Hayes, Cardiff CF1 1JW

J Williamson & Co, Southey House, Coventry CV1 5RU

Our order number 3241 is enclosed for the goods mentioned in our original enquiry. They are urgently needed and as they are available from stock we hope you will arrange prompt delivery.

I appreciate your agreement to allow 2 months' credit on receipt of satisfactory references.

Yours sincerely

GORDON WOOD
Manager

Enc

(b) 訂單

→ p.99

G WOOD & SONS
36 Castle Street
Bristol BS1 2BQ
Telephone 0117 954967

ORDER NO 3241   Date 24 November 200—

Electrical Supplies Ltd
29–31 Broad Street
BIRMINGHAM
B1 2HE

Please supply

Quantity	Item(s)	Price
		£
10	Swanson Electric Kettles (2 litre)	25.00 each
10	Cosiwarm Electric Blankets (single-bed size)	24.50 each
10	Regency Electric Toasters	25.50 each
10	Marlborough Kitchen Wall Clocks	27.50 each

Terms $33\frac{1}{3}$% trade discount

(signed)

for G Wood & Sons

圖表 11.1　訂單

11.6　供應商回函確認

寫信給下單的客戶，尤其是第一次下單的客戶，表示感謝及確認收到訂單和備詢商號資料，是一個很好的生意技巧。接著供應商會聯絡備詢人，而在收到對方表示肯定的回覆後，便開始處理訂單。

→ p.100

ELECTRICAL SUPPLIES LTD
29–31 Broad Street
Birmingham B1 2HE
Telephone 0121–542–6614

HT/JH

1 December 200—

Mr G Wood
G Wood & Sons
36 Castle Street
Bristol
BS1 2BQ

Dear Mr Wood

YOUR ORDER NUMBER 3241

Thank you for your letter of 24 November. We were very pleased to receive your order and confirm that the goods will be supplied at the prices and on the terms stated.

Your order has been passed to our warehouse for immediate despatch of the goods from stock. We hope you will be pleased with them.

Please do not hesitate to contact me if I can be of any further help.

Yours sincerely

Henry Thomas
Sales Manager

11.7　通知書

和商品的出貨與送貨有關的文件包括：裝箱單（packing note）、發貨通知（advice of despatch note）、託運單（consignment note）和送貨單（delivery note）。這些文件都屬於發票的副本，通常使用不可

複寫紙（NCR, no carbon required），和發票一起成套提出。這些作為通知書的文件不會列出關於價格的資料。

通知書或發貨單用來通知買方貨物已在途中，以便貨物抵達時可據此核對。通知書常被發票取代，在商品寄出當天或之前先行寄出，有時候也會寫封信來通知出貨。

如果小型商品是以郵寄，只需用到裝箱單（視為通知單的副本）。有些供應商，特別是使用自家運輸工具的供應商，不用通知書，而以裝箱單或送貨單代替。

11.8　託運單

貨品交由火車託運時，供應商需填妥託運單（consignment note），當成是和鐵路局簽訂的運輸合約。託運單上必須特別註明交寄的商品數量、重量、種類和目的地，並說明運費已付（carriage paid）還是運費到付（carriage forward，如由買方負擔）。託運單一般是使用鐵路局事先印製好的表格，但有的貿易商偏好使用自家的託運單。

當集貨完畢，填好的託運單會交由承運業者與貨物一同運送，當貨品送抵買方手上，買方須在託運單上簽名，作為交貨的證明文件。

11.9　送貨單

有時候要準備兩份送貨單，一份由買方保存，另一份買方簽名後交還給承運業者，作為貨物已經運抵的證明。有的承運業者會請求買方在送貨記錄冊或送貨表格上簽名，以記錄貨物寄送。

由於買方無法在簽名之前先檢查貨物是否完好，因此簽名時要記得加上 not examined 或 goods unexamined（貨物尚未檢查）等字眼，以防萬一。

11.10　發票

發票的開立方式各有不同，有時是隨貨物寄出，有時是分開郵寄。寄出的時間可能比貨物更早（當成通知書用）或更晚。通常貨物如果包成一大綑或為散裝時，會單獨寄出發票。

(a) 發票所附的短信

郵寄發票時不一定要附一封短信做說明，即使需要，也應該簡短且正式。

→ p.101

ELECTRICAL SUPPLIES LTD
29–31 Broad Street
Birmingham B1 2HE
Telephone 0121–542–6614

HT/JH

3 December 200—

G Wood & Sons
36 Castle Street
Bristol
BS1 2BQ

Dear Sirs

YOUR ORDER NUMBER 3241

We enclose our invoice number 6740 for the domestic electrical appliances supplied to your order dated 24 November.

The goods have been packed in three cases, numbers 78, 79 and 80, and sent to you today by rail, carriage paid. We hope they will reach you promptly and in good condition.

If you settle the account within 2 months we will allow you to deduct from the amount due a special cash discount of $1\frac{1}{2}$ %.

Yours faithfully

SALLY YAP (Mrs)
Credit Control Manager

Enc

(b) 發票

當伍德父子公司收到發票後，會根據裝箱單或送貨單，檢查所有的貨物是否符合發票所載。當然，買方在將貨款記入帳簿時，會檢查發票上的商業折扣及總額是否正確。

依據規定，發票並不是用來請求付款，而是作為交易的一項記錄及負債報告書（statement of the indebtedness）。供應商之後會再寄對帳單給買方請款。

→ p.102

ELECTRICAL SUPPLIES LTD
29–31 Broad Street
Birmingham B1 2HE
Telephone 0121–542–6614

INVOICE

G Wood & Sons
36 Castle Street
BRISTOL
BS1 2BQ

Date 3 December 200—

Your order no 3241

Invoice No 6740

發票採用連續編號，以利參考。貨運編號也一併寫上

Quantity	Item(s)	Unit Price	Total Price
		£	£
10	Swanson Electric Kettles (2 litre)	25.00	250.00
10	Cosiwarm Electric Blankets (single-bed size)	24.50	245.00
10	Regency Electric Toasters	25.50	255.00
10	Marlborough Kitchen Wall Clocks	27.50	275.00
			1025.00
	Less 33⅓% trade discount		341.33
			683.67
	VAT @ 17.5%		119.64
			803.31
	3 packing cases (returnable)		15.00
			818.31
	Terms: 1½% two months		

之前已經同意 33⅓% 的商業折扣

在發票日期起算兩個月內付款，可享現金折扣，並在付款時扣除

意指錯誤及遺漏除外，亦即賣方有更正發票上錯誤或疏漏的權利

E & OE   Registered in England No 726549

圖表 11.2　發票

11.11 借項單與貸項單

有關這兩項文件的使用目的，請參考第 148-150 頁。

(a) 買方索取貸項單

在此交易範例中，伍德父子公司要退回發票上索費的三個包裝箱。他們會寫信請供應商針對箱子的費用開立貸項單。至於伍德父子公司是否要在提出這項請求的同時寄發借項單給供應商，則可以沿用慣例。

→ p.103

G WOOD & SONS
36 Castle Street, Bristol BS1 2BQ
Telephone 0117 954967

GW/ST

10 December 200—

Mrs Sally Yap
Credit Control Manager
Electrical Supplies Ltd
29–31 Broad Street
Birmingham
B1 2HE

Dear Mrs Yap

INVOICE NUMBER 6740

We have today returned to you by rail the three packing cases charged on this invoice at a cost of £15.00.

We enclose a debit note for this amount and shall be glad to receive your credit note by return.

All the goods supplied and invoiced reached us in good condition. Thank you for your promptness in dealing with our first order.

Yours sincerely

Gordon Wood
Manager

Enc

→ p.104

G WOOD & SONS
36 Castle Street
Bristol BS1 2BQ
Telephone 0117 954967

DEBIT NOTE

Electrical Supplies Ltd
29–31 Broad Street
BIRMINGHAM
B1 2HE

Date 10 December 200—

Debit Note No D 841

Date	Details	Total
		£
10.12.200—	To　3 packing cases charged on your invoice number 6740 and returned	15.00

圖表 11.3　借項單

(b) 賣方開立貸項單

當電器供應有限公司收到借項單後，他們會先檢查退還的包裝箱，接著準備對方所請求的貸項單，連同（也可不附）一封精簡、正式的短信寄給伍德父子公司。由於這是客戶第一次下單，明智的供應商可撰寫簡箋來鼓勵雙方未來繼續合作。

→ p.104

ELECTRICAL SUPPLIES LTD
29–31 Broad Street
Birmingham B1 2HE
Telephone 0121–542–6614

HT/JH

14 December 200–

Mr Gordon Wood
Manager
G Wood & Sons
36 Castle Street
Bristol
BS1 2BQ

Dear Mr Wood

Thank you for your letter of 10 December enclosing debit note number D841. I confirm receipt of the three packing cases returned. Our credit note number C672 for the sum of £15.00 is enclosed.

Yours sincerely

SALLY YAP (Mrs)
Credit Control Manager

Enc

→ p.105

ELECTRICAL SUPPLIES LTD
29–31 Broad Street
Birmingham B1 2HE
Telephone 0121–524–6614

CREDIT NOTE

G Wood & Sons   Date 14 December 200–
36 Castle Street
BRISTOL
BS1 2BQ   Credit Note No C 672

Date	Details		Total
			£
10.12.200–	To	3 packing cases charged on your invoice number 6740 and returned	15.00

圖表 11.4　貸項單

11.12　對帳單

供應商通常會於一定期間（通常是每個月）寄對帳單給顧客，一則用來請款，一則供買方核對自己帳簿上的帳款。寄對帳單時通常不需附上短信（請參考第 152 頁）。

→ p.105

ELECTRICAL SUPPLIES LTD
29–31 Broad Street
Birmingham B1 2HE
Telephone 0121–524–6614

STATEMENT

G Wood & Sons
36 Castle Street
BRISTOL
BS1 2BQ

Date 31 January 200—

Date	Details	Debit	Credit	Balance
		£	£	£
3.12.200—	Invoice 6740	818.31		818.31
14.12.200—	Credit note C 672		15.00	803.31
	(2 $\frac{1}{2}$ % seven days)			

E & OE　　　　　　　　　　　　　　Registered in England No 726549

圖表 11.5　對帳單

11.13　付款

發票和對帳單通常會指明付款條件。例如：

◆ prompt cash（即期付款）：一個有些彈性的術語，通常為發票或對帳單日期起算十五天內付款。

◆ 2.5% 30 days（三十天內付款享 2.5% 折扣）：如果買方在發票或對帳單開出後三十天內付款，即享有 2.5% 的折扣，否則就必須支付對帳單所列金額。

◆ Net 30 days（三十天內付清）：買方必須於三十天內付清全部的款項。

商業的往來交易上通常是用支票付款。如果款項爲數眾多，可採銀行轉帳方式。在此交易中，買方是寄支票給供應商以結清帳款。

→ p.106

G WOOD & SONS
36 Castle Street, Bristol BS1 2BQ
Telephone 0117 954967

GW/ST

4 February 200—

Mrs Sally Yap
Credit Control Manager
Electrical Supplies Ltd
29–31 Broad Street
Birmingham
B1 2HE

Dear Mrs Yap

We have received your statement of account dated 31 January 200— showing a balance due of £803.31.

From the total amount due on the statement I have deducted the allowable cash discount of $2\frac{1}{2}\%$ and enclose a cheque for £783.23 in full settlement.

Yours sincerely

Gordon Wood
Manager

Enc

11.14 收據

通常支票本身就是付款證明，不需另外開立正式收據。但如果需要收據，仍可依法請求對方開立。

在此項交易中，付款證明可以是供應商的正式收據，或者是銀行兌現後的買方支票。

Unit 3

富創造力與說服力的文件
Creative and persuasive documents

抱怨與調解
Complaints and adjustments

抱怨的處理

無論如何盡心盡力，抱怨總是在所難免，它們可能來自買方或賣方。要抱怨的原因很多，像是：

◆ 收到不對的商品。
◆ 服務品質不佳。
◆ 不滿意商品品質。
◆ 運送延誤交貨。
◆ 商品損毀。
◆ 非當初約定的價格。

對商品的抱怨

確認購買的商品都有保留收據，然後持收據儘快向購買的商家說明商品的問題所在（口氣肯定，但不挑釁），並提出希望的解決方式。能夠圓滿落幕是最好的，萬一得不到滿意答覆，可寫一封抱怨信寄給客服經理，且儘可能找出對方的姓名，直接註明收件人。

對服務的抱怨

給供應商一個解決問題的機會，如果有必要寫抱怨信，請告訴對方你希望怎麼做，並提出一個期限。你也許希望扣留尾款，直到問題獲得滿意的解決。但是，請記得先檢查你所簽訂的合約或信用協議上的每一個附屬細節。

撰寫抱怨信的注意事項

即使滿腔憤怒，下筆還是要克制，因為也許錯不在供應商。以下幾點是寫抱怨信時的應注意事項：

1. 立即處理。拖延除了可能削弱自身立場之外，也會增加供應商調查的困難。
2. 不要一味將過錯歸咎於供應商，對方可能有很好的理由。

3. 避免粗暴、無禮，否則容易引起反感，並導致對方不願意出面解決。
4. 抱怨信的內容應是：
   ◆ 描述你所購買的商品或服務。
   ◆ 說明購買商品（或被服務）的地點、時間以及費用。
   ◆ 解釋出現什麼錯誤、你已採取的行動、跟誰談過，以及結果為何。
   ◆ 解釋你希望對方如何彌補錯誤，例如退費或修理，或是免費再提供一次服務。
5. 利用掛號／快遞將信寄出，如此可確認對方是否有收到信。
6. 將寫好的信影印一份留底，且絕對不要寄原始文件或收據給對方。

對各種抱怨的處理

如果客戶有所抱怨，大多數的供應商自然會想聆聽這些聲音，以免客戶流失或轉與他人交易。聆聽抱怨也讓供應商有機會調查、解釋或解決事情，維持友好關係，也許還能藉此改善商品和服務。在面對不滿或不悅的客戶時，應遵循以下方針：

1. 大家總說「顧客永遠是對的」（The customer is always right），雖然實際情況不見得如此，至少必須假設「顧客或許是對的」（The customer may be right）。

2. 立刻回信確認有收到對方的抱怨。如果暫時無法完全回應對方的要求，應向對方解釋正在著手調查，稍後將完整回覆。

 好的寫作者學習謹慎用字及使用正確的語氣。

有關商品的抱怨

12.1 抱怨送錯商品

如果買方收到的並不是當初訂購的商品或品質不對，可以將它們退回，運費由供應商負擔。

(a) 抱怨

→ p.108

Dear Sirs

訂單編號與日期 —— On 12 August I ordered 12 copies of *Background Music* by H Lowery under my order number FT567.

不滿意的理由 —— On opening the parcel received this morning I found that it contained 12 copies of *History of Music* by the same author. I regret that I cannot keep these books as I have an adequate stock already. I am therefore returning the books by parcel post for immediate replacement, as I have several customers waiting for them.

要求採取何種行動 —— Please credit my account with the invoiced value of the returned copies including reimbursement for the postage cost of £17.90.

Yours faithfully

(b) 回覆

→ p.108

Dear Mr Ramsay

表示歉意 — I was sorry to learn from your letter of 18 August that a mistake was made in dealing with your order.

解釋發生
錯誤的原因 — This mistake is entirely our own and we apologise for the inconvenience it is causing you. This occurred because of staff shortage during this unusually busy season and also the fact that these 2 books by Lowery have identical bindings.

補救措施 — 12 copies of the correct title have been sent to you today.

Your account will be credited with the invoiced value of the books and cost of return postage. Our credit note is enclosed.

結尾再次道歉 — Our apologies again for this mistake.

Yours sincerely

12.2　抱怨商品品質

如果商品品質不佳或與原先所述不符，那麼買方有權拒收。但即使商品正確，卻延遲交貨，買方可能也會拒收。

(a) 抱怨

→ p.109

Dear Sirs

抱怨的理由 — We have recently received several complaints from customers about your fountain pens. The pens are clearly not giving satisfaction and in some cases we have had to refund the purchase price.

進一步細節 — The pens are part of the batch of 500 supplied against our order number 8562 dated 28 March. This order was placed on the basis of a sample pen left by your representative. We have ourselves compared the performance of this sample with that of a number of the pens from this batch, and there is little doubt that many of them are faulty – some of them leak and others blot when writing.

The complaints we have received relate only to pens from the batch mentioned. Pens supplied before these have always been satisfactory.

請求採取的行動 — We therefore wish to return the unsold balance, amounting to 377 pens. Please replace them with pens of the quality which our earlier dealings with you have led us to expect.

結尾 — Please let us know what arrangements you wish us to make for the return of these unsuitable pens.

Yours faithfully

(b) 接受抱怨的回信

→ p.109

Dear

Thank you for your letter dated 10 May pointing out faults in the pens supplied to your order number 8562. This has caused us a good deal of concern and we are glad that you brought this matter to our notice.

We have tested a number of pens from the production batch you mention, and agree that they are not perfect. The defects have been traced to a fault in one of the machines, which has now been rectified.

Please arrange to return to us your unsold balance of 377 pens; the cost of postage will be reimbursed in due course. We have already arranged for 400 pens to be sent to replace this unsold balance. The extra 23 pens are sent without charge, and will enable you to provide free replacement of any further pens about which you may receive complaints.

We apologise for the inconvenience this has caused you.

Yours sincerely

(c) 不接受抱怨的回信

如果不認同客戶提出的抱怨，應該站在客戶的立場，小心解釋不得不拒絕所請的理由。

→ p.110

Dear

有技巧的開場白 — We are sorry to learn from your letter of 10 May of the difficulties you are having with the pens supplied to your order number 8562.

有關品管的解釋 — All our pens are manufactured to be identical in design and performance and we cannot understand why some of them should have given trouble to your customers. It is normal practice for each pen to be individually examined by our Inspection Department before being passed into store. However, from what you say, it would seem that a number of the pens included in the latest batch escaped the usual examination.

圓融地拒絕 — We sympathise with your problem but regret that we cannot accept your suggestion
對方請求 to take back all the unsold stock from the batch concerned. Indeed there should be no need for this since it is unlikely that the number of faulty pens can be very large. We will gladly replace any pen found to be unsatisfactory, and on this particular batch are prepared to allow you a special discount of 5% to compensate for your inconvenience.

提供折扣， — We trust you will accept this as being a fair and reasonable solution of this matter.
以軟化問題
Please give me a call on 4626123 if you have any further questions.

Yours sincerely

12.3　抱怨數量

(a) 數量超出

當供應商交貨的數量超出實際訂購量時，在法律上，買方有權將商品全數退回，或者僅退回超出的部分。另外，買方也可以接受所有商品，再以相同價格買下多送來的商品。以下範例中，買方拒絕接受多出的商品，且無義務退回，供應商必須負責安排退貨事宜。

→ p.110

Dear Sirs

Thank you for your promptness in delivering the coffee we ordered on 30 July. However 160 bags were delivered this morning instead of 120 as stated on our order.

Our present needs are completely covered and we cannot make use of the 40 bags sent in excess of our order. These bags will therefore be held in our warehouse until we receive your instructions.

Yours faithfully

(b) 數量短少

如果供應商送來的數量比當初訂購的少，供應商不能強迫客戶同意分批收貨。客戶可以要求立刻補上不足的部分。

→ p.111

Dear Sir/Madam

OUR ORDER NUMBER 861

We thank you for so promptly delivering the gas coke ordered on 20 March. Although we ordered 5 tonnes in 50-kg bags, only 80 bags were delivered. Your carrier was unable to explain the shortage and we have not received any explanation from you.

We still need the full quantity ordered, so please arrange to deliver the remaining 20 bags as soon as possible.

Yours faithfully

12.4　抱怨製造商

(a) 客戶的抱怨

這封信中，供應商通知買方有關瑕疵品請直接寫信給製造商。

→ p.111

> Dear Sirs
>
> On 15 September I bought one of your 'Big Ben' alarm clocks (mains operated) from Stansfield Jewellers in Leeds. Unfortunately I have been unable to get the alarm system to work and am very disappointed with my purchase.
>
> The manager of Stansfield's has advised me to return the clock to you for correction of the fault. This is enclosed.
>
> Please arrange for the clock to be put in full working order and return it to me as soon as possible.
>
> Yours faithfully

(b) 製造商的回覆

這封信中，製造商對客戶的抱怨深表關切，並盡全力要讓客戶滿意。這種處理抱怨的方式有助於建立可信任與交易公正的聲譽。

→ p.111

> Dear Mrs Wood
>
> Thank you for your letter of 20 September enclosing the defective 'Big Ben' alarm clock.
>
> Your comments on the performance of the clock are very interesting and I have passed it to our engineers for inspection.
>
> Meanwhile we are arranging to replace your clock with a new one that has been tested thoroughly to ensure that it is in perfect working order. This will be sent to you within the next few days.
>
> I am sorry for the trouble and inconvenience this matter has caused you, but am confident that the replacement clock will prove satisfactory and give you the service you are entitled to expect from our products.
>
> Yours sincerely

有關交貨的抱怨

沒有供應商喜歡被指控疏忽或粗心，但這類抱怨常和貨物包裝有關。在提出這一類的抱怨時應該注意遣詞用字，避免激怒對方，正所謂「敬人者人恆敬之」，任何人都不願意被冷嘲熱諷或受辱。所以，首先應對提出抱怨表示歉意，接著解釋因為問題嚴重而不得不這麼做。

12.5　抱怨商品損壞

(a) 抱怨

以下範例是客戶來信指出商品在托運後有所損壞。在未查明緣由之前，應避免做出貨物損壞是因包裝不良所致的暗示。

→ p.112

Dear Sirs

OUR ORDER NUMBER R569

引言與背景細節 — We ordered 160 compact discs on 3 January and they were delivered yesterday. I regret that 18 of them were badly scratched.

詳細解釋收貨後的狀況 — The package containing these goods appeared to be in perfect condition and I accepted and signed for it without question. It was on unpacking the compact discs the damage was discovered; I can only assume that this was due to careless handling at some stage prior to packing.

上受損貨品的完青單並請求更換 — I am enclosing a list of the damaged goods and shall be glad if you will replace them. They have been kept aside in case you need them to support a claim on your suppliers for compensation.

Yours faithfully

(b) 回覆

供應商立刻回覆客戶的請求，並表示會改善服務品質的誠意。

→ p.112

Dear

YOUR ORDER NUMBER R569

告知收到來信
並對損壞表示遺憾

I was sorry to learn from your letter of 10 January that some of the compact discs supplied to this order were damaged when they reached you.

說明更換細節

Replacements for the damaged goods have been sent by parcel post this morning. It will not be necessary for you to return the damaged goods; they may be destroyed.

有關後續的行動

Despite the care we take in packing goods there have recently been several reports of damage. To avoid further inconvenience and annoyance to customers, as well as expense to ourselves, we are now seeking the advice of a packaging consultant in the hope of improving our methods of handling.

對未來的訂購
提出保證

We apologise once again for this, and hope the steps we are taking will ensure the safe arrival of all your orders in future.

Yours sincerely

12.6　抱怨包裝不良

(a) 抱怨

→ p.113

Dear Sirs

說明寫信的理由

The carpet supplied to our order number C395 of 3 July was delivered by your carriers this morning.

抱怨的內容

We noticed that one of the outer edges of the wrapping had been worn through, presumably as a result of friction in transit. When we took off the wrapping it was not surprising to find that the carpet itself was soiled and slightly frayed at the edge.

進一步細節與
對預防措施的疑問

This is the second time in 3 weeks that we have had cause to write to you about the same matter. We find it hard to understand why precautions could not be taken to prevent a repetition of the earlier damage.

建議未來訂單
的處理方式

Although other carpets have been delivered in good condition, this second experience within such a short time suggests the need for special precautions against friction when carpets are packed onto your delivery vehicles. We hope that you will bear this in mind in handling our future orders.

請求特別折扣

In view of the condition of the present carpet we cannot offer it for sale at the normal price and propose to reduce our selling price by 10%. We suggest that you make us an allowance of 10% on the invoice cost. If you cannot do this, we shall have to return the carpet for replacement.

I hope to hear from you soon.

Yours faithfully

(b) 回覆

→ p.113

Dear

對顧客的
不滿表示歉意 — I was very sorry to learn from your letter of 15 August that the carpet supplied to your order number C395 was damaged on delivery.

解釋抱怨的理由 — Our head packer informs us that the carpet was first wrapped in heavy oiled waterproof paper and then in a double thickness of jute canvas. Under normal conditions this should have been enough protection. However on this occasion our delivery van contained a full load of carpets for delivery to other customers on the same day, and it is obvious that special packing precautions are necessary in such cases.

後續行動 — In all future consignments, we are arranging for specially reinforced end-packings which should prevent any future damage.

確認折扣 — We realise the need to reduce your selling price for the damaged carpet and readily agree to the special allowance of 10% which you suggest.

Yours sincerely

12.7　抱怨未收到貨

(a) 抱怨

→ p.114

Dear Sirs

On 25 September we placed our order number RT56 for printed headed notepaper and invoice forms. You acknowledged the order on 30 September. As that is some 3 weeks ago and we have not yet received advice of delivery, we are wondering whether the order has since been overlooked.

Your representative promised an early delivery and this was an important factor in persuading us to place this order with you.

The delay in delivery is causing considerable inconvenience. We must ask you to complete the order immediately, otherwise we shall have no option but to cancel it and obtain the stationery elsewhere.

Yours faithfully

(b) 回覆

面對情緒極端低落的顧客，唯有周延、客氣的應對才不致破壞友好關係。在底下的範例中，印刷商以體諒對方及有具體幫助的行動，消除了客戶的怒氣。

→ p.114

Dear Mr Sargeant

Thank you for your letter of 18 October. I quite understand your annoyance at not yet having received the stationery ordered on 25 September.

Orders for printed stationery are at present taking from 3 to 4 weeks for delivery, and our representatives have been instructed to make this clear to customers. Apparently you were not told that it would take so long, and I apologise for this oversight.

On receiving your letter we put your order in hand at once. The stationery will be sent from here tomorrow by express parcel post, and it should reach you within 24 hours of your receiving this letter.

It is very unfortunate that there should have been this misunderstanding but we hope you will forgive the delay that has been caused.

Yours sincerely

12.8 抱怨經常性的延遲交貨

下面這封信示範的是，寫抱怨信時應該要小心下筆，不去假設是供應商的疏失，這點非常重要。

(a) 抱怨

→ p.115

Dear Sirs

We ordered 6 filing cabinets from you on 2 July on the understanding that they would be delivered within one week. However these were not received until this morning.

Unfortunately there have been similar delays on several previous occasions, and their increasing frequency in recent months compels us to say that business between us cannot continue in such conditions.

We have felt it necessary to make our feelings known since we cannot give reliable delivery dates to our customers unless we can count on undertakings given by our suppliers.

We hope you will understand our position in this matter, and trust that from now on we can rely on punctual delivery of our orders.

I look forward to receiving your comments on this matter.

Yours faithfully

(b) 回覆

供應商在回信中小心解釋錯不在他們，彼此的友好關係應該要維繫
下去。

→ p.115

Dear

Your letter of 18 July regarding delays in delivery came as a surprise as the absence of any earlier complaints led us to believe that goods supplied to your orders were reaching you promptly.

It is our usual practice to deliver goods well in advance of the promised delivery dates; the filing cabinets to which you refer left here on 5 July. We are very concerned that our efforts to ensure punctual delivery should be frustrated by delays in transit. It is possible that other customers are also affected and we are taking up this whole question with our carriers.

We thank you for drawing our attention to a situation of which we had been quite unaware until you wrote to us. Please accept our apologies for the inconvenience you have been caused.

Yours sincerely

12.9　抱怨未如期完工

以下的範例是關於建商無法依照合約所載時間蓋好一棟新的平房。
客戶的語氣堅定但用字適當，而建商的回信也展現出體諒、說服
力、有條理並提供具體協助。

(a) 抱怨

→ p.116

Dear Sirs

BUNGALOW AT 1 CRESCENT ROAD, CHINGFORD

When I signed the contract for the building of this property you estimated that the work would be completed and the bungalow ready for occupation 'in about 6 months'. That was 8 months ago and the work is still only half finished.

The delay is causing inconvenience not only to me but also to the buyer of my present home which I cannot transfer until this bungalow is finished.

I urge you to press forward with this work without any further delay. Please let me know when you expect it to be completed.

Yours faithfully

(b) 回覆

→ p.116

Dear Mr Watson

BUNGALOW AT 1 CRESCENT ROAD, CHINGFORD

Thank you for your letter of 18 June. We are of course aware that the estimated period for completion of your bungalow has already been exceeded and wish to say at once that we realise what inconvenience the delay must be causing you.

We would ask you, however, to remember first that we have had an exceptionally severe winter – work on the site has been quite impossible during several prolonged periods of heavy snow. Secondly, there has been a nationwide shortage of building materials, especially bricks and timber, from which the trade is only just recovering. Without these 2 difficulties, which could not be foreseen, the estimated completion period of 6 months would have been observed.

In the improved weather conditions work on the bungalow is now proceeding satisfactorily. Unless we have other unforeseen hold-ups we can safely promise that the bungalow will be ready for you by the end of August.

Yours sincerely

 提示　如果您不會那樣說，就不要那樣寫。

12.10　抱怨被索取運費

有些客戶會只因為商品不適合他們就提出抱怨；有些則雖有所不滿，但會保持沉默，進而轉向其他供應商購買。底下的範例就是有關這方面的抱怨。

(a) 供應商的詢問

→ p.117

Dear Sirs

We are sorry to notice that we have had no orders from you since last April. As you have at no time notified us of defects in our products or about the quality of our service, we can only assume that we have given you no cause to be dissatisfied. If we have, then we should be glad to know of it.

If the cause of your discontinued orders is the present depressed state of the market, you may be interested in our latest price list showing a reduction of $7\frac{1}{2}\%$ on all grocery items. A copy of this is enclosed.

Should there be any matter in which we have given you cause to be dissatisfied, we hope you will give us the opportunity to put it right so that our custom can be renewed.

Yours faithfully

(b) 客戶的回覆（抱怨）

→ p.117

Dear

Thank you for your letter of 5 July. As you wish to know why we have placed no orders with you recently, I will point out a matter which caused us some annoyance.

On 21 April last year we sent you two orders, one for £274 and one for £142. Your terms at the time provided for free delivery of all orders for £300 or more, but although you delivered these two orders together we were charged with the cost of carriage.

As the orders were submitted on different forms, we grant that you had a perfect right to treat them as separate orders. However for all practical purposes they could very well have been treated as one, as they were placed on the same day and delivered at the same time. The fact that you did not do this seemed to us to be a particularly ungenerous way of treating a regular long-standing customer.

I would welcome your comments on this matter.

Yours sincerely

(c) 供應商的回覆

→ p.118

Dear

合適的引言 — Thank you for your letter of 8 July. Your explanation gives us the opportunity to explain a most regrettable misunderstanding.

詳細解釋情況 — Our charge for carriage on your last two orders arose because they were for goods dealt with by two separate departments, neither of which was aware that a separate order was being handled by another.

進一步保證情況不會重演 — At that time these departments were each responsible for their own packing Fand despatch arrangements. Since then this work has been taken over by a centralised packing and despatch department so a repetition of the same kind of misunderstanding is now unlikely.

技巧性結尾，希望恢復交易 — I hope you will understand that the charge we made was quite unintentional. In the circumstances I hope you will feel able to renew your former custom.

Yours sincerely

12.11 抱怨服務太差

以下書信內容是客戶抱怨未獲得適當的服務。在電話中，供應商建議將損壞的卡式錄音機寄回檢查，以便提供修理的報價，但當客戶依照約定寄回後，供應商就音訊全無。

(a) 客戶寫信告知寄回瑕疵品

在 6 月 28 日與傑克森先生講完電話後，客戶寫信給供應商。

→ p.118

Dear Mr Jackson

STEREO CASSETTE RECORDER, MODEL NUMBER 660

說明電話交談細節 —— Further to our telephone conversation this morning, I am sending my faulty tape recorder. I understand that arrangements can be made for it to be inspected and also a quotation given for its repair.

The following faults will be found:

清楚條列出瑕疵 ——
1   The recorder does not reproduce clearly on the right-hand speaker.
2   Distortion suggests that the recording head may need replacing.
3   The winding mechanism appears to be faulty.

It is possible that an inspection may reveal other faults.

結尾要求立刻
提出報價 —— It would help to speed matters if you would let me have the quotation by telephone as I want this work to be carried out and the recorder returned as quickly as possible.

Yours sincerely

(b) 客戶要求供應商依承諾提出報價

7 月 5 日供應商寄上一張印製好的編號 WE69376 的收據，以確認收到客戶 6 月 2 日寄來的信和錄音機，但是並沒有附上當初承諾提供的報價單。兩星期後，也就是 7 月 18 日，客戶再度寫信給供應商。要注意的是，客戶不去暗示對方尚未寄出報價單，信中反而有技巧地說明自己尚未收到報價單。

→p.119

Dear Mr Jackson

STEREO CASSETTE RECORDER, MODEL NUMBER 660

On 28 June I sent the above recorder to you for inspection and a quotation for servicing. As the matter was of some urgency I requested a quotation by telephone.

On 5 July your form number WE69376 acknowledged receipt of the recorder and my letter, but to date I have not received a quotation.

If a quotation has not already been sent I should be grateful if you would send it immediately to enable work on the recorder to be put in hand without further delay.

A prompt reply will be appreciated.

Yours sincerely

(c) 客戶收到報價並寄出修理費

客戶在 7 月 25 日收到一張標題為「工作參考編號 WE69376」、要求其支付 60.85 英鎊維修費的服務卡。客戶是在於 7 月 28 日寄出支票及一封短信。

→p.119

Dear Mr Jackson

STEREO CASSETTE RECORDER, MODEL NUMBER 660

I am returning your service card WE69376 with a cheque for £60.85 to cover the cost of servicing the above recorder.

This recorder has been with you for over 4 weeks and I am greatly inconvenienced without it. I hope you can arrange for its immediate repair and that it can be returned within the next few days.

Yours sincerely

(d) 客戶收到再度付款的要求

供應商並未函覆確定收到客戶寄來的支票。 8 月 14 日，客戶收到一張通知單表示錄音機已經修復完畢，並請求支付維修款。

(e) 客戶寫信向經理抱怨

供應商不但延遲寄回錄音機，且要求已經付款的客戶再次付款，客戶當然會生氣，於是立刻提筆寫了一封措詞強硬的信給經理。結果對方反而有所回應，並改正這個可能是無心的錯誤。

→ p.120

Dear Mrs Stansfield

STEREO CASSETTE RECORDER, MODEL NUMBER 660

技巧地開頭 — I am sorry to have to write to you personally regarding delay in the return of the above recorder sent in for repair on 28 June. The facts are as follows:

表列事情的經過 —
1. On 28 June I spoke to your Mr Keith Jackson regarding my faulty tape recorder. As a result I sent my letter dated 28 June with the recorder requesting a quotation.
2. On 5 July your Service Department acknowledged receipt of the recorder and my letter.
3. Not having received the quotation I sent a reminder on 18 July, and on 25 July I received a service card (reference WE69376) quoting a charge of £60.85 for servicing.

只陳述事實，沒有感情用事 —
4. This card was returned on 28 July with my cheque for that amount and my letter asking for the service to be carried out and the recorder returned as a matter of urgency.

I heard nothing more until this morning when I was surprised to receive a printed form stating that the work had been completed and asking for payment of the amount due.

技巧地結尾 — I am sure you will appreciate my concern at the length of time involved in this matter. As it is 2 full months since I sent the recorder to you, I hope you will arrange to return it immediately.

Yours sincerely

(f) 經理回信致歉

經理在回信中承認疏失，誠懇的態度將有助於挽回客戶對公司的信心及維繫友好關係。

→ p.120

Dear Mr Richards

STEREO CASSETTE RECORDER, MODEL NUMBER 660

I was very sorry to learn from your letter of 14 August of the problems experienced in the repair and return of your tape recorder.

I have investigated this matter personally, and regret that the delay is due to the absence through illness of the assistant who was dealing with your order initially.

Please accept my apologies for the inconvenience caused. The recorder has been sent to you today by express parcel post, and I hope it will reach you quickly and in good condition.

Please do not hesitate to contact me on 4962123 if I can be of further help.

Yours sincerely

(g) 客戶感謝經理

這個事件可以因為經理的回信而落幕，但是客戶認為應該寫信感謝經理的立即介入及明快處理。

→ p.121

Dear Mrs Stansfield

STEREO CASSETTE RECORDER, MODEL NUMBER 660

Thank you for your letter of 3 September and for dealing so promptly with this matter. I can appreciate the circumstances that led to the delay which was experienced.

My tape recorder has been delivered and appears to be in good working order.

Yours sincerely

取消訂單

在供應商受理訂單之前，客戶依法可以在任何時間取消訂單。如果發生下列狀況，客戶也可以取消訂單：

- 交貨的商品種類或品質有誤（如商品跟樣品不符）
- 未依約定時間交貨（或者在交貨時間未定的情況下，未於合理時間內交貨）
- 交貨數量短少或超出
- 收到的商品損毀（但僅限於供應商負責運送的情況）

除非合約另有規定，否則依法買方需負責從供應商處取貨及運貨，這類提貨包括現場交貨（loco）、工廠交貨（ex works）或其他類似的條件等。而所有運輸途中所造成的損失或遺失均由買方承擔。同樣地，在離岸價格（FOB）或到岸價格（CIF）的合約下，貨物一旦放置到船上時，買方就承擔了所有的責任。

12.12 買方因庫存足夠而取消訂單

(a) 客戶來信

→ p.121

Dear Sirs

On 2 March I ordered 100 tennis rackets to be delivered at the end of this month.

Persistent bad weather has seriously affected sales so I find that my present stock will probably satisfy demand in the present season. I am therefore writing to ask you to cancel part of my order and to deliver only 50 of these rackets instead of the 100 ordered.

I am sorry to make this request so late but hope that you will be able to agree to it in view of our long-standing business association. Should sales improve I will get in touch with you again and take a further delivery.

Yours faithfully

(b) 供應商同意取消訂單

通常供應商會同意取消或修改訂單的原因有：

◆　希望施惠於一位好客戶。
◆　利潤損失不大。
◆　有助建立良好客戶關係。
◆　或許在他處有現成的市場可賣出這批貨。
◆　客戶的財務狀況可疑。
◆　法律訴訟程序昂貴。

→ p.121

Dear

We have received your letter of 2 May asking us to cancel part of the order you placed on 2 March for tennis rackets.

We are naturally disappointed that there should be any need for this request. However we always like to oblige our regular customers and in the circumstances we are prepared to reduce the number of rackets from 100 to 50 as requested.

We do hope that your sales will improve sufficiently to enable you to take up the balance of your order at a later date.

In this respect we hope to hear from you again soon.

Yours sincerely

(c) 供應商拒絕取消訂單

供應商有時候會因為以下狀況而拒絕客戶取消訂單：

◆　希望保有一定的銷售額
◆　該批商品已經開始生產，但又不易在他處販售
◆　有強烈企圖心的企業家或許不願意放棄法律上的權利

在回信拒絕客戶取消訂單時，遣詞用字需謹慎小心，以免激怒對方，把客戶永遠趕跑了。信中應表達理解客戶的立場，並技巧地解釋取消訂單對自己造成的困難。回絕的理由必須具說服力，否則可能會破壞與客戶的友好關係。

→ p.122

Dear

We have received your letter of 2 May asking us to cancel part of your order of 2 March for tennis rackets.

We are sorry you find it necessary to make this request, especially at this late stage. To be able to meet our customers' needs promptly we have to place our orders with manufacturers well in advance of the season. In estimating quantities we rely very largely upon the orders we have received.

We do not like to refuse requests of any kind from regular customers. However on this occasion we have no choice but to do so. All orders, including your own, have already been made up and are awaiting delivery.

I hope you will understand why we must hold you to your order. If we had received your request earlier we should have been glad to help you.

Yours sincerely

12.13 因交貨延遲而取消訂單

→ p.122

Dear

In our order number 8546 dated 18 August we stressed the importance of delivery by 4 October at the very latest.

We have already written to you twice reminding you of the importance of prompt delivery. However as you have failed to make delivery on time we are left with no choice but to cancel the order.

We take this action with regret but as the goods were required for shipment abroad, and as the boat by which they were to be sent sails tomorrow, we have no means of getting them to our client in time for the exhibition for which they were required.

We have informed our client of the action we have taken and should be glad if you would acknowledge the cancellation.

Yours sincerely

個人的抱怨

有很多理由讓你必須寫信抱怨。也許你很生氣，但請記住，對方也許有一個很好的理由或者錯不在他們。信件內容應侷限於陳述事實及強調你的失望之意，然後詢問對方打算如何處置。

12.14　抱怨罐裝湯的品質

(a) 顧客來信

→ p.123

Dear Mr Turner

CHUNKY ROASTED VEGETABLE SOUP

I was recently in your High Street, Sheffield branch and I bought 3 tins of Chunky Roasted Vegetable Soup because I thought the description sounded excellent – Mediterranean flavours of roasted peppers, courgettes and olives with fusilli pasta.

However I was very disappointed when I opened the first tin to find that there was no pasta in the soup at all. This made the soup quite weak and watery, and not very substantial at all.

I am enclosing the label from this tin of soup, and also noted the details on the foot of the can as follows:

BB <0827> MRVI   31.10.2003

I felt you would wish to know about this because you will want to address the issue and find out why this happened. I am used to good quality food products from Manson and Spindlers, so I was very disappointed that this soup fell far short of my expectations.

I look forward to your early reply.

Yours sincerely

(b) 店經理的回覆

→ p.123

稱呼顧客姓名 ── Dear Miss Taylor

公司會想知道
顧客有何不滿 ── Thank you for letting us know that a recent purchase of our Chunky Roasted Vegetable Soup did not contain the stated pasta. Please accept my apologies.

訴顧客目前採取
的確保品質行動 ── We try very hard to make sure that all our products are of the highest quality and they should be correctly prepared. It is obvious from your comments that on this occasion a mistake was made.

解釋做了哪些事 ── I have passed the details of this issue to the department concerned. They will investigate the error and will contact the supplier to prevent it from happening again.

在感謝時
將關係再拉近 ── I am pleased to enclose a voucher for £10 as a gesture of our goodwill, and I hope you will continue to be a valued customer of Manson and Spindlers.

Yours sincerely

提示　在發出或回覆抱怨信時，不要使用 **complaint**（抱怨）這個字眼。

12.15　要求航空公司補上短缺的哩程數

(a) 顧客來信

→ p.124

Dear Sirs

MISSING MILEAGE REQUEST

I attach my missing mileage request form for missing mileage from my Harrisons Car Rental in July this year.

Also attached is a copy of the missing mileage request form faxed to you last week by my travel agent (Travel Shop) who booked this flight for me.

I hope you are able to credit me with the missing miles. This flight back to the UK was arranged very quickly because I received a phone call to say that my mother was ill and was being taken into hospital. I arranged the flight and flew home very quickly – I remember my travel agent telling me that if I paid a few hundred dollars extra, my flight would be eligible for air miles, so I chose to do this. However, when I got to the check-in desk at the airport, I was very upset and anxious, and I don't recall reminding the check-in clerk that I was a Content Club member. Perhaps this is why my account has not been credited with the extra miles?

As you will see from my Harrisons Car Rental receipt, I did mention that I was a Content Club member when I picked up my hire car at Manchester airport. However, again these miles have not been credited to me.

I hope that you can look into this and that I will be credited with the air miles that are due from both my air travel and my hire car rental.

Yours faithfully

(b) 航空公司的回覆

→ p.124

Dear Mr Green

感謝顧客的來信，
並先道歉

Thank you for your letter dated 21 August and many apologies for the printing mistake on your recent Content Club statement.

解釋已針對這種
情況做好措施

Our Information Management team has isolated the error and the problem happened at the printing stage. However I can assure you that your personal data has not been affected and the information stored on the Content Club database is correct, provided your membership number has been recorded in your booking in the usual way.

提供額外的資訊
來向顧客保證

I am pleased to enclose a corrected version of your Content Club statement. If you have any further questions about your statement please feel free to contact me. Alternatively your most recent travel history is available on our website www.contentclub.com.sg.

給予額外哩數

In the circumstances I feel we should make amends for the inconvenience caused, and we will credit your account with 100 bonus air miles.

Thank you for your patience and understanding.

Yours sincerely

12.16　對申請保險理賠的抱怨

(a) 顧客來信

→ p.125

Dear Mr Watson

CLAIM AL54323432 – STORM DAMAGE TO ROOF

I received a cheque for £623 dated 26 January in payment of my recent claim. However I wish to place on record how much upset has been caused by the way your Claims Assessor, Mr Michael Tan, handled this claim.

When Mr Tan first called me he specifically told me that he believed I had been overcharged for this work, and said he would expect to pay that price for work on a double garage rather than a single garage like mine. Mr Tan said that in his opinion I should neither use nor recommend this contractor again. He proceeded to tell me that as such it was unlikely that I would receive payment for the full cost which I had paid out. Never during this conversation did he mention that the reason for not receiving full payment was because of the nature of my insurance policy.

Consequently I wrote to the contractor, Mr Lance Ashe, to complain about his pricing, stating that I was very upset thinking that he could have knowingly taken advantage by overcharging a 73-year-old woman. Mr Ashe telephoned me immediately and explained his charges in detail, as he was very upset that he had caused me some distress. I believe Mr Ashe then called Mr Tan, because he later reported back to me that Mr Tan had told him that the reason I would not receive full payment in regard to my claim was because of the type of policy that I hold, which does not cover wear and tear. This was the first time this issue had been brought to my attention, so you can imagine my surprise.

When I received Mr Tan's letter of 2 February this situation was explained. If this had been explained to me in this way in the first place I would have been able to accept it and would certainly not have questioned Mr Ashe's charges. Instead, by telling me initially that I had been overcharged for this work, it caused a great deal of upset not only for me but also for Lance Ashe who was naturally most upset that anyone should think his work was unfairly priced.

I believe this claim was handled badly by Mr Tan from the beginning in that I was led to believe that I would not be reimbursed in full because I had been overcharged – not because of the nature of my policy, which I now know to be the case. I have been caused a great deal of embarrassment and upset over this issue, and this has caused a lot of upset between me and Mr Ashe.

I felt you should know how disappointed and upset I am. I trust you will look into this and ensure that such claims are handled more appropriately in the future.

Yours sincerely

(b) 保險公司回信確認

保險公司因為需要調查此事，故而無法立即回覆。但良好的商業往來應該寄一份簡短的通知來解釋他們採取了哪些行動。

→ p.126

Dear Mrs Richardson

Thank you for your letter of 4 February. I am sorry to learn of the problems you have experienced recently with your claim.

I am looking into the matter you have raised and I, or one of my colleagues, will write to you again as soon as possible, definitely within the next 7 working days. However, if you would like to discuss this matter further in the meantime, please do not hesitate to call me on 0114 2347827.

Yours sincerely

(c) 保險公司再次詳細回覆

→ p.126

Dear Mrs Richardson

Following my letter of 6 February, I have reviewed our file on your recent claim.

I am sorry that you feel you were given the impression by our claims assessor that there was a problem with the work carried out by your chosen contractor and the price that he charged. It was not the assessor's intention to cause any distress to you by his initial thoughts, and I am sorry about the distress this caused you. However, after discussion with Mr Ashe, the assessor was satisfied that the cost was reasonable and that the work had been completed satisfactorily.

We are always interested in any feedback from our customers on the service that we provide, and are continually looking for ways to improve this. However, on this occasion, I do not feel that it is necessary to adjust our procedure. Our assessors are highly trained to investigate claims and ensure that claims settlements are fair and reasonable. They have a responsibility to ensure that all relevant enquiries are made before settling a claim and I am happy that the assessor has acted properly in this respect. However, it is unfortunate that in the first place he gave you the wrong impression, and I do apologise for this.

Thank you again for writing to us. If I can be of any further help, please let me know.

Yours sincerely

底下這封信顯然是在盛怒及匆忙之下寫的。不但語氣相當無禮，而且內容缺乏邏輯，重要的細節也略過不提，所以這封信無法達到預期的效果。

→ p.127

不要寫一封籠統的信到店裡——不知收信者是誰時，可電話詢問客服經理的姓名

應使用個人化的稱謂

不要用 I am writing, complain, few days ago 等無濟於事的字眼

應提供相關的店員姓名

這個資訊放錯地方，應該放在引言處

一位店員態度不好，並不表示整家店的服務都是差勁的

這樣的結語不太像是永遠不再光顧

The Manager
Robinsons Departmental Store
High Street
Manchester
M20 4HT

Dear Sir/Madam

I am writing to complain about how I was treated when I visited your store a few days ago.

When I asked the sales clerk for help she ignored me and continued gossiping with a colleague. When I interrupted them they both 'tutted' loudly and stared at me. When I persisted, one sales clerk offered some assistance very begrudgingly and when I requested specific help she said, 'You'll have to be quick – I'm due for my break soon.'

I have been a customer of this store for 10 years now but it is obvious that your customer service policy leaves a lot to be desired, otherwise the assistant would not have dared to be so rude. In the circumstances I shall be taking my business elsewhere in future.

Yours faithfully

底下這封信架構清晰，行文有禮。寫信的人清楚說明其不滿意的原因，用詞適當，也提供了所有的細節，以方便經理調查此事。

→ p.127

使用個人化的稱呼 ── Dear Mrs Williams

在寫抱怨信時，以稱讚為開頭永遠是好的 ── I have been a customer of Robinsons for the last 10 years and have always been very happy with the service.

提供所有細節，地、時、人、事、物 ── However when I visited the Ladies' Department around noon on Monday 12 June one of your assistants, Sandra Wong, was very unprofessional. When I asked for help she continued talking to her colleague. Eventually she said abruptly, 'You'll have to be quick – I'm due for my break soon!

不要提出你的期望，只要求她調查 ── This is not the sort of service that I have come to expect from staff of Robinsons, and I hope you will investigate this matter.

以簡單的結尾說明您期待早日收到回音 ── I look forward to your prompt reply.

Yours sincerely

以下是回覆客戶抱怨的信函，信寫得很匆促，且根本談不上禮貌。

→ p.128

From	grace.peng@global.co.cn
Date	25 October 2003　15.29.45
To	robinzhang@midway.co.cn
CC	
Subject	Your Complaint

Your complaint about your fax machine that you bought from us last year has been past to me for my attn. Please be informed that your policy document shows that you only have a one year guarantee for this product and it ran out on 2nd Sept. So if you want it fixing you will have to pay for it.

Let me know what you want to do.

 在回覆抱怨信時，切勿粗暴或譏諷。這會引起對方反感，造成反效果。

以下是同樣的回覆，但語氣上是禮貌的。

→ p.128

From	grace.peng@global.co.cn
Date	25 October 2003　15.29.45
To	robinzhang@midway.co.cn
CC	
Subject	ST101 Fax Machine

Dear Robin

Thank you for your message. I am sorry to hear about the problems you have experienced with this fax machine.

I have checked your policy document and unfortunately our one-year guarantee for this machine ended on 2 September. I am sorry to say that you must pay for any repairs.

We will be pleased to repair the machine for you and can promise immediate attention and reasonable terms.

Please give me a call soon on 2874722 to discuss this.

Grace Peng
Global Communications
www.global.co.cn

檢查清單

【提出抱怨】

☐ 立即採取行動。

☐ 留意措詞，供應商或許會有很好的反駁理由。

☐ 簡短、清楚、正確地陳述事實。

☐ 避免無禮。

☐ 建議希望採取的行動或結果。

【處理抱怨】

☐ 立即調查事件緣由。

☐ 對抱怨者表達充分理解之意。

☐ 面對不合理的抱怨，措詞應堅定、有禮，不要激怒對方。

☐ 如果錯在自己，表達歉意並承認錯誤。

☐ 說明將採取的解決方法或已如何更正錯誤。

☐ 永遠不要責備員工。

☐ 如果適當，可提供額外的努力、資訊及賠償。

☐ 給予個人化的關心。

☐ 再度謝謝來信。

☐ 再度向顧客保證未來會有良好的服務品質，以建立忠誠度。

實用措詞

抱怨信

【開頭】

1. The goods we ordered from you on ... have not yet been delivered.
   我們於（日期）向您訂購的商品目前仍未送達。

2. Delivery of the goods ordered on ... is now considerably overdue.
   於（日期）訂購的商品，到目前已經遲交一段時間了。

3. We regret having to report that we have not yet received the goods ordered on ...
   很抱歉必須通知您，我們於（日期）訂購的商品仍未收到……

4. We regret to report that one of the cases of your consignment was badly damaged when delivered on ...
很抱歉向您報告，於（日期）所交付的商品中，有一箱在運送途中嚴重損壞……

5. When we examined the goods despatched by you on ... we found that ...
當我們檢查您於（日期）寄來的商品，我們發現……

6. We have received a number of complaints from several customers regarding the ... supplied by you on ...
我們收到幾位顧客抱怨有關您於（日期）所供應的……

【實用片語】

1 I am very happy with ...
我很高興……

2. This situation is causing us a great deal of inconvenience.
這種情況造成我們相當大的不便。

3. This standard of workmanship is not what I have come to expect from you.
這種做工的水準不是我從你們這裡所預期的。

4. This service is well below the standard expected.
這種服務遠低於預期標準。

5. I felt you would wish to know about this.
我認為您會想要知道這件事。

6. I am sure you will wish to look into this and find out what happened.
我很確定您會想要調查這件事，並查明發生了什麼事。

7. I am used to good quality from ...
我很習慣從……出產的良好品質。

【結尾】

1. Please look into this matter at once and let us know the reason for this delay.
請立刻調查此事，並且讓我們知道延遲的原因。

2. We hope to hear from you soon that the goods will be sent immediately.
   希望儘快聽到您通知商品將立刻送達的消息。

3. We feel there must be some explanation for this delay and await your prompt reply.
   我們認為您一定對延遲有所解釋，也等待您立即回覆。

4. We hope to learn that you are prepared to make some allowance in these circumstances.
   在這種情況下，我們希望您能提供一些折扣。

5. I hope to receive a complete refund soon.
   我希望能夠儘快收到全部的退款。

回覆抱怨信

【開頭】

1. We are concerned to learn from your letter of ... that the goods sent under your order number ... did not reach you until ...
   從您（日期）信中提到有關（訂單號碼）商品直到（日期）才收到，對此我們表示關切……

2. I am sorry that you have experienced delays in the delivery of ...
   很抱歉您的（商品）運送延遲……

3. I am very sorry to hear about ... in your letter of ...
   很遺憾從您（日期）的來信得知……

4. Thank you for your letter of ..., which has given us the opportunity to rectify a most unfortunate mistake.
   感謝您（日期）的來信，讓我們有機會彌補一個不幸的錯誤。

5. We wish to apologise for the unfortunate mistake pointed out in your letter of ...
   對於您（日期）信中所提的錯誤，在此致上歉意……

【實用片語】

1. We appreciate the opportunity to clarify this issue.
   我們很感激有此機會澄清這件事。

2. From your comments it is obvious that on this occasion a mistake was made.
從您的意見很明顯可以看到，這種情況下錯誤已造成。

3. You have rightly pointed out that …
您正確無誤地指出……

4. In the circumstances I feel we should make amends for the inconvenience caused.
這種情況下，我覺得我們應該為所造成的不便做些修正。

5. Due to an oversight …
由於一時疏忽……

6. It is unfortunate that …
很不幸地……

7. I am sorry about the distress this caused you.
關於對您所造成的苦惱，我感到很抱歉。

【結尾】

1. We assure you that we are doing all we can to speed delivery and offer our apologies for the inconvenience this delay is causing you.
我們向您保證我們正盡全力加快運送速度，並且對這項延遲所造成的不便致歉。

2. We hope you will be satisfied with the arrangements we have made.
希望您能滿意我們所做的安排。

3. We trust these arrangements will be satisfactory and look forward to receiving your future orders.
相信您會滿意我們的安排，並期望日後繼續收到您的訂單。

4. We regret the inconvenience which has been caused in this matter.
因為這件事對您造成不便，在此致歉。

5. We apologise once again for the unfortunate mistake and can assure you that a similar incident will not occur again.
再一次對這令人遺憾的錯誤道歉，並保證類似的意外將不再發生。

6. As a gesture of goodwill I am pleased to enclose ...

為表示友好關係，我樂意附上……

7. Thank you once again for taking the time to write to us.

再一次謝謝您花時間寫信給我們。

親善信
Goodwill messages

1
2
3
4
5
6
7
8
9
10
11
12
13
14
15
16
17
18
19
20
21
22
23
24
25
26
27
28
29
30

溝通最重要的功能之一在於創造良好的商業關係。許多管理者及經營者懂得抓住機會,在下列的場合寫一封親善信給對方:

道歉	接獲不幸消息	慰問	歡迎	晉升	祝賀
死亡	獲得殊榮	感謝	弔唁	感激	結婚

善用每一個寫親善信件的機會,不僅客戶或同事們收到這類信函會感到窩心,對於生意的往來也有很好的幫助。花一點點的成本和努力,不但可以強化現有的關係,還能建立拓展新商機的機會。

親善信應該要及時寄出,內容則宜簡短、扼要,態度誠懇、不流於制式化。適當的話可以用手寫,進一步增加誠懇度和親和力。

一般的親善信

以下是一般日常的親善信範例。信中的語氣禮貌、友善,加上個人的關心,肯定能令對方留下良好印象。

 你的寫作方式反映了你給人的印象——當然要確保你的寫作能力是良好的。

13.1 簡短的個人問候

有時候我們會在信文的最後一段致上個人的問候,以聯絡感情。

→ p.130

Dear Mr Ellis

I am sorry not to have replied sooner to your letter of 25 October regarding the book *English and Commercial Correspondence*. My Export Director is in Lebanon and Syria on business; as I am dealing with his work as well as my own I am afraid my correspondence has fallen behind.

Whether this book should be published in hardback or paperback is a decision I must leave to my Editorial Director, Tracie James, to whom I have passed on your letter. No doubt she will be writing to you very soon.

I hope you are keeping well.

With best wishes

Yours sincerely

13.2　更深的個人問候

在信文的最後一段表達更為個人化的關心。

→ p.130

> Dear Mrs Jenner
>
> *Importing Made Easy*
>
> I have had an opportunity to review the book you sent to me recently.
>
> This book presents a concise and clear account of the new import regulations with good examples of how they are likely to be applied.
>
> More detailed comments are made on my written review which is attached.
>
> I remember you mentioned that you will be spending your summer holiday in the south of France. I hope you have good weather and an enjoyable time.
>
> Yours sincerely

13.3　解釋為何延遲回覆

收到來信最好是當天就回覆，以便讓人留下好印象。若因故拖延，則應及早去函解釋延遲回覆的原因。

→ p.131

> Dear Mrs Jones
>
> I am sorry we cannot send you immediately the catalogue and price list requested in your letter of 13 March as we are presently out of stock.
>
> Supplies are expected from our printers in 2 weeks' time; as soon as they are received, we will send a copy to you.
>
> Yours sincerely

13.4　供應商的友善問候信

客戶通常會在想要合作的交易對象中找尋友善的訊息。例如底下這封信的撰寫者就表達了樂意幫忙的好意，目的在打動潛在客戶，建立一種信任感，贏得他們的關心、友誼，最後上門光顧。

→ p.131

> Dear Mr Jackson
>
> I am pleased to enclose our catalogue and price list as requested in your letter of 12 October.
>
> In this latest catalogue we have taken trouble to ensure it is both attractive and informative; particulars of our trade discounts are shown inside the front cover.
>
> May I suggest that next time you are in Bristol you allow us to show you our factory where you could see for yourself the high quality of materials and workmanship put into our products. This would also enable you to see at first hand the latest fancy leather goods, and to return home with interesting and useful information for your customers.
>
> If I can be of service in any way please do not hesitate to let me know.
>
> Yours sincerely

13.5　歡迎海外訪客

如果客戶是遠從海外來訪，那麼殷勤款待、提供協助及建議，就是最妥善的商業行為。這類歡迎信的語氣必須真誠、友好，讓對方感受到自己樂於提供服務的誠意。

→ p.131

> Dear Mr Brandon
>
> I was pleased to receive your letter of 24 April and to learn that your colleague, Mr John Gelling, is making plans to visit England in July. We shall be very pleased to welcome him and to do all we can to make his visit enjoyable and successful.
>
> I understand this will be Mr Gelling's first visit to England, and am sure he will wish to see some of our principal places of interest. A suitable programme is something we can discuss when he arrives. I would be pleased to introduce him to several firms with which he may like to do business.
>
> When the date of Mr Gelling's visit is settled please let me know his arrival details. I will arrange to meet him at the airport and drive him to his hotel. He may be assured of a warm welcome.
>
> Yours sincerely

道歉函

遇上必須為某事向對方道歉時，用對語氣非常重要。有時候即使你不認為有道歉的必要，但顧及萬一你已造成傷害或激怒對方，恐怕得面臨法律問題時，仍必須放下身段，並說聲對不起。

13.6　為服務不佳致歉

→ p.132

Dear Mrs Taylor

關於抱怨的細節 — Thank you for your letter of 12 June regarding the poor service you received when you visited our store recently.

達歉意並且陳述已經採取的行動 — The incident was most unlike our usual high standards of service and courtesy. The member of staff who was rude to you has been reprimanded; he also expresses his regret.

後續行動 — I am enclosing a gift voucher for £20 which you may use at any Omega store. If I can be of any further assistance to you please do not hesitate to contact me.

再次道歉 — With my apologies once again.

Yours sincerely

13.7　為取消約會致歉

→ p.132

Dear Mr James

I am so sorry that I had to cancel our meeting yesterday at such short notice. As my secretary explained to you I am afraid an urgent matter came up which I had to deal with immediately.

I understand our appointment has been rearranged for next Tuesday 12 May at 11.30.

Perhaps we can extend our meeting over lunch.

Yours sincerely

 提示　請記住，描述事情的方式比事情本身還重要。謹慎考慮你的語氣。

格外講究語氣的信函

生意往來，總會碰上需要寫信拒絕對方請求、提高價格、解釋疏失、為錯誤道歉等的時候。語氣上的斟酌，是這類信函的一個最主要的考量點。語氣不當可能會激怒對方、造成反感，甚至失去交易機會。

13.8　傳達令人不悅的消息

在需要回絕請求或者傳達令人不悅的消息時，應該站在讀信者的立場來思考：利用一段合適的開頭段落並且使用適當的語氣，來為他們的失望做好準備。

→ p.133

> Dear Mr Foster
>
> It was good of you to let me see your manuscript on *English for Business Studies*. I read it with interest and was impressed by the careful and thorough way in which you have treated the subject. I particularly like the clear and concise style of writing.
>
> Had we not recently published *Practical English* by Freda Leonard, a book that covers very similar ground, I would have been happy to accept your manuscript for publication. In the circumstances, I am unable to do so and am returning your manuscript with this letter.
>
> I am sorry to have to disappoint you.
>
> Yours sincerely

13.9　拒絕為損失負責

以下這封信也是在開頭段落讓收件人對自己的保險索賠將被拒絕，有個心理準備。

→ p.133

> Dear Mr Burn
>
> When we received your letter of 23 November we sent a representative to inspect and report on the damage caused by the recent fire in your warehouse.
>
> This report has now been submitted and it confirms your claim that the damage is extensive. However, it states that a large proportion of the stock damaged or destroyed was very old and some of it obsolete.
>
> Unfortunately, therefore, we cannot accept your figure of £45,000 as a fair estimate of the loss as it appears to be based on the original cost of the goods.
>
> Yours sincerely

13.10　拒絕客戶信用交易的請求

要寫一封拒絕客戶採取信用交易，而又不激怒對方的信是很不容易的。如果是對客戶的信用狀況有所懷疑，當然可以拒絕其請求，但信中不能有這類的暗示。如果是基於其他理由，則應該清楚告知對方，並技巧地提出解釋。

批發商在底下這封回給新合作貿易商的信中表示，雖然目前的合作關係不錯，但雙方的生意往來尚未穩固到足以在雙方財務上建立起信心。

→ p.134

Dear Miss Wardle

We were glad you approached us with a view to placing an order, and to learn of the good start of your new business.

The question of granting credit for newly established businesses is never an easy one. Many owners get into difficulties because they overcommit themselves before they are thoroughly established. Although we believe that your own business promises very well, we feel it would be better for you to make your purchases on a cash basis at present. If this is not possible for the full amount, we suggest that you cut the size of your order, say by half.

If you are willing to do this we will allow you a special cash discount of 4% in addition to our usual trade terms. If this suggestion is acceptable to you, the goods could be delivered to you within 3 days.

We hope that you will look upon this letter as a mark of our genuine wish to enter into business with you on terms that will bring lasting satisfaction to us both. When your business is firmly established we will be very happy to welcome you as one of our credit customers.

Yours sincerely

13.11　為疏失致歉

如果你已經犯了錯，或者無論如何是有過失的一方，就應該坦承錯誤，不要有任何藉口。一封帶有歉意的信函，可用來建立友好關係，讓客戶不易繼續對你產生嫌隙。

→ p.134

Dear Mrs Wright

I was very concerned when I received your letter of yesterday stating that the central heating system in your home has not been completed by the date promised.

On referring to our earlier correspondence I find that I had mistaken the date for completion. The fault is entirely mine and I deeply regret that it should have occurred.

I realise the inconvenience which my oversight must be causing you and will do everything possible to avoid any further delay.

I have already given instructions for this work to take first priority; our engineers will be placed on overtime to complete the work. These arrangements should ensure that the work is completed by next weekend.

My apologies once again for the inconvenience caused.

Yours sincerely

13.12 為價格調漲致歉

客戶對於商品價格調漲感到生氣，是很自然的反應，尤其是當他們認為此調漲是不合理時。就漲價理由提出清楚且具說服力的解釋，可以保有友好關係，避免產生裂痕。

→ p.135

Dear

Many businesses have been experiencing steadily rising prices over the past few years and it will come as no surprise to you that our own costs have continued to rise with this general trend.

Increasing world demand has been an important factor in raising the prices of our imported raw materials. A recent national wage award has added to our labour costs which have been increased still further by constantly increasing overheads.

Until now we have been able to absorb rising costs by economies in other areas. We find that we can no longer do so, and therefore increases in our prices are unavoidable. The new prices will take effect from 1 October, and revised price lists are being prepared. These should be ready within the next 2 weeks and copies will be sent to you.

We are sorry that these increases have been necessary but can assure you that they will not amount to an average of more than about 5%. As general prices have risen by nearly 10% since our previous price list, we hope you will not feel that our own increases are unreasonable.

Yours sincerely

感謝函

企業經營者有很多機會書寫表達感激和敦促友好關係的信函。這類感謝信函可以簡短，但必須熱情與誠懇地傳達出你的謝意，讓收件者感受到你的眞心與誠意。

感謝函應避免提及具體的銷售事宜，否則會讓對方覺得你的感謝只不過是推銷業務的藉口。

13.13 感謝第一次下單

→ p.135

Dear Mr Martin

You will have already received our formal acknowledgement of your order number 456 dated 12 July. However as this is your first order with us I felt I must write to say how pleased we were to receive it and to thank you for the opportunity given to us to supply the goods you need.

I hope our handling of your order will lead to further business between us, and to a happy and mutually beneficial association.

Yours sincerely

13.14 感謝大量訂購

→ p.135

Dear Mrs Usher

I understand that you placed an unusually large order with us yesterday, and I want to say how very much your continued confidence in us is appreciated.

The happy working relationship between us for many years has always been valued and we shall do our best to maintain it.

Yours sincerely

13.15　感謝立即結清帳款

→ p.136

Dear Mr Watts

I am writing to say how much we appreciate the promptness with which you have settled your accounts with us during the past year, especially as a number of them have been for very large amounts.

This has been of great help to us at a time when we have been faced with heavy commitments connected with the expansion of our business.

I hope our business relationship will continue in the future.

Yours sincerely

13.16　感謝對方提供的服務

→ p.136

Dear Miss Armstrong

Thank you for your letter of 30 March returning the draft of the catalogue we propose to send to our customers.

I am very grateful for the trouble you have taken to examine the draft and comment on it in such detail. Your suggestions will be very helpful.

I realise the value of time to a busy person like you and this makes me all the more appreciative of the time you have so generously given.

Yours sincerely

13.17　感謝對方提供資訊

→ p.136

Dear Mrs Webster

Thank you for your letter enclosing an article explaining the organisation and work of your local trade association.

I am very grateful for the interest you have shown in our proposal to include details of your association in the next issue of the *Trade Association Year Book*, and for your trouble in providing such an interesting account of your activities. This feature is sure to inspire and encourage associations in other areas.

Yours sincerely

祝賀函

寄發祝賀函給對方，也是提升友好關係的最佳方式之一。祝賀的理由包括升遷、派任新職、獲得殊榮、成立新公司、通過考試，甚至結婚生子等。信函可以簡短、正式，也可以是口語而非正式的，視雙方關係和情況而定。

13.18　祝賀對方獲獎的正式信函

恭賀對方獲此殊榮的道賀信簡短、正式即可。而為了表示個人的關心，信中的稱呼和結尾問候應該都用手寫。

→ p.137

> I was delighted to learn that your work at the South Down College of Commerce has been recognised in the New Year Honours List.
>
> At a time when commercial education is so much in the public eye, it gives us all at the Ministry great pleasure to learn of your OBE.

13.19　祝賀對方獲獎的非正式信函

→ p.137

> On looking through the *Camford Times* this morning I came across your name in the New Years Honours List. I would like to add my congratulations to the many you will be receiving.
>
> The award will give much pleasure to a wide circle of people who know you and your work. Your services to local industry and commerce over many years have been quite outstanding and it is very gratifying to know that they have been so suitably rewarded.
>
> With very best wishes

13.20　祝賀對方升遷

→ p.137

> Dear Dr Roberts
>
> I would like to convey my warm congratulations on your appointment to the Board of Electrical Industries Ltd.
>
> My fellow directors and I are delighted that the many years of service you have given to your company should at last have been rewarded in this way.
>
> We all join in sending you our very best wishes for the future.
>
> Yours sincerely

13.21 祝賀員工任職十週年

→ p.137

> This month marks your tenth anniversary as a member of staff of SingComm Pte Ltd. We would like to take this opportunity to thank you for these past 10 years of fine workmanship and company loyalty.
>
> We know that the growth and success of our company is largely dependent on having strong and capable staff members such as yourself. We also recognise the contributions you make in helping us maintain the position we enjoy in the industry.
>
> We are hoping that you will remain with us for many years to come and would like to offer our congratulations on this special anniversary.

 避免瞎扯，將訊息內容全部讀過一遍，把重複或不合邏輯的部分剔除。

13.22 答謝祝賀

收到他人的祝福也必須禮貌性回覆。大多數的情況下，簡短的正式回覆函即已足夠。

以下信函是回給 13.18 的祝賀信的很好範例。寫信者非常適切地趁此機會感謝同事對她工作上的支持。

→ p.138

> Dear Mrs Fleming
>
> Thank you for your letter conveying congratulations on the award of my OBE.
>
> I am very happy that anything I may have been able to do for commercial education in my limited field should have been rewarded by a public honour. At the same time I regard the award as being less of a tribute to me personally than to the work of my college as a whole – work in which I have always enjoyed the willing help and support of many colleagues.
>
> Thank you again for your good wishes.
>
> Yours sincerely

弔唁與慰問函

撰寫弔唁信並不容易，它並無特定格式，端視寫信者與收信者的關係而定。一般而言，這類書信通常簡短、誠懇。而為了凸顯關心之意，最好是用手寫。

你一旦得知消息就必須立刻提筆，以簡單、溫暖、有力的文字表達慰問之意，並真誠地寫下你想說的話。

13.23　寫給鄰居的弔唁函

→ p.138

> Dear Mrs McDermott
>
> It was not until late last night that my wife and I learned of your husband's tragic death. Coming as it did without warning, it must have been a great shock to you. I want you to know how very sorry we both are, and to send our sincere sympathy.
>
> If there is any way in which we can be of any help, either now or later, do please let us know. We shall be only too glad to do anything we can.
>
> Yours sincerely
>
> Peter Brand

13.24　寫給客戶的弔唁函

→ p.138

> **Dear Mr Kerr**
>
> I have just learned with deep regret of the death of your wife.
>
> There is not much one can say at a time like this, but all of us at Simpsons who have dealt with you would like to extend our sincere sympathy at your loss.
>
> Please include us among those who share your sorrow at this sad time.
>
> Yours sincerely

13.25 寫給商業夥伴的弔唁函

→ p.139

Dear Mrs Anderson

We were distressed to read in *The Times* this morning that your Chairman has died and I am writing at once to express our deep sympathy.

I had the privilege of knowing Sir James for many years and always regarded him as a personal friend. By his untimely passing our industry has lost one of its best leaders. He will be greatly missed by all who knew him.

Please convey our sympathy to Lady Langley and her family.

Yours sincerely

13.26 寫給員工的弔唁函

→ p.139

Dear Maxine

I was very sorry to learn of your father's death. I remember your father very well from the years he served in our company's Accounts Department until his retirement 2 years ago. I well recall his love for his family and the great sense of pride with which he always spoke of his daughters. He has been greatly missed at Wilson's since his retirement. We all join in expressing our sympathy to you and your family at this very sad time.

Yours sincerely

13.27 寫給朋友的弔唁函

→ p.139

Dear Henry

I felt I must write to say how deeply sorry we were at the news of Margaret's passing.

She was a very dear friend and we shall greatly miss her cheerful outlook on life, her generous nature and her warmth of feeling for anyone in need of help. Above all we will miss her for her wonderful sense of fun.

Tom and I send you our love and our assurance of continued friendship, now and always. If there is any help we can provide at any time, just let us know.

Yours

Alice

13.28 寫給商業夥伴的慰問函

→ p.140

Dear Bill

When I called at your office yesterday I was very sorry to learn that you had been in a car accident on your way home from work recently. However I was equally relieved to learn that you are making good progress and are likely to be back at work again in a few weeks.

I had a long talk with Susan Carson and was glad to learn of your rising export orders. I expect to be in Leicester again at the end of next month and shall take the opportunity to call on you.

Meanwhile I wish you a speedy recovery.

Yours sincerely

13.29 答謝弔唁或慰問

收到慰問信函，自然會想寫封信感謝對方。這類的書信只簡短即可，但要能表達出對這樣溫暖的慰問真心感動之意。

(a) 個人的答謝

個人答謝函主要是回覆親戚或親密的朋友。

→ p.140

Dear Mrs Hughes

My mother and family join me in thanking you for your very kind letter on the occasion of my father's death.

We have all been greatly comforted by the kindness and sympathy of our relatives and friends. Both at home and in the hospital, where my father spent 2 weeks prior to his passing, the kindness and sympathy shown by everyone has been almost overwhelming.

Yours sincerely

Laura Darabi

(b) 制式答謝函

如果收到很多弔唁信，可使用事先印製好的答謝函回覆對方。

→ p.140

> Mr and Mrs Ashton and family thank you most sincerely for your kind expression of sympathy at their sad loss.
>
> The kindness of so many friends and the many expressions of affection and esteem in which Margaret was held will always remain a proud and cherished memory.
>
> 97 Lake Rise
> Romford
> Essex
> RM1 4EF

檢查清單

☐ 立刻寫信並寄出。

☐ 使用正確的語氣。

☐ 誠懇。

☐ 使用非正式的文體。

☐ 採用個人化的方式（如果適當的話，用手寫）。

☐ 保持簡短並切中要點。

☐ 問問自己在收到這類信函時的感受為何。

報告與提案
Reports and proposals

簡介報告與提案

商業上會用到許多不同形式的報告，有的十分簡短且不正式，有的篇幅較長又較正式。不論是哪一種，其最終的目的都是提供做成決策及採取行動的依據。

有些報告只是記錄某個活動、某次的訪問或是一些情況的簡單描述及其所採取的行動摘記。有些則包含了事實的詳細解說、結論，也許還加入採取行動的評論。

更詳盡的報告仰賴許多的研究，其中可能包含了訪談、問卷及市調。這些資訊可以用書面、表格或圖像等方式予以呈現，而撰寫者需要提出清楚結論及評論。

提案的寫作技巧與報告相同，但兩者仍存在以下的差異：

報告	提案
◆ 包含的資訊是過去已發生的。	◆ 檢視未來可能發生的事。
◆ 主要目的在提供資訊。	◆ 主要目的在說服閱讀者做出具體決策。
◆ 記錄客觀的事實。	◆ 表達意見：舉客觀的事實來佐證。

在此感謝「簡易英語運動」（Plain English Campaign）網站准許引用其《撰寫報告的簡易英語指南》（*The Plain English Guide to Writing Reports*）中的資料。這是一份很棒的報告寫作指南，當然它們都是用簡單的英語寫成的。如果你想獲得更多資訊，請至以下網站：**www.plainenglish.co.uk**

 一個好的標題，可以為你的報告建立良好印象。

撰寫報告的簡易英語指南

當你在寫報告時，應該要儘量讓讀報告的人能夠很容易就了解它的內容，像是使用主動動詞、句子簡潔，切入重點，就如同其他文件的寫法。

前述網站上的這份指南，涵蓋了撰寫報告的主要步驟：

◆　界定目的。
◆　針對主題做調查。
◆　分區塊（section）組織報告的內容。
◆　呈現的順序。
◆　書寫的順序。
◆　為章節段落加上編號。
◆　擬定寫作計畫。
◆　校訂。

最後會以邱吉爾所寫的備忘錄及這份指南的摘要來做結尾。

界定目的

這樣可以幫助你清楚知道：

◆　為什麼要寫這份報告。
◆　（什麼是）應該要納入的部分。
◆　（什麼是）應該要省略的部分。
◆　讀報告的是誰。

如果你可以用一個句子來說明目的為何，那是再好不過了。

針對主題做調查

如何著手調查，需視主題及目的而定。你也許需要閱讀資料、訪談、做實驗和觀察。如有需要，也可以向有經驗的人士請益，以徵求一些建議。

分區塊組織報告的內容

你的工作是要讀報告的人輕鬆地找到他們想要的資訊。要在一或兩頁長度的報告中找資訊並不難，但若報告篇幅較長（超過四頁或五頁），你就必須更用心地組織、編排你的資訊。

報告內容可分成以下八個部分，但不一定每次都要全部納入。

- ◆ 標題或標題頁 （title or title page）
- ◆ 目錄（contents list）
- ◆ 摘要（abstract）
- ◆ 引言（introduction）
- ◆ 討論（discussion）
- ◆ 概要及結論（summary and conclusions）
- ◆ 建議（recommendations）
- ◆ 附錄（appendix）

一篇短的報告不需標題頁，但標題不可少。而目錄也只有長篇報告才需要。

摘要只用於正式的報告，例如科學研究報告。它是整篇報告的大意，常出現在圖書館檔案及期刊摘要中。摘要通常不會和報告一起印，所以它必須能單獨成立。

將摘要的字數控制在 80 至 120 字之間，不要把它和「執行概要」（executive summary）混淆了。稍後會再說明執行概要的部分。

引言應簡短且能回答下列任一相關問題：

- ◆ 主題為何？
- ◆ 誰要這篇報告？為什麼？
- ◆ 背景為何？
- ◆ 你採用什麼方法？如果方法又長又瑣細，請將它置於附錄中。
- ◆ 資料來源為何？如果來源很多，請將它置於附錄中。

討論是報告的正文，它可能是最長的部分，包含了以主標題及副標題組織之下的所有詳細內容。

很少讀者會逐字逐句閱讀這部分，所以要將重要的部分提到最前面，接著是次重要、次次重要……，依此類推。

每個段落都應該遵循相同的規則，以該段落的主要重點開始，然後鋪陳細節或解釋說明。

概要及結論有時候會置於討論之前。它說明報告的目的、你的結論，以及你是如何得出此一結論的。

結論是你的主要發現，宜簡潔、扼要。此部分旨在指出你認為的最佳選擇及行動，以及可從已發生的案例中學到何事，所以它應該要包含或引導至你的建議：未來應該怎麼做以改善情況？

通常，撰寫者會將概要、結論和建議放在一起，和報告本身分開，單獨傳閱，我們稱之為執行概要。這麼做是方便大家不需閱讀全篇報告就能取得所需資訊。

一個比較好也較省錢的方式是先給每人一份執行概要，等有人要求閱讀全文時再提供完整報告。如此既可減少樹木的砍伐，也能為公司省下許多的時間及金錢。

附錄是擺放一些只有當閱讀者深入研究該篇報告才需要用到的資料，而相關圖表則應置於討論中，以方便閱讀者使用，只有在它們會打亂報告流暢度時才改置於附錄中。

呈現的順序

建議以下的呈現順序，但不一定每次都要全部用到，尤其是有括弧的部分。

長篇報告

◆ 標題或標題頁
◆ （目錄）
◆ （摘要）
◆ 引言
◆ **概要及結論**
◆ 建議
◆ 討論
◆ （附錄）

短篇報告

◆ **標題**
◆ 引言
◆ 討論
◆ **概要及結論**
◆ 建議
◆ （附錄）

書寫的順序

書寫的順序不需要比照呈現的順序。建議採用以下的書寫順序，因為每完成一個區塊都有助於撰寫下一個部分。

◆ 引言
◆ 討論
◆ **概要及結論**
◆ 建議
◆ （摘要）
◆ 標題或標題頁
◆ （目錄）
◆ （附錄）

在寫完所有的區塊之後，要讀一遍並加以校訂。如有必要，可重寫某一區塊。

為章節段落加上編號

如果你的標題清楚，並且在報告開頭附上一份完整的目錄，讀者將可輕易找到每個部分的起始與結尾，如有必要，也可相互參照（cross-refer）。

如果真的有必要標示段落（paragraph），儘可能簡單。如用大寫字母來標示章節，用數字標示段落，如 A1（A 節的第一段）、 A2（A 節的第二段）等。必要時再用小寫字母來表示段落的每個部分。

擬定寫作計畫

常常手邊已經蒐集好大量的資訊，但卻無法決定要從何處著手。在動筆之前，你必須先做好某種計畫。如此可以省下撰寫時間，並協助你製作一個更有組織的報告。

以下是兩種不同的撰寫計畫。

第一種，在一張大的空白紙上勾勒出輪廓。用筆記形式，完全隨意地寫下所有的事實、想法及觀察等等，試著儘快記下每件事。

寫下所有重點後，將重點加以整理、歸納，評估它們的強項、相關度，以及在報告中的位置。

你可以在重點旁標上代表順序的數字，或是加註 Intro（引言）、Discussion（討論）、 Conclusion（結論）等標題。接著用直線或箭頭來連結相關的重點。

漸漸地，你會在各標題下建置出概念群組，這就是你報告的架構。如果可以，先將它擱置一旁，一、兩天後再回頭檢視內容，加進新想法或之前遺漏的重點，或是將不需要的部分刪除。

第二種是「心智圖法」（mind mapping），更適合某些撰寫內容。要領與前一種大約相同，先任意地寫下所有想法，你可以專注在內容上，然後在確定想法後，利用閒暇來組織這些資料。

心智圖法沒有什麼特別的魔力，只是先在紙的正中間畫個方格，將主題放入方格中，以此為中心，將與主題相關的主要想法，拉一條線寫在旁邊。

這個方法讓你很容易加入新資訊，且方便連結主要的想法，自然勾勒出順序及內容結構。

校訂

對於自己書寫的內容，要經常用批判的角度去讀它。如果可以，將它擺上幾天，然後再重讀一遍，或是請別人讀過。然後問：「這份報告清楚、簡潔，有說服力嗎？」做好修正遣詞用字及架構的準備。甚至有些不好的地方，也許需要重寫。

 不要用太多的字型或太常變換字體大小，因為那樣不但沒有吸引力，而且也會令讀者困惑。

14.1　「簡潔」：邱吉爾寫給戰爭內閣的備忘錄

即使是在 1940 年，邱吉爾也已經知道要刪除多餘用字以及過度使用的被動語氣。

→ p.142

> "To do our work, we all have to read a mass of papers. Nearly all of them are far too long. This wastes time, while energy has to be spent in looking for the essential points.
>
> I ask my colleagues and their staff to see to it that their reports are shorter.
>
> The aim should be reports which set out the main points in a series of short, crisp paragraphs.
>
> If a report relies on detailed analysts of some complicated factors, or on statistics, these should be set out in an appendix.
>
> Often the occasion is best met by submitting not a full-dress report, but an aide-memoire consisting of headings only, which can be expanded orally if needed.
>
> Let us have an end of such phrases as these:
>
> 'It is also of importance to bear in mind the following considerations', or 'Consideration should be given to the possibility of carrying into effect'. Most of these woolly phrases are mere padding, which can be left out altogether, or replaced by a single word. Let us not shrink from using the short expressive phrase, even if it is conversational.
>
> Reports drawn up on the lines I propose may first seem rough as compared with the flat surface of officialese jargon. but the saving in time will be great, while the discipline of setting out the real points concisely will provide an aid to clearer thinking."
>
> *Sir Winston Churchill, 9 August 1940*

 提示　問自己：這份報告是否完全不懂的人閱讀後能夠理解內容，而且不必提出問題來釐清疑問。

14.2　備忘錄

→ p.143

MEMORANDUM

To	Jean Lee, Manager
From	Sally Turner, Administration Assistant
Ref	JL/ST
Date	20 April 200—

VISIT OF MR HO CHWEE LEONG, WANCHAI IMPORTING COMPANY, HONG KONG

Mr Ho Chwee Leong is to visit us on (date). As we can expect a large order from his company, Wanchai Importing Company of Hong Kong, it is important that he receives a good impression of our company. The following are the arrangements for the visit.

ARRANGEMENTS MADE

1　Accommodation has been arranged for Mr Ho at Hotel Moderne and I have arranged for a taxi to collect him from the hotel at 9.30 am to bring him to Shazini Shoes factory.

2　When Mr Ho arrives at Shazini Shoes at 10.00 am he will be met by Mr Lee and senior staff who will take him on a visit of the factory.

3　A buffet lunch has been arranged in the guest room at 12.30 am. Vegetarian food has been provided.

4　The boardroom has been booked for a conference for the whole afternoon for Mr Ho, Mr Lee and senior staff. Refreshments have been laid on during the afternoon.

5　A taxi has been booked to take Mr Ho to the airport at 5.30 pm, so he can check in for his flight before 6.00 pm.

ARRANGEMENTS STILL TO BE MADE

1　Up to date price lists, catalogues and samples of shoes will be provided in the boardroom.

2　Staff will be informed that Mr Lee and senior staff will not be available next Friday.

14.3 報告

→ p.144

MARUMAN STORES, NOTTING HILL BRANCH
REPORT ON POSSIBILITY OF OPENING A CRÉCHE

INTRODUCTION

說明誰要求做這份報告，你又被要求做哪些事

I was asked to investigate the opening of a crèche at the Notting Hill branch by Mrs Lillian Cheng. In order to do this the following steps were taken.

列出蒐集資訊所採取的步驟

1　I obtained a breakdown of figures showing the number of customers with young children.
2　I discussed this issue with several customers who brought children to the store.
3　The accommodation, staffing and insurance issues were considered.
4　I investigated the experience of other shops that already have a crèche.

DISCUSSION

以合乎邏輯的順序來說明發現。使用引述方式

1　7.3% of Maruman customers have at least one child under the age of 3.
2　The majority of customers interviewed said they would use a crèche if the cost was reasonable. Some of these customers also commented that other friends who are not presently customers might also consider using the shop if there was a crèche.
3　There are strict laws and regulations concerning accommodation and staffing of a crèche. The site would have to be approved to run a crèche before we could start one.
4　Staff appointed to run the crèche would have to be fully qualified.
5　A suitable space would have to be found. This would require running water as well as toilets. The crèche would have to be close to the store entrance but due to noise levels it should be kept separate from the main store.
6　The company would be required to ensure adequate insurance.
7　Many rival stores in the neighbourhood are offering crèche facilities.

CONCLUSIONS

從以上的發現做出合理的結論

A crèche would be popular and well-used if we decided to go ahead with this.

RECOMMENDATIONS

建議應該採取的行動

I suggest that the company should give further consideration to offering a crèche and investigate the financial aspects that would be involved.

註明姓名及頭銜包含參照號碼及日期

Sally Turner
Customer Services Executive
LC/ST
20 April 200—

提示　確保報告中所有的資訊都經過仔細調查且有憑有據。

14.4 較長的提案

這篇提案是引自羅斯‧傑（Ros Jay）所寫、Prentice Hall 出版的《如何撰寫提案與報告》（*How to Write Proposals and Reports that get Results*）一書。

→ p.145-147

FLEXIBLE WORKING HOURS
An initial study for ABC Ltd

by
Jane Smith

An initial study

Objective

To identify the factors involved in introducing flexible working hours, to examine their benefits and disadvantages and to recommend the best approach to take.

Summary

At present, almost all employees of ABC Ltd work from 9.00 to 5.00. A handful work from 9.30 to 5.30.

Many, though not all, staff are unhappy with this and would prefer a more flexible arrangement. Some are working mothers and would like to be able to take their children to and from school. Some, particularly the older employees, have sick or elderly relatives who make demands on their time which do not fit comfortably with their working hours.

For the company itself, this dissatisfaction among staff leads to low morale and reduced productivity. It also makes it harder to attract and retain good staff.

There are three basic options for the future:

1 *Leave things as they are*. This is obviously less demanding on resources that implementing a new system. At least we know it works even if it isn't perfect.

2 *Highly flexible system*. Employees would clock on and clock off anytime with a $12\frac{1}{2}$ hour working day until they have 'clocked up' 35 hours a week. This would be the hardest system to implement.

3 *Limited flexibility*. Staff could start work any time between 8.00 to 10.00 am and work through for eight hours. This would not solve all employees' problems but it would solve most of them.

（接下頁）

Proposal

Introduce a system of limited flexibility for now, retaining the option of increasing flexibility later if this seems appropriate.

Position

The current working hours at ABC Ltd are 9.00 to 5.00 for most employees, with a few working from 9.30 to 5.30.

Problem

Although this works up to a point, it does have certain disadvantages, both for the organisation and for some of the employees.

The organisation: The chief disadvantage of the current system is that many of the staff are dissatisfied with it. This has become such a serious problem that it is becoming harder to attract and retain good staff. Those staff who do join the company and stay with it feel less motivated: this, as research has shown, means they are less productive than they could be.

The employees: Some employees are satisfied with their current working hours, but many of them find the present system restrictive. There are several reasons for this but the employees most strongly in favour of greater flexibility are, in particular:

- parents, especially mothers, who would prefer to be able to take their children to and from school, and to work around this commitment

- employees, many of them in the older age range, who have elderly or sick relatives who they would like to be more available for.

A more flexible approach would make it easier for many staff to fulfil these kinds of demands on their time.

An initial study questioned nearly 140 employees in a cross-section of ages. A large majority were in favour of a more flexible approach, in particular the women and the younger members of the company. It is worth noting that a minority of staff were against the introduction of flexible working hours. Appendix I gives the full results of this study.

Possibilities

Since this report is looking at the principle and not the detail of a more flexible approach, the options available fall broadly into three categories: retaining the present system, introducing limited flexibility of working hours, and implementing a highly flexible system.

（接下頁）

Although the system is not perfect, at least we know it works. The staff all signed their contracts on the understanding that the company worked to standard hours of business, and while it may not be ideal for them it is at least manageable. Better the devil you know.

Implementing any new system is bound to incur problems and expense, consequently retaining the present working hours is the least expensive option in terms of direct cost.

Highly flexible system: A highly flexible system would mean keeping the site open from, say, 7.30 am to 8.00 pm. All staff are contracted to work a certain number of hours a week and time clocks are installed. Employees simply clock on and off whenever they enter or leave the building, until they have reached their full number of hours each week.

This system has the obvious benefit that it can accommodate a huge degree of flexibility which should suit the various demands of all employees. They could even elect to work 35 hours a week spread over only three days. A further benefit to the company would be that doctors' appointments and so on would no longer happen 'on company time' as they do at present. This system does have several disadvantages, however:

- Many staff regard occasional time off for such things as doctors' appointments or serious family crises as a natural 'perk' of the job. With this system they would have to make up the hours elsewhere. Not only would they lose the time off, but many would also feel that the company did not trust them. This would obviously be bad for company morale.

- It would be difficult to implement this system fairly. The sales office, for example, must be staffed at least from 9.00 to 5.30 every day. What if all the sales staff want to take Friday off? How do you decide who can and who can't? What if the computer goes down at 4 o'clock in the afternoon and there are no computer staff in until 7.30 the following morning?

Limited flexibility: This would make asking employees to continue to work an eight hour day, but give them a range of, say, ten hours to fit it into. They could start any time between 8.00 and 10.00 in the morning, so they would finish eight hours later – between 4.00 and 6.00.

On the plus side, this would give the employees the co-operation and recognition of their problems that many of them look for, and would therefore increase staff motivation. For some it would provide a way around their other commitments.

Proposal

Given the number of staff in favour of more flexible working hours, and the importance of staff motivation, it seems sensible to adopt some kind of flexible

（接下頁）

approach. But it is probably advisable to find a system that allows the significant minority who prefer to stay as they are to do so.

So which is the best system to choose? It is harder to go backwards than forwards in developing new systems: if the highly flexible approach failed it would be difficult to pull back to a less flexible system (in terms of keeping the staff happy). On the other hand, a limited degree of flexibility could easily be extended later if this seemed appropriate.

So at this stage it seems that the most workable system, which contains most of the benefits required by the employees, is the limited flexibility of working hours.

Appendix I

Table of employee responses to the proposal for flexible working hours.

AGE GROUP	MEN Total number consulted	MEN Positive response	MEN Negative response	WOMEN Total number	WOMEN Positive response	WOMEN Negative response
18–30	20	19	1	18	18	0
30–40	23	19	4	29	27	2
40–50	15	8	7	12	8	4
50–60	12	2	10	8	7	1
	70	48	22	67	60	7

檢查清單

☐ 開始撰寫前，要非常謹慎地規畫報告及提案。

☐ 利用副標將文件組織成數個段落。

☐ 使用日常的簡單英文。

☐ 避免使用專業術語，不得不用的術語則應加上註解。

☐ 將句子維持在 15 至 20 個字，每個句子都要有一個主要想法。

☐ 儘量使用主動動詞。

☐ 清楚、簡明。

☐ 以真誠且個人化的方式撰寫，就好像是在跟閱讀的人說話。

☐ 先撰寫草稿。有些報告需要嚴格的編輯、排版及修正措詞等。

☐ 請別人讀一遍，並檢查內容是否符合所有的目標，以及是否容
　易閱讀、是否準確。

公告、廣告與通知單
Notices, advertisements and information sheets

公告

大多數的企業會在辦公室的明顯處設置布告欄，用來告知所有員工需特別注意的事項。這類公告資訊必須以吸引人的方式呈現，才能引起注意並取得配合。公告的訊息可以是：

◆ 公司的新規定。　　　　　　◆ 聯誼活動。
◆ 公司內部的任命啓事。　　　◆ 攸關利益事項的報告。
◆ 公司各項常規程序的提醒。

15.1 公告

→ p.150

用來引起注意的標題	**CAN YOU ACT?** **(OR WOULD YOU LIKE TO TRY?)**
使標題看起來有趣	This year Global Communications celebrates its 10th year of providing quality telecommunications equipment. To mark this special occasion we are holding a 10th Anniversary Celebration at the Regal Prince Hotel in July. Special guests, directors and staff are to be invited.
提供完整的細節	A special 20-minute sketch has been written and we are now looking for aspiring actors and actresses to perform the sketch.
加上另一個相關標題	**INTERESTED?**
使用富吸引力的版面來吸引員工注意特殊重點	If you would like to attend an audition for a part in this sketch please come along and find out more. When?　Monday 15 March Where?　Training Room, Global House Time?　　　　6.00–8.00 pm If you will be coming along to the auditions please call Mandy Jones, Marketing Department, to put your name down.
在公告底部放上姓名／頭銜	**James Porter** **Marketing Manager**
務必加上公告日期	JP/ST 2 March 200–

廣告

大多數的企業會在報紙、商業期刊或雜誌上刊登廣告或啓事，以打動廣大或特定的市場。廣告／啓事的內容可以是：

◆　徵人啓事。　　　　　　　　◆　促銷產品或服務。
◆　宣布特殊活動或盛大集會。　◆　發表組織上的變動。

15.2 徵人啓事

→ p.151

公司商標
引人注意的標題
工作頭衔
公司的相關資訊
註圓點條列事項
說明對應徵者
的要求
強調待遇
說明應徵函
必須用手寫
標示公司名稱
及地址
應徵截止日期

Together

We

Excel

QUALITY ENGINEER

Here's your chance to join a dynamic and rapidly expanding global company. Global Commmunications is a global leader in the world of telecommunications. We are looking for dynamic, self-motivated team players to join us.

Responsibilities
- Ensure Global's major accounts continue to benefit from customer service and support.
- Support major accounts on technical and quality issues.
- Organise pre-sales initiatives on new products.

Pre-requisites
- Experience in telecommunications industry.
- ISO 9000 knowledge.
- Good people skills.

We offer a 5-day week and attractive compensation package commensurate with experience and qualifications.

Please send a handwritten application letter with full resumé and a recent photograph to:

Mr William Wright
Human Relations Manager
Global Communications plc
14 Western Avenue
Highbury
Sheffield S26 2ES

Closing date for applications: 12 July 200–

15.3 職缺公告或啓事

→p.152

GLOBAL COMMUNICATIONS

require a

TEAM LEADER – CUSTOMER SERVICES

Do you have what it takes to build a successful team?
We are looking for someone who can coach, support and develop
individuals to improve team performance.

The successful applicant will have:

- excellent supervisory skills
- proven skills in directing and controlling projects
- good organisational skills
- effective decision-making skills
- first-class leadership skills

Global Communications provide great working conditions:

- flexible working hours
- excellent training and development
- private medical insurance (after one year)
- 20 days' holiday allowance, increasing with length of service
- incentive schemes
- career opportunities.

IF YOU THINK YOU HAVE WHAT IT TAKES

please apply ONLINE ONLY at

www.global.com.sg

 提示 設計搶眼的廣告，以便讓它從其他的廣告中脫穎而出。

傳單及通知單

現今的商業環境創造出各式各樣的傳單(leaflet)與通知單
(information sheet)。這些傳單或通知單在將資訊傳遞給許多人時是
十分有用的。它們可在街上或是在購物中心入口處散發；或是放在
公共區域供民眾取閱，像是在博物館、展覽場、百貨公司及店家；
甚至夾在報紙或雜誌內寄送。老師也可以利用通知單的格式來製作
給學生的講義。

WOW! WHAT A GREAT OFFER !...

15.4 傳單

→ p.153

Most infections get better without antibiotics

In cases where patients will get better without antibiotics,
it makes sense for your doctor not to prescribe them.
Your body's defence system can often protect against
infection without the need for antibiotics.

Listen to your doctor

Your doctor will be able to recognise whether you
have an infection that needs antibiotics, so you
should not always expect to be given a prescription.
Doctors need to prescribe antibiotics with care: This
is because inappropriate use of antibiotics can be
dangerous for individual patients and for the whole
population.

Overuse of antibiotics can also cause resistance and
result in them not working in the future. This is a
very worrying trend, especially for patients with
serious life-threatening infections.

Harmful side-effects

Potential side-effects are another reason why doctors
are cautious about prescribing antibiotics. Some
antibiotic treatment can cause side-effects such as
stomach upset and thrush. For women on the pill,
antibiotics can reduce contraceptive protection.

Antibiotic facts

- Antibiotics have no effect on viral infections (*eg. colds, flu and most sore throats*). Viral infections are much more common than bacterial infections.
- Inappropriate use of antibiotics can encourage the development of resistant bacteria. This could mean that the antibiotic may not work when you really need it.
- Some antibiotics have harmful side-effects such as diarrhoea and allergic reactions.
- Antibiotics do not just attack the infection they are prescribed for – they can also kill useful bacteria which normally protect you against other infections such as thrush.

- There are effective alternative remedies for managing the symptoms of many infections.

If you are prescribed antibiotics ensure you take the medication according to instructions.

- Although you may begin to feel better, you must take the full course of antibiotics to prevent your illness coming back.
- Not taking the full course of antibiotics can lead to future antibiotic resistance.

If you have an infection such as a cold, flu or sore throat

- Take paracetamol according to the instructions to help reduce fever and relieve aches and pains.
- Drink plenty of water to avoid dehydration.
- Ask your pharmacist (*chemist*) for advice. Many infections can be managed effectively with over-the-counter medications. The pharmacist will refer you to your doctor or practice nurse if they think it is necessary.

When to contact your GP

Call your GP's surgery for advice if, after taking
over-the-counter medications as directed, you or
your child are experiencing any of the following:

- symptoms which are severe or unusually prolonged.
- extreme shortness of breath.
- coughing up of blood or large amounts of yellow or green phlegm.

DEVELOPING PATIENT PARTNERSHIP

*Promoting a healthy partnership between
patients and health professionals*

BMA House   Tavistock Square   London   WC1H 9JP
Fax: 0171 383 6403   Internet:www.doctorpatient.org.uk

（引自 *Developing Patient Partnership*）

15.5　講義

→ p.154

使用清楚的標題 ——

PASSIVE vs ACTIVE VOICE

Which is more effective?

#1 Your order was received by us today. The goods you requested have been despatched by courier. You should receive them within 48 hours. Should they not have been received by you tomorrow our despatch department should be contacted as soon as possible.

Why?

#2 Thank you for your order number HT121 dated 21 June. Our special courier service will deliver these goods within 48 hours. If you have not received them by Friday morning please contact me on 254 8777.

Why NOT passive voice?

一些空白，以方 便引導學生寫答案

☺ It makes your writing vague
☺ It denies responsibility
☺ It creates a distance between you and your reader

Why USE active voice?

☺
☺
☺

✎ YOUR TURN

Rewrite these sentences using ACTIVE voice.

提供一些練習 ——

1 The seminar will be conducted by Robert Sim.

2 The leak was fixed by the plumber.

3 Your thoughtful suggestions are accepted graciously.

4 Arrangements have been made for the conference to be held at the Hilton Hotel.

5 The investigation has been concluded by our client, and the paperwork has been signed.

6 The design of our new systems was simplified by the use of hydraulics.

使用副標題 —— **Is passive voice ever appropriate?**

✓ **In minutes of meetings**　Mrs Jones reported that the photocopier had broken down for the third time in a month.

✓ **When tact is important**　A serious mistake was made.

想知道更多有關使用主動及被動語態的問題，請至：
www.shirleytaylor.com/articles.html

通知單的細節說明通常與下列主題有關：

◆ 商品或服務。
◆ 特別的促銷。
◆ 特殊活動或盛大集會。
◆ 指導方針及資訊。

設計技巧

上述這些文件的設計技巧十分相似，底下的 **AIDA** 是非常有用的指導方針：

A 注意（Attention） 你必須引起閱讀者的注意：
— 使用公司商標？
— 具體的標題。
— 在框格或陰影處放上特別的資訊。
— 使用副標題／數字／圓點。

I 興趣（Interest） 藉由提及某件會吸引閱讀者的事來激起他們的興趣：
— 具說服力。
— 使用簡單的語言、簡潔的句子。

D 渴望（Desire） 喚醒閱讀的人購買、參加、找尋更多資訊或與寫作者聯繫的渴望：
— 讓每件事聽起來都很有趣。
— 指出好處。

A 行動（Action） 讓閱讀者在閱讀公告或廣告／啟事之後會想要採取行動。

 提示 中國人會說：好的設計與呈現就是好風水！

檢查清單

☐ 如果適當的話，加入公司的商標並標示於明顯處。

☐ 選用簡單、易記的標題來呈現重點。

☐ 小心地使用空白，以凸顯特別的事項。

☐ 使用副標題及陰影以引起注意。

☐ 用數字和圓點將資訊加以歸類。

☐ 確保所呈現的內容是引人注意且有效的。

☐ 使用直接、簡單的語言和簡潔的句子。

☐ 使用具有說服力的寫作技巧讓每件事聽起來都很實用、令人興奮、有趣或有益。

☐ 與其他文件並排，你的文件必須能脫穎而出。

☐ 說明你要閱讀者採取的行動。如果有必要，註明聯絡人姓名、電話號碼、電子郵件等。

通知函
Circulars

所謂通知函，是用來將同一訊息傳遞給許多人知道。它們被廣泛運用在銷售活動中（參考第 17 章），以及布達企業的重大發展，像是擴大營業、組織重整或地址遷移等。

通知函只需準備一次即可利用複製方式寄給不同的收件人。而為了讓信件個人化，可於複製後再插入姓名、地址和個別的稱呼。

利用電腦或其他文書處理機的合併列印功能將「可更動」的細節，如封內地址及稱呼等合併印出，就可以讓每一封信看起來都像是原創而非複製的。

雖然通知函要寄給很多人，但顧及個人化的特色，仍是很重要的。請牢記以下幾項規則：

1. 簡短：措詞行文不宜太過冗長。
2. 個人化：儘可能將每一封信件寫明是給特定人士，如果你知道的話就加上名字。使用 Dear Mr Smith（親愛的史密斯先生）來取代 Dear Reader（親愛的讀者）或 Dear Subscriber（親愛的用戶）；用 Dear Customer（親愛的顧客）取代 Dear Sir 或 Dear Madam（親愛的先生／夫人）。不要用複數形式的稱呼，記住每位收件人收到的都是一封個別的信件。
3. 建立個人的關心：例如用 you（你、您），而不用 our customers, all customers, our clients, everyone（我們的顧客、所有顧客、我們的客戶、各位）。

使用	不使用
You will appreciate ... 您將感謝……	Our customers will appreciate ... 我們的顧客將會感謝……
We are pleased to inform you ... 我們很高興通知您……	We are pleased to inform all our clients ... 我們很高興通知所有的客戶……
You will be interested to learn ... 您將有興趣知道……	Everyone will be interested to learn ... 每個人將有興趣知道……
If you visit our new showroom you will see ... 如果您參觀我們新的展示室，您將會看到……	Anyone visiting our new showroom will see ... 任何參觀新展示室的人將會看到……

企業組織變更通知

當企業組織變更時，可透過類似底下範例的通知函來布達。而為了讓信件更個人化，有的信件在稱呼處會留白，經過電腦或文字處理機的處理後，收信人姓名、地址及稱呼會以合併方式印出。

16.1 公司更改名稱

→ p.156

Dear Customer

Change of Company Name/Transfer of Business

In November 2001 Merlion Communications was acquired by SingComm Pte Ltd. As a result of this acquisition and renaming the company, we are amending the registered name for direct debit processing.

This change will not affect the service you receive in any way, except that future direct debits will be collected by SingComm Pte Ltd instead of Merlion Communications with immediate effect. The only change you will notice is the different name on your bank/building society statement for this direct debit.

You need not take any action. Details of the change have been sent to your bank/building society. Your rights under the direct debit guarantee are not affected, as detailed on the attached guarantee.

Yours sincerely

提示 在直效行銷或電子郵件中，直接用 **you** 去引起對方注意，使它們看起來更個人化。

16.2　新店開張 (a)

→ p.156

Dear

BEST SUPERSTORE OPENS AT BEDFORD – 12 JULY 200–

Have you seen the great news in the national newspapers recently? Best International are opening a chain of furniture superstores throughout the UK. The first one will be open at Bedford on Monday 12 July 200–.

Special discounts will be given to the first 50 customers who come through our doors from 0900 on our opening day.

Open times are　　　0900–2000 Monday to Saturday
　　　　　　　　　　0900–1700 Sunday

A variety of kitchens, bathrooms, dining rooms and lounges will be on display. A full planning service is available so you can leave it to the experts to design just what you want. Each department in the Superstore is supervised by friendly, qualified staff.

The store will be of particular interest to the DIY enthusiast. You will find everything you may need – paints, wall coverings, tiles, carpets, and so much more. We will deliver free of change any orders over £100 – for smaller orders there will be a minimal charge. Credit facilities are available at low interest rates.

Our car park has spaces for 400 cars but if you prefer to take the bus, number 214 stops right outside the Best Superstore. Don't miss our grand opening on Monday 12 July – **remember there's a special discount waiting for you if you are among the first 50 customers.**

See you at the superstore!

Yours sincerely

16.3　新店開張 (b)

→ p.157

Dear Householder

We are pleased to announce the opening of our new retail grocery store on Monday 1 September.

Mrs Victoria Chadwick has been appointed Manager. She has 15 years' experience of the trade and we are sure that the goods supplied will be of <u>sound</u>[1] quality and reasonably priced.

Our new store will open at 0800 hours on Monday 1 September. As a special celebration offer a discount of 10% will be allowed on all purchases made by the first 50 customers. We hope we can look forward to your being one of them.

Yours sincerely

---

1. sound：可靠的。

16.4　業務擴張

→ p.157

Dear Customer

To meet the growing demand for a hardware and general store in this area we have decided to extend our business by opening a new department.

Our new department will carry an extensive range of hardware and other domestic goods at prices which compare very favourably with those charged by other suppliers.

We would like the opportunity to demonstrate our new merchandise to you so we are arranging a special window display during the week beginning 24 June. The official opening of our new department will take place on the following Monday 1 July.

We hope you will visit our new department during opening week and give us the opportunity to show you that the reputation enjoyed by our other departments for giving sound value for money will apply equally to this new department.

Yours sincerely

16.5　成立分公司

→ p.158

Dear

Owing to the large increase in the volume of our trade with the Kingdom of Jordan, we have decided to open a branch in Amman. Mr Faisal Shamlan has been appointed as Manager.

Although we hope we have provided you with an efficient service in the past, this new branch in your country will result in your orders and enquiries being dealt with more promptly.

This new branch will open on 1 May and from that date all orders and enquiries should be sent to

Mr Faisal Shamlan
Manager
Tyler & Co Ltd
18 Hussein Avenue
Amman
Tel: (00962)6–212421
Fax: (00962)6–212422

We take this opportunity to express our thanks for your custom in the past. We hope these new arrangements will lead to even higher standards in the service we provide.

Yours sincerely

16.6 遷移至新址

→ p.158

> Dear
>
> The steady growth of our business has made necessary an early move to new and larger premises. We have been fortunate in acquiring a particularly good site on the new industrial estate at Chorley, and from 1 July our new address will be as follows:
>
> Unit 15
> Chorley Industrial Estate
> Grange Road
> Chorley
> Lincs CH2 4TH
> Telephone 456453 Fax 456324
>
> This new site is served by excellent transport facilities, both road and rail, enabling deliveries to be made promptly. It also provides <u>scope</u>[2] for better methods of production which will increase output and also improve the quality of our goods even further.
>
> We have very much appreciated your custom in the past and confidently expect to be able to offer you improvements in service when the new factory moves into full production.
>
> Yours sincerely

16.7 門市重整

→ p.159

> Dear
>
> In order to provide you with even better service, we have recently extended and <u>relocated</u>[3] a number of departments in our store.
>
> - On the ground floor we have a wide selection of greetings cards, including both boxed and single Christmas cards.
>
> - In the Children's and Babywear Department on the first floor there is a new 'Ladybird' section.
>
> - Our Fashion Fabrics and Soft Furnishings Departments are together on the second floor. Light Fittings and Electrical Goods are relocated on the third floor.
>
> - The basement displays a good collection of wallpapers, most of which we are able to supply within 24 hours.
>
> We thank you for your past custom and hope we may continue to be of service to you.
>
> Yours sincerely

---

2. scope ：機會。
3. relocated ：移至不同地點。

16.8 同事過世

→ p.159

Dear

It is with much sadness that I have to tell you of the sudden death of our Marketing Director, Michael Spencer. Michael had been with this company for 10 years and he made an enormous contribution to the development of the business. He will be greatly missed by all his colleagues.

I am anxious to ensure continuing service to you. Please contact me directly with any matters which Michael would normally deal with.

Yours sincerely

合夥人變動通知

當合夥的成員有所變動時，必須寫信通知供應商和客戶。這對退出合夥的人尤其重要，因為其對任期內所簽訂的借貸合約，以及將到期的舊債權合約依然擔負法律責任。

這類書信中的簽名應該是公司名稱，不加上任何合夥人的名字。

16.9 合夥人退休

→ p.160

Dear

We regret to inform you that our senior partner, Mr Harold West, has decided to retire on 31 May due to recent extended ill-health.

The withdrawal of Mr West's capital will be made good by contributions from the remaining partners, and the value of the firm's capital will therefore remain unchanged. We will continue to trade under the name of West, Webb & Co, and there will be no change in policy.

We hope that the confidence you have shown in our company in the past will continue and that we may rely on your custom in the future.

Yours sincerely

16.10 指定新合夥人

→ p.160

Dear

A large increase in the volume of our business has made necessary an increase in the membership of this company. It is with pleasure that we announce the appointment of Mrs Briony Kisby as partner.

Mrs Kisby has been our Head Buyer for the past 10 years and is well acquainted with every aspect of our policy. Her expertise and experience will continue to be of great value to the company.

There will be no change to our firm's name of Taylor, Hyde & Co.

We look forward to continuing our mutually beneficial business relationship with you.

Yours sincerely

16.11 從合夥轉為私人公司

→ p.160

Dear

The need for additional capital to finance the considerable growth in the volume of our trade has made it necessary to reorganise our business as a private company. The new company has been registered with limited liability in the name Barlow & Hoole Limited.

We wish to stress that this change is in name only and that the nature of our business will remain exactly as before. There will be no change in business policy.

The personal relationship which has been built up with all customers in the past will be maintained; we shall continue to do our utmost to ensure that you are completely satisfied with the way in which we handle your future orders.

Yours sincerely

更換公司代表通知

16.12　解雇公司代表

→ p.161

> Dear
>
> We wish to inform you that Miss Rona Smart who has been our representative in North-West England for the past 7 years has left our service. Therefore she no longer has authority to take orders or to collect accounts on our behalf.
>
> In her place we have appointed Mrs Tracie Coole. Mrs Coole has for many years had control of our sales section and is thoroughly familiar with the needs of customers in your area. She intends to call on you some time this month to introduce herself and to bring samples of our new spring fabrics.
>
> We look forward to continuing our business relationship with you.
>
> Yours sincerely

如果該名公司代表是自己辭去工作，而且是一位風評不錯的員工，那麼將上面這封信的第一段改成下列方式會更合適：

→ p.161

> It is with regret that we inform you that Miss Rona Smart, who has been our representative for the past 7 years, has decided to leave us to take up another appointment.

16.13 指派新代表

→ p.161

> Dear
>
> Mr Samuel Goodier, who has been calling on you regularly for the past 6 years, has now joined our firm as junior partner. His many friends will doubtless be sorry that they will see him much less frequently and we can assure you that he shares their regret.
>
> Mr Goodier hopes to keep in touch with you and other customers by occasional visits to his former territory.
>
> Mr Lionel Tufnell has been appointed to represent us in the South West and Mr Goodier will introduce him to you when he makes his last regular call on you next week. Mr Tufnell has worked closely with Mr Goodier in the past and he will continue to do so in the future. Mr Goodier will continue to offer help and advice in matters affecting you and other customers in the South West, and his intimate knowledge of your requirements will be of great benefit to Mr Tufnell in his new responsibilities.
>
> Our business relations with you have always been very good, and we believe we have succeeded in serving you well. It is therefore with confidence that we ask you to extend to our new representative the courtesy and friendliness you have always shown to Mr Goodier.
>
> Yours sincerely

內部通知函

有關一般的業務、安全、管理、行政及其他種種事務，可以透過通知函傳達給員工知道。日常事務有時多半採用備忘錄，但是某些情形下較正式的信函會使用印有公司信頭的紙張。

16.14 新工作時間的通知

→ p.162

> NEW WORKING HOURS
>
> With effect from 1 September 200— working hours will be amended to 0930 to 1730 Monday to Friday instead of the present working hours of 0900 to 1700.
>
> I hope you will find these new hours convenient. If you anticipate experiencing any difficulties please let me know before 14 August.

16.15 新停車場啟用通知

→ p.162

NEW CAR PARK

You may be aware that some old buildings on our site have been demolished. A piece of land in this area has been cleared so that it may be used as a car park.

The new car park should be ready for use by 28 October. It will be available between 0730 and 1830 hours Monday to Friday. The company takes no responsibility for loss or damage to vehicles or contents while in the car park.

If you wish to use the car park please obtain an agreement form from Mr John Smithson, Security Officer. This form must be completed and returned to him before using the car park.

Copy　　　John Smithson, Security Officer

16.16 商店折扣資訊

→ p.162

DISCOUNT AT QUANTUM STORES

An agreement has been reached which will allow all our employees to take advantage of the special discount scheme operated by Quantum Stores.

As an employee of Omega International you will receive 10% discount on any goods which are not already reduced in price. A discount of 2 $\frac{1}{2}$% will be given on reduced price or sale goods. If you wish to claim the discount you must show your Omega identification badge.

These discounts will take effect from 1 September 200–.

16.17 給各部門主管的保全訊息

→ p.163

SECURITY

公告理由 — In view of recent bomb threats received by several competitors, please brief your staff on the following points of security.

條列說明
以方便參考用

1　All employees must wear a name badge at all times.
2　All areas must be kept as clean and tidy as possible. This will reduce potential areas where bombs may be hidden.
3　Do not tamper with or move any suspicious object. The Manager should be informed and the police notified.
4　Evacuation should follow established fire drills.

後續行動 — All incidents must be taken seriously and a detailed report must be submitted to me.

最後的強調 — Please stress to all your staff that they have an important part to play in maintaining a high level of security in all areas at all times.

16.18 有關未休完的年假

→ p.163

In the past it has been a policy of the company that all staff must take their holiday entitlement within one calendar year. Any holiday entitlement not taken before 31 December each year has been forfeited.

It has now been decided to amend this rule to provide staff with more flexibility regarding holidays.

With immediate effect anyone who has up to 5 days' holiday entitlement outstanding at 31 December may carry this over to 31 March the following year. Any days that have not been used by 31 March will be forfeited. Unused holiday entitlement may not be converted to pay in lieu.

The approval of staff leave is still subject to agreement with your manager/supervisor. This will take into account the business and operational needs of the department and especially clashes with other staff.

If you have any questions about this new policy, please telephone the Human Resource Department on extension 456.

16.19 有關健康及安全政策的提醒

→ p.164

In view of the recent unfortunate accident involving a visitor to our premises, I would like to remind you about our health and safety policy.

Whenever you have a visitor to the building, you are responsible for his/her health and safety at all times. For his/her own safety, a visitor should not be allowed to wander freely around the building. If, for example, a visitor needs to use the washroom, you should accompany he or she and escort he or she back.

For security reasons, if you see someone you do not recognise wandering around the building unaccompanied, do not be afraid to ask questions. Ask politely why he or she is here, which member of staff he or she is visiting, and if that person knows the visitor has arrived.

All SingComm employees have a responsibility to take reasonable care of themselves and others and to ensure a healthy and safe workplace. If you notice any hazard or potential hazard, please bring it to the attention of the Health and Safety Manager, Michael Wilson, who will investigate the issue.

A copy of the company's health and safety policy is attached. Please take a few minutes to read it through to remind yourself of the main points.

Thank you for your help in ensuring the health and safety of all employees and visitors to SingComm.

附回條的通知函

如果需要對方回覆，通常回函會採用「沿虛線撕開」（tear-off）的方式，當然也可用分開回覆的表格。回函部分必須包含以下重點：

◆ 開頭一定要寫上 Please return by ... to ...（請於……前寄至……），此舉是以防有人將回函撕下，或另附的回函與信件分開時的因應之道。
◆ 需要回覆的部分採雙行的格式。
◆ 在每一個問題或標題後預留足夠的空間，方便填寫。
◆ 在需要回覆處加上虛線做區隔。

16.20　正式典禮的邀請（沿虛線撕開回函）

→ p.165

10TH ANNIVERSARY CELEBRATION

Omega International is celebrating its 10th year of providing quality communications equipment. Approximately 50 representatives from Omega clients are expected to attend a special 10th Anniversary Celebration on Friday 29 October 200—.

The directors have decided to invite all employees who have been with Omega for at least 5 years to attend this special function. I am pleased to extend to you an invitation to join us at Omega's 10th Anniversary Celebration. Cocktails and a buffet supper will be provided.

This special function will take place from 1800 to 2300 hours at The Mandarin Suite, Oriental Hotel, West Street, London.

Please let me know whether you will be attending by returning the tear-off portion before 31 August.

I hope you will be able to join us.

Please return to Mrs Judy Brown, Administration Manager, before 31 August.

I shall/shall not* be attending the 10th Anniversary Celebration on Friday 29 October.

Name ....

Designation/Department ....

Signature ....　　　　　Date ....

* Please delete as applicable.

如果是內部公告，只需註明姓名／職稱，無須完整地址

保持簡單、明確的敘述

使用兩行間距

適當的話，加上註記

16.21　回函格式

（此節取自 Shirley Taylor 的 *Communication for Business* 一書）

這是一封寄給訓練機構客戶的回覆表格，目的在詢問客戶是否要參加為期一天的管理研討會，如果需要安排住房則附上住宿費支票。

→ p.166

REPLY FORM

若是對外公告，則應　—　Please complete and return by 15 February 200— to
註明公司完整地址。
不要忘了回覆日期

Mr Edward Teoh
Personnel Manager
Professional Training Pte Ltd
126 Buona Vista Boulevard
KUALA LUMPUR
Malaysia

與說明文件上　—　ONE-DAY MANAGEMENT CONFERENCE
的標題一樣　　　SATURDAY 3 APRIL 200—

數字條列　—　1　I wish/do not wish* to attend this conference.

使用個人化措詞，如　—　2　I require accommodation on
I wish..., I require... 等
　　　　　　　　　　　　　☐ Friday 2 April

用選項／方塊供勾選　—　　　☐ Saturday 3 April　　(Please tick)

　　　　　3　My cheque for M$400 is attached (made payable to Professional
　　　　　　　Training Pte Ltd)

Signature...　　　Date.................

Name (in caps) ....

在回函下方放上　—　Title ....
所需的詳細資料

Company ....

Address ....

留足夠的填寫空間　—　...

　　　　　　　　　　　　　　　　　　　　　　Post code.......................

Telephone...　　Fax...............................

不要忘了註記　—　* Please delete as necessary.

 **檢查清單**

【傳單】

☐ 利用加入個別的封內住址而讓通知函變得更個人化。

☐ 如果知道對方姓名，則直接稱呼收件人姓名，否則用單數型的 Dear Customer（親愛的客戶）、 Dear Reader（親愛的讀者），不要用 Customers（客戶們）、 Readers（讀者們）。

☐ 適當的話，可以加入手寫的稱呼。

☐ 用 you（您）代替 all customers（所有客戶）、 everyone（各位）等稱呼，以顯示個人的關心。

【附回函的書信】

☐ 註明回覆日期。

☐ 提及回函的收件人是誰：

　　內部格式：只寫姓名及頭銜。

　　外部格式：姓名、頭銜、公司名稱和地址。

☐ 使用與說明文件相同的標題。

☐ 使用雙行格式。

☐ 使用個人化的措詞，如： I wish, I shall/shall not 等。

☐ 適當的話，使用選項／方塊供勾選。

☐ 留足夠的填寫空間。

☐ 確保所有必要的資訊都涵蓋在表格中。

銷售信與主動報價
Sales letters and voluntary offers

銷售信

銷售信是所有廣告格式中最具選擇性的。不像報刊或海報廣告，銷售信的目標是將特定商品或服務賣給選定的顧客。目的在於說服讀信者需要你試圖推銷的商品，並勸服他們購買。

你應該試著將商品變得有吸引力並使之成為必需品，或者將必需品變得更吸引人。

 記住，雖然銷售信會在眾人之間傳閱，但在書寫時，仍需使用個人化的口吻。用 **you**（您）而不用 **all of you**（各位）。

銷售信的七個最弱環節

以下是一般人撰寫銷售信時容易出現的問題，也是必須多加留意的事項。

1. 標題不吸引人

標題也許是銷售信最重要的部分，它是第一眼吸引閱讀者注意，並讓他們對你提供的商品感興趣的機會。一個有力的標題可以穩定提升你的利潤。

2. 內容薄弱

如果銷售信讓人看了想睡覺，表示有某個地方出問題了。你的銷售信用字應當有趣、令人興奮，風格則應犀利、活潑，從頭到尾都能留住閱讀者的目光。

3. 購買方式受限

一個可以吸引人購買的簡單方式是提供比較多種的付款方式。基於方便，大多數顧客希望用信用卡付帳。但仍有部分顧客偏好其他付款方式，如支票、借方卡（debit card，編注：立即從帳戶中扣款，與現金卡不同）或網路購物等，你當然也想吸引這一類的客戶。

4. 銷售主張不夠有力

是什麼讓你的產品或服務不同於競爭對手？售價較低、品質較好、出貨較快，或是產品較多樣化呢？顧客希望有一個合理且具體的理由來跟你做生意，你需要琢磨出一個獨特的銷售主張：你可以提供競爭對手無法做到的事。務必在廣告或銷售信中提到這一點。

5. 無人背書或背書太弱

有人推薦、背書真的可以提高業績。一個好的背書等於好口碑，潛在顧客會信任那些滿意你產品或服務的顧客所說的話。如果你收到顧客的稱讚，一定要請他們准許你在銷售信中引用，將他們的意見拿來做保證。

6. 保固期太短

顧客不喜歡保固期太短的商品，因為他們未必有那麼多時間去發現產品或服務是否能正常運作的時間不夠。較長的保固期通常可以提高銷量，並降低退貨次數。

7. 後續追蹤做得不夠

大多數到你網站瀏覽的人不太可能第一次就下單。你必須設計一個有效的追蹤計畫，以便將潛在銷量放到最大。建議可以用免費的樣品來促使對方留下聯絡資料。

成功的銷售信

一封好的銷售信，必須依據下列四點來架構內容：

◆ 引起興趣（arouse interest）
◆ 創造渴望（create desire）
◆ 有說服力（carry conviction）
◆ 誘發行動（induce action）

以下逐一詳細探討每個要點。

引起興趣

第一段必須引起讀者興趣，並激勵他們去注意你想表達的內容。如果未用心處理這開頭段落，你的銷售信最終可能淪爲沒人要讀的垃圾。你可以用問句、指引或引述起頭，以下是一些例子：

(a) 訴諸自尊

Are you nervous when asked to propose a vote of thanks, to take the Chair at a meeting, or to make a speech? If so this letter has been written specially for you!

您是否對公開致謝、當會議主席，或對演講覺得緊張？如果您有以上情況，那麼這封信就是特地為您而寫的。

(b) 訴諸實惠

Would you like to cut your domestic fuel costs by 20 per cent? If your answer is 'yes', read on ...

您想削減 20% 的家用燃料費嗎？如果您的答案是肯定的，請閱讀……

(c) 訴諸健康

'The common cold,' says Dr James Carter, 'probably causes more lost time at work in a year than all other illnesses put together.'

詹姆士‧卡爾特醫生說：「一般的感冒在一年內所造成的工時損失，也許比所有其他疾病加起來還多。」

(d) 訴諸恐懼

More than 50 per cent of people have eye trouble and in the past year no fewer than 16,000 people in Britain have lost their sight. Are your eyes in danger?

超過 50% 的人都有眼睛方面的疾病，而在過去幾年當中，有多達一萬六千名的英國人喪失視力。您的眼睛是否處於危險中呢？

創造渴望

在開頭段落引起讀者興趣後，接下來是具體指出你所銷售的產品或服務能帶給收件人什麼樣的好處及影響，也就是創造渴望。

如果收件人對該產品一無所知，那麼就必須清楚地描述產品的內容及功能。詳細研究產品，找出可超越同類產品的特色，並從收件人的觀點去強調此一特色。

例如，用「市場首選」或「最新電子科技產品」之類的口號來宣傳高立體傳真音響，效果相當有限。不如去強調使用的材質有多好，以及有哪些特色是此產品比競爭對手更方便或有效的。下列的形容就強調了這些重點：

This hi-fi system is carefully designed and incorporates the latest technological developments to give high-quality sound including full stereo recording and playback on the twin-cassette deck. Its clearly arranged controls make for very simple operation. It is supplied with two detachable loudspeakers separately mounted in solid, polished teak cabinets, as finely finished as a Rolls-Royce.

此一高立體傳真音響系統經過精心設計，並結合最新科技發展，提供高品質音效，包括立體音響的雙卡匣錄放裝置。它的按鍵清楚排列，操作簡單，搭配一組可分離、具柚木堅固外殼的揚聲器，宛如汽車界的勞斯萊斯。

有說服力

接下來是說服收件人，產品就如同你所宣稱的一樣好。你必須以事實或評價等證據來佐證你的主張，方法有下列數種：

◆ 邀請對方參觀工廠或展示間。
◆ 提供「包退包換」的商品。
◆ 提供一個保證。
◆ 引用你在業界多年的經驗。

Remember, we have manufactured cotton shirts for 50 years and are quite confident that you will be more than satisfied with their quality.

This offer is made on the clear understanding that if the goods are not completely to your satisfaction you can return them to us without any obligation whatever and at our own expense. The full amount you paid will be refunded immediately.

> 請記住，我們生產棉質襯衫已長達 50 年，十分有信心您會相當滿意該產品的品質。
>
> 在聲明中已經清楚表示，如果您對該產品有任何不滿，無須任何理由，我們將無條件讓您退貨，並且立刻全額退款。

然而，要注意的是，任何誇大不實的主張都是違法的。要記住，企業的好名聲和事業基礎，就和成功一樣，都仰賴誠實的交易行為。

誘發行動

結尾段落必須說服收件人採取你想要的行動，包括參觀展示間、接見公司代表、寄出樣品或者下單訂購產品。

最後一段必須提供收件人為什麼要回覆的合理理由

> If you will <u>return the enclosed request card</u> we will show <u>you how you can have all the advantages of cold storage and at the same time save money</u>.

> 如果您將回函卡寄回本公司，我們將示範如何在享有冷藏櫃的各項好處之外，又能省錢的方法。

你必須讓收件人容易採取行動，例如提供可沿虛線撕下的回函或附上郵資已付的卡片。

在書寫銷售信時應牢記：收件人真正感興趣的不是你銷售的產品、服務或想法，而是他們可從中獲得什麼好處。要設法說服收件人可從你的銷售中享有什麼好處，以及可以為他們做些什麼。

有時候結尾必須告知收件人為什麼必須立刻採取行動的特殊理由

> The special discount now offered can be allowed only on orders placed by 30 June. So hurry and take advantage of this limited offer while there is still time.

> 本次特別折扣僅限於 6 月 30 日以前的訂購者。所以，趁現在還來得及，趕緊把握此次有限的機會。

 提示 避免用過分誇飾的文字，如 **totally fantastic**（絕佳的）、**truly awesome**（真了不起）、**extraordinary**（非凡的）、**incredible**（難以置信的）、**astounding**（異常的）。

銷售信範例

以下是依照興趣、渴望、說服和行動四要點寫成的銷售信。

17.1　訴諸實惠

→ p.168

Dear Mr Reading

興趣 — Have you ever thought how much time your typist wastes in taking down your dictation? It can be as much as a third of the time spent on correspondence. Why not record your dictation – on our Stenogram – and she can be doing other jobs while you dictate?

渴望 — You will be surprised at how little it costs. For 52 weeks in the year your <u>Stenogram</u> works hard for you, and you can never give it too much to do – all for less than an average month's salary for a secretary! It will take dictation anywhere at any time – during lunch-hour, in the evening, at home – you can even dictate while you are travelling or away on business. Simply post the recorded messages back to your secretary for typing.

說服 — The <u>Stenogram</u> is efficient, reliable, time-saving and economical. Backed by our international reputation for reliability, it is in regular use in thousands of offices all over the country. It gives superb reproduction quality with every syllable as clear as a bell. It is unbelievably simple to use – just slip in a preloaded cassette, press a button, and it is ready to record your dictation, interviews, telephone conversations, reports, instructions or whatever. Nothing could be simpler! And with our unique after-sales service contract you are assured lasting operation at the peak of efficiency.

行動 — Some of your business friends are sure to be using our <u>Stenogram</u>. Ask them about it before you place an order and we are sure they will back up our claims. If you prefer, return the enclosed prepaid card and we will arrange for our representative to call and arrange a demonstration for you. Just state the day and time that will be most convenient for you.

Yours sincerely

17.2　訴諸效率

→ p.169

Dear Mr Wood

興趣 —— Reports from all over the world confirm what we have always known – that the RELIANCE solid tyre is the fulfilment of every car owner's dream.

渴望 —— You will naturally be well aware of the weaknesses of the ordinary air-filled tyre – punctures, outer covers which split under sudden stress, and a tendency to skid on wet road surfaces, to mention only a few of motorists' main complaints. Our RELIANCE tyre enables you to offer your customers a tyre which is beyond criticism in those vital[1] qualities of road-holding and reliability.

說服 —— We could tell you a lot more about RELIANCE tyres but would prefer you to read the enclosed copies of reports from racing car drivers, test drivers, motor dealers and manufacturers. These reports really speak for themselves.

行動 —— To encourage you to hold a stock of the new solid RELIANCE, we are pleased to offer you a special discount of 3% on any order received by 31 July.

Yours sincerely

17.3　訴諸安全

→ p.169

Dear Mr Goodwin

興趣 —— A client of mine is happier today than he has been for a long time – and with good reason. For the first time since he married 10 years ago he says he feels really comfortable about the future. Should he die within the next 20 years, his wife and family will now be provided for. For less than £2 a week paid now, his wife would receive £50 per month for a full 20 years, and then a lump sum of £10,000.

渴望 —— Such protection would have been beyond his reach a short time ago, but a new and novel scheme has enabled him to ensure this security for his family. The scheme does not have to be for 20 years. It can be for 15 or 10 or any other number of years. And it need not be for £10,000. It could be for much more or much less so that you arrange the protection you want.

說服 —— For just a few pounds each month you can buy peace of mind for your wife, your children and for yourself. You cannot – you dare not – leave them unprotected.

行動 —— I would appreciate an opportunity to call on you to tell you more about this scheme which so many families are finding so attractive. I shall not press you to join; I shall just give you all the details and leave the rest to you. Please return the enclosed prepaid reply card and I will call at any time convenient to you.

Yours sincerely

1.　vital：不可或缺的；必要的；基本的。

17.4　訴諸舒適

→ p.170

Dear Mrs Walker

興趣 — What would you say to a gift that gave you a warmer and more comfortable home, free from draughts, and a saving of over 20% in fuel costs?

渴望 — You can enjoy these advantages, not just this year but every year, simply by installing our SEALTITE panel system of <u>double glazing</u>.[2] Can you think of a better gift for your entire family? The enclosed brochure will outline some of the benefits which make SEALTITE the most completely satisfactory double-glazing system on the market thanks to a number of features not provided in any other system.

說服 — Remember that the panels are <u>precision-made</u>[3] by experienced craftsmen to fit your own particular windows. Remember too that you will be dealing with a well-established company which owes its success to the satisfaction given to scores of thousands of customers.

行動 — There is no need for you to make up your mind right now. First why not let us give you a free demonstration in your own home without any obligation whatsoever? If you are looking for an investment with an annual average return of over 20%, then here is your opportunity. If you post the enclosed card to reach us by the end of August, we can complete the installation for you in good time before winter sets in.

Secure your home with SEALTITE!

Yours sincerely

17.5　訴諸休閒

→ p.170

Dear Mrs Hudson

興趣 — 'Modern scientific invention is a curse to the human race and will one day destroy it,' said one of my customers recently. Rather a <u>rash statement</u>[4] and quite untrue for there are modern inventions which, far from being a curse, are real blessings.

渴望 — Our new AQUAMASTER washer is just one of them. It takes all the hard work out of the weekly wash and makes washing a pleasure. All you have to do is put your soiled clothes in, press a button and sit back while the machine does the work. It does everything – washing, rinsing and drying – and we feel it does it quicker and better than any washing machine on the market today.

說服 — Come along and see the AQUAMASTER at work in our showroom. A demonstration will take up only a few minutes of your time, but it may rid you of your dread of washing day and make life much more pleasant.

行動 — I hope you will accept this invitation and come along soon to see what this latest of domestic time-savers can do for you.

Yours sincerely

---

2. double glazing ：雙層氣密窗。
3. precision-made ：精確製成。
4. rash statement ：不加思索的鹵莽說法。

17.6 訴諸同情心

以下這封信和傳單一併寄出，希望收件人可以捐獻。

→ p.171

Dear Reader

You can walk about the house, at work, in the streets, in the country. You take this ability for granted, yet it is denied to thousands of others – those who are born crippled, or crippled in childhood by accident or illness.

It is estimated that every 5 minutes in Britain a deformed child is born or a child is crippled by accident or illness. This means that every day there could be 288 more crippled children.

Does this not strike you as unfair? Most of what is unfair in life is something we can do little about but here is one very important inequality which everyone can help with. The enclosed leaflet explains how you can help. Please read it carefully while remembering again just how lucky you are.

Yours faithfully

17.7 訴諸舒適

→ p.171

Dear Home-owner

At half the actual cost you can now have SOLAR HEATING installed in your home.

As part of our research and development scheme introduced two years ago we are about to make our selection of a number of properties throughout the country as 'Research Homes' – yours could be one of them.

The information received from selected 'Research Homes' in the past 2 years has proved that SOLAR HEATING is successful even in the most northern parts of the United Kingdom. This information has also enabled us to modify and improve our designs, which we will continue to do.

If your home is selected as one of the properties to be included in our research scheme, we will bear half the actual cost of installation.

If you are interested in helping our research programme in return for a half-price solar heating system, please complete the enclosed form and return it by the end of May. Within three weeks we will inform you if your home has been selected for the scheme.

Yours sincerely

17.8　訴諸保暖

→ p.172

Dear Madam

Thousands of people who normally suffer from the miseries of cold, damp, changeable weather wear THERMOTEX. Why? The answer is simple – tests conducted at the leading Textile Industries Department at Leeds University have shown that of all the traditional underwear fabrics THERMOTEX has the highest warmth insulating properties.

THERMOTEX has been relieving aches and pains for many years, particularly those caused by rheumatism. It not only brings extra warmth but also soothes those aches caused by icy winds cutting into your bones and chilling you to the marrow. THERMOTEX absorbs much less moisture than conventional underwear fabrics, so perspiration passes straight through the material. It leaves your skin dry but very, very warm.

Don't just take our word for it – take a good look at some of the testimonials shown in the enclosed catalogue. The demand for THERMOTEX garments has grown so much in recent years that we often have to deal with over 20,000 garments in a single day.

The enclosed catalogue is packed with lots of ways in which THERMOTEX can keep you warm and healthy this winter. Just browse through it, choose the garment you would like, and send us your completed order form – our FREEPOST address means there is even no need for a postage stamp!

Warmth and health will soon be on their way to you. If you are not completely satisfied with your purchase, return it to us within 14 days and we will refund your money without question and with the least possible delay.

Let THERMOTEX keep you warm this winter!

Yours faithfully

主動報價

這是一方主動報價，而非應對方要求才寄送的信函。寄發對象是特定的個人或少數一群人，屬於銷售信的一種，所以和銷售信有著相同的目的和基本的撰寫原則。

這類主動報價信的形式不一，包括：

◆ 提供免費的樣品。
◆ 提供含鑑賞期之試用品。
◆ 提供特定期間的特別折扣。
◆ 只要寄回卡片（通常郵資已付），就會提供宣傳小冊子、產品目錄、價目表或產品樣式等。

17.9 提供給新客戶

→ p.172

Dear Sir

We would like to send our best wishes for the success of your new shop specialising in the sale of toys. Naturally you will wish to offer your customers the latest toys – toys that are attractive, hard wearing and reasonably priced. Your stock will not be complete without the mechanical toys for which we have a national reputation.

We are sole importers of VALIFACT toys and as you will see from the enclosed price list our terms are very generous. In addition to the trade discount stated, we would allow you a special first-order discount of 5%.

We hope that these terms will encourage you to place an order with us and feel sure you would be well satisfied with your first transaction.

We will be happy to arrange for one of our representatives to call on you to ensure that you are fully briefed on the wide assortment of toys we can offer. Please complete and return the enclosed card to say when it would be convenient.

Yours faithfully

17.10 提供給固定往來客戶

→ p.173

Dear Mr Welling

We have just bought a large quantity of high quality rugs and carpets from the bankrupt stock of one of our competitors.

As you are one of our most regular and long-standing customers, we would like you to share in the excellent opportunities which our purchase provides. We can offer you mohair rugs in a variety of colours at prices ranging from £55 to £1500; also premier quality Wilton and Axminster carpeting in a wide range of patterns at 20% below current wholesale prices.

This is an exceptional opportunity for you to buy a stock of high-quality products at prices we cannot repeat. We hope you will take full advantage of it.

If you are interested please call at our warehouse to see the stock for yourself not later than next Friday 14 October. Or alternatively call our Sales Department on 0114-453 2567 to place an immediate order.

Yours sincerely

17.11 提供給新住戶

→ p.173

Dear Newcomers

Welcome to your new home! We have no wish to disturb you as you settle in but we would like to tell you why people in this town and the surrounding areas are very familiar with the name BAXENDALE.

Our store is situated at the corner of Grafton Street and Dorset Road and we invite you to visit us to see for yourself the exciting range of goods which have made us a household name.

Our well-known shopping guide is enclosed for you to browse through at your leisure. You will see practically everything you need to add to the comfort and beauty of your home.

As a special attraction to newcomers into the area we are offering a free gift worth £2 for every £20 spent in our store. The enclosed card is valid for one calendar month and it will entitle you to select goods of your own choice as your free gift.

We sincerely hope that you enjoy living in your new home.

Yours faithfully

17.12 提供示範

→ p.174

Dear Mrs Thornton

The Ideal Home Exhibition opens at Earls Court on Monday 21 June and you are certain to find attractive new designs in furniture as well as many new ideas.

The exhibition has much to offer which you will find useful, but we would like to extend our special invitation to our own display on Stand 26 where we shall be revealing our new WINDSOR range of <u>unit furniture</u>.[5]

WINDSOR represents an entirely new concept in luxury unit furniture at very modest prices and we hope you will not miss the opportunity to see it for yourself. The inbuilt charm of this range comes from the use of solid elm and beech, combined with expert craftsmanship to give a perfect finish to each piece of furniture.

I enclose two admission tickets to the Ideal Home Exhibition. I am sure you will not want to miss this opportunity to see the variety of ways in which WINDSOR unit furniture can be arranged to suit any requirements.

I look forward to seeing you there.

Yours sincerely

5.　unit furniture：以標準規格製成的家具、家具組。

這封信沒有符合前面提及的四點原則，無法激起收件人找出更多有關全球行動電話資訊的慾望。

→ p.174

這樣的引言單調、乏味，無法引人注意

風格無趣，難以引起興趣

不會喚醒收件人任何的渴望

結語無法激勵收件人採取購買行動

Dear Customers

Staying in touch is easy with Global Mobile.

We would like to tell you all about new Connect Cards. With the Connect Card you can enjoy the benefit of our network without worrying about monthly bills. This month's issue of *In Touch* magazine explains how it works. In *In Touch* you can also read about our improved international roaming services. Roam-a-round allows you to roam anywhere – take Global Mobile with you all over the world.

In Touch also explains how you can make savings when you call another GM customer, also details of our website and you can see and read about our performance at a recent Communications Exhibition. I'm sure you'll be very impressed.

Inside *In Touch* we have also included a contest for you to win things like a free subscription to our services, a free Connect Card and also some restaurant privileges.

Enjoy the magazine and we look forward to your custom continuing in the future.

Yours faithfully

Maxine Pearson
Customer Services

現在，請看以下所做的修改。

→ p.175

C* Aurora Mobile

it's important
to stay ... in touch

Dear Valued Customer

With the introduction of our new **Connect Card**, Aurora Mobile has brought a new era of convenience in mobile communications. With the **Connect Card** you can enjoy all the benefits of Aurora Mobile's leading-edge network without worrying about monthly bills. Find out how in this month's issue of **In Touch**.

In Touch also introduces you to our vastly expanded international roaming services – Roam-a-round – which allows you to roam to all corners of the globe. Inside **In Touch** you will find out why no one covers the world better than Aurora Mobile.

Many more features can be found inside **In Touch** ...

© generous savings when you call another Aurora Mobile customer
© what's new at our website
© see and read about our performance at a recent Communications Exhibition.

Inside **In Touch** we have also included an exciting contest for you to win fabulous prizes such as a free subscription to our value-added services, a free **Connect Card** worth £20 and restaurant privileges in leading restaurants.

With your continued support we have become the UK's leading network service provider. Thank you for staying with us.

Yours sincerely

Lesley Bolan (Ms)
Senior Director
Marketing, Sales and Customer Service

C Aurora Mobile, Aurora House, Temple Street, London SE1 4LL
Tel: +44(0)181 542 4444 Fax: +44(0)181 555 4444 Email: auroramobile@cfb.co.uk

檢查清單

☐ 開頭段落引起興趣。

☐ 創造對產品或服務的渴望。

☐ 如有需要，對產品做一描述。

☐ 指出好處。

☐ 強調品質與特色。

☐ 說服對方你的銷售聲明是正確的。

☐ 提供證據來支持你的主張。

☐ 說服對方採取適當的行動。

實用措詞

【開頭】

1. We are enclosing a copy of our latest catalogue and price list.
    隨函附上一份最新的產品目錄及價目表。

2. As you have placed many orders with us in the past, we would like to extend our special offer to you.
    因為您過去曾經多次向我們訂購，我們將提供給您這項特別的優惠。

3. We are able to offer you very favourable prices on some goods we have recently been able to purchase.
    我們可以針對最近買入的一些商品提供您優惠的價格。

4. We are pleased to introduce our new ... and feel sure that you will find it very interesting.
    很高興為您介紹我們新的……，相信您會對它感興趣。

5. I am sorry to note that we have not received an order from you for over ...

    很抱歉我注意到，我們已經超過（一段時間）未曾收到您的訂單了。

【結尾】

1. We hope you will take full advantage of this exceptional offer.

    希望您能夠充分利用這次特惠。

2. We feel sure you will find a ready sale for this excellent material and that your customers will be well satisfied with it.

    我們相信您會找到一個現成的銷路來銷售此一優質素材，而且您的客戶將會很滿意。

3. We should be pleased to provide a demonstration if you would let us know when this would be convenient.

    如果您可以告訴我們您方便的時間，我們樂意為您提供示範。

4. We feel sure you will agree that this product is not only of the highest quality but also very reasonably priced.

    我們相信您一定認同這項產品不僅品質卓越，價格也非常合理。

We are sorry to note that we have not received an order from you for over...

採購信函..

【譯文】

1. We hope you will take full advantage of this exceptional offer.

我們希望您充分利用這次特別優惠。

2. We feel sure you will find a ready sale for this excellent material and that your customers will be well satisfied with it.

我們確信，這種優質材料您一定會很快銷售出去，您的顧客一定會十分滿意。

3. We should be pleased to provide a demonstration if you would let us know when this would be convenient.

如果您能告訴我們何時方便，我們將很高興進行示範表演。

4. We feel sure you will agree that the product is not only of the highest quality but also very reasonably priced.

我們確信您會認為，該產品不僅質量上乘，而且價格十分合理。

宣傳品
Publicity material

新聞稿

在報紙或其他媒體上發表文章或專欄常常是必要的,而此時擬一份新聞稿也是不可避免的。新聞稿是一個宣傳或發布以下訊息的好方法:

◆ 辦公室遷移。
◆ 擴大營業。
◆ 發表新產品/服務。
◆ 高層人事異動。
◆ 人們關注的事件。

想要讓新聞稿有報導價值,內容必須包含一般大眾感興趣或是特殊的觀點,也必須以客觀的角度寫作,就好似另外有人為你寫作一般。最重要的是必須謹記,你是在提供訊息,而不只是在販賣產品而已。

18.1　宣布新店開張的新聞稿

→ p.178

℮ Turner Communications　　　Mobile Phone specialists

21 Ashton Drive
Sheffield　　　　　　　　Tel　　+44 114 2871122
S26 2ES　　　　　　　　Fax　　+44 114 2871123
　　　　　　　　　　　　Email　TurnerComm@intl.uk

參考編號 —— ST/BT

日期 —— 15 June 200—

發布日期是指在此 —— PUBLICATION DATE: Immediate
日前不可對外公布

NEW JOBS IN TURNER SUPERSTORE

引言中簡要陳述 —— Mobile phone specialists, Turner Communications, have today announced the
主要訊息　　　opening of their new store Turner's Office Supplies. More than 50 new jobs have
　　　　　　been created.

使用簡短獨立的 —— Turner Communications have established themselves as leaders in the field of
段落，納入所有　mobile communications in the UK. Roaming agreements have been set up with
必要細節　　　many countries throughout the world.

使用間隔一行方式 —— The company has now announced that it is diversifying. Their new Office Supplies
書寫新聞稿　　superstore will sell everything from stationery and office sundries to computers and
　　　　　　other office equipment. It will be situated in a prime location at Meadowhall Retail
　　　　　　Park on the outskirts of Sheffield, very close to the M1 motorway.

A grand opening ceremony is planned to take place on Monday 1 July with special
offers to the first 100 customers and a grand draw at 5.00 pm.

以結論或引述結尾 —— Sally Turner, Managing Director, said, 'We are very excited about this new office
　　　　　　superstore and feel confident that it will prove to be an overwhelming success.'

註明聯絡細節 —— Contact: Susan Gingeu, Marketing Manager, Turner Communications
（利提供更進一步
的資訊／照片）　　　　　　　　　Telephone: 0114 2871122

18.2　飯店擴建的新聞稿

→ p.179

FK/ST

14 September 200—

EMBARGO DATE: Immediate

NEW SERVICE CONCEPTS AT PAGODA SINGAPORE

Service, the magic word in today's hotel industry, gains a new perspective when the new Regency Suites wing of the Pagoda Hotel Singapore opens in early 2004.

The hotel's new upmarket product is targeted at the corporate traveller. In line with this, a range of personalised services in major areas can now be expected by the discerning traveller.

The Business Centre, a vital facility for businessmen on the move, will operate 24 hours 7 days a week. With this extension of operating hours, busy executives will enjoy the convenience of conducing business at any time of the day. Whether it is an urgent fax required at 1 am or an e-mail, fax or letter by send in the middle of the night, time is no longer an issue. The Business Centre is well equipped with a complete range of secretarial services including a comprehensive reference library, personal computer, access to the Internet, private offices and conference room with lounge.

Housekeeping and laundry services will also be available 24 hours daily. Guests arriving late at night will no longer worry about getting a suit pressed for the next morning. Requests for extra pillows, shampoo or stationery, or any other item, will be met regardless of the hour.

A professional concierge team will answer queries and provide the wealth of information often required, from dinner reservations to theatre shows, or even finding the best shoe-maker in town.

The hotel's airport representatives will not only greet guests upon arrival at the airport but also meet them during departure too. In addition to its 2 limousines, a fleet of 14 other cars are available at all times for a city tour or business trips.

With 148 Pagoda Hotels and resorts around the world, the Pagoda Singapore is positioning itself as a top deluxe hotel, making it the perfect choice for any traveller.

-end-

Contact:　　　Florence Cheung, Public Relations Manager

　　　　　　　Telephone 3432343 Extension 145.

 提示　一封平淡無趣又冗長的新聞稿最後的命運是被編輯扔進垃圾桶。

時事通訊

各部門的時事通訊（newsletter），是一個發布員工們關心的話題或事項的極佳管道，同時還能增進公司與各部門員工間的關係。有些公司會另外發行時事通訊給他們的顧客。

時事通訊可以包含下列資訊：

◆ 促銷活動。

◆ 同仁生日／結婚／逝世等消息。

◆ 退休。

◆ 運動及社會新聞。

◆ 員工投稿。

◆ 產品／服務的最新訊息。

◆ 某一特定產業的發展。

◆ 來自分公司／部門的消息。

18.3　員工通訊上的一篇文章

→ p.180

動人的標題 ——　**SUPERSTARS TEAM GAIN SECOND PLACE**

在第一段迅速
點出主要訊息 ——　The stamina and strength of 3 Global employees were put to the test when they competed in the European finals of the Tech-stars competition held in Rotterdam, Holland.

使用簡短、
有力的段落 ——　Global Holdings was invited to the European finals after winning the regional heat at Leeds and being runners-up in the British final.

要編輯時
間隔一行書寫 ——　All entrants must work with information technology in some way, and Global has entered a team every year since 1985 when they won the European final. This year's competition consisted of 8 strenuous, athletic-based events in one day, in which 3 of the 5 team members had to compete.

編寫成
有人情味的故事 ——　Unfortunately due to holiday commitments, this year's Global team entered without 2 of their top athletes, leaving John Holmes, Martin Wilson and Andrew Johnson to compete in this event. After a long day's work the team then had to face the final event, which was a 2000 metre steeplechase, and all team members performed extremely well in this.

以活潑的結論結尾 ——　The final result was that Global put in a very creditable performance and achieved second place. Well done to the team!

寫作技巧

新聞稿的寫作技巧和文章一樣：

標題（Headline）　　以一行有趣、活潑的標題勾勒出整個故事。

開頭（Opening）　　一個好的開頭段落可以抓住編輯或閱讀者的目光。將訊息主旨納入此段。

中間段（Middle）	段落簡短、具獨立性，並以第三人稱的方式書寫，就好像在與編輯在說話。牢記以下 5W： What is happening?（發生何事？） Who is involved?（誰牽涉其中？） Where is it happening?（何處發生？） When is it happening?（何時發生？） Why is it newsworthy?（為何它具新聞？）
結尾（Closing）	引用關鍵人物的話來結尾是非常有用的，也可用摘要或結論來作結尾。

18.4 宣布晚宴及舞會的文章

→ p.180

ARE YOU READY FOR THE GLOBAL DINNER AND DANCE?

The year has flown and it's time once again to get ready for the Global Annual Dinner and Dance. Put these details in your diary now:

Where?	Dynasty Suite, Shangri La Hotel
When?	Saturday 17 December 200—
What time?	7.30 pm until late

As usual there will be a 10-course Chinese dinner (we can of course cater for any special requirements). Carmen Fashions will be entertaining us with a fashion show as we eat. With lucky draws, spot prizes and after-dinner entertainment and dancing, it's sure to be a great evening that you will not want to miss.

This company-sponsored dinner dance will cost you only S$50 each. Partners pay the same price too. If it's anything like previous years' functions, you can be assured of a fabulous time. Get your registration forms from Reception or the Human Resource Department – and book early.

If you have any queries please contact:

Caroline Marshall
Human Resource Department
Extension 216
E-mail: carolinemarshall@global.com.my

 永遠吹毛求疵地看待你所寫的每一個字。

檢查清單

☐ 在新聞稿上註明發布日期（embargo/publication date），代表在該日期之前，報紙或是雜誌不能登出此篇新聞稿。

☐ 撰寫一個活潑的標題，並控制在一行以內。這麼做可以吸引編輯的注意，並為新聞稿的內容提供一個有趣的粗略印象。

☐ 用好的開頭段落來抓住編輯的注意，它包含所有關鍵細節，並直接切入重點。

☐ 中間段落保持簡潔、具獨立性，方便編輯於必要時做刪減。確定所有細節流暢連貫。

☐ 確定納入所有細節，像是何人（who）、何事（what）、何時（when）、何處（where）、為何（why），以及如何（how）。

☐ 筆觸趣味、活潑、有力。即使是表面上看似無趣的事件，也可以透過靈巧的文字化為動人、令人印象深刻的故事。

☐ 以客觀的語調書寫，彷彿你與該公司無關，而是這份報紙或雜誌在「發聲」。

☐ 中間段落使用間隔一行的編排方式。

☐ 藉著再次陳述主要訊息中令人興奮的部分來作為新聞稿的結尾。而結尾引用關鍵人物的話是非常有用的。

☐ 記得加上聯絡人姓名、網址和電話號碼。

行銷
Marketing matters

企業的成敗取決於顧客。網際網路及其他激勵人心新技術的問世，使得企業與顧客的溝通變得愈來愈重要。四、五十年前，只要產品好用，就能取信大部分的消費者，是個「賣方市場」（sellers' market），至於購買動機多半出自「需要」，而非「想要」。而今，隨著企業組織的擴展與全球化，情況已有所改觀。競爭加劇，顧客的期望也相對提高，結果是企業體悟到想要生存，就必須與顧客保持良好的互動。

找出你的群眾

在規畫與外部群眾的溝通策略時，首要之務是找出你的目標群眾。不是所有人都需要相同的資訊，所以此一步驟很重要。找到目標群眾後，才能想清楚要和他們溝通些什麼。圖表 19.1 列出一些公司可能需要面對的外部溝通群眾。

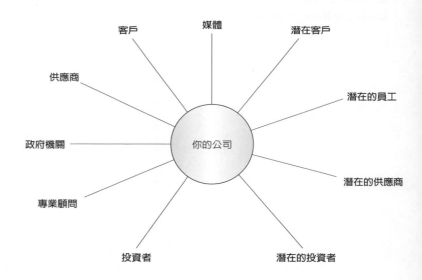

圖表 19.1　外部溝通群眾

客服為何如此重要？

愈來愈多的企業體認到必須採取積極的行動，才能讓客戶的滿意度成為他們的主要訴求。如果要在競爭激烈的市場搏鬥，要確保產品或服務的品質不只能夠符合顧客的要求，且必須是優秀、卓越的。

當前的企業應該要將重點放在與市場溝通、提供優質的客服，以及售後服務之上，如此才可以長期留住顧客的心。有更多的理由可說明優質客服的重要性：

◆ 競爭加劇。
◆ 產品雷同度高。
◆ 顧客消息更靈通。
◆ 顧客願意掏錢購買有價值的東西。
◆ 對更好支援的期待增高。
◆ 人人想要昨天的東西（卻沒時間想到未來）。

成功的客服，其最終目標是藉由提高顧客的滿意度來提升市場占有率，而所有員工都有責任協助達成這個目標。

以前的客服	現今的客服
最好的價格	最好的品質
顧客滿意度	超出顧客的期望
把工作做好	迅速做好工作
工作的勝任	真誠的聯繫與關懷

 提示 企業要生存，應該要將目標放在努力超越顧客的期望……即便他們的期待不斷地提高。

19.1　公司名稱變更

→ p.182

Dear

CHANGE OF COMPANY NAME

We are pleased to announce that further to the 100% acquisition by FGB Insurance (Asia Pacific) Holdings Limited, Ruben Insurance Pte Ltd has been renamed FGB Insurance (Singapore) Pte Ltd. General insurance operations will start using this new name from 2 August 200–.

You will continue to enjoy the same high level of service that you have previously received from Ruben Insurance Pte Ltd. You will also see additional benefits arising from the wide-ranging expertise, products and services of the FGB Group, as well as the strong financial standing that FGB brings to our 34 million customers all over the world.

With effect from 2 August 200– we will be relocating to this new address:

45 Robinson Road, #02-04-06 Wisma Supreme, Singapore 234381

Our new telephone number will be +65 63453456

Please visit our website at <u>www.fgbins.com.sg</u> for the latest information.

Your current insurance policy remains legally valid and we will honour all our obligations and liabilities under documents bearing our former corporate name.

If you have any questions at any time please call us on 63453456.

We thank you for your support and look forward to being of great service to you.

Yours sincerely

19.2　新合夥關係通知

→ p.183

Dear Client

It gives us great pleasure to announce that on 1 April we have entered into a close association with Garner Accountancy Co Ltd of 22 High Street, Cheltenham.

We have formed a new company that will practise as Garner and Barret Accounting Co Ltd, and as a result we will be moving to bigger premises at:

21 Hillington Rise
Sheffield
S24 5EJ

Telephone:　　0114 2874722
Fax:　　　　　0114 2874768
Website:　　　**www.garnerbarret.co.uk**

This association provides us with a much bigger base that will enable us to offer improved services to our customers. We will of course ensure that we retain the close personal contact and interest in our clients' affairs.

We also take this opportunity to announce that Mr Robin Wilson, who is already known to many clients, will become a partner in the new company with effect from the same date.

Yours sincerely

19.3　任命新總經理通知

→ p.183

Dear

NEW MANAGING DIRECTOR

We are pleased to announce the appointment of Richard Wilson as Managing Director with effect from 2 September 200—. His appointment follows the early retirement in July of Francis Billington due to ill health.

Richard is already known to many of you through his position as Marketing Director. He has 12 years' experience with Yangon Electrics, and he is looking forward to taking over this more challenging role in the company.

We are happy to assure you that we shall continue to provide the high-quality service for which we are proud to enjoy such a good reputation.

If you have any urgent queries please do not hesitate to contact me personally.

Yours sincerely

19.4 客戶意見調查

→ p.184

Dear

Mansor Communications are committed to providing quality service, and as such we like to keep in touch with customer needs and views on the products that we sell.

To maintain our high standard of quality products and services to you, I hope you will take a few moments to complete the enclosed questionnaire. In appreciation of your trouble, I shall be pleased to send you one of our superb Mansor Pens on receipt of your completed questionnaire.

I look forward to receiving your reply, and can assure you of our continued good service to you in the future.

Yours sincerely

19.5 價格調漲通知

→ p.184

Dear

I am sorry to inform you that, due to an unexpected price increase from our manufacturers in Europe, we have no option but to raise the prices of all our imported shoes by 4% from 6 October 200—.

Orders received before this date will be invoiced at the old price levels.

We sincerely regret the need for these increased prices. However we know you will understand that this increase is beyond our control.

We look forward to a continuing association with you, and can assure you of our continued commitment to good-quality products and service.

Yours sincerely

19.6　特殊宴會的邀請

→ p.185

Dear

10th ANNIVERSARY CELEBRATION

Omega International is commemorating its 10th year of providing quality communications equipment. We are planning to hold a special celebration in August.

As one of our major clients, we are pleased to invite you to join over 100 of our management and staff to attend this celebration. Details of the function are:

Where?	Orchid Suite, Merlion Hotel, Orchard Road
When?	Friday 27 August 200—
What time?	Cocktails 6.30 pm
	Dinner 7.30 pm

There will be many highlights during this special evening, including speeches and special awards to clients and employees, plus lucky draw prizes and a cabaret act.

Please let us know whether you will be able to attend by returning the enclosed reply form before 31 July or by telephoning Suzanne Sutcliffe on 64545432.

We do hope you will join us to help make this evening a success.

Yours sincerely

透過網路與電子郵件傳遞的客服

網際網路的使用不斷地普及，再沒有一個像網路如此難得的機會，可以讓你利用它來提升銷售量及加強客戶服務。

就顧客關係而言，全球資訊網的驚人成長帶來了一個全新的環境。當顧客為某一特定的產品或服務上網瀏覽時，他們面臨了數百種的選擇。顯而易見地，顧客會選擇的是能夠提供最佳服務、擁有完整配套的電子商務機制及卓越售後服務的公司。

本書主要是談寫作，不是教你如何使用網路來提高公司業績。然而了解你的顧客們對電子世界的期待，以及如何將網路的功能最大化，仍是必要的。

底下是一些可以讓你的線上銷售及服務更方便顧客使用，更具網路智慧的原則：

1. 容易在線上找到

曝光度是最基本的，務必確認顧客可以簡單就找到你。以下是一些基本要素：

◆ 登入搜尋引擎中的名冊。網頁行銷專家可協助你做到這一點。
◆ 與其他網頁做連結。與其他目標客群類似的網頁建立線上連結關係。
◆ 在地方性和全國性的報刊及任何商業類媒體發布新聞稿，告知大家你的網站。

2. 吸引人的視覺設計

在包裝新產品時，大家都知道要讓產品看起來既搶眼，又能迎合顧客喜好。同樣地，你必須在網站上適當地展示你的公司，帶給瀏覽者良好的第一印象，以吸引他們再度上門光顧。

3. 簡易的網頁導覽

人們通常是沒耐性的，他們希望可以快速、簡單地找到自己所要的資料。為了幫助自己及你的顧客，網頁上各區塊的名稱必須易於辨識，並給予清楚的連接說明。

4. 附上連絡網址

在每個網頁加入聯絡用的電子郵件地址，方便任何人輕易、快速地與你聯絡。

5. 提供額外的資訊

你可以在網站上提供額外資訊，給上網者一個極好的經驗：

◆ 連結更多有關你公司及產品資訊的相關文章。
◆ 增加問題集錦（FAQs），並定期更新。

◆ 附上聯絡方式及意見欄，以方便顧客寄訊息給你。要包含電話、傳真以及郵寄地址等詳細資料。

◆ 免費送贈品。訪客填妥表格，即可免費收到贈品。這是一個蒐集有價值資料的好方法。

 精簡呈現內容，避免凌亂。

透過網站行銷

廣告及直效行銷（direct marketing）可以讓潛在顧客輕易找到你。方法包括：

◆ 給所有的顧客你的電子郵件地址，並以電子郵件回答所有的問題。顧客會很感激，因為他們可以省下電話詢問的時間及費用（有時還挺貴的）。

◆ 在公司的名片、文具、工商名錄和電話簿、廣告、海報、通知函，以及所有的促銷資料上，加入網址及電子郵件地址做宣傳。

◆ 建立一個潛在客戶的網路社群。電子商務行銷的第一個挑戰是建立一個願意收取特定主題（像是產品及服務）的電子郵件收件人名冊，即所謂的「自願加入郵寄名單（opt-in）」。你可以藉著詢問潛在客戶的電子郵件地址，或是在網站上加入一個按鈕讓使用者表明有無興趣加入來建立名單。

◆ 行銷，行銷，行銷！一旦有了名單後，即可將電子郵件當成一個行銷工具，利用它來寄發有關新產品、促銷、新辦公室、內部任命、特別公告及電子報（e-newsletter）。另外，也可試著依據顧客的喜好來為每位收件人編製訊息內容。

◆ 有關定期寄發電子報，請參照 19.7。

電子郵件行銷是當前最重要、最有效的直效行銷手法。有許多軟體可協助架設資料庫、建立訊息範本，進而幫你設計一個有效的電子郵件行銷活動。你需要做的是仔細規畫內容，其餘由軟體包辦，包

括有多少人上網瀏覽、點閱連結的人數，以及其他更多的工作。電子郵件行銷活動比傳統的直效行銷郵件高出十至二十倍的效力，其結果會因活動策略、頻率及專業度而不同，更別提資料庫的起源資料了。

 成功的電子商務行銷（**e-marketing**）不只在架設一個網站，更涉及活用網路的力量，以及利用電子郵件來創造、建立和維護活絡且有利潤的線上客戶關係。

19.7 電子報摘錄

→ p.186

 SHIRLEY TAYLOR
Training and Consultancy

bringing out the best in you

Shirley Says

Greetings!

E-Newsletter Issue 2
December 2002

Shirley Says

First of all, a huge **thank you** to all who wrote to me after receiving my first e-newsletter. It was fantastic to receive such a great response, and to know you enjoyed the first issue.

Special thanks to all those who wrote in with suggestions for a name for my e-newsletter. There were so many suggestions – including Wise Words from the Wise One (thanks for that!), Cool Shirley, Shirley's Tete-a-Tete and Shirl's Whirl'd (very clever, that one!) I chose **Shirley Says** because it seemed simple, brief and straight to the point – rather like our business writing should be these days.

This month I'm pleased to introduce the new <u>Links to Learning</u> channel on my website. Every month I will be adding new pages so that you can learn more about good business writing skills.

I hope you enjoy this month's e-newsletter, and don't forget to write to me at <u>news@shirleytaylor.com</u> with your comments.

Shirley

It's official!
My e-newsletter now has a name. Here I am raising a toast to René Patat from ABN AMRO Bank in Sydney, Australia who suggested the name **Shirley Says.** Congratulations, René.

營運計畫書
Business plans

營運計畫書的組成要素
Components of a business plan

檢查清單
Checklist

當你在籌組新公司或是邀人投資時，你需要擬定一份營運計畫書（business plan），界定出公司的業務範圍，並說明經營模式及目標。具體且有組織的指出公司各項資訊的營運計畫書，就像是一家公司的履歷表。

營運計畫書有兩個主要訴求：

1. 提供詳細計畫，以協助新事業的成長。
2. 讓投資者相信你及這家公司是值得他們投資的。

營運計畫書的組成要素

在撰寫營運計畫書時，儘可能閱讀類似範例是有幫助的。這並不困難，因為網路上有很多網站有提供各類公司的營運計畫書範本，而大部分範本都包含了以下數個要件：

1. 執行概要（Executive summary）

這是營運計畫書的第一個部分，顧名思義整個計畫的簡要提綱。在這部分中你應當說明：

◆ 公司的本質。
◆ 你所提供的產品／服務。
◆ 產品／服務的特色為何？
◆ 經營團隊是哪些人？
◆ 你需要多少錢？用於何處？

大多數的人只閱讀此部分，所以你的執行概要必須要有振奮人心的效果，凸顯出公司及經營團隊的獨特性。

2. 目錄（Table of contents）

試著將目錄保持在一頁之內，列出計畫中的每一件事以及頁碼。

3. 公司描述（Company description）

◆ 如何著手？
◆ 公司如何發展？
◆ 提供過去的銷售數據、獲利及其他重要資訊。
◆ 公司目前的進展爲何？
◆ 未來有何計畫？

4. 產品／服務（Products/Services）

站在投資者的立場問自己：在拿錢投資一家公司之前，你會想要知道什麼資訊？問題包括：

◆ 你提供什麼產品或服務？
◆ 你的產品或服務有何特色？
◆ 它如何改善人們的生活？
◆ 你需要何種設備？

5. 市場分析（Market analysis）

列出你所有已經做的研究和調查，像是銷售流通問題、政府規章、技術機會、產業特性及趨勢、預估發展、顧客行爲、搭配的產品／服務等等。

6. 行銷計畫（Marketing plan）

在探討過市場面之後，你必須說明你及你的經營團隊要如何攻占市場。列出你將採取的步驟，以確保顧客知道你的產品／服務，以及顧客爲什麼會在競爭產品中選擇它們的理由。列出所有你會使用的策略，從花費最便宜到最貴的。

7. 營運計畫（Operations plan）

這是營運計畫的基本要素。對於公司運作所牽涉的地點、實體部分、需要的設備、員工需求等事項，都必須提出精確的資訊。

8. 財務計畫（Financial plan）

財務計畫中必須包含銷售預測、損益表、現金流量預估、資產負債表等細部資料。

9. 管理（Management）

列出管理公司的細節，包括董事會的成員、各個部門由誰管理及理由為何。

10. 附錄（Appendices）

附錄中可以包含經營團隊的簡歷、促銷資料、產品的圖片及說明、詳細財務資料等等。

關於營運計畫書的範本，請參考 **www.bplans.com**

 現今的商業寫作講求簡單、精確及有條理，也就是逗點愈少愈好。

檢查清單

☐ 閱讀大量的營運計畫書範例。只要連上任何一個搜尋引擎，就可以找到很多實用的網頁。

☐ 翻翻書櫃。很多書籍都提供如何撰寫營運計畫書的優秀、詳細建議。

☐ 不要等到最後一分鐘才動筆。如果你有一些想法，那麼一個堅實的規畫，可以讓你更有系統地陳述你所有的想法。

☐ 將重點放在凸顯長處而非獨創性。投資者通常會聚焦在經營團隊有哪些優勢更勝於原創性。

☐ 儘可能的簡潔。營運計畫書基本上屬於長篇文件，可能在 40 至 60 頁之間。

☐ 集中焦點。忠於基本事實，刪除多餘的廢話。

☐ 在編排上花點心思。活用標題、色彩明暗、表格、條列，以及各類圖形等，增添版面的活潑度。

☐ 適當地包裝營運計畫書，但不必花費大筆金錢用昂貴的皮革來裝訂。投資者希望的是易讀且可平放在桌上的計畫書。

☐ 編輯、編輯、編輯。將內容做對了，就達到你想要的結果。

☐ 小心地校對執行概要。這是最重要的部分，確定它是令人興奮、有趣且正確無誤的。大家應該都會閱讀它的內容，同時想要知道更多的資訊。

會議文件
Meetings documentation

生意往來經常需要開會，一場有效率的會議提供了分享資訊、提出建議、做出建議、提案與決議，以及得到即時回應的機會，是溝通上的一項利器。

公告與議程

任何會議的成功都仰賴基本的準備工作。確保所有的開會用文件均按適當順序排列是其中一項。公告與議程通常置於同一份文件，上半部放公告，內容包括會議型態、地點、日期、時間等詳細資料。至於議程則列出會議中要討論的主題。

公告與議程需在召開會議之前寄發，這點很重要。如此所有的與會者才可以事先知道討論的主題，並據此做必要的準備。

21.1 詢問有無其他議程的備忘錄

→ p.188

MEMORANDUM

To   Departmental Heads

以平常方式呈現 —— From Steven Broom, Administration Manager
備忘錄的標題

Ref   SB/ST

Date   2 July 200—

說明會議的名稱 —— OPERATIONS MEETING – 14 JULY
及日期

詳列會議的地點、 —— The next Operations Meeting will be held in the Conference Room at 1000 hours
時間及日期　　　on Monday 14 July.

Follow-up items from our last meeting which will be included under Matters Arising are:

提及已列入 ——
議程中的議題
- New brochure (Suzanne Sutcliffe)
- Annual Dinner and Dance (Mandy Lim)

對於額外要討論 —— If you wish to add any further items to the agenda please let me know before 8
的議題，訂出　　July.
提交期限

21.2　包含議程的備忘錄

→ p.189

MEMORANDUM

To   Departmental Managers

From   Steven Broom, Administration Manager

Ref   SB/ST

Date   2 July 200—

OPERATIONS MEETING

The next monthly Operations Meeting will be held in the Conference Room at 1000 hours on Monday 14 July 200—.

AGENDA

1 Apologies for absence

2 Minutes of last meeting

3 Matters arising from the Minutes

    3.1   New brochure (Suzanne Sutcliffe)

    3.2   Annual Dinner and Dance (Mandy Lim)

4 New branches (Suzanne Sutcliffe)

5 Far East Trip (Sally Turner)

6 European Telecommunications Conference (John Stevens)

7 5th Anniversary Celebrations (Suzanne Sutcliffe)

8 Any other business

9 Date of next meeting

以平常方式呈現備忘錄的標題

確認有關地點、日期及時間等細節

出「議程」一字

項為一般事項，應列入每次議程

特別事項，只在這個會議中討論

最後兩項也是一般事項

21.3 公告與議程

→ p.190

公司名稱 —— ✆ **Turner Communications**

會議標題 —— **OPERATIONS MEETING**

公告部分：
列出會議的地點、
時間及日期 —— The monthly Operations Meeting will be held in the Conference Room at 10.00 hours on Monday 14 July 200—

AGENDA

1 Apologies for absence

以一般事項開頭 —— 2 Minutes of last meeting

3 Matters arising from the Minutes

    3.1   New brochure (Suzanne Sutliffe)

    3.2   Annual Dinner and Dance (Mandy Lim)

特別事項
（用括弧註明全名）—— 4 New branches (Suzanne Sutcliffe)

5 Far East Trip (Sally Turner)

6 European Telecommunications Conference (John Stevens)

7 5th Anniversary Celebrations (Suzanne Sutcliffe)

最後的一般事項 —— 8 Any other business

9 Date of next meeting

ST/BT

會議記錄

會議記錄（minute）是將開會的過程做成書面記錄。準備一份正確的書面記錄是必要的，不但要發給那些參加會議的人，也要發給沒參加會議的人。會議記錄應該使用過去式，並以第三人稱及引述方式來書寫。

會議記錄的種類

逐字記錄

這種會議記錄主要是用於法院的報告，每一件事都需要逐字逐句地記下來。

21.4　決議式會議記錄

只記錄會中得出的主要結論，而不記錄討論過程。通常用於年度大會（AGM）及其他法定會議。最重要的是措詞正確地寫下所通過的決議。

→ p.190

> **PURCHASE OF PHOTOCOPIER**
>
> The Company Secretary submitted a report from the Administration Manager containing full details of the trial of the AEZ photocopier.
>
> **IT WAS RESOLVED THAT** the AEZ photocopier be purchased at a cost of £11,500.

21.5　敘述式會議記錄

這類記錄是將會中的所有討論、收到的報告、所做的決議，以及將採取的行動，做個簡潔的摘要。

→ p.191

> **PURCHASE OF PHOTOCOPIER**
>
> The Company Secretary submitted a report from the Administration Manager containing full details of the trial of the AEZ photocopier. The machine had been used for a period of 4 weeks in the Printing Room. Its many benefits were pointed out, including reduction/enlarging features and collating. After discussion it was agreed that such a machine would be extremely valuable to the company.
>
> The Company Secretary was asked to make the necessary arrangements for the photocopier to be purchased at the quoted price of £11,500.

21.6 會議記錄

→ p.191~192

AURORA HOLDINGS plc

WELFARE COMMITTEE

MINUTES OF A MEETING OF THE WELFARE COMMITTEE HELD IN THE CHAIRMAN'S OFFICE ON TUESDAY 21 OCTOBER 200– AT 1630.

PRESENT: Eileen Taylor (Chairman)
Jim Cage
Robert Fish
Ellen McBain
Wendy Sheppard
Georgia Thomas
Will Thomas

1   APOLOGIES FOR ABSENCE

Apologies were received from Anthony Long who was attending a business conference.

2   MINUTES OF LAST MEETING

The minutes had already been circulated and the Chairman signed them as a correct record.

3   MATTERS ARISING

Will Thomas reported that he and Georgia had visited Reneé Simpson in hospital on 16 October to deliver the committee's basket of flowers and good wishes for a speedy recovery. Reneé said she hopes to return to work on Monday 4 November and will be able to attend the next committee meeting.

4   STAFF RESTAURANT

Jim Cage distributed copies of the accounts for the half year ending 31 July. He pointed out that a profit of £1300 was made over the first 6 months of the year. He suggested that some of this be used to buy a new coffee machine as the present one is old and unreliable. It was agreed that he would obtain some estimates and discuss this further at the next meeting.

5   WASHROOM FACILITIES

Mr Taylor announced that several complaints had been received about the female toilets on the second floor. He had investigated the complaints and agreed that the need upgrading. Several locks were reported to be faulty, plus chipped tiles and poor decoration.

Miss McBain volunteered to arrange for some local workmen to provide an estimate on the cost of repairs and to report back at the next meeting.

（接下頁）

6 STUDY LEAVE FOR YOUNG TRAINEES

Mr Robert Fish reported that examinations would be held in December for the company's trainees who presently attend evening courses at Cliff College. He suggested that they should be allowed 2 weeks' study leave prior to their examination.

The Chairman pointed out that it was not within the committee's power to make this decision. She advised Mr Fish to write formally to the Board of Directors asking them to include this item on the agenda of the November Board Meeting. An answer should be obtained before the next meeting.

7 CHRISTMAS DINNER AND DANCE

Miss Wendy Sheppard passed around sample menus which had been obtained from hotels. After discussion it was agreed that arrangements should be made with the Marina Hotel for Saturday 21 December. Miss Sheppard agreed to make all the necessary arrangements.

8 ANY OTHER BUSINESS

There was no other business.

9 DATE OF NEXT MEETING

It was agreed that the next meeting would be held on Wednesday 20 November at 2000.

(Chairman)

(Date)

ET/ST
30 June 200—

  提示　記得在會議記錄中使用過去式及引述方式。

用 **was** 不用 is
用 **would be** 不用 will be
用 **had been** 不用 has been
用 **were** 不用 are

會議用語

底下資料是經 Desk Demon（英國首屈一指的祕書資源、資訊及社群）的同意，節錄自其網站 www.deskdemon.co.uk。

Ad hoc：特別的（地）
源自拉丁語，意思是「為了……的目的」，例如設立一個特別小組委員會來組織某件事。

Adjourn：延期
將會議延至更晚的日期。

Adopt minutes：通過會議記錄
在獲得會員的同意並由主席簽字後，會議記錄就算「通過」了。

Advisory：諮詢
提供忠告或建議，不是採取行動。

Agenda：議程
就會議中要討論的項目擬定計畫。

AGM：年度大會（Annual General Meeting）
通常所有的會員都合乎參加資格。

Apologies：致歉
對於無法參加會議事先致歉。

Articles of Association：公司章程
公司法所要求的章程，用於管理公司活動。

Attendance list：出席名冊
有些委員會以傳遞的方式來簽名，作為出席的記錄。

Bye-laws：內部規則
規範一個組織活動的規則。

Casting vote ：決定票
贊成票和反對票相等時，按照常規，有些委員會的主席可以使用「決定票」來做成決議。

Chairman ：主席
領導者或是授權召開會議的人。

Chairman's agenda ：主席議程
以委員會的議程為主，但加上註釋。

Collective responsibility ：集體責任
所有委員會的成員同意遵守多數人決定的協議。

Committee ：委員會
被選出或被任命的一群人，以開會方式來處理議定的業務，並向更高層的組織報告。

Consensus ：一致合意（達成共識）
取得全體贊同，但未進行正式的投票。

Constitution ：章程
一套用來規範組織、團體活動的法規。

Convene ：召集（會議）

Decision ：決議
決議式會議記錄（resolution minutes），有時候也稱為 decision minutes。

Eject ：逐出
將某人驅離（如果必要，可動用武力）會場。

Executive ：執行者
有職權依據決議來行動者。

Extraordinary meeting：特別大會
全體會員召開會議，共同商討影響全體會員的重大議題，稱之為特別大會（Extraordinary General Meeting）。除此以外，也可以說是一個針對特別目的而召開的非例行性會議。

Ex officio：依據職權
依照職務而被賦予的權利。

Guillotine：截止辯論以付表決法
打斷辯論，通常是在議會中。

Honorary post：名譽職位
未給薪的職務，如名譽祕書長（Honorary Secretary）。

Information, point of：在會議中對相關的事項引起注意。

Intra vires：個人或法人權限內的
在委員會或會議的職權內探討、執行。

Lie on the table：擱置或延期提議案
將事項留待下次會議再予以考慮（參考 Table 一字）。

Lobbying：遊說
在開會前，尋求會員支持、贊同的做法。

Minutes：會議記錄
會議的書面記錄；決議式會議記錄只有在達成決議時才會記錄，而敘述式會議記錄（narrative minutes）則是提供決議過程的記錄。

Motion：動議；提議
正在會議中討論的提案。

Mover：發起人；提案人
以提議的名義而發言的人。

Nem con：無異議地；全體一致地
源自拉丁語，按照字面上的解釋是「沒有人反對」。

Opposer：反對者；提出異議者
反對提議而發言的人。

Order, point of：針對違反規則或程序引起注意。

Other business：上次會議所留下的議題，或是在會議的主體之後所要討論的議題。

Point of order：程序問題
如果會議沒有遵守程序或規則，則可能因「程序問題」而被中斷。

Proposal：提議；提案
在會議舉行之前，提交討論（通常是書面）的議題。

Proxy：代理人；代理權（代理委託書）
按照字面上的解釋是「以其他人的名義」──代理投票（proxy vote）。

Quorum：法定最低人數
會議要具合法性才能召開，與會者必須達一定人數。

Refer back：將議案交回以進行更進一步考慮。

Resolution：決議
提議（motion）被通過或採納，稱為決議。在會議達成決議時使用。

Seconder：贊同者；附議者
藉由「贊成」（seconding）來支持提議者（proposer）的人。

Secretary：書記；祕書；幹事
委員會的職員，負責委員會內部及外部的行政事務。

Secret ballot ：無記名投票
印有候選人名單而投票人不記名的選票（祕密投票）。

Shelve ：擱置；暫緩考慮
放棄沒有被贊同的提議。

Sine die ：無限期地
源自拉丁語，按字面的解釋是「沒有日期」，也就是無限期的意
思，例如：「無限期休會」（adjourned sine die）。

Standing committee ：常任委員
無任期限制的委員。

Standing orders ：會議常規
管理公部門會議的程序規則。

Table ：提出（議案等）；把……列入議程。
提出記錄的文件或預定表。

Taken as read ：為節省時間，假定會員們已經讀過會議記錄。

Treasurer ：司庫（會計；出納員）
委員會幹事，負責委員會的財務資料檔案以及各項交易。

Ultra vires ：超越權限
超越會議考量權之外。

Unanimous ：全體一致的；一致同意的；無異議的
全體一致同意。

人事
Personnel

求職函

基本上，求職函是推銷信的一種。你要試著推銷自己，所以你的求職函必須是：

◆ 能引起注意的良好寫作風格。

◆ 讓人感興趣的資歷。

◆ 善用經歷和推薦函的說服力。

◆ 引導雇主採取你期望的行動——得到面試機會，並爭取到這份工作。

求職函的風格

除非徵人啓事中註明你必須用手寫，或者應徵的工作完全是書記或簿記性質，否則求職函應該用打字的。一封編排良好、容易閱讀的求職函能夠馬上引起注意，創造有利的第一印象。

有些應徵者的求職函篇幅很長，包含很多有關教育、經歷和資格的資訊。這是很不智的做法，反而會不容易找到所需資訊，且看起來像是在自吹自擂。

較好的方式是寫一封短信（covering letter）來應徵該項職務，並說明履歷表（curriculum vitate or resumé）已隨函附上。履歷表上應詳列個人背景、教育、取得資格和經歷，而這些就不必於短信中重複提及。

遵循重點

◆ 記住，求職函的目的在於取得面試機會，而不是獲得工作。

◆ 確保你的求職函看起來簡潔又夠吸引人，有別於其他的求職函。

◆ 精簡。儘可能用最少的文字來提供所有相關資訊。

◆ 誠懇。語氣友善但又不過分熱絡。

◆ 勿誇大其詞或給人老王賣瓜之嫌，簡單合宜地表達自己的能力即可。

◆ 不要暗示自己是因為厭倦目前工作才來應徵這份工作。

◆ 如果你在乎薪水，建議先不要寫出期望待遇，只需提及你目前的薪資是多少。

◆ 在寄出求職函時不要附上原始推薦函，只需附上影本，面試時再提出正本。

檢查清單

忙碌的雇主沒有太多時間去瀏覽冗長、雜亂的求職函，因此應該避免提及收件人可能不感興趣的內容，即使這些資訊對自己很重要。另外就是略過一般資訊，只提較具體的部分，例如與其說「我在一家知名企業有多年的工程師相關經驗」，不如直接告訴對方你工作了多少年、有哪些工作經驗，以及服務公司的名稱。

寫完求職函後要仔細重讀一遍，並試著問自己以下問題：

(a) 讀起來像是一封好的商業書信嗎？

(b) 開頭第一段是否能夠引起雇主興趣，促使其往下閱讀？

(c) 信中是否提及你真正感興趣的是該項職務與工作內容？

(d) 陳述是否合乎邏輯，同時簡短扼要？

如果以上問題的答案都是肯定的，那麼就可以安心的將求職函寄出去了。

22.1 應徵廣告上的職位

(a) 求職函

如果你的求職函是回應報紙或雜誌上的廣告，那麼應該在開頭段落或是標題中提及這個部分。

→ p.194

寄件人的地址置於 — 信件的右上角

26 Windsor Road
CHINGFORD
CH4 6PY

15 May 200—

在完全齊頭式 — 的書信中，所有其他細節必須靠左對齊（日期也可以寫在右邊）

Mrs W R Jenkinson
Personnel Manager
Leyland & Bailey Ltd
Nelson Works
CLAPTON
CH5 8HA

Dear Mrs Jenkinson

PRIVATE SECRETARY TO MANAGING DIRECTOR

提到該職務 — 及從何處得知

I was interested to see your advertisement in today's *Daily Telegraph* and would like to be considered for this post.

概述目前職務與 — 工作內容

I am presently working as Private Secretary to the General Manager at a manufacturing company and have a wide range of responsibilities. These include attending and taking minutes of meetings and interviews, dealing with callers and correspondence in my employer's absence, and supervising junior staff, as well as the usual secretarial duties.

說明自己為何 — 有興趣應徵該職務會有一些幫助

The kind of work in which your company is engaged particularly interests me, and I would welcome the opportunity it would afford to use my language abilities which are not utilised in my present post.

如果可以，附上履 — 歷表和數封推薦函

A copy of my curriculum vitae is enclosed with copies of previous testimonials.

合適的結尾 —

I hope to hear from you soon and to be given the opportunity to present myself at an interview.

Yours sincerely

Jean Carson

JEAN CARSON (Miss)

Encs

(b) 履歷表

履歷表應該包含所有個人基本資料、教育、取得資格和工作經歷等資訊。但長度不宜超過兩頁、且儘量用標題和欄位加以分類，在呈現上要力求吸引人，以便在眾多履歷中脫穎而出。

→ p.195-196

CURRICULUM VITAE

NAME	Jean Carson
ADDRESS	26 Windsor Road Chingford Essex CH4 6PY
TELEPHONE	020 8529 3456
DATE OF BIRTH	26 May 1965
NATIONALITY	British
MARITAL STATUS	Single

在開頭就列出個人細節

EDUCATION

列出全日制或半日制的受教課程

19— to 19—	Woodford High School
19— to 19—	Bedford Secretarial College (Secretarial Course)

QUALIFICATIONS

列出完整的資格(不只是 4A level's)

GCE* A Level	English Language	19—
	Mathematics	19—
	Spanish	19—
	French	19—
GCE O Level	Biology	19—
	Philosophy	19—
	Commerce	19—
	History	19—
LCCI	Private Secretary's Diploma	19—
LCCI 3rd level	Text Production	19—
	Audio	19—
	Shorthand	19—
	English for Business	19—

（接下頁）

RSA**	140 wpm Shorthand	19—
PITMAN	160 wpm Shorthand	19—

指出任何具體 — **SPECIAL AWARDS**
的成就

RSA Silver medal for shorthand 140 wpm
Governors' prize for first place in college examinations

依時間序描述 — **WORKING EXPERIENCE**
目前工作及各
項工作資歷

April 200— to present	Personal Secretary to General Manager	Reliance Cables Vicarage Road Leyton LONDON E10 5RG
Sept 19— to March 19—	Shorthand Typist	Bains, Hoyle & Co Solicitors 60 Kingsway LONDON WC2B 6AB

興趣、嗜好 — **INTERESTS**
或其他相關資訊

Music; Languages; Hockey; Golf; Swimming

REFEREES

至少提供兩位 — 1 Dr R G Davies
推薦人，如前雇主　　　Principal
或老師等　　　　　　Bedford Secretarial College
　　　　　　　　　Righton Road
　　　　　　　　　Bedford MH2 2BS

2 Ms W Harris
　 Partner
　 Bains, Hoyle & Co
　 60 Kingsway
　 London WC2B 6AB

3 Mr W J Godfrey OBE***
　 Managing Director
　 Reliance Cables
　 Vicarage Road
　 Leyton
　 London E10 5RG

提出此份履歷的 — June 200—
日期（月／年）

* GCE：General Certificate of Education（英國）普通教育證書

** RSA：Royal Society of Arts（英國）皇家藝術學會

*** OBE：Officer of the Order of the British Empire　大英帝國官佐勳章

22.2 透過介紹的求職信

有時，你是因為朋友或同事的介紹來應徵。你可在開頭段落中提及此事，這是引起注意的好方法。

→ p.197

Dear Mr Barker

Mrs Phyllis Naish, your Personnel Officer, has told me that you have a vacancy for a Marketing Assistant. I should like to be considered for this post.

As you will see from my enclosed curriculum vitae I have several A levels as well as secretarial qualifications gained during an intensive one-year course at Walthamstow College of Commerce.

I have been Shorthand Typist in the Marketing Department of Enterprise Cables Ltd for 2 years and have been very happy there, gaining a lot of valuable experience. However the office is quite small and I now wish to widen my experience and hopefully improve my prospects.

My former headmistress has written the enclosed testimonial and has kindly agreed to give further details should they be needed. If you are interested in my application my present employer has agreed to provide further information.

I am able to attend an interview at any time and hope to hear from you soon.

Yours sincerely

22.3 應徵業務經理一職

→ p.197

Dear Sir

提及該職務
及看到的廣告 — I was very interested to see your advertisement for a Sales Manager in yesterday's *Daily Telegraph* and should like to be considered for this post.

附上履歷表並
簡述工作經驗 — My full particulars are shown on my enclosed curriculum vitae, from which you will see that I have had 10 years' experience in the sales departments of two well-known companies. My special duties at Oral Plastics Ltd include the training of sales personnel, dealing with the company's foreign correspondence and organising market research and sales promotion programmes. I thoroughly enjoy
提及應徵的理由 — my work and am very happy here but feel that the time has come when my experience in marketing has prepared me for the responsibility of full sales management.

提供推薦人 — Mr James Watkinson, my Managing Director, and Ms Harriet Webb, Sales Manager of my former company, have both agreed to provide references for me: their details can be found on my curriculum vitae.

合適的結尾 — I shall be pleased to provide any further information you may need and hope I may be given the opportunity of an interview.

Yours faithfully

22.4 申請教職

這封信是一位受訓教師寄給當地的教育局長，詢問是否有合適的教師職缺。

→ p.198

Dear Sir

At the end of the present term I shall complete my one-year teacher training course at Garnett College of Education. For domestic reasons, I would like to obtain a post at a school or college in the area administered by your authority.

From my curriculum vitae which is attached you will see that I have 6 O level and 2 A level passes, as well as advanced qualifications in many secretarial subjects. I have held secretarial positions in the London area for a total of 8 years, during which time I studied for my RSA Shorthand and Typewriting Teachers' Diplomas. Having enjoyed the opportunity to teach these subjects in evening classes at the Chingford Evening Institute for 2 years, I was prompted to take up a full-time Certificate in Education at Garnett.

I like young people and get on well with them, and I am looking forward to helping them in the very practical way which teaching makes possible. If there is a suitable vacancy in your area, I hope you will consider me for it.

Yours faithfully

22.5 應徵資料實習生一職

這封信的應徵者不另附履歷表、直接在求職信中提供詳細的教育背景及取得資格。若沒有足夠的工作經驗寫成一份履歷表，這是較為有利的作法。

→ p.198

Dear Sir

I would like to apply for the post of Management Trainee in your Data Processing Department advertised today in *The Guardian*.

I obtained A level passes in Mathematics, Physics and German at Marlborough College, Wiltshire. The College awarded me an open scholarship to Queens College, Cambridge, where I obtained a first in Mathematics and a second in Physics. After leaving university last year I accepted a temporary post with Firma Hollander & Schmidt in order to improve my German and gain some practical experience in their laboratories at Bremen. This work comes to an end in 6 weeks' time.

My special interest for many years has been computer work and I should like to make it my career. I believe my qualifications in Mathematics and Physics would enable me to do so successfully.

I am unmarried and would be willing to undertake the training courses away from home to which you refer in your advertisement.

My former Housemaster at Marlborough, Mr T Gartside, has consented to act as my referee (telephone 0117 234575), as has Dr W White, Dean of Queens College, Cambridge (telephone 01246 453453). I hope that you will take up these references and grant me the opportunity of an interview.

Yours faithfully

22.6　毛遂自薦

毛遂自薦（unsolicited，直譯爲未經請求、主動提供）的求職信是最難寫的，因爲既無徵人廣告，也不是經人介紹，甚至不知道是否眞有這樣的職缺。在這種情況下，你必須試著找出與該公司有關的活動訊息，再來思考該如何於求職信中呈現你的資格及工作經歷。

→ p.199

Dear Sir

For the past 8 years I have been a Statistician in the Research Unit of Baron & Smallwood Ltd, Glasgow. I am now looking for a change of employment which would widen my experience and at the same time improve my prospects. It has occurred to me that a large and well-known organisation such as yours might be able to use my services.

I am 31 years of age and in excellent health. At the University of London I specialised in merchandising and advertising, and was awarded a PhD degree for my thesis on 'Statistical Investigation in Research'. I thoroughly enjoy working on investigations, particularly where the work involves statistics.

Although I have had no experience in consumer research, I am familiar with the methods employed and fully understand their importance in the recording of buying habits and trends. I should like to feel that there is an opportunity to use my services in this type of research and that you will invite me to attend an interview. I could then give you further information and bring testimonials.

I hope to hear from you soon.

Yours faithfully

 提示　在第一次寫信給對方時，切記要創造第一印象的機會只有一次。

推薦函

在寄出附有履歷表的求職信時，如果能附上幾份前幾位雇主的推薦函，會有一定的幫助。推薦函的開頭可以寫上 TO WHOM IT MAY CONCERN（敬啓者）。推薦函通常是由前雇主提供，正本要保留，只將影本寄給未來的可能雇主參閱。

是否一定要附推薦函，法律上並無明文規定，但是陳述的資訊必須屬實，否則推薦人可能要負法律責任，不是被應徵者告以誹謗罪（libel，即破壞名譽），就是因推薦函內容不實遭雇主控告。

任何的推薦函必須遵循以下四點原則：

1. 說明任職時間及職稱。
2. 詳細說明工作內容。
3. 描述工作態度和個人特質。
4. 以推薦做結尾。

22.7 為前任祕書所寫的正式推薦函

以下是一位工作八年的員工在接受教師訓練後，請求前雇主為她撰寫的推薦函。

→ p.199

TO WHOM IT MAY CONCERN

任職期間／職位 — Miss Sharon Tan was employed as Shorthand Typist in this Company's Sales Department when she left secretarial college in July 19—. She was promoted to my Personal Secretary in 200—.

工作內容 — Her responsibilities included the usual secretarial duties involved in such a post as well as attending meetings, transcribing minutes and supervising and advising junior secretaries.

工作態度 — Sharon used her best endeavours at all times to perform her work conscientiously and expeditiously. She was an excellent secretary, an extremely quick and accurate shorthand typist and meticulous in the layout, presentation and accuracy of her work. I cannot overstress her exceptional work rate which did not in any way detract from the very high standards she set for herself.

個人特質 — Sharon enjoyed good health and was a good time-keeper. She was very personable, friendly, sociable and quick to share in a joke. It was a great loss to both myself and the company when Sharon took up teacher training.

推薦 — In my opinion, Sharon has the necessary character, dedication and approach to be suitable for the position of personal secretary or to enter the teaching profession. I can recommend her highly and may be contacted for further information.

IAN HENLEY
Deputy Chairman

22.8 為系主任所寫的推薦函

這是為依約做滿兩年系主任後、離開該所私立學院的教員所寫的有
利推薦函。

→ p.200

TO WHOM IT MAY CONCERN

Norman Tyler has been employed by this College as Head of Business Studies from August 200— to 9 March 200—.

As well as capably handling the responsibilities for the overall administration of his department Norman ably taught Economics, Commerce and Management Appreciation to students of a wide range of ability and age groups on courses leading to Advanced LCCI examinations.

Norman is a highly competent and professional teacher whose class preparation is always thorough and meticulous. His committed approach to teaching is matched by his administrative abilities. He has made a substantial contribution to course planning, student counselling, curriculum development and programme marketing.

Norman possesses an outgoing personality and he mixes well. He makes his full contribution to a team and is popular with his students and colleagues alike.

In view of his dedication and ability I am confident that Norman will prove to be a valuable asset to any organisation fortunate enough to employ him. It is with pleasure that I recommend him highly and without hesitation.

FAISAL SHAMLAN
Principal

22.9 為同事所寫的推薦函

→ p.200

April 200—

TO WHOM IT MAY CONCERN

說明你如何
認識這個人 I have known Sonja Bergenstein for several months in her capacity as Business Development Executive of SingaJobs.com, Singapore.

As a freelance Training Consultant, I have worked with SingaJobs.com on many occasions. They have acted as my agent in marketing and promoting my 2-day workshops 'Transform your Business Writing Skills', and Sonja has been one of the team working on this.

提及一些有關工作
及職務的關鍵事項 My contact with Sonja has been mainly on the days of the workshops, when Sonja has always been well organised, helpful and friendly. She has a very sociable and pleasant personality, and she always goes the extra mile in making sure that all participants are kept happy during each workshop. She has been an expert in public relations during breaks, when it is important to mix with participants and make sure they are well looked after. When it has been necessary to address groups, Sonja has always been confident and able to express herself clearly and with interest.

針對個性及態度
提供額外的評語 Working with many different nationalities in the Singaporean scene has been no problem for Sonja. She had adapted well to the different cultures, and she has been able to mix and get on well with people from all races. From my experience, she has been very well liked and respected, a hard-working member of the team at SingaJobs.com who will be sorely missed.

以推薦做結尾 I have certainly enjoyed working with Sonja, and wish her every success in her future career, in which I am sure she will do extremely well.

SHIRLEY TAYLOR
Author and Training Consultant

有利的推薦函

即使推薦函是和求職信一併寄出，通常仍會在履歷表或是短信上註明一至兩位同意推薦者的姓名。未來的可能雇主若認為有需要，會進一步透過電話或信函向推薦人詢問更詳細的資料，像是應徵者的工作表現及性格特質等。

22.10 寫信向推薦人求證

→ p.201

Dear Mrs Lambert

提及應試者姓名 — Mr James Harvey, at present employed by you as Foreign Correspondent, has
及其應徵職務 applied to us for a similar post and has given your name as a referee.

詢問應徵者的 — I should be grateful if you would state whether his services with you have been
工作狀況 entirely satisfactory and whether you consider he would be able to accept full
responsibility for the French and German correspondence in a large and busy
department.

包括具體的 — I am aware that Mr Harvey speaks fluent French and German but I am particularly
工作能力 interested in his ability to produce accurate translations into these languages of
letters that may be dictated to him in English.

保證保密 — Any other information you can provide would be appreciated, and of course will be
treated as strictly confidential.

Yours sincerely

22.11 有利的回覆

推薦者在回信中高度推薦該名員工,且毫不猶豫地肯定該員工能夠
勝任未來的職務。

→ p.201

Dear Mr Brodie

I am pleased to be able to reply favourably to your enquiry of 6 April concerning Mr
James Harvey.

Mr Harvey is an excellent linguist and for the past 5 years has been in sole charge
of our foreign correspondence, most of which is with European companies,
especially in France and Germany.

We have been extremely pleased with the services provided by Mr Harvey. Should
you engage him you may rely upon him to produce well-written and accurate
transcripts of letters into French and German. He is a very reliable and steady
worker and has an excellent character.

We wish him success, but at the same time shall be very sorry to lose him.

Yours sincerely

22.12 謹慎的回覆

推薦者在底下這封回函中，小心翼翼地暗示該名應徵者缺乏控管部門所需的經驗。推薦者很謹慎，既不直接點出此人並不適合，也不多加贅述。

→ p.202

Dear Mr Brodie

Thank you for your letter of 6 April concerning Mr James Harvey.

Mr Harvey is a competent linguist and for the past 5 years has been employed as senior assistant in our foreign correspondence section. He has always been conscientious and hard-working. Whether he would be capable of taking full responsibility for a large and busy department is difficult to say; his work with us has always been carried out under supervision.

Should you require any further information please do not hesitate to contact me.

Yours sincerely

22.13 請求推薦人提供資訊

在這封信中，另一位雇主請求對方提供應徵者的工作表現和特質等資訊。

→ p.202

Dear Mr Jones

Mr Lionel Picton has applied to us for an appointment as Manager of our factory in Nairobi. We are leading manufacturers of engineered components used in the petrochemical industry and are looking for a qualified engineer with works manager's experience in medium or large batch production.

Mr Picton informs us that he is employed by you as Assistant Manager of your factory in Sheffield. We should be grateful for any information you can give us about his competence, reliability and general character.

Any information provided will be treated in strictest confidence.

Yours sincerely

22.14　表示贊同的回覆

→ p.202

表示收到來信
並提供背景資料

詳細說明有關
應徵者的工作、
資格及態度

結尾提出評語及
做出個人推薦

Dear Mr Gandah

Thank you for your letter of 6 August regarding Mr Lionel Picton, who has been employed by this company for the past 10 years.

Mr Picton served his apprenticeship with Vickers Tools Ltd in Manchester, followed by a 3 course for the Engineering and Work Study Diploma of the Institution of Production Engineers. He is technically well qualified and for the past 5 years has been our Assistant Works Manager responsible for production and associated activities in our Sheffield factory. In all aspects of his work he has shown himself to be hard-working, conscientious and in every way a very dependable employee.

I can recommend Mr Picton without the slightest hesitation. I feel sure that if he was appointed to manage your factory in Nairobi he would bring to his work a genuine spirit of service, which would be found stimulating and helpful by all who worked with him.

Yours sincerely

22.15　條列問題請推薦人回答

底下這封詢問信，寫信者為了解應徵者的某些特質，並確保對方能逐一回覆，特意將問題條列出來。

→ p.203

引言中說明
應徵者的姓名和
應徵的職位

條列關於應徵者
的具體問題

保證會保密

Dear Miss French

Miss Jean Parker has applied for a post as Administrator in our Sales Department. She states that she is presently employed by you and has given your name as a referee.

I should be grateful if you would answer the following questions regarding her abilities and character:

1　Is she conscientious, intelligent and trustworthy?
2　Is she capable of dealing with any difficult situations?
3　Are her keyboarding and administrative skills satisfactory?
4　Is she capable of dealing accurately with figure work?
5　Is her output satisfactory?
6　Does she get on well with her colleagues?
7　Are her health and time-keeping satisfactory?

Any information you are kind enough to provide will be treated in strict confidence.

Yours sincerely

22.16 回覆

→ p.203

Dear Mr Kingston

In reply to your letter of 15 April I have nothing to say but good about Miss Jean Parker. She has been employed as Assistant Sales Administrator in our general office for the past 2 years and I feel sure that you will find her in every way satisfactory.

In reply to each of the questions in your letter, I have no hesitation in saying that Miss Parker meets all these requirements.

We will be sorry to lose Miss Parker, but realise that her abilities demand wider scope than is possible at this company.

Yours sincerely

22.17 有利的推薦函——為以前的學生做推薦

→ p.204

Dear Mrs Thompson

MISS CAROLINE BRADLEY

In reply to your enquiry of 3 June I welcome the opportunity to support Miss Bradley's application for the post of your Marketing Assistant.

Miss Bradley was a student at this college during the year 200– to 200–. Admission to this intensive one-year course is restricted to students with good school-leaving qualifications. The fact that Miss Bradley was admitted to the course is in itself evidence of excellent academic ability. Upon completing her course she was awarded the title 'Student of the Year', being the student gaining highest qualifications over the one-year course.

In all other respects Miss Bradley's work and attitude were entirely satisfactory, and I can recommend her to you with every confidence. I feel sure that if she was appointed she would perform her duties diligently and reliably.

Yours sincerely

22.18 有利的推薦函──為部門經理做推薦

→ p.204

Dear Mr Lee

In reply to your letter of yesterday Mr Leonard Burns is both capable and reliable. He came to us 5 years ago to take charge of our Hardware Department.

Leonard knows the trade thoroughly and does all the buying for his department with notable success. I know that for some time he has been looking for a similar post with a larger store. While we would be sorry to lose his services, we would not wish to stand in the way of the advancement which could be offered by a store such as yours.

Yours sincerely

22.19 應徵者給推薦人的感謝信

那些願意提供推薦函的人士自然樂於知道應徵者的進展與是否順利獲得該份工作。應徵者應將結果告知推薦人,並感謝他們的支持。

→ p.204

Dear Mr Freeman

I would like to thank you for supporting my application for the post as Manager of the Barker Petrochemical Company in Nairobi.

I know that the generous terms in which you wrote about me had much to do with my being offered the post and I am very grateful to you for the reference you provided for me.

Your help and encouragement have always been much appreciated and this will always be remembered.

Yours sincerely

實用的推薦函用語

◆ Mr John Smith was employed by this company from ... to ...
約翰・史密斯自……到……（期間）受雇於本公司

◆ I am very glad of this opportunity to support Miss Lim's application for a position in your company.
我很高興有這個機會支持林小姐申請貴公司的一項職務。

◆ Mr Johnson has proven to be an efficient, hard-working, trustworthy and very personable employee.
強生先生已證明是一位有效率、工作努力、值得信賴，以及人品佳的員工。

◆ Sharon used her best endeavours at all times to perform her work conscientiously.
莎朗總是盡最大的努力謹慎對自己的工作負責。

◆ In my opinion, Harrison has the necessary character, dedication and approach to be suitable for the position of personal secretary.
以我的觀點，哈里遜擁有適合擔任個人祕書的必要人格特質、專心努力及方法。

◆ Nigel has an outgoing personality and he mixes well.
耐吉個性外向並擅於交際。

◆ He makes his full contribution to a team and is popular with his colleagues and clients.
他全心貢獻團隊，而且在同事與客戶間很受歡迎。

◆ Geetha made a substantial contribution to the work of the Sales Department and always performed her work in a businesslike and reliable manner.
姬瑟對業務部門的工作有非常重要的貢獻，她總是以認真及可靠的態度工作。

◆ It was great loss to both myself and the company when Miss Turner moved abroad.
當透納小姐搬到海外時，對我及公司來說都是一大損失。

- We were very sorry to lose Miss Fisher and she will be greatly missed.
  我們很遺憾費許小姐的離開，她令人懷念。
- It is with great pleasure that I recommend Martha Tan for this position in your company.
  很高興在此推薦瑪莎‧湯應徵貴公司這項職務。
- I can recommend Mr Cheong without hesitation, and know you will find him an excellent addition to your staff.
  我毫不遲疑地推薦章先生，你會發現他是一位優秀的員工。
- We were very sorry to lose Miss Franks and are pleased to recommend her highly and without hesitation.
  我們很遺憾失去了法蘭克小姐，但我們也很樂意在此毫不猶豫地推薦她。

不利的推薦函

對於表現不盡理想的員工，前任或現任雇主不太會為其撰寫推薦函，而只是讓員工將他們的姓名提供給對方作為推薦人之用。遇到這類請求，較安全的做法是透過電話或親自向詢問者傳達一些不利的評語，而不要用寫的。如果一定要用寫的，必須小心措詞，並且有所節制，儘可能提供愈少的細節愈好。萬一被未授權的人看到這些評語，總是危險的。

22.20　不利的推薦函

→ p.205

近似這樣的推薦函幾乎令該員工無法在其他地方謀得好職務。但如果寫信者相信自己所言，就不必害怕將信寄出。

Dear Ms Samson

Thank you for your letter of 18 January regarding Mr Ian Bell.

Mr Bell was employed as Clerk in this company from February to October last year. We released him because his work fell below the standards we normally require. His punctuality also left a lot to be desired and he had a disturbing influence on other members of our staff.

Mr Bell is an intelligent young man and with the exercise of a little self-discipline he could do well. However, from my personal experience I am afraid that I cannot conscientiously recommend him.

Yours sincerely

22.21 另一封不利的推薦函

→ p.205

22.20 的信函對應徵者的不適任相當明顯，然而較安全且明智的做法是使用更一般的措詞，少做具體的批評，如同這封信所示。

Dear Ms Samson

I am replying to your letter of 18 January in which you enquire about Mr Ian Bell.

This young man was a member of our clerical staff from February to October last year but I am sorry to say that we did not find him suitable. It is quite possible that he may do better in another office.

Yours sincerely

面試函

當很多人寫信來應徵一項職缺時，不太可能所有應徵者都能得到面試的機會。在此情況下，公司會挑出合適的人選來參與面試。至於未能獲得面試機會的人，公司也應該寄封信告知對方。

22.22 邀請應徵者參加面試

邀請應徵者參加面試的信函，首先是答謝對方來函應徵，接著告知面試日期、時間和地點，以及要找誰報到。另外也常要求應徵者確認是否前來面試。

→ p.206

Dear Miss Wildman

SENIOR SECRETARY TO TRAINING MANAGER

Thank you for your application for this post.

You are invited to attend for an interview with me and Mrs Angela Howard, Training Manager, on Friday 29 May at 3.30 pm.

Please let me know either by letter or telephone whether this appointment will be convenient for you.

Yours sincerely

22.23　應徵者確認參加面試

→ p.206

Dear Mrs Graham

SENIOR SECRETARY TO TRAINING MANAGER

Thank you for your letter inviting me to attend for interview on Friday 29 May at 3.30 pm.

I shall be pleased to attend and look forward to meeting you and Mrs Howard.

Yours sincerely

22.24　致函未能參加面試的應徵者

如果應徵者未被列在面試名單上，回函的措詞必須謹慎，避免冒犯應徵者或引發負面情緒。

→ p.206

Dear

Thank you for your application for the post of Senior Secretary to the Training Manager.

We have received many applications for this post. I am afraid that your experience and qualifications do not match all our requirements closely enough so we cannot include you on our shortlist for this post.

I realise you will be disappointed but would like to thank you for the considerable time and effort you put into preparing your application. You have a lot of useful experience and I am sure that you will soon find suitable employment.

Yours sincerely

工作說明書

22.25　資深祕書的工作說明書

工作說明書記載了該項職務的詳細工作內容及責任，包括所有的監督工作、具體職權，以及職務特性。

→ p.207

如果是用空白
紙張，必須寫上
公司名稱。有時會
使用印有信頭
的信紙

© Turner Communications

JOB DESCRIPTION

使用與該職位
相關的適當標題

JOB TITLE	Senior Secretary
REPORTS TO	Training Manager
LOCATION	Head Office, Sheffield
MAIN PURPOSE	To provide a confidential secretarial and support service to the Training Manager

REQUIREMENTS

有時會列出對該
職務的具體要求

1 Abilities: use initiative, decide priorities, work without supervision

2 Previous experience at senior level

3 Skills: Microsoft Office, notetaking skills, minute-taking skills, good organiser, good interpersonal skills

4 High standard of education with appropriate secretarial/administration qualifications

MAIN DUTIES AND RESPONSIBILITIES

條列主要工作與責任

1 To provide secretarial support to the Training Manager.

2 To deal with mail, answer telephone enquiries, take messages and compose correspondence.

3 To take shorthand dictation and deal with instructions from manuscript, audio or disk and to transcribe documents accurately and consistently.

確認各要點的
格式一致，例
如都用 To 開頭

4 To maintain the diary of the Training Manager.

5 To arrange meetings and produce accurate minutes.

6 To arrange training courses and seminars.

7 To make travel and accommodation arrangements as may be required.

8 To ensure the security of the office and confidential documents.

用標準的句子來結尾

9 To carry out any other duties as may be expected in a post of this level.

ST/BT

June 200—

22.26　電話行銷員的工作說明書

→ p.208

JOB DESCRIPTION

Job Title	Telephone Executive (Marketing)
Location	Marketing Department, Head Office
Responsible to	Marketing Manager
Main Purpose of Job	To telephone customers with the objective of identifying opportunities where business can be increased

MAIN DUTIES AND RESPONSIBILITIES

1 To achieve daily call rate targets and any target set for sales campaigns.
2 To have a good telephone manner and be courteous to customers at all times.
3 To carry out any administrative requirements generated by the telephone calls in an accurate and efficient manner. This may include sending letters, fax messages, e-mails, reports, product literature, etc.
4 To undertake training courses to make good use of telephone selling techniques.
5 To undertake training on the company's products and services and to promote associated products where appropriate.
6 To carry out competitor market research by contracting their branches to gather information on pricing, product availability, etc, as directed by your supervisor.
7 To carry out any other tasks as requested by your supervisor.

任用函

任用函中必須清楚說明員工的薪水和其他任用條件。但如果已附上詳載職務內容的工作說明書，可不必在信中重複陳述。

22.27 確認聘雇函

如果面試時已經口頭聘雇，必須在之後立刻再以書信確認一次。

→ p.208

Dear Miss Wildman

工作聘用與到職日 — I am pleased to confirm the offer we made to you yesterday of the post of Senior Secretary to the Training Manager, commencing on 1 August 200–.

具體說明工作內容 — Your duties will be as outlined at the interview and as described on the attached
或附上工作說明書　　Job Description.

薪資及休假的細節 — This appointment carries a commencing salary of £15,000 per annum, rising to £16,500 after one year's service and thereafter by annual review. You will be entitled to 4 weeks' annual holiday.

提及終止聘雇規定 — The appointment may be terminated at any time by either side giving 2 months' notice in writing.

請對方確認 — Please confirm that you accept this appointment on the terms stated and that you will be able to commence your duties on 1 August.

Yours sincerely

22.28 任用函

如果面試時未明確告知應徵者是否已被聘用，之後才決定予以聘用，則應儘快以信函通知對方。

→ p.209

Dear Miss Jennings

Thank you for attending the interview yesterday. I am pleased to offer you the post of Secretary in our Sales Department at a starting salary of S$1200 (Singapore dollars) per month. Your commencement date will be Monday 1 October.

As discussed, office hours are 0900 to 1730 with one hour for lunch. You will be entitled to 3 weeks' annual paid holiday.

Please confirm in writing by return that you accept this appointment on these terms and that you can take up your duties on 1 October.

Yours sincerely

22.29　接受聘雇

任何接受聘雇的信函都必須馬上回覆。

→ p.209

> Dear Miss Tan
>
> Thank you for your letter of 24 August offering me the post of Secretary in your Sales Department.
>
> I am pleased to accept this post on the terms stated in your letter and confirm that I can commence work on 1 October.
>
> I can assure you that I shall do everything I can to make a success of my work.
>
> Yours sincerely

22.30　婉拒聘雇

如果您不接受該項職務，還是要立刻回覆對方，說明拒絕的理由才是有禮貌的做法，以方便對方儘快安排其他人選。

→ p.209

> Dear Miss Tan
>
> Thank you for your letter of 24 August offering me the post of Secretary to the Sales Department.
>
> I am sorry that I will be unable to take up this position. My present company have discussed with me their plans for expansion and I have been offered the new post of Office Manager. You will appreciate that this post will offer me a challenge which I feel I must accept.
>
> I wish you every success in appointing a suitable candidate.
>
> Yours sincerely

22.31 致函未錄取者

錄取者接受聘雇後，接下來是儘速禮貌性地寫信通知其他參加面試、但未被錄取的應徵者。

→ p.210

感謝對方，
並提及該職務

委婉解釋，
態度有禮

祝福應徵者
謀職成功

Dear

Thank you for attending the interview for the post of Senior Secretary to the Training Manager.

I am sorry to have to inform you that we are unable to offer you this position. Although you have excellent qualifications we have decided to appoint someone with more experience.

I feel sure that you will soon be successful in finding suitable employment.

With best wishes

Yours sincerely

終止聘雇

22.32 員工請辭函

除非雙方同意延長聘雇時間，否則員工的聘雇在聘雇合約（Contract of Employment）屆滿就必須終止。如果合約書中說明期限，那麼任何一方都可以在雙方同意的期限內寄發通知來終止聘雇關係。

→ p.210

Dear Miss Ward

I regret to inform you that I wish to give 2 weeks' notice of my resignation from the company. My last day of work will be 30 June 200—.

I have been very happy working here for the past 2 years and found my work challenging and enjoyable. However I have obtained a post in which I will have more responsibilities and greater career prospects.

Thank you for your help and guidance during my employment.

Yours sincerely

22.33　雇主終止聘雇關係（員工表現不佳）

根據英國 1996 年就業權利法（Employment Rights Act 1996），如果員工自認為受到不公平的解雇時，有權上訴工業裁決所（Industrial Tribunal）。此時雇主必須提出解雇的合理證據，例如員工的行為不當或無法勝任工作等。

事實上，即使已經決定要解雇表現不佳的員工，但身為雇主，先以口頭告知是比較恰當的做法。至於解雇確認函的措詞則必須謹慎、委婉。

→ p.211

表示遺憾並提出終止日期

說明員工令人不滿的行為

措詞必須小心

適當的結尾

Dear Miss Anderson

Following our discussion earlier this week I regret to inform you that your services with the company will not be required with effect from 31 August 200—.

As you know there have been a number of occasions recently when I have had to point out the unsatisfactory quality of your work. Together with your persistent unpunctuality in spite of several warnings, this has led me to believe that you will perhaps be more successful in a different kind of work.

I hope you will be successful in finding suitable employment elsewhere. If another employer should wish you to start work before the end of the month, arrangements can be made for you to be released immediately.

Yours sincerely

22.34 雇主終止聘雇關係（人力過剩）

根據前述的英國就業權利法，企業因爲歇業或人員過剩等因素而解雇員工，員工有權可以拿到失業的補償金（compensation）。至於補償金額則依員工年齡、服務年資和週薪來計算。

→ p.211

Dear Mr White

As you are aware the reorganisation of our office has been the subject of an investigation by a firm of management consultants. They have made a number of recommendations which will result in a decrease in staff.

I very much regret having to inform you that your position as Ledger Clerk is one which will become redundant on 30 June. I am giving you as much notice as possible so that you can immediately begin looking for alternative employment.

You will be entitled to a redundancy payment which will amount to 2 weeks' salary for each of your 5 years' service, at the rate prevailing when your services end. This is calculated as follows:

£200 x 2 x 5 = £2000

I would like to take this opportunity to say that your work has always been entirely satisfactory and I shall be pleased to provide any prospective employer with a reference if required.

I do hope you will soon find another suitable post and wish you all the best for the future.

Yours sincerely

22.35 警告函

一般來說，員工在被解雇之前會收到公司發給的警告函（Warning letter）。公司有關警告和解雇的相關法令，則應該在就業條件（Conditions of Employment）或聘雇合約中載明。

實務上良好的處理方式是先與員工個別討論其不好的工作表現及態度，接著才將討論的內容以信函告知。

解雇的理由必須明確，如果可以的話，最好是說明其違反公司的任用條件或是工作說明書的哪一部分。至於從通知到離職的期間長短則視任用合約而定，法律上針對資深員工的最短通知期限也視國情而異，有關這些正式的要求，應事先調查清楚並考慮在內。

→ p.212

詳述背景

具體說明
事件／日期

表達希望對方
改進之意

說明後續行動

Dear Mark

Further to our meeting today I am sorry to say that your conduct has been found to be unsatisfactory recently.

There have been two occasions during the past month in which you were found to be breaching our company rules. On 12 March you were found smoking in a prohibited area, and on 24 March you were rude to a customer. On both occasions you received a verbal warning from your supervisor.

I hope there will be no repeat of either of these incidents, or indeed any other breach of the company's rules or standards of conduct.

I will review the situation again in one month's time.

Yours sincerely

22.36 第二次警告

→ p.212

Dear Mark

At our meeting today I gave you a second warning for unsatisfactory conduct. This occurred after your supervisor informed me that you had been caught taking money from the petty cash till this morning. This follows the 2 previous incidents mentioned in my letter of 12 June.

The sum involved was very small but I stressed to you that integrity and trust are vital in any business. You have appealed to me to give you another chance and against my better judgement I have agreed to do so. However any further unsatisfactory conduct will result in immediate dismissal.

Yours sincerely

22.37 做出解雇決定

→ p.212

> Dear Mark
>
> I confirm that you are dismissed from the company with immediate effect following the discovery that you were caught stealing money from a colleague's drawer. This action follows my warning letters dated 25 March and 5 April about unsatisfactory conduct.
>
> Our cheque for one week's salary in lieu of notice is enclosed.
>
> Yours sincerely

22.38 要求員工一個月內離職的通知

→ p.213

> Dear Mark
>
> I confirm that you have agreed to leave the company at the end of this month, ie 30 June. This follows my warning letters to you dated 25 March and 5 April and further instances of breaching company rules, smoking in prohibited areas and rudeness to customers. All these incidents have been discussed with you and officially reported under the company's general conditions of employment.
>
> If you find another position before the end of the month we will be happy to release you.
>
> Yours sincerely

各式人事函

當公司基於某種因素必須將在某職位上勝任愉快的員工調至其他工作崗位時，必須將調職理由解釋清楚，並強調任何可能的優點和好處，包括工作性質更有趣和更具責任感、更多經驗、薪水更高或見識更廣等等。如果處理得體，那麼就有可能在對員工傳達不受歡迎或令人失望的消息時，不致令員工感覺受傷或受到冒犯。說不定情勢還可因此扭轉，讓原本不受歡迎的消息變成好消息。

底下這封信是寫給原本安逸穩定、不希望工作有所調動的資深員工，但因科技進步，有時調職仍是勢在必行。

22.39 員工調職

→ p.213

Dear Mr Turner

As Mrs Williamson has already discussed with you, we have arranged to appoint you as Section Supervisor in the Stores Department with effect from Monday 1 July. Your salary will be £19,200 per annum.

In your new post you will report directly to Mr James Freeman, Storekeeper, and you will be responsible for the work of the clerical staff employed in the department.

Your 30 years of loyal service in the Invoice Department have been greatly appreciated by the management, and we are sorry that it is necessary to move you from a department with which you are so familiar. Our only reason for doing so is that invoicing will be completely changed by the introduction of computerised methods. We feel sure that you will understand that it is uneconomic for us to retrain our long-standing employees who might find difficulty in adjusting to new ways of working.

In your new post you will find ample scope for your experience. I know you will do a good job and hope you will find it enjoyable.

Yours sincerely

22.40 透過仲介招募員工

對於經常性的招募，有時候雇主會委託人力仲介公司處理。仲介公司會介紹全職、兼職或臨時人員，且從受雇者薪水中抽取佣金。

→ p.214

Dear Sir/Madam

I hope you will be able to help me to fill a vacancy which has just arisen in my department.

My Secretary needs secretarial help on a part-time basis. This will be an interesting post and ideal for someone who wishes to work for only a few hours each week. Applicants should be able to undertake normal secretarial duties and have shorthand and typewriting speeds of about 100 and 45 wpm respectively. Applicants of any age would be considered, but willingness and reliability are preferable to someone with high qualifications.

The successful applicant will be required to work for 3 hours on 5 mornings each week. We would be willing to consider an alternative arrangement if necessary.

I propose payment based on an hourly rate of £5 to £6 according to age and experience.

Please let me know whether you have anyone on your register who would be suitable.

Yours faithfully

22.41　請求加薪

任何要求調薪的信函措詞都必須相當小心。你必須技巧的解釋為什麼你覺得加薪是合理的。

→ p.214

> Dear Mr Browning
>
> My present appointment carries an annual salary of £18,500; this was reviewed in March last year.
>
> During my 5 years with this company I feel I have carried out my duties conscientiously and have recently acquired additional responsibilities.
>
> I feel that my qualifications and the nature of my work justify a higher salary and I have already been offered a similar position with another company at a salary of £20,000 per annum.
>
> My present duties are interesting and I thoroughly enjoy my work. Although I have no wish to leave the company, I cannot afford to turn down the present offer unless some improvement in my salary can be arranged.
>
> I hope a salary increase will be possible, otherwise my only course will be to accept the offer made to me.
>
> Yours sincerely

22.42　辭呈

如果是主動離職，一定要提出通知。通常提出通知並附上正式辭呈的程序是根據公司的雇用條件而定。

→ p.215

> Dear Mr McKewan
>
> Please accept notice of my intention to leave the company in one month's time, ie 28 July.
>
> As I have discussed with you I have accepted a position with another company which will allow me greater responsibilities and improved opportunities for advancement.
>
> Thank you for your support during my 2 years with Turner Communications. I have gained a lot of valuable experience which will be very useful.
>
> Yours sincerely

22.43　歡迎新員工

→ p.215

It is with great pleasure that I welcome you as a new employee to SingComm Pte Ltd, Singapore. I am very pleased that you have chosen to accept our offer of employment and hope that this will be the beginning of a mutually beneficial association.

We encourage our personnel to take advantage of selected courses that are available in Singapore, so as to improve their skills and learn new skills in related areas. The current list of courses and their corresponding registration dates are posted on the employee bulletin board. If you decide to attend one of these courses, please advise your supervisor and s/he will make the necessary arrangements.

If you have any questions at any time that I may be able to answer, please do not hesitate to give me a call on [telephone number].

Once again, welcome to SingComm Pte Ltd.

22.44　有關健康及安全政策的提醒

→ p.216

In view of the recent unfortunate accident involving a visitor to our premises, I would like to remind you about our health and safety policy.

Whenever you have a visitor to the building, you are responsible for their health and safety at all times. For his/her own safety, a visitor should not be allowed to wander freely around the building. If, for example, a visitor needs to use the washroom, you should accompany them and escort them back.

For security reasons, if you see someone you do not recognise wandering around the building unaccompanied, do not be afraid to ask questions. Ask politely why he or she is here, which member of staff they are visiting, and if that person knows the visitor has arrived.

All SingComm employees have a responsibility to take reasonable care of themselves and others and to ensure a healthy and safe workplace. If you notice any hazard or potential hazard, please bring it to the attention of the Health and Safety Manager, Michael Wilson, who will investigate the issue.

A copy of the company's health and safety policy is attached. Please take a few minutes to read it through to remind yourself of the main points.

Thank you for your help in ensuring the health and safety of all employees and visitors to SingComm.

22.45 有關未休完的年假

→ p.216

In the past it has been a policy of the company that all staff must take their holiday entitlement within one calendar year. Any holiday entitlement not taken before 31 December each year has been forfeited.

It has now been decided to amend this rule to provide staff more flexibility with holidays.

With immediate effect anyone who has up to 5 days' holiday entitlement outstanding at 31 December may carry this over to 31 March the following year. Any days that have not been used by 31 March will be forfeited. Unused holiday entitlement may not be converted to pay in lieu.

The approval of staff leave is still subject to agreement with your manager/ supervisor. This will take into account the business and operational needs of the department and especially clashes with other staff.

If you have any questions about this new policy, please telephone Human Resource Department on extension 456.

實用措詞

求職信

【開頭】

1. I wish to apply for the post ... advertised in the ... on ...
   我希望應徵貴公司在（日期）於……廣告中刊登的……職務……

2. I was interested to see your advertisement in ... and wish to apply for this post.
   我對貴公司在……廣告中刊載的……職務表示興趣，希望能應徵該職。

3. I am writing to enquire whether you have a suitable vacancy for me in your organisation.
   我寫信的目的在於詢問貴公司是否有適合我的職缺。

4. I understand from Mr ..., one of your suppliers, that there is an opening in your company for ...
   我從……先生，您的一位供應商那兒得知，目前貴公司有……的職缺。

5. Mrs ... informs me that she will be leaving your company on ... and if her position has not been filled, I should like to be considered.

……女士通知我她將於……（日期）離開貴公司，如果她的職務尚無人遞補，我希望您們能夠考慮我。

【結尾】

1. I look forward to hearing from you and to being granted the opportunity of an interview.

期待收到您的回信，並且有機會參加面試。

2. I hope you will consider my application favourably and grant me an interview.

我希望您能考慮我，並且准許我參加面試。

3. I look forward to the opportunity of attending an interview when I can provide further details.

我期待有參加面試的機會，屆時我將提供更詳盡的資訊。

有利的推薦函

【開頭】

1. Mr ... has applied to us for the above post/position of ... We should be grateful if you would give us your opinion of his character and abilities.

……先生向我們申請上述……的職務。如果您能提供我們有關他的個人特質和能力等相關資料，我們將非常感激。

2. We have received an application from Miss ... who has given your name as a referee.

我們收到……小姐的應徵函，她提供您的名字作為推薦人。

3. I am very glad of this opportunity to speak in support of Miss ...'s application for a position in your company.

很高興利用這個機會為……小姐應徵貴公司……職務一事表示支持。

4. In reply to your recent enquiry Ms ... has been employed as ... for the past 2 years.

回覆您最近的詢問，……小姐過去兩年在公司擔任……一職。

【結尾】

1. Any information you can provide will be much appreciated.
   您所提供的任何資訊，我們均將感激不盡。

2. Any information you are kind enough to provide will be treated in strictest confidence.
   您提供的任何訊息都會被嚴加保密。

3. I am sure you will be more than satisfied with the work of Mr ...
   我相信您一定會對……先生的表現感到滿意。

4. I shall be sorry to lose ... but realise that her abilities demand wider scope than are possible at this company.
   我們對失去……表示遺憾，但是可以了解，以她的能力需要比我們公司所能提供的更大發揮空間。

不利的推薦函

1. I find it difficult to answer your enquiry about Mr ... He is a very likeable person but I cannot conscientiously recommend him for the vacancy you mention.
   有關您對……先生的詢問，我很難回答。他是一位令人喜愛的人，但是我無法憑良心推薦貴公司聘用他。

2. The work produced by ... was below the standards expected and we found it necessary to release him.
   ……先生的工作表現低於預期的標準，因此我們認爲有必要讓他離開。

3. Her poor time-keeping was very disturbing and caused some disruption to the work of the department.
   他對時間觀念的忽視令人相當困擾，而且也讓部門工作有一些中斷的情形。

4. We found her attitude quite a bad influence on other staff within the department.
   我們發現她的態度對部門的其他員工有相當不好的影響。

5. Although ... possesses the qualifications to perform such work, I have seen no evidence that she has the necessary self-discipline or reliability.
雖然……符合這類工作的資格要求，但沒有證據顯示她具備必要的責任感和可靠度。

聘雇

【開頭】

1. Thank you for attending the interview last ..., I am pleased to offer you the position of ...
謝謝您上……（時間）參加面試，很高興聘雇您擔任……職務。

2. I am pleased to confirm the offer we made to you when you came for interview on ...
很高興向您確認，在您於……參加面試後，我們決定聘雇您。

3. Following your interview with ..., I am pleased to offer you the position of ... commencing on ...
在……先生與您面試後，很高興聘雇您擔任……一職，從……（日期）開始。

【結尾】

1. Written confirmation of your acceptance of this post would be appreciated as soon as possible.
如果您接受這項職務，請儘快以書面確認。

2. Please confirm in writing that you accept this appointment on the terms stated and that you can commence your duties on ...
請以書面確認您接受這項所述條件的職務，並且於……（日期）上班。

3. We look forward to welcoming you to our staff and hope you will be very happy in your work here.
期待您成為公司一員，希望您未來在此工作愉快。

終止聘雇

【開頭】

1. I regret that I wish to terminate my services with this Company with effect from ...
   很抱歉，我希望我的工作可以在 ⋯⋯（日期）終止

2. I am writing to confirm that I wish to tender my resignation. My last date of employment will be ...
   我寫信的目的在於確認我要提出辭呈，我最後一天上班日爲⋯⋯。

3. As my family have decided to emigrate I am sorry to have to tender my resignation.
   因爲全家決定移民，因此很抱歉必須提出辭呈。

4. It is with regret that I have to inform you that your position with this company will become redundant on ...
   很抱歉必須通知您，目前您在公司的職務在⋯⋯（日期）之後將被裁撤。

5. There has been no improvement in your work performance and attitude despite our letters dated ... and ... As a result we have no option but to terminate your services with effect from ...
   儘管公司在⋯⋯（日期）以及⋯⋯（日期）的信中請您改善您的工作表現及態度，但未見效果。我們不得不終止您的聘用，自⋯⋯（日期）起生效。

【結尾】

1. I have been very happy working here and am grateful for your guidance during my employment.
   我這一段時間在公司工作非常愉快，也很感謝您的指導。

2. I am sorry that these circumstances make it necessary for me to leave the company.
   很抱歉我因爲這些情形而必須離開公司。

3. We have been extremely satisfied with your services and hope that you will soon find another suitable post.
   我們對您的工作表現非常滿意，也希望您能早日找到合適的工作。

4. I hope you will soon find alternative employment, and extend my best wishes for your future.
    希望您早日找到其他工作，預祝未來一切順利。

推薦函

【開頭】

1. Mr ... has been employed by this company from ... to ...
    ……先生從……（日期）……到（日期）受雇於本公司。

2. Miss ... worked for this company from leaving college in 200— until she emigrated to Canada in March 200—.
    ……小姐自 200—年大學畢業後就在本公司上班，直到 200—年 3 月因移民到加拿大而離職。

【內文】

1. Miss ... enjoys good health and is a good time-keeper.
    ……小姐非常健康，而且相當守時。

2. She uses her best endeavours at all times to perform her work expeditiously and has always been a hard-working and conscientious employee.
    她總是迅速完成工作，是一位工作認真、負責的員工。

3. Miss ... made a substantial contribution to the work of the ... department, and always performed her work in a businesslike and reliable manner.
    ……小姐對……（部門）的貢獻相當大，而且工作相當認真、可靠。

4. Mr ... gave considerable help to his colleagues in improvements of teaching methods and materials and also produced many booklets of guidance which are proving valuable to other teachers.
    ……先生在改進教學方法和教材方面為同事提供很多協助，而且也編製很多實用的教學手冊提供給其他老師。

【結尾】

1. I have pleasure in recommending ... highly and without hesitation.
   我很高興也毫無猶豫地高度推薦……

2. We hope that ... meets with the success we feel he deserves.
   我們希望……可以獲得聘雇，他非常適任。

3. I shall be sorry to lose his services but realise that his abilities demand wider scope than are possible at this company.
   對於他的離職表示遺憾，但是也能理解以他的能力需要比我們公司所能提供更大的發揮空間。

4. I can recommend Miss ... to you with every confidence.
   我有信心向您推薦……小姐。

旅行與飯店
Travel and hotels

1
2
3
4
5
6
7
8
9
10
11
12
13
14
15
16
17
18
19
20
21
22
23
24
25
26
27
28
29
30

在處理商務旅行的過程中，可能需要辦理護照或簽證（如有必要），以及預訂機票、船票及飯店等事務。行程表（itinerary）對商務人士而言是必要的，而這一類相關事務一般會委託給旅行業者，由其代爲出面，雙方之後再以書面做確認即可。

本章將介紹與旅遊有關的書信，其中也包括了商務人士的旅程計畫在內。

護照

護照是政府發給的身分證明文件，目的在保護他們的海外旅遊安全。英國國民可以在主要的郵局或大型旅行社取得護照申請表。填妥後連同相關證明文件和費用，寄至外交部護照處的各地方辦公室（London, Liverpool, Peterborough, Glasgow, Newport, Belfast 等）。通常用郵件辦理約需 3 至 5 星期的作業時間，如果是急件，可親自送件，只需 5 天即可完成。一般護照的有效期是 10 年。新規定不再核發夫婦共同護照，小孩應列名在父母雙方的護照中。有關護照的詳細規定可於護照申請表中取得（編注：以上爲英國的相關規定）。

23.1　請求提供護照申請表

→ p.218

Dear Sir

Early next year I intend to visit a number of countries in the Far East and Australasia. Please send me a passport application form and a list of the addresses to which applications for visas for the various countries should be sent.

I have not previously held or applied for a passport of any description.

Yours faithfully

23.2　正式提出申請

→ p.218

> Dear Sir
>
> I have completed and enclose my application form for issue of a United Kingdom passport. Also enclosed are two passport photographs (one certified at the back), my birth certificate and a cheque for the passport fee.
>
> I propose to leave England on 15 January. Please ensure that my passport is prepared and sent to me in good time to enable me to obtain the necessary visas.
>
> Yours faithfully

簽證

到很多國家旅行需要先取得簽證，可交由旅行社代辦，他們通常可取得任何需要的簽證。另外也可逕自向辦理簽證的相關部門洽詢。

申請簽證需繳交必要的文件和費用，可能包括申請人的護照、照片、疫苗接種證明或其他健康證明、機票，或者出具雇主或贊助者的證明文件（擔保申請人在海外旅遊期間的財務保障）等等。

23.3　請求提供簽證申請表

→ p.218

> Dear Sir
>
> Our Sales Director, Mr Robert Dickson, proposes to visit Australia in 2 months' time on company business.
>
> As I understand a visa is necessary, please send me the appropriate application form, together with details of your visa requirements.
>
> Yours faithfully

23.4　正式提出申請

→ p.219

Dear Sir/Madam

I enclose the completed application form for an entry visa to enable Mr Robert Dickson, Sales Director of this company, to visit Australia.

Mr Dickson will be leaving London on 5 August for a business tour of Singapore and Hong Kong. Subject to issue of the necessary visa, he proposes to fly to Perth, Western Australia, on 7 August. Thereafter he will be visiting Melbourne, Sydney and Cairns.

The purpose of Mr Dickson's visit to Australia is to gain information about recent developments in education there, with special reference to the use of our publications. He intends to visit departments of education, universities, commercial and technical colleges and other educational organisations as well as leading booksellers. This company guarantees Mr Dickson's financial security during his stay as well as payment of all expenses incurred.

The following supporting documents are enclosed:

1　Mr Dickson's passport.
2　A cheque for the visa fee.
3　A registered stamped addressed envelope for return of the passport.
4　A copy of the company's publications catalogue for your reference.

If you require any further information please do not hesitate to let me know.

Yours faithfully

搭飛機或船旅行

搭飛機的乘客主要有兩種：商務人士及度假者。商務人士通常是在很短時間內排定的行程，所以會直接透過電話向航空公司訂票。至於度假者則常是事先透過旅行社做安排。

23.5　詢問班機

(a) 詢問

底下的傳真是向英國航空公司票務組詢問有關倫敦飛往紐約的航班事宜。

→ p.219

My company will be arranging a number of business trips to New York during the next 3 months.

Please send me information concerning flights (outward and return) including departure times and cost of single and return fares.

We are particularly interested in information relating to reduced fares.

(b) 回覆

底下的回覆既有禮貌又提供實質幫助，給人相當的信心。

→ p.220

Many thanks for your enquiry of 5 September.

I enclose a timetable giving details of outward and return flights between London and New York together with a price list in which you will find details of both ordinary and discounted fares. As you will see from this list discounted fares can be as little as one-third of the normal fare.

A visa is necessary for all visitors to the United States.

If I can be of any further assistance please call me.

23.6　汽車海運

汽車海運（car ferry）是往來英國與歐陸的方式之一。在這封信中，寄件人向一家知名營運業者詢問有關汽車海運的詳細資訊。

(a) 詢問

→ p.220

Dear Sir/Madam

Later this year I propose to tour Western Europe with friends and I wish to take a car with me.

Please send me details of your car ferry service including your terms and conditions for transporting a Mercedes-Benz and three passengers from Dover to Calais.

As this would be my first use of the car ferry service I am not familiar with Customs and other formalities involved. I should be grateful for any information you can provide.

Yours faithfully

(b) 回覆

→ p.221

Dear Mr Hanley

Thank you for your letter of 4 August requesting details of our car ferry service.

A brochure is enclosed giving all the information you require together with prices and a timetable.

Formalities for touring Europe by car are now simpler than ever before. All that is necessary is for you to check in at our Dover office one hour before departure time and to produce the following documents:

1　Your travel ticket
2　Your passport
3　Your car registration papers
4　A valid British driving licence
5　An international insurance 'green card'[1]

Your car must carry a GB nationality plate.

If you require further details please contact me. Meanwhile I hope you enjoy travelling with British Car Ferries Ltd.

Yours sincerely

23.7　海上旅遊

在這封信中，寄件人詢問有關定期郵輪之旅的事項。

(a) 詢問

→ p.221

Dear Sir/Madam

I am interested in your sailings to New York during August or September this year. Please let me have any available literature giving information about the ships scheduled to sail during this period.

Please also let me have details of fares (single and return) for both first- and second-class travel.

I look forward to hearing from you soon.

Yours faithfully

1.　**green card**：綠色保險卡，為駕駛在國外遭遇意外時提供保險。

(b) 回覆

→ p.222

Dear Mrs Morrison

Thank you for your letter of 11 June enquiring about sailings to New York.

In the enclosed copy of our Queen Elizabeth 2 sailing list you will find details of sailings and of first-class and tourist fares including excursion fares in both classes.

A valid passport is necessary for all passengers, but an international certificate of vaccination is no longer necessary. All passengers other than United States citizens and holders of re-entry permits will also require a visa issued by a United States consul.

As the company's liability for baggage is limited under the terms of the passenger ticket, we strongly urge passengers to insure against all risks for the full period of their journey. I shall be glad to supply details on request.

Please let me know if I can be of further assistance.

Yours sincerely

(c) 預定舖位

→ p.222

Dear Sir

Thank you for sending me information about the sailings of Queen Elizabeth 2.

Please make a reservation in my name for a first-class single cabin on 3 August sailing to New York. Full payment is enclosed.

I look forward to receiving confirmation of my reservation, together with travel ticket.

Yours faithfully

23.8　度假郵輪

這封信是詢問度假郵輪的相關事項。

(a) 詢問

→ p.222

Dear Sir

I am interested in learning more about 10–14-day holiday cruises offered by your organisation for this summer.

Please let me have the relevant brochure as well as costs for tourist-class travel.

Yours faithfully

(b) 回覆

→ p.223

Dear Mrs McFarlane

Thank you for your enquiry of 10 February.

I have pleasure in enclosing our illustrated brochure which contains full details of our summer cruises, as well as tourist-class fares. Also enclosed is a leaflet showing the accommodation available for the coming summer; as the booking position is constantly changing this leaflet can serve only as a broad guide to what we can offer.

Please let me know if you require further information or help.

Yours sincerely

飯店住宿

大部分的大型飯店都以公司型態經營，所有詢問信都應該要寫給經理。至於私人旅館，因為規模較小，可直接洽詢業主，他們通常身兼旅館的所有人及管理者。

在寫信詢問有關訂房的資訊時，必須注意以下原則：

◆ 內容簡潔，切入重點。

◆ 清楚、扼要說明自己的需求。為避免造成誤解，應註明住房日期、天數及確切的停留期間（如果知道的話），例如 from Monday 6 to Friday 10 July inclusive（從7月6日星期一至7月10日星期五，含7月10日）。

◆ 知道的話註明抵達和離開時間。

◆ 如果有時間，可請求做訂房確認。

23.9　預訂商務房

在這封詢問信中，公司寫信給一家倫敦飯店的經理，請求提供住宿方面的資訊。

(a) 詢問

→ p.223

> Dear Sir/Madam
>
> My company will be displaying products at the forthcoming British Industrial Fair at Earls Court and we shall require hotel accommodation for several members of staff.
>
> Please send me a copy of your current brochure and details of terms for <u>half board</u>.[2] Please also indicate if you have one double and three single rooms available from Monday 13 to Friday 17 May inclusive.
>
> I hope to hear from you soon.
>
> Yours faithfully

(b) 回覆

→ p.224

感謝 —— Dear Miss Johnson

Thank you for your letter of 15 March.

附上小冊子 —— As requested I enclose a copy of our brochure in which you will find all the details required.

重複房間和日期等細節，以避免誤會 —— We presently have one double and three single rooms available from Monday 13 to Friday 17 May inclusive. However as we are now entering the busy season and bookings for this period are likely to be heavy, we suggest that you make your reservation without delay.

提到飯店的優點，既建立和善關係也能擴展未來的業務 —— You will see from our brochure that this is a modern hotel and I am sure your staff would be very comfortable here. We are well served by public transport to Earls Court, and it should be possible to reach there within 15 minutes.

I hope to receive confirmation of your reservation soon.

2.　half board：只附早餐和晚餐。

(c) 訂房確認

通常你會先透過電話訂房，隨後應立即再以書面做確認。

→ p.224

Dear Mr Nelson

Thank you for your letter of 17 March and our telephone conversation today.

I confirm reservation of one double and three single <u>en suite</u>[3] rooms from 13–17 May inclusive, with half-board. Names of guests are:

Mr & Mrs Philip Andersen
Mr Geoffrey Richardson
Miss Lesley Nunn
Mr Jonathan Denby

The account will be settled by Mr Philip Andersen, our Company's General Manager.

Yours sincerely

23.10 個人訂房

(a) 詢問

→ p.225

Dear Sir/Madam

I shall be passing through London next week and would like to reserve a single room for Wednesday and Thursday 18 and 19 October.

My previous stays at the Norfolk Hotel have always been very enjoyable; I particularly like the rooms overlooking the gardens. If one of these rooms is available I hope you will reserve it for me.

I expect to arrive at the hotel in time for lunch on the 18th and shall be leaving immediately after breakfast on the 20th.

Yours faithfully

---

3. en suite：附有浴室的房間。

(b) 回覆

→ p.225

Dear Mr Robinson

Thank you for your letter of 10 October.

I was glad to learn that you have enjoyed your previous visits to the Norfolk Hotel. Unfortunately a room overlooking the garden is not available for the dates you requested. However I have several pleasant rooms on the south side of the hotel, away from traffic noise and with an open view of the nearby park and lake.

The charge for these rooms is £85 per night. You will find all details in the enclosed brochure.

I have provisionally reserved for you one of the rooms mentioned for the 2 nights of Wednesday and Thursday 18 and 19 October.

Please let me have your confirmation soon.

Yours sincerely

23.11 國外訂房

底下這封信是因為朋友推薦而向海外的飯店預訂房間。

(a) 詢問

→ p.226

Dear Sir/Madam

Your hotel has been highly recommended by a friend who stayed there last year.

I will be arriving in Singapore at 1730 hours on Monday 15 April on flight SQ24, accompanied by 3 friends. We wish to stay in Singapore for 4 nights, ie 15–18 April inclusive before arranging independent travel by land in Malaysia.

Please let me know if 2 twin-bedded rooms are available for this period, and what the charges would be. I also understand that your hotel arranges local tours; full details would be appreciated.

I hope to hear from you soon.

Yours faithfully

(b) 回覆

因爲是朋友住過而來信詢問，所以訂房專員在回函中不厭其煩地說明該飯店的地理位置及本身的優點。

→ p.226

Dear Mr Hill

I am pleased to learn from your letter of 2 February that The Lion Hotel was recommended to you.

A copy of our illustrated brochure is enclosed showing the hotel's many facilities. You will note the recent improvements made to our pool area, with adjoining gym and leisure facilities.

Our hotel's tour operator is Century Tours and a brochure is attached giving details of their half- and full-day tours. There would be no problem in reserving places on any of these tours when you arrive in Singapore.

I have taken the liberty of making a provisional reservation of 2 twin-bedded rooms from 15–18 April at a cost of S$120 per night. This reservation will be held until 1 March and your confirmation would be appreciated before that date.

Arrangements can be made for our courtesy pick-up service to meet your flight SQ24 at 1730 on 15 April if you mention this at the time of confirming your reservation.

You will find The Lion Hotel very convenient for transport both by MRT (Mass Rapid Transport) and bus. It is also within 5 minutes walking distance of Orchard Road.

I look forward to extending the hospitality of The Lion Hotel to your party and hope to receive confirmation of your reservation before 1 March.

Yours sincerely

假期住宿與旅行計畫

有關飯店、賓館或度假公寓（holiday flat）的資訊，可以從度假景點的宣傳部門所編製的年度度假指南中取得。指南中包含度假景點的魅力所在——有趣的名勝、遊樂設施、運動、博物館、藝術中心或文化活動等詳細資訊。通常可免費索取這些指南。

23.12　索取度假指南

索取度假指南的信函簡短、正式即可，除非是對方要求付費，否則可使用明信片。度假指南通常會連同敬贈便條（compliment slip）一併起寄出，而不用正式的信函。

→ p.227

> Dear Sirs
>
> Please send me a copy of your official holiday guide and a list of hotels and guest houses.
>
> I enclose a large stamped addressed envelope.
>
> Yours faithfully

23.13　詢問飯店住宿

(a) 詢問

→ p.227

> Dear Sir/Madam
>
> 基本資料介紹 ── I found the name of your private hotel in the holiday guide received from the Bridlington Information Centre.
>
> 提到房間、日期，以及特定需求 ── Please let me know if you have accommodation for a family of 5 for 2 weeks commencing Saturday 10 August. We shall require 2 twin-bedded rooms and 1 single room – the single room should be on the ground floor or near to the lift as it is for my elderly mother.
>
> 要求確認並提供詳細資料 ── If you can provide this accommodation please send me a copy of your brochure and also your terms for <u>full board</u>.[4]
>
> Yours faithfully

4.　full board：包含三餐。

(b) 回覆

→ p.227

Dear Mr Leeson

感謝 ── Thank you for your enquiry dated 15 April.

確認房間與日期，並回應特定請求 ── I am pleased to say that the accommodation you require is available for the 2 weeks commencing Saturday 10 August. We can offer you two adjacent[5] twin-bedded rooms on the first floor, with a single room on the same floor conveniently located about 10 metres from the lift. Should this distance present a problem we can place a wheelchair at your disposal.

說明為何要早日訂房 ── Early confirmation of this accommodation is necessary as bookings for August are always heavy and I should not wish you to be disappointed.

附上小冊子並以個人的關懷結尾 ── A brochure containing details of our charges is enclosed. We hope you will give us the opportunity to welcome your family to the Northcliffe.

Yours sincerely

23.14　私人小旅館

(a) 詢問

→ p.228

Dear Sir/Madam

Your hotel has been recommended to me by Mr & Mrs John Windsor who tell me they spent a very happy fortnight with you last summer.

I am planning to bring my family to St Annes for 2 weeks between mid-July and the end of August, and hope you will be able to accommodate us. We need one double and one twin-bedded room for my wife and myself and our two young children.

Our holiday arrangements are fairly flexible and any 2 consecutive[6] weeks within the period mentioned would be suitable.

An early reply would be appreciated so that our holiday arrangements can be completed as soon as possible.

Yours faithfully

5.　adjacent：鄰近的。
6.　consecutive：連續的。

(b) 回覆

→ p.228

Dear Mr Wilkinson

Thank you for your letter of 10 April. I remember Mr & Mrs Windsor very well; please pass on my thanks for their recommendation.

We are already fully booked for the month of August but the flexibility of your arrangements enables us to offer you one double and one twin-bedded room for 2 full weeks from Saturday 18 July.

We are provisionally reserving this accommodation for you, but would appreciate your written confirmation within one week.

Our current brochure is enclosed for your information.

We look forward to welcoming you to St Annes and assure you that everything possible will be done to make your stay here a very happy one.

Yours sincerely

23.15　度假公寓

(a) 詢問

→ p.229

Dear Sir/Madam

We wish to arrange a family holiday for 2 weeks from Saturday 14 August. Please let me know whether you have accommodation available which would be suitable for my husband and myself, as well as our two teenage children. We also wish to bring our dog, a clean and well-trained Irish Setter.

If you are able to accommodate us during this period, please let me know the facilities available in your holiday flats, together with your charges.

Yours faithfully

(b) 回覆

→ p.229

Dear Mrs Turner

Thank you for your recent enquiry regarding holiday accommodation for your family for 2 weeks from Saturday 14 August.

I am pleased to say that we have a holiday flat available which would be suitable for your family. This flat is on the first floor and comprises one double and two bunk beds, as well as cooker, fridge, sink, wardrobes and bedside drawers.

We do allow dogs in our holiday flats and refer you to the rules contained in our enclosed brochure. Schedules of prices are also shown on the separate leaflet.

We hope to welcome you to Thornton Holiday Flats and advise you to make an early reservation.

Yours sincerely

23.16 旅行計畫

旅行計畫是依據日期順序所安排的詳細行程。計畫中說明所有旅行安排、住宿和約定行程等。通常會使用副標題和欄位方式表示，既可打動人心且一目了然。

→ p.230

使用空白紙張，但
必須標示公司名稱

包含旅行者的
名字、預計參觀的
地點和旅行期間

© Turner Communications

ITINERARY FOR MRS SALLY TURNER

TOUR OF SINGAPORE AND MALAYSIA
7–19 JULY 200—

將日期作為
段落標題

SUNDAY 7 JULY

1530	Depart London Heathrow (flight SQ101)

MONDAY 8 JULY

1830	Arrive Singapore Changi Airport (Met by Christine Winters, Communications Asia) Accommodation: Supreme International Hotel, Scotts Road.

使用二或三欄格式
方便參考

TUESDAY 9 JULY

1030	Miss Joy Chan, Communications Asia, Funan Centre
1430	Mr Andre Misso, TalkTime, Bugis Junction

WEDNESDAY 10 JULY

0930–1730	5th International Telecommunications Conference

SUNDAY 14 JULY

使用 24 小時制
的時刻表

1545	Depart Singapore Changi Airport Terminal 2 (flight MH989)
1700	Arrive Kuala Lumpur Accommodation: Royal Hotel, Petaling Jaya

MONDAY 15 JULY

1030	Mr Keith Walker, KL Talk
1530	Mrs Ong Lee Fong, Malaysia Communications

TUESDAY 16 JULY

1130	Miss Sylvia Koh, Talklines

FRIDAY 19 JULY

2330	Depart Kuala Lumpur (BA 012)

SATURDAY 20 JULY

0830	Arrive London Heathrow

ST/BT
15 June 200—

實用措詞

【開頭】

1. I wish to visit ... and would be pleased to know if you have a single room available on ...
   我希望參訪……（地方），希望您能告訴我……（日期）是否有一間單人房

2. I should be grateful if you would forward a copy of your current brochure.
   如果您能寄給我一份貴公司最新手冊，我將十分感激。

3. Please let me know if you have available a first-class single cabin on the ... leaving for ... on ...
   請讓我知道……（日期）前往……（目的地）的……（船名）是否有頭等艙的單人舖位

4. I was pleased to hear that our hotel was recommended by ... after his visit in ...
   很高興聽到……（人名）在……（時間）住宿之後，向您推薦我們飯店

【結尾】

1. When replying please include a copy of your current brochure.
   回覆時，請寄上貴公司最新小冊子。

2. I hope to receive an early reply.
   希望早日收到您的回覆。

3. I look forward to hearing that you can provide this accommodation.
   期待得知您能提供住宿。

4. As we wish to make arrangements in good time I should appreciate an early reply.
   因為我們希望儘早做好安排，您能早日回覆將十分感激。

祕書與行政往來書信
Secretarial and administrative correspondence

在任何公司，內部溝通都扮演一個重要的角色。祕書、特助（PA），現在有時稱爲行政助理（Administrative Assistant），常需要撰寫書信、傳眞或電子郵件，其中很多是和安排會面、會議、面談、研討會，以及其他特殊的集會有關。

本章將列舉一些祕書或行政助理所經手的典型書信。

有關超級祕書的最高祕訣，請至：
www.shirleytaylor.com/index.html

安排與籌劃

24.1 要求見面的信函

(a) 要求見面【範例 1】

→ p.232

> Dear Mr Harrison
>
> Our Mr Chapman has informed me that you have returned home from your visit to the Middle East. There are a number of points that have arisen on the book I am writing on *Modern Business Organisation*. I should like the opportunity to discuss these with you.
>
> I shall be in London from 16 to 19 September and will telephone you on Monday 15 September to arrange a day and time which would be convenient for us to meet.
>
> I look forward to the opportunity of meeting you again.

(b) 回覆

→ p.232

> Dear Mr Alexander
>
> Thank you for your letter regarding *Modern Business Organisation*.
>
> I will look forward to meeting you again to discuss this. I note you will be telephoning me on Monday morning and hope that it will be possible to arrange to meet on either Tuesday or Wednesday afternoon.
>
> I look forward to meeting you again.

(c) 要求見面【範例 2】

→ p.232

Dear Mr Jones

I am very concerned about the difficulties you are having with the goods we supplied earlier this year.

I should very much like the opportunity to discuss this matter with you personally and wonder whether it would be convenient to see you while I am in your area next month. My secretary will telephone you soon to make a convenient appointment.

(d) 回覆

→ p.233

Dear Mrs Graham

I should very much like to see you to discuss various matters of mutual interest. As I shall be in Bradford next week, I wonder if it will be convenient to meet you on Thursday 12 September.

My secretary will call you within the next few days to confirm this appointment or if necessary arrange an alternative appointment.

I look forward to seeing you.

24.2 邀請研討會的演說者

(a) 邀請函

→ p.233

Dear Miss Forrester

提及會議、地點、日期及預期參加人數 — Our Society will be holding a conference at the Moat House Hotel, Swansea from 4 to 6 October the theme of which will be 'Changes in the Role of the Secretary'. Approximately 100 delegates are expected, comprising mostly practising secretaries as well as some lecturer members.

包含演講題目、時間及報酬 — We would be delighted if, once again, you would accept our invitation to speak on the subject of 'Effective Communication' on 5 October from 1030 to 1130. We would of course be prepared to pay you the usual fee of £100 and your travel expenses.

附上詳細活動內容並提及住宿安排 — A copy of the detailed draft programme is enclosed. You will of course, be welcome to attend other sessions of the conference on that day. Overnight accommodation will be provided for you on 4 October.

請求確認參加與否及需要哪些設備 — We look forward to hearing that you can accept our invitation. At the same time please let us know if you will need any visual aids or other equipment.

Yours sincerely

(b) 活動流程

→ p.234

CHANGES IN THE ROLE OF THE SECRETARY

DRAFT PROGRAMME

DAY ONE – MONDAY 4 OCTOBER 200—

0800	Registration and morning coffee
0900	Chairman's opening remarks (Hayati Abdulla, Core Services)
0915	The new secretary (Sally Turner, Author)
1030	Refreshments
1100	Business writing skills (Janice Lim, STTC Training Consultancy)
1230	Lunch
1400	Working with different cultures (Nigel Lau, StaSearch International)
1530	Refreshments
1600	Convincing presentation skills (Ricky Lien, Mindset Media)
1715	End of Day One

DAY TWO – TUESDAY 5 OCTOBER 200—

0800	Morning coffee
0900	Chairman's opening remarks (Janice Lim, STTC Training Consultancy)
0915	IT and the new economy (Sarah Cowles, D&P International)
1000	Refreshments
1030	Effective communication (Pamela Forrester)
1130	Lunch and fashion show
1400	Effective time management (Ian Norton, Leighton Industries)
1515	Refreshments
1545	Projecting the right image (Louisa Chan, C&G Fashion House)
1630	How to be a super secretary (Sally Turner, Author)
1715	End of Day Two

(c) 回覆

→ p.234

Dear Ms Bolan

感謝 — Thank you for your letter inviting me to speak at your conference on 5 October on the subject of 'Effective Communication'.

接受與確認 — I am delighted to accept your invitation, and confirm that I shall require overnight accommodation on 4 October.

提及所需的設備 — I will require use of an overhead projector for my presentation and hope this can be made available.

結尾附上
個人的關心 — I look forward to meeting you and other members of your Society again at your conference and wish you every success.

Yours sincerely

(d) 回函婉拒邀請

→ p.235

Dear Mr Woodhead

I was very pleased to receive your letter of 2 July.

Much as I should like to be able to speak at your conference in October, I am sorry to say that I will be unable to do so as I shall be abroad at the time. I must therefore regretfully decline your kind invitation.

I do hope that the day will be a great success.

Yours sincerely

24.3　詢問研討會所需設備

→ p.235

Dear Sir

提及會議、日期、時間及寫信的理由 — Our company will be holding a one-day conference on Saturday 18 May from 1000 to 1730, and we are looking for suitable accommodation.

預計參加人數 — About 200 delegates are expected to attend and our requirements are as follows:

條列特定需求 —

1　A suitable conference room with theatre-style seating

2　A small adjacent room for the display of equipment and accessories

3　A reception area for welcoming and registering delegates

4　Morning coffee at 1130 and afternoon tea at 1530

5　A buffet luncheon to be served from 1300 to 1400

詢問可否提供相關設備與收費明細 — If you have suitable facilities available please let us know the costs involved. At the same time please send specimen menus for a buffet-style luncheon.

We hope to hear from you soon.

Yours faithfully

24.4 研討會的活動流程

→ p.236

公司名稱 ——— © **Turner Communications**

主標題 ——— **5TH ANNIVERSARY CELEBRATIONS**

日期與地點 ——— to be held on Wednesday 17 September 200—
at Supreme Hotel, Aston, Sheffield

副標說明該節目單 ——— PROVISIONAL PROGRAMME
是暫定的或是
定案的

1800	Arrival of Directors and staff

使用 24 小時制， ——— 1830　Arrival of guests
hours 一字　　　　　　　　5th Anniversary folders will be issued to guests on arrival
可省略　　　　　　　　Cocktails will be served

條列各節目 ——— 1900　Introduction by Suzanne Sutcliffe, Marketing Manager
及額外細節　　　　　　　who will act as Master of Ceremonies

括弧內為主持人 ——— 1915　Opening address (Sally Turner, Managing Director)

1930　Slide presentation (Mandy Lim, Administration Manager)

2000　Buffet supper

2130　Toastmaster (John Stevens, Public Relations Manager)

標示結束時間 ——— 2145　Closing address (Suzanne Sutcliffe, Marketing Manager)
Drinks will be served until 2300

SS/ST

5 July 200—

有關祕書的好網站，請至：
www.deskdemon.com
www.executaryinternational.co.uk
www.pa-assist.com

24.5　召開董事會的電子郵件

→ p.236

Dear All

I confirm that there will be a board meeting on Monday 5 April 200—.

The scheduled board meeting dates for the remainder of 200— are:

Wednesday 5 May
Wednesday 7 July
Wednesday 1 September
Wednesday 3 November

All meetings will start at 1030 am and will be held in the board room in Atrium Towers. Lunch will follow the meetings, hosted by the Chairman, Mr Graham Newman.

Please inform your directors of these arrangements.

Mary

24.6　敲定行事曆日期的電子郵件

(a) 建議日期

→ p.237

Good morning Ladies

The Chairman has decided to hold an extra board meeting in August to discuss urgent issues. The suggested dates are:

Tuesday 10 August
Thursday 12 August
Friday 13 August

Timing: Between 11 am and 2 pm or 2 pm and 5 pm

Please let me know if your director is available.

An urgent response will be appreciated.

Joy

 不要因為趕時間而忽略書信開頭與結尾的問候語。

(b) 回覆

→ p.237

Hi Joy

The Finance Director will be available on Thursday 12 or Friday 13 August. His diary is free all day on both these dates.

Please let me have confirmation of the exact date for this extra board meeting soon.

Thanks

Sandra

祕書機構的好網站，請至：
美國國際行政專業人才協會（International Association of Administration Professionals, USA）
www.iaap-hq.org

英國合格私人祕書協會（Institute of Qualified Private Secretaries, UK）
www.iqps.org

澳洲辦公室專業人才協會（Australian Institute of Office Professionals）
www.aiop.com.au

英國醫學祕書、執業經理、行政人員以及接待員協會（Association of Medical Secretaries, Practice Managers, Administrators and Receptionists, UK）
www.amspar.co.uk

新加坡專業與行政祕書協會（Signapore Association of Professional and Executive Secretaries）
www.sapes.org.sg

邀請函

很多公司會召開特殊會議來發布特定活動，例如：

◆ 分公司開幕。
◆ 介紹新產品或業務。

◆　資深主管退休。

◆　特別的週年紀念日。

正式的邀請函通常印在 A5 或 A6 大小的高品質紙張或卡片上。

→ p.238

24.7　正式的邀請函

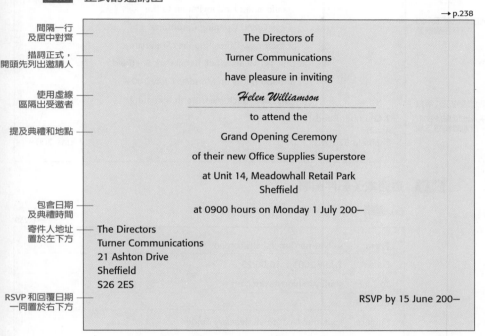

間隔一行
及居中對齊

措詞正式，
開頭先列出邀請人

使用虛線
區隔出受邀者

提及典禮和地點

包含日期
及典禮時間

寄件人地址
置於左下方

RSVP 和回覆日期
一同置於右下方

The Directors of

Turner Communications

have pleasure in inviting

Helen Williamson

to attend the

Grand Opening Ceremony

of their new Office Supplies Superstore

at Unit 14, Meadowhall Retail Park
Sheffield

at 0900 hours on Monday 1 July 200—

The Directors
Turner Communications
21 Ashton Drive
Sheffield
S26 2ES

RSVP by 15 June 200—

回覆邀請

收到邀請函，無論參加與否都必須做回覆。回覆的形式和邀請函類
似。若不克前往，最好說明理由。

24.8 接受正式的邀請

→ p.238

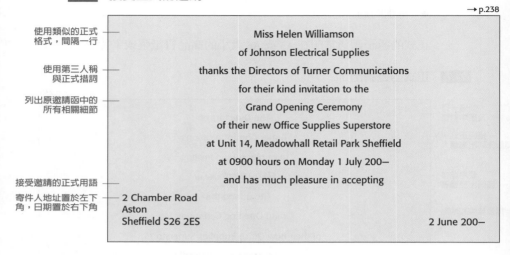

使用類似的正式格式，間隔一行

使用第三人稱與正式措詞

列出原邀請函中的所有相關細節

接受邀請的正式用語

寄件人地址置於左下角，日期置於右下角

> Miss Helen Williamson
>
> of Johnson Electrical Supplies
>
> thanks the Directors of Turner Communications
>
> for their kind invitation to the
>
> Grand Opening Ceremony
>
> of their new Office Supplies Superstore
>
> at Unit 14, Meadowhall Retail Park Sheffield
>
> at 0900 hours on Monday 1 July 200—
>
> and has much pleasure in accepting
>
> 2 Chamber Road
> Aston
> Sheffield S26 2ES   2 June 200—

24.9 透過電子郵件邀請

(a) 邀請

→ p.239

From	sallyturner@marshalls.com.id
Date	2 July 2003　16:06:29
To	shirley@shirleytaylor.com
CC	
Subject	Invitation to 10th anniversary dinner

Hi Shirley

I hope you remember meeting me in Jakarta earlier this year when you conducted a 2-day workshop for Marshalls employees.

I was interested to see from your e-newsletter that you will be in Jakarta next month conducting some more workshops. My company will be celebrating its 10th anniversary by holding a dinner at the Aryaduta Hotel on Wednesday 29 August.

It would be great if you could join us at our special celebration. Please let me know as soon as possible so that I can add your name to our VIP list.

Best wishes

Sally Turner
HR Manager
Marshalls Indonesia Sdn Bhd
Telephone: 6782 3742

(b) 接受邀請

→ p.239

From	shirley@shirleytaylor.com
Date	3 July 2003 17:02:45
To	sallyturner@marshalls.com.id
CC	
Subject	Re: Invitation to 10th anniversary dinner

Hi Sally

Of course I remember meeting you. I really enjoyed my workshop at Marshalls and hope you have seen your photographs in the Photo Gallery on my website.

Thank you so much for your kind invitation to join you at your company's 10th anniversary dinner on Wednesday 29 August. I should normally be flying into Jakarta that evening for some public workshops later that week. However I am going to change my travel plans and fly in one day early so that I can accept your invitation.

I will certainly look forward to seeing you and your colleagues again.

Shirley
http://www.shirleytaylor.com/
Mobile: +65 96355907

(c) 婉拒邀請

→ p.240

From	shirley@shirleytaylor.com
Date	3 July 2003 17:02:45
To	sallyturner@marshalls.com.id
CC	
Subject	Re: Invitation to 10th anniversary dinner

Hi Sally

Of course I remember meeting you. I really enjoyed my workshop at Marshalls and hope you have seen your photographs in the Photo Gallery on my website.

Thank you so much for your kind invitation to join you at your company's 10th anniversary dinner on Wednesday 29 August. However, I shall only be in Jakarta from Sunday 26th for one night – I have to fly back to Singapore straight after my one-day workshop on the 27th due to commitments in Singapore later that week.

I am so sorry that I cannot join you on what will, I know, be a wonderful evening. Please pass on my apologies to all my friends at Marshalls.

I hope to see you again when I am back in Jakarta for a longer trip.

Best wishes

Shirley
http://www.shirleytaylor.com/
Mobile: +65 96355907

24.10　下列是邀請客戶參加一個特別的午後座談會的邀請函。

→ p.240

Invitation to Rendezvous with Shirley

How would you like to transform your business writing style in just 5 simple steps? Learn modern terminology instead of yesterday's jargon? Overcome common problems in today's business writing? Learn the art of writing as you speak?

Imagine all this in just 2 hours!

What's more amazing is that it will cost you nothing except your time. If that's not good enough for you, we will even give you a free book – Shirley Taylor's *Model Business Letters*.

Rendezvous is our way of getting great minds to converge in a pleasant setting. Hopefully we will all learn a thing or two as well, and best of all we can network with peers in an afternoon of learning fun.

Event	Workshop and tea reception
Topic	Make writing your most powerful tool
Venue	Room 1, STTC Training Centre, Wisma Atrium
Date	Friday 26 March 2004
Time	3 to 5 pm

Please secure your place at our Rendezvous early by calling me on 6532341.

See you at Rendezvous.

Unit 4

分類商業書信
Classified business letters

代理
Agencies

很多擁有龐大海外貿易的企業都是自行處理買賣業務。例如，大型的製造商通常會有自己的出口部門，當交易量夠大時，則會考慮設立海外分公司。但是仍有很多的小型公司認為透過代理商（commission agent）、代理行（commission house）、行紀商（factor，或稱代理融通公司）、仲介商（broker），以及其他形式的代理商交易，會是比較經濟實惠的做法。

任何一家公司在指定代理商之前，應該要事先就代理商的資格、經驗與個人品格等，進行徹底的調查，例如：

◆ 可靠性及財務健全度。
◆ 產品行銷的專業能力。
◆ 與市場的關係及業務組織的效率。
◆ 目前代理的產品性質與範圍，特別是有沒有代理其他競爭者的產品。

在指定國外代理商時，因為無法親至當地予以監督與管控，以上幾點更顯重要。在此建議以書面方式來正式指定，並且於合約中詳細記載代理商方面的條款才是明智之舉。

徵求代理商

對於想尋找合適代理商的企業，有一些可取得實用資訊的管道可資利用。舉例來說，如果一位英國供應商希望擴展海外業務，可以到以下地方取得所需資訊：

◆ 出口服務部門或貿易部門的區辦公處。
◆ 大使館的領事處。
◆ 相關國家的貿易局。
◆ 商會（The Chamber of Commerce）。
◆ 銀行。
◆ 相關國家的期刊廣告。

申請代理

另一方面，在申請成爲他人的代理商時，應該強調兩件事：

◆　當地的市場商機正待開發。
◆　本身具備的優勢。

提出代理要求時，通常會向對方展示本身所累積的市場知識、充沛的人脈、長期建立的地位及豐富的經驗、高效率的業務組織，以及可提供展示間陳列代理產品等優勢，另外還會提供個人或企業名單，供對方徵信之用，同時表明佣金的比例。

25.1　申請國內代理

(a) 申請

→ p.242

Dear Sir/Madam

引言 — We understand from Knowles Hardware Ltd of Glasgow that you are looking for a reliable firm with good connections in the textile trade to represent you in Scotland.

這封信的背景說明 — For some years we have acted as Scottish agents for one of your competitors, Jarvis & Sons of Preston. They have recently registered as a limited company and in the reorganisation decided to establish their own branch in Edinburgh. As they no longer need our services we are now free to offer them to you.

有關經驗、員工及設備等細節 — As we have had experience in marketing products similar to your own, we are familiar with customers' needs, and are confident that we could develop a good market for you in Scotland. We have spacious and well-equipped showrooms not only at our Glasgow headquarters but also in Edinburgh and Perth, plus many experienced sales representatives who would energetically promote your business.

順勢說明你的需求並提議雙方見面 — We hope you will be interested in our proposal and will let us know on what terms you would be willing to conclude an agreement. I will be visiting your town in 2 weeks' time and hope it will be possible to discuss details with you then.

在結尾處提供備詢人 — We can provide first-class references if required, but for general information concerning our standing in the trade we suggest you refer to Knowles Hardware Ltd.

We hope to hear from you soon.

Yours faithfully

(b) 回覆

→ p.242

Dear Mrs Matthews

Thank you for your letter of 10 September. We are very interested to discuss further your proposal for an agency in Scotland.

Your work with Jarvis & Co is well known to us and in view of your connections throughout the trade in Scotland we feel there is much you could do to extend our business there.

Our final decision would depend upon the terms and conditions. As you will be visiting our town soon it would be better to discuss these in person rather than to enter upon what may become lengthy correspondence.

Please give me a call on 2684632 to discuss a convenient time to talk.

Yours sincerely

(c) 指定代理

→ p.243

Dear Mrs Matthews

提及會面並提供口頭討論的約定條件 —— It was a pleasure to meet you yesterday. We are now pleased to offer you an appointment as our sole agents for Scotland on the terms and conditions agreed verbally with you.

有關期限及佣金的詳細資料 —— This appointment will be for a trial period of 12 months initially. We will pay you a commission of 7% on the net value of all sales against orders received through you, to which would be added a del credere commission[1] of 2 $\frac{1}{2}$%.

庫存和樣品的進一步細節 —— As we are able to facilitate quick delivery there will be no need for you to maintain stocks of our goods, but we will send you full ranges of samples for display in your showrooms.

提及正式合約的必要性 —— Please confirm these terms in writing as soon as possible, after which we will arrange for a formal agreement to be drawn up. When this is signed a circular will be prepared for distribution to our customers in Scotland announcing your appointment as our agents.

鼓勵性的結尾 —— We look forward to a successful business relationship.

Yours sincerely

---

1. del credere commission：保信佣金，指支付給保證付款的代理商的佣金。

25.2 申請海外代理

(a) 電子工程

→ p.243

Dear Sir/Madam

引言中說明寫信
的原因

I was interested to see your advertisement in *The Daily Telegraph* and wish to offer my services as representative of your company in Morocco.

公司背景介紹

I am 35 years old, a chartered electrical engineer, and have a good working knowledge of Spanish and German. For the past 5 years I have acted in Egypt as agent for Moxon & Parkinson, electrical engineers in Warrington, Cheshire. This company has recently been taken over by Digital Equipment Ltd and is now being represented in Egypt by its own representative.

經驗與能力
的進一步細節

I have been concerned with work in the electronic field[2] since I graduated in physics at Manchester University at the age of 22. During my agency with Moxons I also had first-hand experience of marketing electronic and microprocessing equipment.[3] I feel I am well able to promote the sale of your products in the expanding economies of the African countries.

備詢人資料

For references I suggest you contact Moxon & Parkinson, as well as the 2 companies named below, both of which I have had close business connections for several years:

Fylde Electronic Laboratories Ltd, 4 Blackpool Road, Preston, Lancs

Sexton Electronic Laboratories Ltd, 25 Deansgate, Manchester

建議會面
進一步討論

I look forward to being able to give you more information at a personal interview.

Yours faithfully

---

2. **electronic field** ：電子產業。
3. **microprocessing equipment** ：如電腦等在尺寸上已大幅縮小的微處理設備。

(b) 紡織（來自海外的代理商）

→ p.244

Dear Sir/Madam

We would like to offer our services as agents for the sale of your products in New Zealand.

Our company was established in 1906 and we are known throughout the trade as agents of the highest standing. We are already represented in several West European countries including France, Germany and Italy.

There is a growing demand in New Zealand for British textiles especially for fancy worsted suitings and printed cotton and lycra fabrics. The prospects for good quality fabrics at competitive prices are very good. According to a recent Chamber of Commerce survey the demand for British textiles is likely to grow considerably during the next 2 or 3 years.

If you would send us details of your ranges with samples and prices, we could inform you of their suitability for the New Zealand market and also indicate the patterns and qualities for which sales are likely to be good. We would then arrange to call on our customers with your collection.

You will naturally wish to have references and may write to Barclays Bank Ltd, 99 Piccadilly, Manchester, or to any of our customers, whose names we will be glad to send you on request.

We feel sure we should have no difficulty in arranging terms to suit us both, and look forward to hearing from you soon.

Yours faithfully

25.3　申請獨家代理權

(a) 進口商提出申請

→ p.244

Dear Sir/Madam

We recently attended the International Photographic Exhibition in Cairo and were impressed by the high quality, attractive design and reasonable prices of your cameras. Having since seen your full catalogue, we are convinced that there is a promising market for your products here in Jordan.

If you are not already represented here we should be interested in acting as your sole agents.

As leading importers and distributors of more than 20 years' standing in the photographic trade, we have a good knowledge of the Jordanian market. Through our sales organisation we have good contacts with the leading retailers.

We handle several other agencies in non-competing lines and if our proposal interests you we can supply first-class references from manufacturers in Britain.

We firmly believe that an agency for marketing your products in Jordan would be of considerable benefit to both of us and we look forward to learning that you are interested in our proposal.

Mr Semir Haddad, our Purchasing Director, will be in England during May and will be pleased to call on you if we hear from you positively.

Yours faithfully

(b) 製造商的回覆

→ p.245

Dear Mr Jamal

Thank you for your letter of 18 March and for your comments on our cameras.

We are still a young company but are expanding rapidly. At present our overseas representation is confined to countries in Western Europe where our cameras are selling well. However we are interested in the chance of developing our trade further afield.

When your Mr Semir Haddad is in England we should certainly like to meet him to discuss your proposal further. If Mr Haddad will get in touch with me to arrange a meeting, I can also arrange for him to look around our factory and see for himself the quality of the materials and workmanship put into our cameras.

Yours sincerely

25.4　提議擔任保信代理商

除了一般正常的責任之外，有時候代理商還必須擔負買方無法付款的責任。這類的代理商就是所謂的「保信代理商」（del credere agent），有權利獲取額外的佣金以承受額外的風險。

(a) 提議

→ p.245

Dear Sir/Madam

The demand for toiletries in the United Arab Emirates has shown a marked increase in recent years. We are convinced that there is a considerable market here for your products.

There is every sign that an advertising campaign, even on a modest scale, would produce very good results if backed by an efficient system of distribution.

We are well-known distributors of over 15 years' standing with branches in most of the principal towns. With knowledge of the local conditions we feel we have the experience and the resources necessary to bring about a market development of your trade in this country. Reference to the Embassy of the United Arab Emirates and to Middle East Services and Sales Limited would enable you to verify our statements.

If you were to appoint us as your agents we should be prepared to discuss the rate of commission. However as the early work on development would be heavy we feel that 10% on orders placed during the first 12 months would be a reasonable figure. As the market would be new to you and customers largely unknown we would be quite willing to act on a del credere basis in return for an extra commission of 2 $\frac{1}{2}$% to cover the additional risk.

We hope you will see a worthwhile opportunity in our proposal, and look forward to your early decision.

Yours faithfully

(b) 回覆

→ p.246

Dear

We are interested in your proposals of 8 July and are favourably impressed by your views. However we are concerned that even a modest advertising campaign may not be worthwhile. We therefore suggest that we first test the market by sending you a representative selection of our products for sale on our account.

In the absence of advertising we realise that you would not have an easy task, but the experience gained would provide a valuable guide to future prospects. If the arrangement was successful we would consider your suggestion for a continuing agency.

If you are willing to receive a trial consignment we will allow commission at 12 $\frac{1}{2}$% cent, with an additional 2 $\frac{1}{2}$% del credere commission, expenses and commission to be set against your monthly payments.

Please let us know soon if this arrangement is satisfactory to you.

Yours sincerely

25.5 提議擔任進口商的採購代理

→ p.246

Dear Sir/Madam

引言：
背景資料說明

We understand from our neighbours, Firma Karl Brandt, that you have conducted your past buying of hardware in the German market through Firma Neymeyer and Schmidt of Bremen, and that in view of the collapse of their business you now require a reliable agent to take their place.

自我介紹
並提供服務

We are well known to manufacturers of hardware in this country and believe we have the experience and connections necessary to meet your needs. We therefore would like to offer our services as your buying agents in Germany.

是供有關個人經驗
及服務的進一步
詳細資料

Before transferring our business to Germany we had many years in the English trade. Knowing the particular needs of the English market, we can promise you <u>unrivalled service</u>[4] in matters of prices, discounts and freights.

As Firma Brandt have promised to write to you with a recommendation, we would like to summarise the terms we should be willing to accept if we acted for you:

清楚條列細節

1　We would have complete freedom in placing your orders.
2　All purchases would be made on your behalf and in your name.
3　All accounts would be passed to you for settlement direct with suppliers.
4　Commission at 5% payable quarterly would be allowed us on <u>CIF values</u>[5] of all shipments.
5　You would have full benefit of the very favourable terms we have arranged with the shipping companies and of any special rates we may obtain for insurance.

鼓勵性的結尾

We hope you will accept our offer and look forward to receiving your decision very soon.

Yours faithfully

4.　unrivalled service ：至高的服務。
5.　CIF values ：包含成本、保險費和運費在內的價格。

25.6　製造商確認代理條件

草擬正式合約時必須十分小心、謹慎，過程可能相當耗時，尤其是
當草約完成後，雙方對於條款產生歧見時。也因此在擬定合約前，
雙方應就所有必要列入的條款和條件清楚地達成共識。建議可以先
寫一封類似下列的信函作為預防之用。草擬合約時可加入相關法律
條文。

→ p.247

Dear Sirs

提及傳真以及業務
代表召開的會議

We were pleased to learn from your fax of 14 November that you are willing to
accept an agency for marketing our goods in Saudi Arabia. Set out below are the
terms discussed and agreed with your Mr Williams when he called here earlier this
month, but before drafting the formal agreement we should like you to confirm
them.

清楚簡短的
列出條件

1　The agency will operate as from 1 January 200— for a period of 3 years, subject
to renewal.
2　The agency will be a sole agency for marketing our goods in Saudi Arabia.
3　No sales of competing products will be made in Saudi Arabia either on your
own account or on account of any other firm or company.
4　All customers' orders will be transmitted to us immediately for supply direct.
5　Credit terms will not be given or promised to any customer without our
express consent.[6]
6　All goods supplied will be invoiced by us direct to customers with copies to
you.
7　A commission of 5% based on FOB values[7] of all goods shipped to Saudi
Arabia, whether on orders placed through you or not, will be payable at the
end of each quarter.
8　A special del credere commission of 2 $\frac{1}{2}$% will be added.
9　Customers will be required to settle their accounts with us direct. A statement
will be sent to you at the end of each month of all payments received by us.
10　All questions of difference arising under our agreement will be referred to
arbitration.

請求確認

Please confirm your agreement to these terms. A formal agreement will then be
drafted and copies sent for your signature.

Yours faithfully

6.　express consent：明確表示許可。
7.　FOB values：船上交貨價。

委託代理

有時候企業在找代理商時，會直接將代理權交給熟悉或他人推薦的人選。就如同代理商在爭取代理權的做法一樣，尋找代理商的企業除提供待開發市場的相關資料外，還要著眼於產品的特殊優勢，並努力說服潛在代理商該項產品一定會有很好的銷路，因為它品質佳、用途特殊、新穎、價格合理，而且有廣告做後盾等。

也許一時間無法將所有細節一一向代理商說明清楚，但一定要提供重要的基本資訊，以便對方評估是否值得代理，否則將會在謀合過程中增加不必要的書信往返。

25.7　委託地區代理

(a) 提供代理權

→ p.248

Dear Sirs

We have recently received a number of enquiries from dealers in the North of England for information about our range of <u>haberdashery</u>.[8] This leads us to believe there is a promising market waiting to be developed in that part of the country. Sales of our goods in other parts of the United Kingdom have greatly exceeded our expectations, but the absence of an agency in the North has meant poor sales in that region to date.

From our experience elsewhere we believe that an active agent would have little difficulty in expanding sales of our goods in the North of England. As we understand you are well experienced and have good connections in this area we would like to know if you are interested in accepting a sole agency. We are prepared to offer you a 2-year agreement with a commission of 7 $\frac{1}{2}$% on net invoice values.

As we wish to reach a quick decision I hope you can let me know whether this offer interests you. If so then I suggest an early meeting at which details of an arrangement agreeable to both of us could be discussed.

Yours faithfully

---

8. haberdashery：緞帶、蕾絲或其他衣服配件。

(b) 回覆

→ p.248

Dear Mr Thompson

Thank you for your letter of 5 April offering us the sole agency for your haberdashery products in the North of England.

We are very interested in your proposal and are confident that we should be able to develop a good demand for your products.

Your basic terms are agreeable so please let me know when it will be convenient for me to call on you. It would be helpful if you could offer a choice of dates.

I look forward to meeting you.

Yours sincerely

25.8　委託海外代理

(a) 提供代理權

→ p.249

Dear Sir/Madam

We understand that you deal in stationery and related products, and would like to know if you are interested in marketing our products in your country on a commission basis.

We are a large and well-established firm specialising in the manufacture of stationery of all kinds. Our products sell well in many parts of the world. The enclosed catalogue will show you the wide range of our products, for which enquiries suggest a promising market for many of them waiting for development in your country.

If you are interested in our proposal please let us know which of our products are most likely to appeal to your customers, and also terms for commission and other charges on which you would be willing to represent us. Please give us some idea of the market prospects for our products and suggest ways in which we could help you to develop the market.

We hope to hear favourably from you soon.

Yours faithfully

(b) 回覆

→ p.249

> Dear
>
> I read with interest your letter of 15 May enclosing a copy of your catalogue and inviting me to undertake the marketing of your products in Zambia.
>
> Provided we can agree on terms and conditions, I shall be pleased to accept your offer.
>
> I already represent Batson & Sons of Manchester in office equipment. As my customers include many of the principal dealers in Zambia I am sure they would provide a promising outlet for stationery and related products of the kind described in your catalogue.
>
> I shall be in London in July and would like to take the opportunity to discuss arrangements with you in detail. Meanwhile I suggest the following terms and conditions as the basis for a formal agreement:
>
> 1 All goods supplied to be invoiced direct to buyers with copies sent to me.
> 2 Accounts to be made up and statements sent to me monthly, in duplicate, for distribution to buyers.
> 3 An agency commission of 5% to be payable on net amounts invoiced.
> 4 A del credere commission of 2 $\frac{1}{2}$% in return for my guarantee of payments due on all accounts.
>
> As initial expenses of introducing your products are likely to be heavy, I feel it reasonable to suggest an agreement extending over at least 3 years, but this is a matter we can discuss when we meet.
>
> Please let me know if you are in general agreement with these suggestions.
>
> Yours sincerely

25.9　提供保信代理

當代理商允諾要成為保信代理商時，委託人必須檢視其財務健全度，有時候來自代理商往來銀行的推薦即已足夠。其他情況下，有時代理商也許必須提供保證人或存款保證，如以下的例子：

→ p.250

Dear

Thank you for your letter of 20 June. We are pleased to hear that you think a good market can be found for our goods in your country. We must confess, however, that credit on the scale you mention opens up a far from attractive prospect.

Nevertheless, we are willing to offer you an appointment on a del credere basis of 12% commission on the net value of all orders received through you, provided you are willing to lodge adequate security with our bankers here.

If security is deposited we shall be willing to protect your interests by entering into a formal agreement giving you the sole agency for a period of 5 years.

Please let me know if you are willing to accept the agency on these terms.

Yours sincerely

正式代理合約

有時候代理條件會透過書信往來確定，但對於規模較大的交易，一份正式的合約書是必要的。合約書應透過律師或者根據雙方的協議來草擬。合約的內容可能包含以下全部或部分事項：

◆ 代理商的性質與期限（亦即獨家代理、僅負責移轉訂單的保信代理商）。
◆ 代理區域。
◆ 代理商與委託人的責任。
◆ 採購與銷售的方式。例如代理商是以自己的名義下單，採買斷或「寄售」（on consignment [9]）的方式。
◆ 佣金與費用支出的明細。
◆ 管轄合約的該國法律。
◆ 報表、帳單與貨款的寄送
◆ 爭端發生時的仲裁（arbitration [10]）協定。

以下範例為典型的代理合約，是經出口協會同意而引用。

---

9. **on consignment**：以出口商的名義銷售，即寄售。
10. **arbitration**：透過中立的第三者解決爭端。

25.10　海外製造商的獨家代理合約範例

→ p.250~251

SPECIMEN AGREEMENT 1

Suitable for exclusive and sole agents representing manufacturers overseas

AN AGREEMENT made this　　　　　　　　day of
200— BETWEEN
whose Registered office is situate at
　　　　　　　　　　　　　　　　　　　　　　　　　　(hereinafter
called 'the Principal') of the one part and
　　　　　　　　　　　　　　　　　　　　　　　　　　(hereinafter
called 'the Agent') of the other part

WHEREBY IT IS AGREED as follows:

1. The Principal appoints the Agent as and from the
    to be its sole Agent in
    (hereinafter called 'the area') for the sale of manufactured by the Principal and
    such other goods and merchandise (all of which are hereinafter referred to as
    'the goods') as may hereafter be mutually agreed between them.
2. The Agent will during the term of　　　　　　years (and thereafter until
    determined by either party giving three months' previous notice in writing)
    diligently and faithfully serve the Principal as its Agent and will endeavour to
    extend the sale of the goods of the Principal within the area and will not do
    anything that may prevent such sale or interfere with the development of the
    Principal's trade in the area.
3. The Principal will from time to time furnish the Agent with a statement of the
    minimum prices at which the goods are respectively to be sold and the Agent
    shall not sell below such minimum price but shall endeavour in each case to
    obtain the best price obtainable.
4. The Agent shall not sell any of the goods to any person, company, or firm
    residing outside the area, nor shall he knowingly sell any of the goods to any
    person, company, or firm residing within the area with a view to their
    exportation to any other country or area without the consent in writing of the
    Principal.
5. The Agent shall not during the continuance of the Agency hereby constituted
    sell goods of a similar class or such as would or might compete or interfere
    with the sale of the Principal's goods either on his own account or on behalf
    of any other person, company, or firm whomsoever.
6. Upon receipt by the Agent of any order for the goods the Agent will
    immediately transmit such order to the Principal who (if such order is accepted
    by the Principal) will execute the same by supplying the goods direct to the
    customer.
7. Upon the execution of any such order the Principal shall forward to the Agent
    a duplicate copy of the invoice sent with the goods to the customer and in like
    manner shall from time to time inform the Agent when payment is made by
    the customer to the Principal.
8. The Agent shall duly keep an account of all orders obtained by him and shall
    every three months send in a copy of such account to the Principal.

（接下頁）

9. The Principal shall allow the Agent the following commissions (based on FOB United Kingdom values) in respect of all orders obtained direct by the Agent in the area which have been accepted and executed by the Principal. The said commission shall be payable every three months on the amounts actually received by the Principal from the customers.

10. The Agent shall be entitled to commission on the terms and conditions mentioned in the last preceding clause on all export orders for the goods received by the Principal through Export Merchants Indent Houses, Branch Buying offices of customers, and Head Offices of customers situate in the United Kingdom of Great Britain, Northern Ireland and Eire for export into the area. Export orders in this clause mentioned shall not include orders for the goods received by the Principal from and sold delivered to customers' principal place of business outside the area although such goods may subsequently be exported by such customers into the area, excepting where there is conclusive evidence that such orders which may actually be transmitted via the Head Office in England are resultant from work done by the Agent with the customers.

11. Should any dispute arise as to the amount of commission payable by the Principal to the Agent the same shall be settled by the Auditors for the time being of the Principal whose certificate shall be final and binding on both the Principal and the Agent.

12. The Agent shall not in any way pledge the credit of the Principal.

13. The Agent shall not give any warranty in respect of the goods without the authority in writing of the Principal.

14. The Agent shall not without the authority of the Principal collect any moneys from customers.

15. The Agent shall not give credit to or deal with any person, company or firm which the Principal shall from time to time direct him not to give credit to or deal with.

16. The Principal shall have the right to refuse to execute or accept any order obtained by the Agent or any part thereof and the Agent shall not be entitled to any commission in respect of any such refused order or part thereof so refused.

17. All questions of difference whatsoever which may at any time hereafter arise between the parties hereto or their respective representatives touching these presents or the subject matter thereof or arising out of or in relation thereto respectively and whether as to construction or otherwise shall be referred to arbitration in England in accordance with the provision of the Arbitration Act 1950 or any re enactment or statutory modification thereof for the time being in force.

18. This Agreement shall in all respects be interpreted in accordance with the Laws of England.

AS WITNESS the hands of the parties hereto the day and year first hereinbefore written.

(Signatures)

指定代理商的一般程序

本段舉一家出版社希望在黎巴嫩尋找合適的代理商，以便在當地銷售其出版品的過程為例做說明。

這家出版社決定透過其往來銀行取得所需資料。讀者可將以下的各種信函應用於詢問其他資料來源的場合。

25.11　出版社寫給銀行的信（收件人為銀行經理）

→ p.252

> Dear Sir
>
> At a meeting of our Directors yesterday it was decided to try to develop our trade with the Lebanon. We hope to appoint an agent with an efficient sales organisation in that country to help us to market our publications.
>
> I wonder if your correspondents in Beirut would be able to put us in touch with a suitable and reliable firm. Any help you can provide will be appreciated.
>
> I hope to hear from you soon.
>
> Yours faithfully

25.12　銀行回信給出版社

→ p.252

> Dear Miss Roberts
>
> Thank you for your letter of 24 August regarding the possibility of appointing a local agent in the Lebanon.
>
> Our correspondents in Beirut are the Banque Nationale whose postal address is:
>
> Banque Nationale
> PO Box 25643
> Beirut
>
> I have today sent a fax to their Manager explaining that you intend to appoint an agent in the Lebanon and asking him to provide you with any assistance possible.
>
> No doubt you will now write to them direct and I have told them to expect to hear from you.
>
> Yours sincerely

25.13 出版社感謝銀行

→ p.253

Dear Mr Johnson

Thank you for your letter of 26 August and for introducing our name to your correspondents in Beirut.

I have today written to the Banque Nationale, and would like to thank you very much for your help.

Yours sincerely

25.14 出版社給貝魯特銀行的傳真（收件人為銀行經理）

→ p.253

The Manager of Midminster Bank Ltd, London, has kindly given us your name. We are interested in appointing an agent to represent our interests in the Lebanon and wonder if you can recommend a reliable person or company.

We specialise in publishing educational books, including students' text books and workbooks. If you could put us in touch with a distributor who has good connections with booksellers, libraries and educational institutions, we would be very grateful.

Thank you in advance for any help you can provide.

25.15 貝魯特銀行的回覆

→ p.253

Dear Miss Roberts

Thank you for your fax of 28 August. The Manager of Midminster Bank, London, has already faxed me to explain your proposal to appoint a representative to further your trading interests in the Lebanon.

We are pleased to introduce you to Habib Suleiman Ghanem & Co of Beirut. This company has been our customer for many years. They are a well-known, old-established and highly reputable firm with some 20 years' experience of the book trade in this part of the world. We can recommend them to you with the certain knowledge that they would serve you well.

We have taken the opportunity to contact Mr Faisal Ghanem, General Manager, who has expressed interest in your proposal. I believe he will be writing to you soon.

I wish you much success in your venture, and if I can be of any further help please do not hesitate to contact me.

Yours sincerely

25.16　出版社向貝魯特銀行致謝

→ p.254

Dear Mr Jenkins

Thank you for your fax of 30 August giving us the name of Habib Suleiman Ghanem & Co. I wish to express my company's sincere thanks for your recommendation and the trouble you have so kindly taken to help us.

This company appears to be well equipped to provide the kind of service we need in the Lebanon, and we shall now look forward to hearing from them.

Yours sincerely

25.17　來自潛在代理商的傳真

→ p.254

Dear Miss Roberts

在引言中簡介背景資料 —— Our bankers, the Banque Nationale, inform us that you require an agent to assist in marketing your publications in the Lebanon. Subject to satisfactory arrangements as to terms and conditions we should be pleased to represent you.

詳述本身的經驗及知識 —— As publishers and distributors in Syria and the Lebanon for over 20 years we have a thorough knowledge of the market. We are proud to boast an extensive sales organisation and well-established connections with booksellers, libraries and educational institutions in these 2 countries.

相關利益及未來合作 —— We must mention that we are already acting as sole representatives[11] of several other publishers, including two American companies. However, as the preference in the educational field here is for books by British publishers, the prospects for your own publications are excellent, especially those intended for the student market. Adequate publicity would of course be necessary.

佣金與交易條件 —— Before making any commitment we shall require details of your proposals for commission and terms of payment, and also some idea of the amount you are prepared to invest in initial publicity.[12]

We look forward to receiving this information from you very soon.

Yours sincerely

---

11. sole representatives：獨家代理。
12. initial publicity：早期階段的廣告。

25.18　出版社回給潛在代理商的傳真

→ p.255

Dear Mr Ghanem

提及傳真 — I was pleased to learn from your fax of 3 September that you will consider an appointment as our agent.

關於先前在該地區
貿易的背景資料 — Although we transact a moderate amount of business in the Middle East we have so far not had much success in the Lebanon and are now hoping to develop our interests there.

寄送目錄和價目表 — I am sending by Swiftair today a copy of our complete catalogue of publications. The published prices quoted are subject to the usual trade discounts.

I would reply to your various points as follows:

以小標題列示
確保清晰度 — 1　COMMISSION
The commission at present allowed to our other agents is 10% on the invoice value of all orders, payable quarterly, and we offer you the same terms. We presume your customers would be able to settle their accounts direct with us on the basis of <u>cash against documents</u>,[13] except of course for supplies from your own stocks.

2　PUBLICITY
We feel that perhaps an initial expenditure of approximately £4000 to cover the first 3 months' publicity would be reasonable. However as we are not familiar with conditions in your country this is a matter on which we would welcome your views.

如果接受條件
的後續行動 — If you accept these proposals we will send by courier 2 copies of our standard agency contract. I am enclosing a copy for your reference and comments.

We look forward to the prospect of welcoming you as our agents.

鼓勵性的結尾 — Yours sincerely

---

13. cash against document：根據交貨單據付款。

25.19　接受代理的傳真

→ p.255

Dear

提及傳真並感謝收到文件 — Thank you for your fax of 10 September enclosing a copy of your standard form of agency agreement and for the copy of your catalogue which arrived very promptly. The catalogue covers an extensive range of interesting titles which appear to be very reasonably priced.

對所提供資料的建議 — With the proposed initial expenditure of £4000 on advertising, backed by active support from our own sales staff, we feel that the prospects for many of your titles are very good, particularly where they are suitable for use in schools and colleges.

說明是否接受條件並請求寄發合約 — We take it that you are prepared to leave the choice of advertising media[14] to us.

We are grateful for this opportunity to take up your agency here. As your proposed terms are satisfactory we shall be pleased to accept the conditions in the agreement. I presume you will forward this to me without delay.

Yours sincerely

25.20　出版社回覆已收到合約

→ p.256

Dear Mr Ghanem

Thank you for returning a signed copy of the agency contract with your letter of 26 September.

It is important that you carry stocks of those titles for which there is likely to be a steady demand. When you have had an opportunity to assess the market please let us know the titles and quantities you feel will be needed to enable you to meet small orders quickly.

We will follow the development of our trade with keen interest and look forward to a happy and lasting working relationship with you.

Yours sincerely

---

14. advertising media：廣告媒體。

與代理商的往來書信

25.21　代理商要求提高佣金

想向他人要求更多的錢並不容易，能順利拿到則更加困難，尤其是在金額已固定，且清楚載於合約的情況下。也因此，任何提高佣金的請求，都必須有很好的理由，並有技巧的表達。

在底下的書信中，代理商在陳述個案時，既有說服力又知所節制，促使對方能平心靜氣聆聽原委並公平對待。而任何收到這樣書信的人，也不希望因此失去這份友好關係。

(a) 代理商的請求

→ p.256

Dear Sir/Madam

有技巧地介紹主題並解釋緣由 — We would like to request your consideration of some revision in our present rate of commission. This may strike you as unusual since the increase in sales last year resulted in a corresponding increase in our total commission.

提供進一步詳細內容並完整說明情況 — Marketing your goods has proved to be more difficult than could have been expected when we undertook to represent you. Since then German and American competitors have entered the market and firmly established themselves. Consequently we have been able to maintain our position in the market only by enlarging our force of sales staff and increasing our expenditure on advertising.

需要圓滑的技巧，並給予清楚的正當理由 — We are quite willing to incur[15] the additional expense and even to increase it still further because we firmly believe that the required effort will result in increased business. However we feel we should not be expected to bear the whole of the additional cost without some form of compensation. After carefully calculating the increase in our selling costs we suggest an increase in the rate of commission by say, 2%.

鼓勵性的結尾並請求對方考慮 — You have always been considerate in your dealings with us and we know we can rely on you to consider our present request with understanding.

Yours faithfully

---

15. incur：負責。

(b) 委託人的回覆

→ p.257

Dear

提及傳真並對其所經歷的問題表示感激 — Thank you for your fax of 28 August.

We note the unexpected problems presented by our competitors and appreciate the extra efforts you have made with such satisfactory results.

對於代理商所提出的事實表示意見 — We feel sure that, <u>in the long run</u>,[16] the high quality of our goods and the very competitive prices at which they are offered will ensure steadily increasing sales despite the competition from other manufacturers. At the same time we realise that, in the short term, this competition must be met by more active advertising and agree that it would not be reasonable to expect you to bear the full cost.

建議調整的方式 — To increase commission would be difficult as our prices leave us with only a very small profit. Instead we propose to allow you an advertising credit of £4000 in the current year towards your additional costs. This amount will be reviewed in 6 months' time and adjusted according to circumstances.

請求確認 — We hope you will be happy with this arrangement and look forward to your confirmation.

Yours sincerely

25.22 委託人提議降低佣金比例

委託人如果要提議降低代理佣金，同樣需要良好的理由及謹慎處理，否則會引起反感，並讓雙方的合作關係更形緊張。如果佣金的比例記載在具法律效力的合約內，那麼調整佣金就必須取得代理商的同意才行。而即使之前的協議不受法律約束，委託人仍必須做些讓步，作為回報。

→ p.257

Dear

It is with regret that I must ask you to accept a temporary reduction in the agreed rate of commission. I make this request because of an increase in manufacturing costs due to additional duties on our imported raw materials, and to our inability either to <u>absorb these higher costs</u>[17] or to pass them on to consumers. In the event, our profits have been reduced to a level which no longer justifies continued production.

This situation is disturbing but we feel sure it will be purely temporary. In the circumstances we hope you will accept a small reduction of, say, $1\frac{1}{2}\%$ in the agreed rate of commission. You have our promise that as soon as trade improves sufficiently we shall return to the rate originally agreed.

Yours sincerely

---

16. in the long run ：最終、終究。
17. absorb these higher costs ：不提高價格而自行吸收成本。

25.23 代理商抱怨交貨延遲

買方決定下單的理由不外乎品質、價格和送貨狀況。通常準時交貨又會比價格便宜更受重視，但兩者都很重要。由此推知，在日益競爭的環境下，經常拖延交貨的製造商當然會處於不利的一邊，甚至失去交易機會。

→ p.258

Dear

We enclose our statement showing sales made on your account during March and commission and expenses payable. If you will confirm our figures we will credit you with the amount due.

These sales are most disappointing but this is due entirely to late arrival of goods we ordered from you last January. Not having received the goods by mid-February, we faxed you on the 18th but found on enquiry that the goods were not shipped until 3 March and consequently did not reach us until 20 March.

This delay in delivery is most unfortunate as the local agents of several of our competitors have been particularly active during the past few weeks and have taken a good deal of the trade that would normally have come our way had the goods been here. What is more disturbing is that these rival firms have now gained a good hold on the market which until now has been largely our own.

We have reminded you on a previous occasion of the competition from Japanese manufacturers, whose low prices and quick deliveries are having a striking effect on local buyers. If you wish to keep your hold on this market prompt delivery of orders we place with you is essential.

Yours sincerely

25.24 代理商建議的降價策略

指定海外代理商的一項重要理由，就是取得當地市場狀況和運作的竅門（know-how）。你的代理商知道什麼是最適合這個地區的產品，以及什麼價格是該市場所能接受的。聰明的出口商不會輕忽代理商對這些事項的建議及其特殊經驗。

→ p.258

Dear

We are enclosing our customer's order number 252 for card-index and filing equipment.

To secure this order has not been easy because your quoted prices were higher than those which our customer had been prepared for. The quotation was eventually accepted on the grounds of your reputation for quality, but I think we should warn you of the growing competition in the office-equipment market here.

Agents of German and Japanese manufacturers are now active in the market, and as their products are of good quality and in some cases cheaper than yours we shall find it very difficult to maintain our past volume of sales unless you can reduce your prices. For your guidance we are sending you copies of the price lists of competing firms.

Concerning the present shipment please send a draft bill of exchange for acceptance at 2 months for the net value of your invoice after allowing for commission and expenses.

Yours

25.25 代理商建議採取信用交易

(a) 代理商的建議

→ p.259

Dear

We have studied the catalogue and price list received with your letter of 31 March, and have no doubt that we could obtain good orders for many of the items. However, we feel that it would not be advantageous to either of our companies to adopt a cash settlement basis.

Nearly all business here is done on credit, the period varying from 3 to 6 months. Your prices are reasonable and your products sound in both design and quality. We therefore believe that you could afford to raise your prices sufficiently to cover the cost and fall into line with your competitors in the matter of credit.

In our experience this would be sound policy and would greatly strengthen your hold on the market. With the best will in the world to serve you, we are afraid it would be neither worth your while nor ours to continue business on a cash basis.

If it would help you at all we should be quite willing to assume full responsibility for unsettled accounts and to act as del credere agents for an additional commission of $2 \frac{1}{2}\%$.

We hope to hear from you soon.

Yours

(b) 製造商的回覆

→ p.259

Dear

Thank you for your letter of 10 April. We are glad that you think a satisfactory market could be found for our goods but are not altogether happy at the prospect of transacting all our business on a credit basis.

To some extent your offer to act in a del credere capacity meets our objectives, and for a trial period we are prepared to accept on the terms stated, namely an extra commission of 2 $\frac{1}{2}$%. We make the condition, however, that you are willing either to provide a guarantor acceptable to us or to lodge adequate security with our bankers.

Please let us know your decision on this matter.

Yours sincerely

25.26　委託人對代理商的抱怨

抱怨總不是件愉快的事，遇到不得不提出抱怨時，必須小心處理，內容有所節制。絕對不要假設代理商或是對方一定有錯，如果報怨信行文有禮、體諒，就能得到合理的答覆或讓事情獲得改善。

(a) 業績不佳

→ p.260

Dear Sirs

We are very concerned that your sales in recent months have fallen considerably. At first we thought this might be due to the disturbed political situation in your country. However, on looking into the matter more closely we find that the general trend of trade during this period has been upwards.

Of course, it is possible that you are facing difficulties of which we are not aware. If so, we should like to know of them since it may be possible for us to help. Please let us have a detailed report on the situation and also any suggestions of ways in which you feel we may be of some help in restoring our sales to at least their former level.

Yours faithfully

(b) 支出過高

→ p.260

Dear Sirs

We have received your October statement of sales and are concerned at the high figure included for expenses. This figure seems much too high for the volume of business done.

It is of course possible that there are special reasons for these high charges. If so we feel it is reasonable to ask you to explain them. We are particularly concerned because, under pressure of competition, the prices at which we offered the goods was cut to a level which left us with only a very small profit.

We shall be glad to receive your explanation and your assurance that expenses on future sales can be reduced. If for any reason this is not possible we should be left with no choice but to discontinue our business with you, for which we sincerely hope there will be no need.

Yours faithfully

 如果你是使用電子郵件進行跨國性溝通，那麼最好小心謹慎，訊息內容也最好使用較正式的語氣。等更了解對方之後，語氣上可以較輕鬆、親近。

實用措詞

申請代理

【開頭】

1. We should be glad if you would consider our application to act as agents for the sale of your ...
   如果您能考慮讓我們成為您……（產品）的代理商，我們將十分感謝。

2. Thank you for your letter of ... asking if we are represented ...
   謝謝您……（日期）來信，詢問我們是否已有代理……

3. We have received your letter of ... and should be glad to offer you a sole agency for the sale of our products in ...
   我們已經收到您……（日期）來信，很高興提供您我們在……（地區）產品的獨家代理……

【結尾】

1. We hope to hear favourably from you and feel sure we should have no difficulty in arranging terms.
    我們希望聽到您的好消息，並且確信在條件的協定上也應毫無困難。

2. If you give us this agency we should spare no effort to further your interests.
    如果您願意讓我們成為代理人，我們一定竭誠為您服務。

3. If required, we can provide first-class references.
    如果需要的話，我們可以提供最好的徵信資料。

指定代理

【開頭】

1. Thank you for your letter of ... offering us the sole agency for your products in ...
    謝謝您……（日期）的來信指定我們成為貴公司在……（地區）的獨家代理商。

2. We thank you for your letter of ... and are favourably impressed by your proposal for a sole agency.
    感謝您……（日期）的來信，對於您希望成為我們獨家代理人的提案，留下良好印象。

3. Thank you for offering us the agency in ... we appreciate the confidence you have placed in us.
    謝謝您給予我們在……（地區）的獨家代理權，並感謝您對我們的信心。

【結尾】

1. We hope to receive a favourable response and can assure you of our very best service.
    我們希望收到正面回覆，並保證為您提供最好的服務。

2. We look forward to a happy and successful working relationship with you.
    我們期望與您有一個愉快且成功的合作關係。

國際貿易
International trade

有些出口商會直接與海外買主進行交易，但更常見的是下列的交易方式：

1. 海外買主在出口國雇請代理商。
2. 出口商雇請居住於買方國家的代理商。
3. 出口商將商品寄給進口國的代理商，以寄售方式銷售。此時，出口商是所謂的寄售人（consignor），而進口商是代銷人（consignee）。

與國外聯絡買賣事宜，通常採傳真方式，主要是因為快速。而拜新科技之賜，我們有了電子資料交換（Electronic Data Interchange, EDI），它可大幅減少買賣雙方的文書作業。只要出口商與進口商擁有相容的 EDI 系統，就可以大量節省時間與文書作業。

進／出口流程圖

圖表 26.1 的流程圖，說明了傳統自國外採購商品所需的文件及作業流程。

Importer 進口商	Exporter 出口商
Contact exporters requesting quotations/samples 接洽出口商，請求報價／樣品	
	Provide quotations/samples 提供報價／樣品
Place order with supplier (or indent with agent) 向供應商下單（或向代理商訂購）	
	(If agent, send enquiries to manufacturers in own country and place orders with them for goods) （如果是代理商：向該國的製造商詢問及下單訂貨）
	Arrange with shipping company for goods to be shipped (or arrange for freight forwarder to do this) 安排船公司（或由攬貨業者）運送
	Arrange transport of goods to dock 安排貨物運至碼頭
	Arrange insurance 安排保險事宜
	Shipping company issues Bill of Lading 船公司提供提單
	Arrange insurance (if CIF) 安排保險事宜（如果為到岸價格）
	Send shipping documents (invoice, Bill of Lading, insurance policy or certificate) to importer (directly or through bank) 直接或透過銀行將裝船文件（發票、提單、保單或其他證明文件）寄給進口商
	Notify importer of date of sailing and arrival 通知進口商船期與抵達日期
On receipt of goods, pay dock charges if necessary, plus any customs charges 收到貨時，必要時支付港務及通關等費用	
Arrange transport from docks to own premises 安排運輸工具將貨物從碼頭運回自己公司	
Send payment to exporter 寄貨款給出口商	

圖表 26.1 自國外採購商品的傳統流程

代理商

代理商可以用個人或公司的型態來為委託人採購或銷售產品。在國際貿易上，當代理商以自己的名義代委託人買賣商品時，要做的工作包括取得報價、下單、監督對方履行約定，以及安排出貨等事宜。另外，還要協助委託人收款，萬一買主倒債，佣金代理商有時還得扛起償債責任。

26.1　巴林買主與倫敦代理商的交易

(a) 代理商回覆收到訂單

→ p.262

Your order number C75 of 10 February for 1500 fibreglass wash basins in assorted colours will be placed without delay. We have already written to a manufacturer in North London and will do everything we can to ensure early shipment.

We note your request for the basins to be arranged in tens and packed in cartons rather than wooden containers in order to save freight.

We shall arrange insurance on the usual terms and the certificate of insurance will be sent to you through our bankers along with our draft bill and other shipping documents.

(b) 代理商請求製造商報價

→ p.262

We have received an order for 1500 (fifteen hundred) 40 cm circular fibreglass wash basins in assorted colours for shipment to Bahrain. Please quote your lowest price FOB London and state the earliest possible date by which you can have the consignment ready for collection at your factory.

Your price should include arrangement of the basins in tens and packing in cartons of a size convenient for manual handling.

(c) 代理商寄出裝運通知

在接受製造商的報價及取得出貨日期後，代理商會以電話向攬貨業者（freight forwarder，貨運承攬業者、運輸承攬商）查詢到巴林的船期及交寄貨物的截止日。同時告知攬貨業者委託運送的貨物才積、重量及價格。待攬貨業者給齊船期資料後，代理商會寫信給客戶，告知船運的詳細情形。

→ p.262

YOUR ORDER NUMBER C75

The 1500 fibreglass wash basins which you ordered on 10 February will be shipped to you by the SS Tigris sailing from London on 25 March and due to arrive in Bahrain on 15 April.

The bill of lading, commercial invoice, consular invoice[1] and certificate of insurance, together with our draft[2] drawn at sixty (60) days sight,[3] have been passed to the Barminster Bank Ltd, London, and should reach you within a few days. The enclosed copy of the invoice will give you advance information of the consignment.

We hope the goods will prove to be satisfactory.

(d) 代理商將裝船文件轉給銀行

這筆交易的付款方式是 60 天期匯票，代理商將此匯票透過自己的往來銀行寄給國外買主，巴林的通匯銀行在收到買方同意於 60 天出示此匯票時願意付款的承諾後，才會將裝船文件交給買主。

在收到 26.1 的通知函後，客戶在巴林的往來銀行會將裝船文件出示給客戶，並要求其在匯票背面簽名以表示接受此付款條件。接下來銀行會將裝船文件交給買方，以利清關、提貨。

→ p.263

We enclose a bill of lading, consular invoice, certificate of insurance and our invoice relating to a consignment of fibreglass wash basins for shipment by SS Tigris to Mr Ahmed Ashkar of Bahrain.

Please forward these documents to your correspondent in Bahrain with instructions to hand them to the consignee against acceptance of our 60 days draft, also enclosed.

寄售商品

所謂的寄售是指出口商將商品寄交給進口商，但不會馬上開立發票請款。進口商可保留這些商品直到賣完，屆時出口商再據此開立發票。

---

1. consular invoice：由進口國領事所簽發的發票，為領事簽貨證書。
2. draft：必須經過承兌的匯票。
3. sixty (60) days sight: 六十天的付款期限。

26.2 位於奈洛比的公司請求寄售

(a) 買方請求寄售

→ p.263

自我介紹
並提供背景資料

We are the largest department store in Nairobi and have recently received a number of enquiries for your stainless steel cutlery. There are very good prospects for the sale of this cutlery, but as it is presently unknown here we do not feel able to make purchases on our own account.

建議可行的安排

We would like to suggest that you send us a trial delivery for sale on consignment terms. When the market is established we would hope to place firm orders.

有關款項、支出、
佣金及信用查核等
進一步細節

If you agree we would render monthly accounts of sales and send you the payments due after deducting expenses and commission at a rate to be agreed. Our bankers are the Nairobi branch of Midminster Bank Ltd, with whom you may check our standing.[4]

鼓勵性的結尾

We believe our proposal offers good prospects and hope you will be willing to agree to a trial.

(b) 賣方同意寄售

→ p.263

謝謝代理商的來信

Thank you for your letter proposing to receive a trial delivery of our cutlery on consignment which we have carefully considered.

附上樣品。說明
是否接受代理商的
提議並提及佣金

We are sending you a representative selection[5] of our most popular lines and hope you will find a ready sale for them. Your suggestion to submit accounts and to make payments monthly is quite satisfactory, and we will allow you commission at 10% calculated on gross profits.

貨物與文件的細節

The consignment is being shipped by SS Eastern Prince, leaving Southampton for Mombasa on 25 January. We will send the bill of lading and other shipping documents as soon as we receive them. Meanwhile a pro forma invoice is enclosed showing prices at which the goods should be offered for sale.

鼓勵性的結尾

We are confident that this cutlery will prove popular in your country and look forward to trading with you.

(c) 代理商交付銷貨清單

當商品賣出後，代理商會寄一份銷貨清單（account sales，參見圖表 26.2）給出口商，清單上明列銷售數量、價格、扣除佣金及其他費用後應付給出口商的淨額。該筆淨額可存入出口商在進口國的銀

---

4. check our standing：查詢我們的商譽、信用。
5. representative selection：具代表性的精選商品。

行帳戶，或是以銀行匯票付給出口商（除非採用第 11 章所討論的其他付款方式）。

→ p.264

We enclose our account sales for the month ending 31 March showing a balance of £379.20 due to you after deducting commission and charges. If you will draw on us for this amount at two months we will add our acceptance and return the draft immediately.

ACCOUNT SALES
by U Patel & Co
15–17 Rhodes Avenue, Nairobi

25 October 200—

In the matter of stainless steel cutlery ex SS Eastern Prince sold for account of E Hughes & Co Ltd, Victoria Works, Kingsway, Sheffield.

Quantity	Description	@ per 100 £	£
100	Knives	170.00	170.00
100	Forks	170.00	170.00
50	Table Spoons	150.00	75.00
200	Tea Spoons	105.00	210.00
			625.00

Charges:
Ocean Freight	92.55	
Dock Dues and Cartage	37.40	
Marine Insurance	20.50	
Customs Dues	32.85	
Commission	62.50	
		245.80

Net proceeds, as per banker's draft enclosed　379.20

Nairobi, 28 October 200—
(signed) U Patel & Co

E & OE

圖表 26.2　銷貨清單
（銷貨清單是代理商為委託人銷售商品的明細。在扣除相關費用與佣金後，即為應付給委託人的帳款金額。）

(d) 委託人（供應商）寄出款項

Thank you for sending your account sales for March. Our draft for the balance shown of £379.20 is enclosed.

謝謝您寄來的 3 月份銷貨清單。隨函附上給付餘額 379.20 英鎊的匯票乙張。

委託採購單

若國外買主透過供應商所在國的代理商下單，這種訂單稱爲委託採購單（indent，如圖表26.3 所示），上面列有訂購商品的明細，包括價格、包裝、裝運指示，以及付款方式。委託採購單不是訂單（order），而是國外買主授權給代理商採購商品的單據。

若委託採購單有指定特定的供應商，稱爲限定委託訂單（closed indent, specific indent）。反之，未限制供應商的稱爲不限定委託訂單（opened indent）。而代理商在下單之前，會要求一些供應商報價。

→ p.265

INDENT
No 64

N WHARFE & CO LTD
19–21 Victoria Street
CAIRO, EGYPT

10 February 200—

H Hopkinson & Co
Commission Agents and Shippers
41 King Street
MANCHESTER
M60 2HB

Dear Sirs

Please purchase and ship on our account for delivery not later than 31 March the following goods or as many of them as possible. Insurance should be arranged for the amount of your invoice plus 10% to cover estimated profit and your charges.

Yours faithfully
for N WHARFE & CO LTD

J G Gartside
Director

Identification Marks etc	Quantity	Description of Goods	Remarks
NW 64 Nos 1–12	48	HMV Stereo Model 1636 Walnut finish	Pack 4 per case
NW 64 Nos 13–37	25 bales	Grey Shirting Medium weight About 1,000 metres per bale	Pack in oil bags
NW 64 Nos 38–39	500 pairs	Assorted House Slippers Men's (200) Women's (200) Children's (100)	Pack in plain wooden cases

Ship:	By Manchester Liners Ltd
Delivery:	CIF Alexandria
Payment:	Draw at 60 days from sight of documents through Royal Bank, London

圖表 26.3　委託採購單

（委託採購單為交付代理商的訂單，請其代為採購商品。）

26.3 國外買主與代理行

(a) 在埃及的買方寄委託採購單給英國的代理行

→ p.266

We have received the manufacturer's price list and samples you sent us last month and now enclose our indent number 762 for goods to be shipped by the SS Merchant Prince due to leave Liverpool for Alexandria on 25 July. The indent contains full instructions as to packing, insurance and shipping documents.

It is important for the goods to be shipped either by the vessel named, or by an earlier vessel; if there are any items which cannot be supplied in time for this shipment they should be cancelled. When we receive the goods we shall pay you the agreed agency commission of 5%. The account for the goods will be settled direct with the manufacturers.

This is a trial order and if it is met satisfactorily we shall probably place further orders.

(b) 代理行下單給曼徹斯特的公司

→ p.266

We have just received an order from Jean Riachi & Co of Mansura, Egypt. Particulars are shown in the enclosed official order form together with details of packing and forwarding, case marks, etc.

The goods are to be ready for collection at your warehouse in time to be shipped to Alexandria by SS Merchant Prince due to sail from Liverpool on 25 July or by an earlier vessel if possible. Prompt delivery is essential and if there are any items which cannot be included in the consignment they should be cancelled.

Invoices priced ex warehouse should be in triplicate and sent to us for forwarding to our customers with the shipping documents. The account will be settled by our customers direct with you. As del credere agents, we undertake to be responsible should the buyer fail to pay.

This is a trial order and if it is completed satisfactorily it is likely to lead to further business. Your special care would therefore be appreciated.

Please confirm by return that you can accept this order, and arrange to inform us when the goods are ready for collection.

提單

提單由船公司出具，註明船公司承載該批商品的合約條件，作為承運業者將商品交船託運的憑證。此外，它也是貨物所有權的證明文件，當提單轉交給收貨人時，也就賦予其權利來聲稱提單所載貨物為其所有。

通常，一份提單是三張正本和三張副本，上面會註明船名、船期、貨物的嘜頭與標識、收件地址，以及描述商品沒有損害且確實在船板完好無瑕疵（clean shipped on board）。

承運業者必須檢查船公司開出的提單上所載事項是否正確無誤，並確定上面有船長簽名。之後，提單和其他出貨文件會經由銀行轉交給收貨人。

 請參照 *Essential Communication Skills —— the Ultimate Guide to Successful Business Communication*。本書是一本自我學習手冊，有助於發展及改善商業寫作技巧。

進口文件與程序

無論商品是以寄售或下單採購方式進口，進口的程序大致相同。在船隻抵達前，進口商（自行處理的商號或代理商）通常都會收到裝船（出貨）文件。文件正本會透過銀行轉交給進口商，但實務上，出口商會先以快遞寄一套副本給進口商，以便進口商在貨物抵達前先辦理進口手續，簡化作業，省下許多時間。

裝船文件包括：

1. 出貨通知：明列商品、船名、船期和預計抵達日期。
2. 提單。
3. 發票〔若進口的商品採寄售方式則為預估發票（pro forma，或稱形式發票）〕。

當船隻抵達時，進口商必須拿著提單並進行下列步驟：

1. 進口商必須在提單上背書，提示給到岸港口的船公司或其代表。
2. 支付運費（如果不是由出口商預先支付的話）及船公司所請求的其他費用。
3. 準備並提交海關提供的正式表格，填妥必要的進口登記事項。

進口稅的課徵方式可能是從量稅（specific，即依數量等為標準，每單位課一定金額的關稅，例如酒和香煙）或者是從價稅（ad valorem，即按發票金額課稅，例如電視機或其他製成品）。如果立刻要提取全部或部分商品，則必須事先繳交稅金才可取貨。有些進口至英國的商品要支付加值稅（value added tax, VAT），通常是在商品通關時支付。

26.4 進口交易

(a) 倫敦進口商下單到日本

→ p.267

Our order for 20 Super Hitachi Hi-Fi Systems (SDT 400) is enclosed at the CIF price of £550 each, as quoted in your letter of 10 June.

Through the Midminster Bank Ltd, 65 Aldwych, London WC2, we have arranged with the Bank of Japan, Tokyo, to open a credit in your favour for £6000 (six thousand pounds) to be available until 30 September next.

Please let us know when the consignment is shipped.

(b) 進口商開立信用狀

進口商寫信給倫敦的 Midminster 銀行請求開立信用狀。

→ p.267

I have completed and enclose your form for an irrevocable credit of £6000 to be opened with the Bank of Japan, Tokyo, in favour of Kikuki, Shiki & Co, Tokyo, for a consignment of music systems, the credit to be valid until 30 September next.

When the consignment is shipped the company will draw on the Bank of Japan at 30 days after sight; the draft will be accompanied by bills of lading (3/3), invoice and certificate or policy of insurance.

Please confirm that the credit will be arranged.

(c) 在日本的供應商提交文件給東京的日本銀行

→ p.267

We enclose a 30 days' sight draft together with bill of lading (3/3), invoice, letter of credit and certificate of insurance relating to a consignment of music centres for shipment by SS Yamagata to Videohire Ltd, London.

Please send draft and documents to the Midminster Bank Ltd, 65 Aldwych, London WC2 4LS, with instructions to hand over the documents to Videohire Ltd against their acceptance of the draft.

(d) 供應商寄發裝船通知

→ p.268

YOUR ORDER NO 825

We thank you for your order for 20 Super Hitachi Music Centres. I am glad to say we can supply these immediately from stock. We have arranged to ship them to your London warehouse at St Katharine Docks, London by SS Yamagata sailing from Tokyo on 3 August and due to arrive in London on or about the 25th.

The shipping documents will be delivered to you through the Aldwych Branch of the Midminster Bank Ltd against your acceptance of the 30 days' sight draft as agreed in our earlier correspondence.

We hope you will find everything satisfactory.

(e) 進口商回覆確認交貨

→ p.268

ORDER NO 825

Your consignment of Music Centres reached London on 27 August.

Thank you for the care and promptness with which you have fulfilled our first order. We expect to place further orders soon.

保稅倉庫

如果進口的商品要課稅，但對這些商品沒有即刻的需求，可先暫放在保稅倉庫中。保稅倉庫是倉庫所有人取得海關發給的執照，專門用來儲存未經通關納稅的進口貨物之用，並保證商品會在完稅後才移出。

這種作法可以讓進口商延後繳稅，一直到有需求時（可能是分批取貨）才繳稅。會放在保稅倉庫的商品，主要有茶葉、煙草、啤酒、酒，以及烈酒。當商品存放在保稅倉庫或免稅倉庫時，貨物所有人會拿到一張倉單（warehouse warrant）或是倉庫保管收據。要提貨時，必須出具一張有貨物所有人簽名的提單（delivery order）才能把貨提出來。

26.5 從倉庫中完稅提貨

底下是茶葉商寫給其代理人的信，該代理人買了一些茶葉，且持有進口商所開出的提單。

→ p.268

We refer to the 12 chests of Assam, ex City of Bombay, which you bought for us at the auctions yesterday and for which we understand you hold the delivery order.

Please clear all 12 chests at once and arrange with Williams Transport Ltd to deliver them to our Leman Street warehouse.

實用措詞

詢價與訂購

【開頭】

1. Thank you for your quotation of ... and for the samples you sent me.
   謝謝您對……（商品）的報價以及您寄來的樣品。

2. One of our best customers has asked us to arrange to purchase ...
   我們最好的一位顧客請我們安排訂購……（商品）

3. Your letter of ... enclosing indent for ... arrived yesterday.
   貴公司……（日期）來信所附的……（商品名稱）委託採購單
   已於昨天收到了。

【結尾】

1. Please deal with this order as one of special urgency.
   請以特殊急件方式來處理此訂單。

2. We look forward to receiving further indents from you.
   我們期望再收到您的委託採購單。

3. We thank you for giving us this trial order and promise that we will
   give it our careful attention.
   感謝您給予我們這次的試銷訂單，我們承諾一定會謹慎處理。

寄售品

【開頭】

1. We regret that we cannot handle your goods on our own account, but
   would be willing to take them on a consignment basis.
   很抱歉，我們無法以自己的帳戶名義來銷售您的商品，但是願
   意以寄售的方式來處理。

2. We have today sent a consignment of ... by SS Empress Victoria, and enclose the shipping documents.
   我們今天已經委託 SS 維多利亞皇后號將……（商品）運出，隨函附上裝船文件。

3. The consignment you sent us has been sold at very good prices.
   您寄售的商品已經以很好的價格賣出去了。

【結尾】

1. Please of course credit our account with the amount due.
   當然，請將所有應付的帳款記入我們的帳戶中。

2. We look forward to hearing that you have been able to obtain satisfactory prices.
   我們期望聽到您能獲得好價錢。

3. We will send you our account sales, with banker's draft, in a few days.
   我們會在幾天後將銷貨清單及銀行匯票寄給您。

4. We enclose our account sales and shall be glad if you will draw on us at 2 months for the amount due.
   隨函附上本公司的銷貨清單，對於應付的金額，如果您可以開立兩個月到期的支票，我們將十分感激。

銀行業務（國內）
Banking (home business)

1
2
3
4
5
6
7
8
9
10
11
12
13
14
15
16
17
18
19
20
21
22
23
24
25
26
27
28
29
30

商業銀行提供四種主要的服務：

1. 接受客戶存款。
2. 支付客戶開出的支票票款。
3. 貸款給客戶。
4. 提供客戶一個不同銀行間的資金轉帳支付平台。

帳戶種類

活期存款帳戶（current account）是最常見的銀行帳戶形態。客戶將錢存入帳戶，有需要時，可從帳戶中提領出來。客戶可以充分利用銀行的資金轉移功能來使用支票、轉帳、定期扣款費用（standing order [1]），以及直接扣款（direct debit [2]）等主要服務。活期存款帳戶原本是不支付利息的，但現在已經有一些銀行提供低利存款利息。而除了上述的服務項目外，銀行也提供各式各樣的其他服務，包括保管業務、夜間金庫、提供徵信資料、財產及遺囑信託、退休金和保險服務，以及創業輔導等等。

活期儲蓄存款（deposit account）是近幾年銀行用來吸引顧客的手法之一，提供了各種天期的利率。存戶如果要將錢提出來需在七天前通知銀行。一般來說，利息的多寡視存入的金額和解約通知所需天數長短而定。

開戶

有意開戶者必須提供令人滿意的推薦函，或者經由銀行客戶介紹。然而實務上，銀行為尊重客戶，多半不會要求客戶提供推薦函，但可能會檢視身分證明及某種形式的信用資料。

---

1. standing order：定期扣繳費用，指在約定時間定期支付特定款項的約定。
2. direct debit：類似定期扣繳費用的約定，但付款金額和付款時間不是由客戶指定，而是由消費商號通知銀行。

對帳單

銀行會定期提供活頁式的對帳單（statement）給客戶。對帳單上記錄了客戶存款帳戶各筆的交易與餘額。

支票

支票（cheque）是接受度極高的付款方式。但在以下任一情況，銀行有權拒絕兌現支票，將它退回給受款人或是支票持有人，並說明拒付原因。

◆ 開票人撤銷付款時。
◆ 開票人的存款餘額不足支付支票金額時。
◆ 支票兌現日未到，也就是提前兌現時。
◆ 支票過期，即超過兌現日六個月時。
◆ 支票有違法情事，例如偽造或變更時。
◆ 銀行發現開票人已經死亡或宣告破產時。

銀行手續費

個人客戶只要維持良好的信用，就不會被銀行索取手續費。企業型客戶則通常會與銀行協商手續費，一般為每季支付一次。
（編注：以上的說明都是以英國銀行為例。）

與銀行的往來書信

銀行與客戶之間的書信往來，傾向於標準化且十分正式，如本章中所列的範例。

27.1 給銀行的授權簽字通知

只有經公司董事會授權的員工才可以簽發公司支票。銀行會核對董事會的決議副本，內容詳載授權開戶支票的簽名方式、由誰簽名和簽名的樣本。

→ p.270

Dear Sir

At a meeting of the Board yesterday it was decided that cheques drawn on the company's account must bear two signatures instead of one as formerly.

One of the signatures must be that of the Chairman or Secretary; the other may be any member of the Board. This change takes place as of today's date.

There have been no changes in membership of the Board since specimen signatures were issued to you in July.

A certified copy of the Board's resolution is attached.

Yours faithfully

27.2 帳戶透支──與銀行之間的書信往來

以下為銀行經理寫給帳戶透支客戶的信。在謙恭有禮的同時，也將非經授權而透支的嚴重性傳達給客戶。

(a) 銀行來信

→ p.270

Dear Mrs Wilson

On a number of occasions recently your account has been overdrawn. The amount overdrawn at close of business yesterday was £150.72. Please arrange for the credits necessary to clear this balance to be paid in as soon as possible.

Overdrafts are allowed to customers only by previous arrangement and as I notice that your account has recently been running on a very small balance, it occurs to me that you may wish to come to some arrangement for overdraft facilities. If so perhaps you will call to discuss the matter. In the absence of such an arrangement I am afraid it will not be possible to honour future cheques drawn against insufficient balances.

Yours sincerely

(b) 客戶回覆

→ p.270

Dear

Thank you for your letter of yesterday. I have today paid into my account cheques totalling £80.42. I realise that this leaves only a small balance to my credit and as I am likely to be faced with fairly heavy payments in the coming months I should like to discuss arrangements for overdraft facilities.

I have recently entered into a number of very favourable contracts, which involve the early purchase of raw materials. As payments under the contracts will not be made until the work is completed I am really in need of overdraft facilities up to about £1500 for 6 months or so.

I will call your secretary in the next few days to arrange a convenient time for me to call to see you.

Yours sincerely

27.3　開票人止付

當支票因為郵寄途中不小心遺失等因素而必須停止付款時，我們稱為「撤回付款」（countermanded）或止付。只有開票人有權止付，且須以書面通知銀行取消付款。僅做口頭告知（oral notification），即使是開票人親自打了電話，仍須立即再以書面確認。

→ p.271

Dear Sir

I wish to confirm my telephone call of this morning to ask you to stop payment of cheque number 67582 for the sum of £96.25 payable to the St Annes Electrical Co Ltd.

This cheque appears to have been lost in the post and a further cheque has now been drawn to replace it.

Please confirm receipt of this authority to stop the payment.

Yours faithfully

27.4 抱怨支票被拒付

(a) 客戶給銀行的信

→ p.271

> Dear Sir
>
> The Alexandria Radio & Television Co Ltd inform me that you have refused payment of my cheque number 527610 of 15 August for £285.75. The returned cheque is marked 'Effects not cleared'. I believe this refers to the cheques I paid in on 11 August, the amount of which was more than enough to cover the dishonoured cheque.
>
> As there appears to have been ample time for you to collect and credit the sums due on the cheques paid in, please let me know why payment of cheque number 527610 was refused.
>
> Yours faithfully

(b) 銀行的回覆

→ p.271

> Dear
>
> In reply to your letter of yesterday, I am sorry that we were not able to allow payment against your cheque number 527610. One of the cheques paid in on 11 August – the cheque drawn in your favour by M Tippett & Co – was post-dated to 25 August and that the amount cannot be credited to your account before that date.
>
> To honour your cheque would have created an overdraft of more than £100 and in the absence of previous arrangement I am afraid we could not grant credit for such a sum.
>
> I trust this explanation clarifies this matter.
>
> Yours sincerely

27.5 請求銀行進行信用查核

銀行不會隨意將客戶的資料洩露給個人。商業上，當買方要求供應商提供信用交易時，買方會提供其往來銀行讓供應商進行信用查核。此時，供應商必須請自己的往來銀行（非買方的銀行）代爲進行必要的信用查核。銀行在回覆這類信用查核時，所提供的資訊通常是簡短、正式，且比透過備詢商號所能取得的更不個人化。

(a) 供應商請求其往來銀行協助

→ p.272

Dear Sir

We have received an order for £1200 from Messrs Joynson and Hicks of 18 Drake Street, Sheffield. They ask for credit and have given the Commonwealth Bank, 10 Albert Street, Sheffield S14 5QP, as a reference.

Please make enquiries and let us know whether the reputation and financial standing of this firm justify a credit of the above amount.

Yours faithfully

(b) 銀行的回覆

→ p.272

Dear Sir

As requested in your letter of 18 April we have made enquiries as to the reputation and standing of the Sheffield firm mentioned.

The firm was established in 1942 and its commitments have been met regularly. The directors are reported to be efficient and reliable and a credit of £1200 is considered sound.

This information is supplied free from all responsibility on our part.

Yours faithfully

銀行貸款與透支額度

銀行在核定個人客戶墊款額度(advance)，尤其是透支額度 (overdraft) 時，可能會要求客戶提供某種形式的擔保品 (security)。這類擔保品應該要易於評估價值、銀行容易取得法定所有權，同時可以快速脫手或變現。最常見的擔保品有壽險保單、股票，以及土地抵押權和抵押物等。

透支額度是以日計息，而個人貸款則是依貸款總額計息。

27.6　申請透支額度

(a) 客戶的請求

→ p.273

Dear Sir

With the approach of Christmas I am expecting a big increase in <u>turnover</u>,[3] but unfortunately my present stocks are not nearly enough for this. Because my business is fairly new wholesalers are unwilling to give me anything but short-term credit.

I hope you will be able to help me by making me an advance on overdraft until the end of this year.

As security I am willing to offer a life policy, and of course will allow you to inspect my accounts, from which you will see that I have promptly met all my obligations.

Please let me know when it will be convenient to discuss this matter personally with you.

Yours faithfully

(b) 銀行的回覆

→ p.273

Dear Mr Wilson

Thank you for your recent letter requesting overdraft facilities.

We are prepared to consider an overdraft over the period you mention, and have made an appointment for you to see me next Friday 11 November at 2.30 pm. Please bring with you the life policy mentioned together with your company's accounts.

Yours sincerely

---

3. turnover：交易量。

27.7 請求信用貸款額度

→ p.273

Dear Sir

In April 200— you were good enough to grant me a credit of £5000, which was repaid within the agreed period. I now require a further loan to enable me to proceed with work under a contract with the Waterfoot Borough Council for building an extension to their King's Road School.

I need the loan to purchase building materials at a cost of about £6000. The contract price is £20,000, payable immediately upon satisfactory completion of the work on or before 30 September next.

I hope you will be able to grant me a loan of £5000 for a period of 9 months.

I enclose a copy of my latest audited balance sheet and shall be glad to call at the bank at your convenience to discuss the matter.

Yours faithfully

27.8 請求擔保貸款額度

→ p.274

Dear Sir

I am considering a large extension of business with several firms in Japan and as the terms of dealings will involve additional <u>working capital</u>,[4] I should be glad if you would arrange to grant me a loan of, say, £6000 for a period of 6 months.

You already hold for safe keeping on my behalf £5000 Australian 3% stock and £4500 4% <u>consols</u>.[5] I am willing to pledge these as security. At current market prices I believe they would provide sufficient cover for the loan.

You would be able to rely upon repayment of the loan <u>at maturity</u>[6] as, apart from other income, I have arranged to take into the business a partner who, under the terms of the partnership agreement, will introduce £5000 capital at or before the end of the present year.

If you will arrange a day and time when I may visit you, I will bring with me evidence supporting my request.

Yours faithfully

---

4. working capital ：營運資金。
5. consols ：一種由英國政府發行的長期債券。
6. at maturity ：到期。

27.9　請求延長貸款期限

→ p.274

> Dear Sir
>
> On 1 August you granted me a loan of £2500 which is due for repayment at the end of this month.
>
> I have already taken steps to prepare for this repayment but due to a fire at my warehouse 2 weeks ago I have been faced with heavy unexpected payments. Damage from the fire is thought to be about £4000 and is fully covered by insurance. However, as my claim is unlikely to be settled before the end of next month, I hope the period of the loan can be extended until then.
>
> I am sure you will realise that the fire has presented me with serious problems and that repayment of the loan before settlement of my claim could be made only with the greatest difficulty.
>
> Yours faithfully

27.10　請求清償未經授權的透支

(a) 銀行的要求

→ p.275

> Dear Mr Hendon
>
> I notice that since the beginning of last September there have been a number of occasions on which your current account has been overdrawn.[7] As you know it is not the custom of the bank to allow overdrafts except by special arrangement and usually against security.
>
> Two cheques drawn by you have been presented for payment today, one by Insurance Brokers Ltd for £27.50 and one by John Musgrave & Sons for £87.10. As you are one of our oldest customers I gave instructions for the cheques to be paid although the balance on your current account, namely £56.40, was insufficient to meet them.
>
> I am well aware that there is a substantial credit balance on your deposit account. If overdraft facilities on your current account are likely to be needed in future, I suggest that you give the bank the necessary authority to hold the balance on deposit as overdrawn security.
>
> Yours sincerely

---

7. **overdrawn**：透支，即提款超過結餘。

(b) 客戶的回覆

→ p.275

Dear Mr Stannard

Thank you for your letter of 2 December.

I am sorry to have given you cause to write to me concerning recent overdrafts on my current account. Although the amounts involved are not large I agree that overdraft facilities should have been discussed with you in advance and regret that this was not done. I am afraid I had overlooked the fact that the balance carried on my current account in recent months had been smaller than usual.

Later this month I expect to receive payment for several large contracts now nearing completion. No question of overdraft facilities will then arise. Meanwhile I am pleased to authorise you to treat the balance on my deposit account as security for any overdraft incurred on my current account. Once again my apologies for the inconvenience caused.

Yours sincerely

其他的銀行業務書信

27.11　客服

→ p.276

Dear Miss Turner

It has been 4 months since you opened your account with us. I trust that the service you have experienced during this time has been of the highest standard.

Customer Service is a top priority at the Royal International Bank, and that is why we invite all our customers to have a Customer Service Review. This service can take place in person at this branch or over the telephone. It gives customers the opportunity to ensure that they have the most suitable accounts to meet their requirements.

This review is free of charge. If you would like to take advantage of this service, or to discuss any other matters, please contact Kelly Sherman on 01245 343234 to arrange a mutually convenient appointment.

I look forward to speaking to you very soon.

Yours sincerely

27.12 促銷

→ p.276

Dear Miss Wright

MAXIMUM SAVINGS, MINIMUM EFFORT

Now that you have opened a Bonus 90 Account, why not build up your savings the hassle-free way with a standing order?

This simple arrangement makes everything so easy – just decide how much you would like to transfer from your current account each month, then complete and sign the attached form. We will do the rest. There is no need to visit your branch, and no need to send any cheques.

WATCH YOUR SAVINGS GROW

If you pay money regularly into a savings account with a high interest rate, you will be surprised at how quickly your nest egg builds up. With tiered rates of interest, you will earn more depending on how much you save.

Take advantage of this great opportunity now by completing the standing order form below and returning it in the enclosed reply-paid envelope.

We really can make saving simple!

Yours sincerely

實用措詞

【開頭】

1. I have entered into partnership with Mr ... and we wish to open a current account in the name of ...
   我已經和……先生成爲合夥關係，因此我們希望以……的名義開立活期存款帳戶。

2. I enclose a standing order for payment of £15 on the first day of each month to ...
   隨函附上定期扣繳費用單，以便於每月 1 日轉出 15 英鎊至……

3. I shall be moving to ... at the end of this month and should be glad if you would transfer my account to your branch in that town.

   本月底我將搬到……，希望您可以將我的帳戶轉到該地的分行。

4. According to the statement received from you yesterday ...

   根據您昨天寄來的對帳單……

5. The statement you sent me recently shows that my account was overdrawn ... during July.

   您最近寄給我的對帳單顯示我的帳戶在 7 月透支……。

6. On referring to the statement just received I notice that ...

   根據我剛收到的對帳單，我注意到……

7. This is to confirm my telephone message this morning asking you to stop payment of cheque number ...

   這封信是確認今天早上我在電話中要求您止付……號支票一事。

8. I am writing to ask you to consider a loan of ... for a period of ... months.

   寫這封信的目的在請您考慮給我為期……（個月）的貸款，（金額）……。

9. Please arrange to buy for me the following securities within the price ranges shown:

   請在所示的價格區間內替我購買下列有價證券：

【結尾】

1. If you require further information please let me know.

   如果您需要進一步的資料，請讓我知道。

2. I shall be glad to call on you should you need any further information.

   如果您需要進一步的資料，我很樂意去拜訪您。

3. I feel that the charges are excessive and should be glad of your explanation.

我認為這些費用超收，希望您提出解釋。

4. I should be most grateful if you could grant the credit asked for.

如果您准許我的信用額度，我將十分感激。

5. If you require a guarantor Mr ... of ... has kindly consented to act.

如果您需要一位保證人，……（公司）的……（先生）同意擔任。

銀行業務（國際）
Banking (international business)

支票是國內貿易的主要付款工具，但因為支票只能在開票人的國家使用，因此不適用於國際貿易。國際貿易的付款方式有以下幾種：

◆ 銀行匯票（bankers draft）、銀行匯款／轉帳（以郵件、電傳或電報進行）。
◆ 信用狀（letter of credit）。
◆ 匯票（bill of exchange）及本票（promissory note）。

進口商的付款方式，依其在下單時與出口商的約定而定，而約定的方式則取決出口商對進口商的了解及雙方的信任程度。

二十多年前成立的全球銀行財務電信協會（Society for Worldwide Inter Bank Financial Telecommunication, SWIFT），讓加入該組織的全球各主要銀行，可透過電子化機制彼此溝通，進而加速資金轉帳機制，減少紙張作業。但傳統的付款方式仍被沿用，所以本章還是會加以說明。

銀行匯票

和支票一樣，銀行匯票也是見票即付，但和支票不同的是，銀行匯票因為有發行銀行的資產做背書，所以幾乎沒有風險。想用匯票付款的進口商，會在當地的銀行購買後寄給出口商，出口商只要將匯票存入自己的銀行帳戶即可。

28.1 以銀行匯票付款

(a) 出口商請求付款

→ p.278

We enclose your statement for the month of November showing an outstanding balance of £580.50.

We assume you will settle this outstanding amount by banker's draft in UK Pounds Sterling and hope to receive payment soon.

(b) 進口商的回覆

→ p.278

Thank you for your letter together with our November statement.

Our banker's draft for UK Pounds five hundred and eighty and 50 pence (UK£580.50) is enclosed.

銀行匯款（郵件、電傳及電匯）

銀行匯款是一種簡單的資金移轉方式，也是從債務人所在國的銀行帳戶，將錢轉給債權人所在國銀行帳戶最安全的海外匯款方式之一。債務人先透過書信或特殊表格來指示其通匯銀行進行匯款，銀行收到指示後，再將匯款金額轉換成當地貨幣後記入債權人的通匯銀行。匯率以匯款當時的匯率爲基準。

匯款是由雙方銀行直接進行，不會有遺失問題。爲免延遲，現在銀行習慣以傳眞、電匯及網路來聯絡匯款事宜。匯款的匯率可從當天的報紙取得。

28.2　電匯付款

→ p.278

Dear Sir

We have received your statement for the quarter ended 30 September and find that it agrees with our books. As requested we have instructed our bankers, the Midland Bank Ltd, 2 Deansgate, Manchester, to telegraph the sum of £2182.89 for the credit of your account at the Bank Nationalé, Sweden.

This payment clears your account up to 31 August. The unpaid balance of £623.42 for goods supplied during September will be telegraphed by our bankers on or before 15 November.

Yours faithfully

匯票

匯票是由債權人（出票人，drawer）簽發給債務人（承兌人、受票人，drawee），委託承兌人在指定的日期支付匯票上的金額給指定的個人或公司（即受款人，payee）。目前匯票大部分已被其他付款方式，尤其是銀行信用狀所取代，現在幾乎只用在國際貿易上。

當承兌人同意匯票上的條件，並「承兌」（也就是保證支付）及簽名後，一旦匯票到期，他們就有義務承擔。

在以下範例中：
開票人是 Trevor Gartside（崔佛・賈提賽）
承兌人是 C. Mazzawi（C. 馬查威）
受款人是 E. Hughes & Co.（E. 修奇公司）

→ p.279

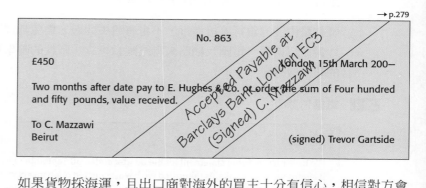

如果貨物採海運，且出口商對海外的買主十分有信心，相信對方會依合約所載條件付款，出口商就會直接寄出裝船文件。買方一旦同意承兌出口商開立的匯票，在收到貨並將匯票寄回給出口商後，就有權保留裝船文件。

出口商常會要求進口商以銀行或金融機構來承兌匯票，這對匯票持有人來說更有保障。即使進口商接受並答應承兌該張匯票，出口商也會要求在匯票上註明承兌的銀行名稱（如上例所示）。匯票持有人可向該銀行出示匯票以請求付款，這種方式稱為「外埠付款貼現」

（'domiciling' a bill，或稱間接匯票），如 Bills domiciled in London 表示匯票指定在倫敦付款，可由英格蘭銀行直接承兌貼現（rediscount）。

→ p.279

28.3　匯票付款

(a) 與可信賴的客戶直接交易

→ p.279

> Dear Sir
>
> We thank you for your order of 25 June for 1000 metres of poplin shirting at the quoted price of £0.86 per metre.
>
> The shirting is now ready for despatch and will be shipped by the SS Tripoli sailing from Liverpool on 18 July.
>
> We are pleased to enclose shipping documents. Also enclosed is our sight draft[1] drawn at 30 days as agreed. Please accept and return it immediately.
>
> Yours faithfully

(b) 與陌生的客戶直接交易

→ p.279

> Dear Sirs
>
> We are pleased to inform you that we can supply the fancy leather goods included in your order number 582 of 6 August and in accordance with our draft at 30 days for acceptance by your bankers.
>
> Immediately we receive the accepted draft we will arrange to ship the goods. Meanwhile we are holding them for you.
>
> Yours faithfully

---

1. **sight draft**：即期票據，付款人在見票時就付款的匯票。

28.4 買方請求展延票期

(a) 買方的請求

→ p.280

Dear Sirs

You informed me on 25 November that you intended to draw on me at 2 months for the amount due on your invoice number S 256, namely £961.54.

Until now I have had no difficulty in meeting my obligations and have always settled my accounts promptly. I could have done so now had it not been for the bankruptcy of one of my most important customers. I should therefore be most grateful if you could draw your bill at 3 months instead of the proposed 2. This would enable me to meet a temporarily difficult situation which has been forced upon me by circumstances that could not be foreseen.

Yours faithfully

(b) 賣方回覆同意展延

→ p.280

Dear Sir

I am replying to your letter of 30 November in which you ask for an extension of the tenor[2] of my draft from 2 to 3 months.

In the special circumstances you mention and because of the promptness with which you have settled your accounts in the past, we are willing to grant the request. Our draft, drawn at 3 months, is enclosed. Please add your acceptance and return it to me.

Yours faithfully

(c) 賣方拒絕展延票期

拒絕客戶提出的要求，很容易會得罪對方，甚至失去日後交易的機會。底下這一封信寫的圓滑又體貼，結果雖然令客戶失望，但不致引起反感。

---

2. **tenor**：票期，即匯票的付款期限。

→ p.280

Dear Sir

I am sorry to learn from your letter of 30 November of the difficulty in which the bankruptcy of an important customer has placed you. I should like to say at once that I fully appreciate your wish for an extension of my draft and would very much like to help you. Unfortunately, I cannot do so because of commitments which I have to meet in 2 months' time.

In the circumstances you mention your request is not at all unreasonable. If it had been at all possible I would gladly have done so. As matters stand I am left with no choice but to ask you to accept the draft, as drawn at 2 months. This is enclosed for your signature and return.

Yours faithfully

28.5　匯票到期拒付

當匯票經買方同意承兌的手續，但卻無法在到期時兌現，就變成所謂的「拒付」（dishonoured）匯票。如此一來，買方立刻會出現欠款。此時，出票人或匯票持有人有權對 (1) 匯票的承兌人；(2) 債款的承諾者採取法律行動。

(a)　出票人請求解釋

→ p.281

Dear Sirs

We were very surprised this morning when our bankers returned the bill we drew on you for £325 on 5 August marked 'Refer to drawer'.

Since we are aware from personal knowledge that your firm is financially sound, we presume that failure to honour the bill was due to some mistake. We shall therefore be glad if you will explain the reason. At the same time we must ask you to send by return the sum due on the bill.

Yours faithfully

(b) 出票人聲稱將採取法律行動

→ p.281

Dear Sir

I regret to say that our bill number 670 for £462.72 of 15 December was not met when we presented it to the bank today.

In view of your earlier promise to meet your obligations on the bill, we are both surprised and disappointed that payment has not been made. We should like to feel that there has been some misunderstanding and ask you to explain why the bill was not <u>honoured</u>.[3]

At the same time we are making a formal request for payment of the sum due and shall be glad to receive your remittance. If payment is not made I am afraid we shall have no choice but to start proceedings for dishonour.

Yours faithfully

28.6 對拒付匯票提出聲明

如果國外匯票（非國內匯票）遭拒付，必須先提出「聲明」（protest），作為訴諸法律的第一步。所謂的「聲明」就是公證人（notary public[4]）正式宣稱該匯票的條件未被兌現，目的在防止承兌人否認該匯票已被提示付款或承兌（如果該匯票之所以跳票是因未能承兌的話）。

供應商在下面這封書中提出聲明後，又給了買主一次付款的機會。

---

3. honoured ：承兌，到期付款。
4. notary public ：公證人，通常指經授權對合約及其他重要文件作證的事務律師。

→ p.281

Dear Sir

Although you gave your <u>unqualified acceptance</u>[5] to our bill number 670 of 15 December for £462.72, this was not met when presented for payment yesterday.

Non-payment has obliged us to make formal protest of the bill. We now offer you this final opportunity to meet your obligations by payment of the sum of £465.22 to cover the amount for which the bill was accepted and the expenses of protest as follows:

Nominal value of the bill	£462.72
Expenses of protest	2.50

We hope to receive payment within the next few days so as to avoid our having to take further proceedings.

Yours faithfully

跟單匯票

以上範例是進口商和出口商直接進行交易，但更常見的是出口商利用銀行的服務來取得保障。主要的方法有三種，任一種出口商都需要準備跟單匯票（匯票連同裝船文件）交給銀行，銀行會將文件轉給其海外分行或通匯銀行，而他們會再與進口商接洽。

1. 進口商支付匯票金額擇一給出口商、指定受款人或銀行。
2. 出口商開跟單匯票給進口商，但會請銀行以收到的裝船文件作為擔保品，將匯票貼現。
3. 出口商請求進口商開立信用狀，目的在出示裝船文件時，出口商可以開立匯票給指定的銀行。針對匯票所開出的信用狀必須說明最高金額、信用期間、匯票的兌現期限（即期限），以及與匯票一起寄出的裝船文件。

5. unqualified acceptance：無條件承兌，指到期即全部付款之意。

當開給進口商的匯票有期限，例如 60 天，出示匯票的銀行只會在進口商承兌時，才將裝船文件交出（即承兌交單， D/A terms）。但如果開出的是見票即付匯票，那麼銀行只能在付款時交出裝船文件（即付款交單， D/P terms）。

實務上，出口商給銀行的指示通常是寫在銀行所提供的特殊表格上，以確保所有重點均無遺漏。之後的書信來往則通常用於未提供特殊表格的場合。

28.7 透過銀行出示的跟單匯票

(a) 出口商給進口商的信（付款交單）

→ p.282

Dear Sirs

We were pleased to receive your faxed order of 29 June and have arranged to ship the electric shavers by SS Tyrania leaving London on 6 July and due to arrive at Sidon on the 24th.

As the urgency of your order left no time to make the usual enquiries, we are compelled to place this transaction on a cash basis and have drawn on you through Midminster Bank Ltd for the amount of the enclosed invoice. The bank will instruct their correspondent in Sidon to pass the bill of lading to you against payment of the draft.

Special care has been taken to select items suited to your local conditions. We hope you will find them satisfactory and that your present order will be the first of many.

Yours faithfully

(b) 出口商給進口商的信（承兌交單）

→ p.282

Dear Sirs

YOU ORDER NO B 614

We are pleased to inform you that arrangements have now been made to ship the dress goods you ordered on 15 October. The consignment will leave London on 1 November by SS Manchester Trader and is due to arrive at Quebec on the 22nd.

In keeping with our usual terms of payment we have drawn on you at 60 days and passed the draft and shipping documents to our bankers. The documents will be presented to you by the National Bank of Canada against your acceptance of the draft in the usual way.

Yours faithfully

28.8 出口商給銀行的指示（付款交單）

（搭配 28.7 (a) 一起閱讀）

→ p.282

Dear Sirs

On 6 July we are shipping a consignment of 2000 electric shavers to the Sidon Electrical Co of whom we have little knowledge and whose standing we have been unable to check. We therefore think it would be unwise to surrender the enclosed documents on a D/A basis and enclose a sight draft on the consignees, with bill of lading and insurance certificate attached.

Will you please arrange for your correspondent in Sidon to obtain payment of the amount due before handing over the documents, and let us know when payment has been made.

Yours faithfully

28.9 透過出口商的銀行寄出的跟單匯票

有時出口商會將跟單匯票直接寄給進口商的國內銀行，但是較常見的作法是與自己的往來銀行交易，銀行再透過其分行或海外通匯銀行將匯票出示給國外買主。

(a) 出口商給銀行的信

→ p.283

Dear Sirs

We have today shipped by SS Seafarer a consignment of haberdashery to the Nigerian Trading Co, Lagos. Since the standing of this company is unknown to us we do not wish to hand over the shipping documents against their mere acceptance of a bill of exchange. Therefore we enclose a sight draft on them, together with bill of lading and the other shipping documents. In the circumstances we shall require payment of the draft in full before the documents are handed over. Please instruct your correspondent in Lagos to arrange for this.

Yours faithfully

(b) 出口商給奈及利亞貿易公司的裝船通知

在寄出以上的信函給銀行時，出口商會寄發裝船通知給奈及利亞貿易公司，並針對付款事宜進行解釋。

→ p.283

Dear Sirs

The goods which you ordered on 2 October have been shipped to you today by SS Seafarer, due at Lagos on 2 December.

We have taken special care to include in the consignment only items suited to conditions in Nigeria. We hope you will be pleased with our selection and that your first order will lead to further business between us.

From the enclosed copy invoice you will see that the price of £865.75 is well within the maximum figure you stated. We have drawn on you for this amount at sight through the Barminster Bank, who have been instructed to hand over documents against payment of the draft. We hope you will understand that the urgency of your order left us with insufficient time to make the usual enquiries. Therefore we had no choice but to follow our standard practice with new customers of placing the transaction on a cash basis.

We look forward to your further orders. Subject to satisfactory references and regular dealings, we would be prepared to consider open-account terms with quarterly settlements.

Yours faithfully

28.10　直接寄跟單匯票給進口商的銀行

→ p.283

Dear Sir

We enclose shipping documents for 10,000 bags of rice shipped by SS Thailand which left Bangkok for London on 15 October.

Please hand the documents to Messrs B Stephenson & Co of London EC2P 2AA, as soon as they are ready to take them up against payment of £4260 (four thousand two hundred and sixty pounds) less interest at 2 $\frac{1}{2}$% from date of payment to 31 December next. Our account should be credited with the proceeds after deducting your charges.

Yours faithfully

急需資金的出口商有時候會請求銀行先行墊款跟單匯票的款項，銀行則會要求其簽訂「出口押匯總質權書」（letter of hypothecation，也稱為質押權書、抵押證書等），授權銀行可在進口商拒絕承兌匯票時，出售該批貨物。定期要求這一類預付款項的出口商會簽訂一份通用出口押匯總質權書以涵蓋未來所有交易。

銀行的商業信用狀

站在出口商的角度，跟單匯票有其缺點，因為國外買主可能無力承兌。為了避免這種風險而發展出所謂的「銀行信用狀」（banker's commercial credits，也稱為銀行信用狀）或「跟單信用狀」（documentary credits，也稱為單據信用狀或押匯信用狀）。目前使用廣泛，方法如下：

1. 進口商請求往來銀行開立信用狀給出口商，通常是使用特定的制式申請表。
2. 接著，進口商的往來銀行將信用狀寄給出口商，而常見的作法是由該銀行的分行或在出口商國家的通匯銀行來執行這項工作。
3. 從這一點起，出口商開始與通匯銀行交易，當貨物裝船時，出口商會備妥裝船文件並出示給通匯銀行（多半附上通匯銀行開

立的匯票），通匯銀行即在已授權的信用額度內「付款」，並將裝船文件寄給進口商的銀行。

4. 進口商的銀行依照付款交單或承兌交單的條件，將文件交給進口商。

實際上，進口商的銀行只是暫時將貨款付給出口商，通常仍會要求進口商維持足夠的帳戶餘額作為信用擔保。

信用狀分為「可撤銷」（revocable）與「不可撤銷」（irrevocable）。如果是可撤銷信用狀，進口商不需通知出口商，可自由修改甚至取消信用狀。但對於不可撤銷信用狀，除非取得出口商許可，否則不能修改，也不能撤銷，出口商可藉此確認對方會付款。

以上是大略的程序，有時會出現稍許差異，但並不影響一般的運作原則。與信用狀有關的書信往來相當專門，這點可從銀行使用的制式表格的複雜度窺知，也因此這方面的業務最好是交由熟悉的人員來處理。

28.11 跟單信用狀——交易階段

學習銀行信用狀或跟單信用狀制度最好的方式也許是跟著交易過程走一遍。在底下這個交易中，麥薩 AH 布魯克父子公司是一家倫敦的毛皮商，他們同意每月向北美貿易公司採購毛皮，為期六個月，並且以信用狀做交易。雙方的書信往來如下：

(a) 買方接洽銀行

→ p.284

Dear Sirs

We have just concluded an agreement to purchase monthly shipments of furs from Canada over the next 6 months and would like to make use of foreign-payment facilities by opening a series of monthly credits for £2000 each in favour of the North American Trading Company. It has been agreed that we provide credits with a bank in Quebec against which our suppliers would draw for the value of shipments as they are made.

Please let us know on what terms your bank would be prepared to arrange necessary credits and to handle the shipping documents for us.

Yours faithfully

(b) 銀行提供信用狀

→ p.284

Dear

Thank you for your enquiry of 15 March. We shall be pleased to handle the shipments and to arrange for the necessary documentary credits with our Quebec branch against deposit of bill of lading and other shipping documents. Please complete and return the enclosed form so that we can make the arrangements.

Our commission charges for revocable documentary credits would be $\frac{1}{8}$ to $\frac{1}{4}$% on each of the monthly credits, to which must be added $\frac{1}{4}$% for irrevocable credits and also our charges for such items as telegrams and postages. In return for these charges you have our assurance that your interests would be carefully protected.

Yours sincerely

(c) 買方指示銀行

→ p.284

Dear

Thank you for your letter of 17 March. I have completed and enclose the form of application for a documentary credit. Please arrange to open for our account with your office in Quebec irrevocable credits for £2,000 a month in favour of the North American Trading Company, the credits to be valid until 30 September next.

To enable them to use the credits the company must present the following documents: bills of lading in triplicate, one copy of the invoice, the certificate or policy of insurance and certificate of origin, and draw on your Quebec office at 60 days after sight for each consignment. The documents relate to five cases of mixed furs in each consignment at the value of about £350 per case, CIF London.

Yours sincerely

(d) 銀行同意開立信用狀

如果銀行同意開立信用狀，通常會使用制式表格通知買方。如果是以書信代替，書寫的方式如下：

→ p.285

Dear

As instructed in your letter of 20 March we are arranging to open a documentary credit with our branch in Quebec in favour of the North American Trading Company, valid until 30 September. Enclosed is a copy of our instruction opening the credit. Please check it to ensure that it agrees with your instructions. As soon as the credits are used we shall debit your account with the amount notified to us as having been drawn against them.

We shall take all necessary steps to make sure that your instructions are carefully carried out. Please note, however, that we cannot assume any responsibility for the safety of the goods or for delays in delivery since these are matters beyond our control.

Yours sincerely

(e) 買方通知出口商

倫敦的銀行寄一份由麥薩AH布魯克父子公司授權開立信用狀的申請表給魁北克分行。

→ p.285

Dear

We have opened irrevocable credits in your favour for £2000 a month with the Royal Bank of Canada, Quebec, valid until 30 September next.

The terms of the credit authorise you to draw at 60 days on the bank in Quebec for the amount of your invoices after each shipment of five cases. Before accepting the draft, which should include all charges to London, the bank will require you to produce the following documents: bills of lading in triplicate, one copy of the invoice covering CIF London, a certificate or policy of insurance and certificate of origin. We will expect your first consignment around the middle of next month.

Yours sincerely

(f) 銀行開出信用狀

下一步是魁北克分行通知北美貿易公司信用狀已經備妥。銀行也許會使用制式表格做通知，但若改用信件或傳真通知，且倫敦的銀行要求確認信用狀，那麼信件內容可能會像這樣：

→ p.285

Dear

On instructions from Messrs A H Brooks & Son received through our London office, we have opened monthly irrevocable credits for £2000 in your favour valid until 30 September next. You have authority to draw on us at 60 days against these credits for the amount of your invoices upon shipment of furs to Messrs A H Brooks & Son.

Your draws must be accompanied by the following documents which are to be delivered to us against our acceptance of the drafts: bills of lading in triplicate, commercial invoice, insurance certificate or policy and certificate of origin.

Provided you fulfil the terms of the credit we will accept and pay at maturity the drafts presented to us under these credits and, if required, provide discounting facilities at current rates.

Yours sincerely

在這封信中，不可撤銷的信用狀是由加拿大皇家銀行的倫敦分行開立，並且在給出口商信中的最後一段由魁北克分行加以確認。如果開立信用狀的銀行在出口商的國內沒有分行，那麼就必須透過通匯銀行來通知出口商。除非開立信用狀的銀行已授權或請求其通匯銀行確認信用狀（一般會如此做），否則通匯銀行沒有義務接受承兌出口商的匯票。一旦通匯銀行確認信用狀之後，如果符合條款，他們對出口商就有一定的承諾要接受承兌這樣的匯票。這種約定承諾不受開立不可撤銷信用狀的銀行所支配，如此可讓出口商有雙重的付款保障。

(g) 出口商出示文件

→ p.286

Dear

Referring to your advice of 30 March, we enclose shipping documents for the first of the monthly consignments to Messrs A H Brooks & Son.

As required by them we have included all charges in our invoice, which amounts to £1725.71 and enclose our draft at 60 days for this sum. We shall be glad if, after acceptance, you will discount it at the current rate and send the net amount to our account with the Banque de France, Quebec.

We thank you for your help in this matter.

Yours sincerely

備註：此時魁北克分行寄裝船文件及開立信用狀所收取的匯票金額報告書給其倫敦的辦公室。

(h) 銀行將款項記入買方帳戶

→ p.286

Dear Mr Jones

As instructed by your letter of 20 March, our Quebec office has just accepted for your account a bill for £1725.71 drawn by the North American Trading Company for a first consignment of furs to you by SS Columbia. We have debited your account with this amount and our charges amounting to £15.30.

The ship left Quebec on 22 April and is due to arrive in London on 2 May. The shipping documents for this consignment are now with us and we shall be glad if you will arrange to collect them.

Yours sincerely

實用措詞

買方給出口商

【開頭】

1. We have received your invoice number ... and agree to accept your draft at 60 days after sight for the amount due.
   收到您……（號碼）的發票，並且同意見票 60 天內付款。

2. As requested in your letter of ... we have instructed the ... Bank to open a credit for £ ... in your favour.
   根據您……（日期）信中的請求，我們已經指示……（銀行名稱）開立信用狀給您，金額為……（英鎊）。

3. We are sorry to have to ask for the term of your bill dated ... to be extended for one month.
   很抱歉必須請求將……（日期）所開的匯票票期展延一個月。

4. I regret that at the moment I cannot meet in full my acceptance, which is due for payment on ...
   很抱歉，目前我無法全額支付應該在……（日期）付款的匯票。

【結尾】

1. Please let us know whether you are prepared to give us open-account terms.

   請讓我們知道您是否願意提供我們定期結帳的記帳條件。

2. Please draw on us for the amount due and attach the shipping documents to your draft.

   請開立應付金額的匯票給我們，並附上裝船文件。

3. We should like to pay by bill of exchange at 60 days after sight and should be glad if you would agree to this.

   如果您同意，我們希望可用見票 60 天內付款的匯票來支付。

4. As requested we will arrange to open an irrevocable credit in your favour.

   依據您的請求，我們將安排開立不可撤銷的信用狀給您。

5. Our acceptance will be honoured upon presentation of the bill at the ... branch of the ... Bank.

   只要您將匯票出示給……（銀行名稱）銀行的……（分行名稱），我們就會支付匯票款項。

出口商給買方

【開頭】

1. We have considered your letter of ... and are pleased to grant the open-account terms asked for.

   我們已考慮過您……（日期）的來信，並且樂於同意您的記帳條件。

2. As requested in your letter of ... we have drawn on you for the amount of our April account at 3 months from ...

   依據您……（日期）的來信所請，我們已經將 4 月份的帳款開立 3 個月期的匯票給您，從……（日期）開始起算。

3. As agreed in our earlier correspondence we have drawn on you for the amount of the invoice enclosed.

   依據之前通信中所協議的，我們已經將所附的發票金額開立匯票給您。

【結尾】

1. Please accept the draft and return it as soon as you can.
   請允諾承兌匯票並且儘快寄回。

2. We are quite willing to put your account on a documents-against-acceptance basis.
   我們很願意採取承兌交單的交易方式。

3. We have instructed our bank to hand over the shipping documents against acceptance (payment) of our draft.
   我們已經指示我們的銀行依承兌交單（付款交單）的方式將裝船文件交給您。

4. Shipping documents, and our draft for acceptance, have been passed to the ... Bank.
   裝船文件及要允諾承兌的匯票已經交給⋯⋯（銀行名稱）。

5. As arranged, we have instructed our bank to surrender (hand over) the documents against payment (acceptance) of our draft.
   如之前所安排的，我們已經指示我們的銀行依承兌交單（付款交單）的方式交出文件。

6. As soon as the credit is confirmed, we will ship the goods.
   一旦信用狀確認之後，我們就會將貨裝上船。

買方給銀行

【開頭】

1. I enclose accepted bill, drawn on me by ... and should now be glad to receive the shipping documents.
   隨函附上我已同意承兌的匯票，請將裝船文件寄給我。

2. Please accept and pay the following drafts for me and, at maturity, debit them to my account.
   請替我承兌與支付下列匯票，並且在到期時從我的帳戶中扣款。

3. Please arrange with your correspondents in ... to open a credit in favour of ...

請安排您在……的通匯銀行開立受款人為……的信用狀。

【結尾】

1. Please accept the above draft for me and debit your charges to my account.

請替我同意承兌以上匯票，並將你們的收費從我的帳戶扣款。

2. Please state the amount of your charges for arranging the necessary credits.

請告知開立信用狀所需的費用。

出口商給銀行

【開頭】

1. We enclose our sight draft on ... of ... and also the shipping documents.

隨函附上開給……天的匯票和裝船文件。

2. Please surrender the enclosed documents to ... of ... when they accept our draft, also enclosed.

當對方承兌所附的匯票時，請將裝船文件交給……。

3. Please instruct your correspondent in ... to release the documents only on payment of our sight draft for £ ...

請指示您在……（地區）的通匯銀行，在支付我們……（英鎊）的見票即付匯票後，才能夠交出文件。

【結尾】

1. Please obtain acceptance of this draft before surrendering the shipping documents.

請先取得承兌後，再交出裝船文件。

2. Please present the bill for acceptance and then discount it for the credit of our account.

請出示承兌的匯票，然後將匯票貼現，再將款項記入我們的帳戶中。

3. Please present this acceptance for payment at maturity and credit us with the proceeds.

請在到期時，出示承兌的匯票以取得款項，並將實收額記入我們的帳戶中。

運輸
Transport

海運

由於貨船的規模擴大、速度加快，以及貨櫃的使用大幅提升，所以透過海運來送貨仍是吸引人的方式。現在有些船隻特別建造用來承載大宗物資，如石油、礦石、肉品及水果等。

定期與不定期航線

船舶通常分成定期航線（liner，有固定的航線和航期）和不定期航線（tramp，沒有固定的航線和航期，只要有適當的貨物就可出發）。目前，除了在英國海域內，不定期航線幾乎不用於長途運輸。

基本上，不定期航線是貨船，隨時可進行特定的航程。而定期航線可以是客輪或貨輪。通常客輪也會裝載一定量混雜的貨物，貨輪則只提供有限的座位給乘客。

船東與貨主（也就是託運人）之間的合約可以採包租（charter party，租用整艘船）或者提單託運（a bill of lading，船隻所載貨物屬於不同的貨主）方式。

包船

如果託運的貨物數量龐大，符合所謂的大宗物資（bulk cargoes[1]），就適合租用整艘船行駛特定航線的包航（voyage charter），或者以期租（a time charter）方式，租下一段經過協議的時間。

註明提供船隻的船東及租船者雙方約定條件的文件，稱之為期租合約（charter party）。雖然此合約有標準格式可用，但許多船東偏好自行擬定。

通常，期租是透過船隻仲介商來安排。倫敦的波羅的海交易所（Baltic Exchange），就是仲介商專門處理船隻仲介業務的特殊場所。

---

1. bulk cargoes：貨物沒有打包，只有散裝裝貨。

海運聯合承攬

海運聯合承攬（The shipping conference system）是由英國和國外運輸航線共同組成的組織，用於提供特定航線的服務。類似的協會大約有300個，每個協會負責自己特定的航線，例如北大西洋、南非和澳洲等。成立的目的是在一定的獲利水準下訂定運費（freight rates），並確保能隨時有最低運貨量來供給航行於該航線的定期船。該組織藉由與貨主之間的約定(ties)來推動這樣的運作模式。約約定中包括對只使用聯合承攬會員船隻託運的貨主給予「遞延折扣」（deferred rebate[2]），但這種折扣制多半已被「優惠費率制」（preferential rate system[3]）所取代。

海運聯合承攬對船東和貨主都有利。對貨主來說，它提供了固定的航程和可靠的交貨日期；對船東而言，可確保貨主會因酬謝其維持固定航班而將貨物交由託運，不會另尋他家船公司。如此一來，加入聯合承攬的船隻等於被長期雇用。

貨櫃服務

貨櫃為陸路、鐵路和航空運輸提供了極高的運作效率。其中最明顯的好處是運輸成本大幅降低。貨櫃通常由金屬製成，標準長度從10到40英呎不等（大約3至12公尺）。

貨櫃有下列優點：

◆ 可在靠近貨櫃中心的工廠裝貨並上鎖，避免遭竊。
◆ 減少貨物在運輸途中遺失或錯置的風險。
◆ 裝卸次數大為減少，成本降低，風險也減少了。
◆ 以機械方式裝卸貨物，只需數小時而非數日即可完成，因而可減少船隻停留在港口的時間，並大幅增加航行量。
◆ 為有需求的貨物提供控溫貨櫃。

---

2. deferred rebate：於使用約定期滿後，退回全期運費的固定百分比，當作折扣。
3. preferential rate system：一種提供聯合承攬會員較低運費的制度。

29.1 詢問船期與運費

這類的詢問通常以電話或傳真進行，貨主（或代理商）想要知道運費和船期。

→ p.288

We shall shortly have ready for shipment from Liverpool to Alexandria,4 cases of crockery. The cases measure $1\frac{1}{4}$ x $1\frac{1}{4}$ x l m, each weighing 70 kg.

Please quote your rate for freight and send us details of your sailings and the time usually taken for the voyage.

29.2 船公司的回覆

→ p.288

The SS Princess Victoria will be loading at number 2 dock from 8 to 13 July inclusive. Following her is the SS Merchant Prince, loading at number 5 dock from 20 to 24 July inclusive.

The voyage to Alexandria normally takes 14 days. The freight rate for crockery packed in wooden cases is £97.00 per tonne.

We shall be glad to book your 4 cases for either of these vessels and enclose our shipping form. Please complete it and return it as soon as possible.

29.3 代理商發出託運指示

當供應商告知貨品已經備妥，代理商會安排集貨並發貨至碼頭，或是請供應商處理。之後，裝船表格會交回給船公司，以便安排在碼頭收貨。

(a) 代理商通知供應商

→ p.288

Thank you for informing us that the items ordered on 16 June are now ready for collection.

Please arrange to send the consignment by road to Liverpool for shipment by SS Merchant Prince due to sail for Alexandria on 25 July and to load at number 5 dock from 20 to 24 July inclusive. All cases should be clearly marked and numbered as shown in our official order. Invoices, in triplicate, and your account for transport charges should be sent to us.

All the necessary arrangements have been made with the shipping company.

(b) 代理商指示船公司

→ p.288

We have today arranged for H J Cooper & Co. Ltd, Manchester, to forward to you by road the following cases to be shipped to Alexandria by SS Merchant Prince on 25 July.

4 cases of crockery, marked ⟨JR⟩ numbers 1–4

The completed shipping form is enclosed together with 4 copies of the bill of lading. Please sign and return 3 copies of the bill and charge the amount to our account.

貨運承攬商

貨運承攬商（shipping and forwarding agent）負責集貨與運送客戶託運的商品，這些服務承攬了繁複的作業，在國際貿易上更顯重要。對出口商而言，船公司將貨物取走、安排裝船事宜，並向進口國的攬貨業者（forwarding agent，又稱攬貨公司等）寄發發貨通知。攬貨業者負責將貨物運給買方，或者如果買方不急著馬上取貨，則安排將貨物存放到倉庫。

包裝、貨運承攬商都是專家，他們懂得如何打包特殊貨品，使用最合適的方式將貨品運至目的地。

貨運承攬商將送至相同目的地的小型貨品重新包裝組合成大批貨品，可藉以取得較低的運費，也就是說供應商雇請這些業者會比直接交由海運或陸運公司處理來得便宜、簡便。但很多進口商與出口商較喜歡直接與供應商（如果他們是進口商）或客戶（如果他們是出口商）的國內攬貨業者交易，以降低成本。

→ p.289

29.4　給買方所在國的攬貨業者的裝運通知

Please note that we have shipped the following goods to you by SS Merchant Prince which left Liverpool yesterday and is due to arrive at Alexandria on 9 August.

Mark and Numbers	Goods	Gross Weight	Value
JR 1–4	4 cases crockery	280 kg	£3250

Insurance in the sum of £2200 is provided as far as Alexandria only.

A copy of the bill of lading and the invoice are enclosed. Please arrange to handle the consignment and deliver it to Messrs Jean Riachi & Co, Mansura, who will be responsible for all charges.

The consignment is urgently required so your prompt attention will be appreciated.

29.5　給買方的裝運通知

當貨物已經裝船送出，並通知買方的攬貨業者，攬貨業者會寫信通知買方收貨。底下這封信採裝運通知的形式。

→ p.289

YOUR INDENT NO 762

We are pleased to inform you that all goods ordered on your above indent have now been shipped by SS Merchant Prince which sailed from Liverpool yesterday and is due to arrive in Alexandria on 9 August.

The consignment will be handled on arrival by Messrs Behren & Co who will make all the arrangements for delivery.

The bill of lading, invoice, and our account for commission and charges are enclosed. The suppliers have been informed that you will settle their account direct.

We hope to hear from you soon that the goods have arrived safely.

攬貨業者

如果出口商透過國內的攬貨業者安排裝運，攬貨業者會負責處理整筆交易，包括安排集貨、運至碼頭並支付費用、安排船公司、支付運費、爲貨品保險、準備提單，以及處理其他必要文件，例如領事

簽證、原產地證明（certificate of origin[4]）、價值與重量證明、出口證明等等。

當貨品裝運後，出口商的代理商會通知買主國內的攬貨業者，當貨品抵達港口時則改由他們負責。簡單地說，攬貨業者負責打理一切瑣事，善盡專家責任。

29.6 供應商尋求攬貨業者的服務

→ p.289

> We have a consignment of tape recorders now waiting to be shipped to Messrs Tan & Co of Kuala Lumpur. Will you please arrange for the consignment to be collected from the above address and arrange shipment to Klang by the first possible sailing. When it arrives at Klang the consignment will be handled for our customers by Mr J Collins with whom you should make the necessary arrangements.
>
> The recorders are packed in 3 cases and the enclosed copy of the invoice shows quantities and a total value of £2800. Insurance should be taken out for £2900 to include cover for expenses.
>
> When the goods are shipped please send the original bill of lading and one copy to us, together with the certificate or policy of insurance and any other necessary documents.

空運

提單（bill of lading）用於海運而不用在空運，因為空運的貨物通常會在提單備妥前即已抵達目的地。空運的貨主必須準備的是空運提單（airway bill），以告知貨品的詳細項目。通常，空運提單有好幾份，被當成正本的其中一份交給空運公司，一份給收件人，另一份給貨主，其餘的副本可以給其他的運輸業者、海關，或作爲記錄存檔之用等等。

---

4. certificate of origin：進口商有權可以取得優惠關稅的文件。

習慣上，航空公司或其代理商會準備空運提單，詳細資料由貨主填寫在一張特殊表格上（也就是貨品發貨指示表，由航空公司或其代理商提供）。

和海運提單一樣，空運提單代表貨品已經登機，它也是運輸合約的證明，合約條款詳列於提單背面。但與海運提單不同的是，空運提單並不是代表所有權的文件。

採用空運，貨主可能請攬貨業者代勞，也或許會直接與航空公司的貨物預訂部門交涉，實務上前者較常見。

除非是以量計費的大批貨物，否則空運貨物是以重量來計價。為了鼓勵採用空運，航空公司對不同種類的貨物皆提供優惠，貴重物品則會額外收費，以負擔額外的處理成本。

`29.7` 透過攬貨業者詢問空運運費

→ p.290

We shall shortly have a consignment of electric shavers, weighing about 20 kg, for a customer in Damascus. We wish to send this by air from London.

Please let us have details of the cost and any formalities to be observed. The invoice value of the consignment is £1550 and we should require insurance cover for this amount plus the costs of sending the consignment.

`29.8` 攬貨業者的回覆

→ p.290

Thank you for your enquiry regarding your consignment to Damascus. All our charges including freight, airway bill fee, insurance and our own commission are shown on the attached schedule.

To enable us to prepare your airway bill we shall need the information requested in the enclosed form. Three copies of a certified commercial invoice and a certificate of origin will also be necessary.

Your consignment should be in our hands by 10 am on the morning of departure day. Please telephone me when you are ready to deliver the consignment to our officer at the airport so that we can prepare to receive it and deal with it promptly. Alternatively we can make arrangements to collect the goods.

We hope to receive instructions from you soon.

陸運

雖然石油、沙和木材等大宗物資採鐵路運輸是比較便宜的，但對於乘客和貨品來說，道路運輸一般會比鐵路便宜。

陸運最重要的特徵是：

◆ 能輕鬆適應各種不同的情況，且提供直接送貨服務。
◆ 可以根據交通流量隨時改變路線。
◆ 對於易碎和需要簡單包裝的貨品，其安全性高於鐵路運輸。
◆ 尤其適合短程，主要是因為小型卡車可以輕鬆且快速地處理貨物。

陸運單據

當貨交給貨運公司後，託運收據或運貨單（如果是以陸路、鐵路或航空運輸）會被當成運輸合約。原始單據會交給託運人作為收據，運輸業者自己保留一份，而另一份則和貨物一起交給收貨人。

29.9　詢問運費

→ p.291

> Early next month we shall have a consignment of motor-car spares for delivery from our warehouse to a company in Aberdeen.
>
> These spares will be packed in 2 wooden cases, each measuring 1 x 1 x 0.75 m and weighing about 80 kg.
>
> Please let us know as soon as possible:
>
> 1　Your charge for collecting and delivering these cases.
> 2　If you can collect them on the 3rd of next month.
> 3　When delivery would be made to the consignee.
>
> An early reply would be appreciated.

29.10　供應商通知發貨

→ p.291

> Your Order No 825
>
> We have today despatched by Williams Transport Ltd 2 wooden cases containing the motor-car spares which you ordered recently.
>
> Would you please unpack and examine them as soon as possible after delivery and in the event of any damage notify us and also the carriers at once.
>
> We understand the goods will be delivered to you in 3 days' time.

29.11　買方通知收到貨

→ p.291

> Our Order No 825
>
> The 2 cases of motor-car spares despatched with Williams Transport Ltd were delivered yesterday in good condition.
>
> The cases are being returned to you by Williams Transport. Please credit us with the amount charged for them on your invoice.

29.12　家具搬運

(a) 詢價

→ p.292

> Early next month we will be moving from the above address to 110 Normanshire Drive, Chingford. I would like a quotation on the cost of your removal services.
>
> Our present house has 6 rooms, all of which are fully furnished. You will no doubt wish to inspect our furniture so please arrange for one of your representatives to call as soon as possible.
>
> I hope to hear from you soon.

(b) 報價

→ p.292

> We are writing to confirm the removal of your furniture from St Annes to Chingford on 3 May.
>
> Our charge for the removal will be £950, including insurance cover in the sum of £45,000. We enclose an agreement form setting out the terms and conditions and shall be glad if you will sign and return it.
>
> Our van with three workmen will arrive at your house at 7.30 am on 3 May. The loading should be completed in about three hours. We should be able to deliver to your Chingford address and complete unloading by 4.30 pm on the following day.
>
> Please let me know if you have any queries.

(c) 運送中財產損害求償

→ p.292

> When your workmen removed the furniture from my house in St Annes on 3 May the staircase was badly damaged. The new owner of this house has obtained an estimate for the repair in the sum of £220 and he is now claiming this amount from me.
>
> I realise the insurance policy you provided only covered damage to furniture. However, as the damage now reported is claimed to have been caused by your workmen I have advised the new owner to contact you directly.

鐵路運輸

對於長距離像是石油、沙及木材之類的大宗物資而言，鐵路運輸會比陸路便宜，只是鐵路運輸必須借助其他的交通工具，進行集貨和發貨的作業，有時會因此造成延誤，原因包括雙倍的處理過程、更複雜的包裝，加上被竊和損害的風險提高，成本也會因此墊高。有愈來愈多的鐵路公司利用「貨櫃」來克服上述的問題。

貨物運輸的風險可以由貨主或運輸公司來承擔，前者的保險費較低廉。保險費也會依貨物的等級有所差異。

除非買賣雙方事先協議，否則集貨和運輸的責任都將由買方承擔。如果雇用了運輸公司，那麼運輸公司就變成買方的代理商。一旦貨物由代理商接收之後，賣方的責任就告終止，買方必須承擔所有可能的遺失或損壞責任。

29.13 失竊損失求償

(a) 買方的抱怨

→ p.293

OUR ORDER NO 328

The consignment of cotton shirts despatched on 21 June was delivered yesterday in a very unsatisfactory condition.

It was clear that 2 of the cases (numbers 4 and 7) had been <u>tampered with</u>.[5] Upon checking the contents we found that case number 4 contained only 372 shirts and case number 7 contained only 375 shirts instead of the 400 invoiced for each case.

Before reporting the matter to the railway please confirm that each of these cases contained the invoiced quantity when they left your warehouse. At the same time please replace the 53 missing shirts with others of the same quality.

You will no doubt be claiming <u>compensation</u>[6] from the railway, in which case we shall be glad to assist you with any information we can provide. Meanwhile, the cases are being held for inspection, together with the contents.

(b) 供應商的回覆

→ p.293

We were sorry to learn from your letter of 27 June that 2 of the cases sent to you on 21 June had been tampered with. We confirm that when they left our warehouse each of these cases contained the full quantity of 400 shirts. The cases were in good order when they left our premises; in support of this we hold the carrier's clean receipt.

As we sent the goods by rail at your request, the railway company must be regarded as your agents. We cannot, therefore, accept any responsibility for the losses and can only suggest that you make the claim for compensation directly with the railway company. We are quite willing to support your claim in whatever way we can.

The 53 missing shirts will be replaced but we will have to charge them to your account. In the circumstances we will allow you an extra discount of 10%.

Please let us know in what way we can help in your claim for compensation.

---

5. tampered with ：任意遭翻動。
6. compensation ：賠償商品損失。

(c) 買方向鐵路局求償

→ p.294

We regret to report that 2 of the cases covered by your consignment receipt number S5321 were delivered to us in a condition that left no doubt of their having been broken into during transit. The cases in question are numbers 4 and 7.

This was noticed when the cases were delivered by your carrier and accordingly we added to our receipt 'Cases 4 and 7 damaged; contents not examined'. A later check of the contents revealed a shortage of 53 shirts.

The consignment was sent by our suppliers on carrier's risk terms. Therefore we must hold you responsible for the loss. Our claim is enclosed for the invoiced value of the missing shirts (at £4.00 each) which is £212.00. In support of our claim we enclose a certified copy of our supplier's invoice.

The 2 cases and their contents have been put aside to await your inspection.

實用措詞

開頭

【詢問】

1. Thank you for your enquiry of ... we are pleased to quote as follows for the shipment of ... to ...
   謝謝您詢問……。很高興回答您從……運至……的報價如下：

2. Thank you for your enquiry regarding sailings to Johannesburg in August.
   謝謝您詢問有關 8 月份至約翰尼斯堡的航程。

3. We are due to ship a large quantity of ... to ... and need you to obtain a ship of about ... tons capacity.
   我們預計要運送大量的……貨物至……，我們需要一艘可以容納……噸的船。

4. Please let us know the current rates of freight for the following:
   請讓我們知道以下……的最新運費：

5. Please quote an inclusive rate for collection and delivery of ... from ...
   請提供包含從……取貨以及運到……的運費報價。

【商品運輸】

1. We have today sent to you a consignment of ... by SS ...
   今天我們委託 SS ……將……貨物運送給您。

2. We have given instructions to ... to forward the following consignment to you by rail:
   我們已經指示……將以下貨物以鐵路運送給您：

結尾

1. Please inform us of the date on which the ship closes for cargo.
   請通知我們船隻截止收貨的日期。

2. Please complete and return the enclosed instructions form with a signed copy of the invoice.
   請將所附的表格填妥，並連同簽名的發票副本寄回給我們。

3. We hope to receive your shipping instructions by return.
   我們希望立刻收到您的裝船指示。

保險
Insurance

30

保險為可能造成損失的各種事故提供一層安全的防護網，使遭逢損失或傷害的人可以得到一定的賠償。換句話說，保險是讓受損害者儘量恢復至原先狀態的一種合約。

然而，保險理賠金額不能高出所損失的總價值。例如，一艘價值50,000 英鎊的船隻，即使投保金額為 60,000 英鎊，萬一因船隻損毀而提出索賠，那麼船主最多只能獲得 50,000 英鎊的理賠金。

另一種保險是當被保險人到達約定年齡時，即可領回一筆固定的錢，或者是被保險人身故後由受益人支領。這種保險在英國稱為人壽保險（assurance），是對必然會發生的事提供保障，而一般的保險（insurance）則是關於損失的賠償，這種損失不一定會發生。

保險合約

保險合約的雙方立約人是：

1. 承保人（insurer，或稱為保險人、保險業者）：同意接受風險的一方。
2. 被保險人（insured）：尋求風險保護的一方。

被保險人需支付保險費（premium），相對的，承保人承諾當被保險人發生事故時，支付被保險人一定或部分的金額。在英國，保險費是依保險總額的百分比來計算（例如 25p%，意指每 100 英鎊收 25便士的保費）。

想投保壽險或意外險的人，通常需要填寫「要保書」（proposal form），並誠實回答列在上面的問題。對於會影響保險業者對其風險判定的其他資訊，被保險人也必須誠實告知，否則保險業者可以認定保險合約無效。海運保險不需填寫要保書，火險也很少用到要保書。但是如同其他的保險表格，所有會影響風險的資訊都不能有所隱瞞。

保險業者一旦接受了要保書，就必須依法核發保單。保單上註明合約的條款，包括承擔的風險、保險金額，以及保險費等。如果日後

要修改保險條款，通常只需在原來的保單背面批註（endorsing）即可，而不需要核發新保單。

任何人都不能爲「不具法定利益」者投保。我們可以爲自己的財產投保，但不能爲鄰居投保。船東可以爲自己的船隻投保，但不能爲承載的貨物投保，除非是貨物遺失而導致運費上的損失。

30.1　詢問保險費率

(a) 爲在途現金投保

→ p.296

> Dear Sirs
>
> 說明有關業務及與銀行往來的背景資料
>
> We normally pay into the bank each morning our takings for the preceding business day. The sums involved are sometimes considerable especially at the weekends: takings on a Saturday may amount to as much as £6000.
>
> We bank with the local branch of the Barminster Bank on West Street, Milton – about half a mile from our premises.
>
> We therefore wish to take out insurance cover for the following:
>
> 條列重點
>
> 1　Against loss of cash on the premises, by fire, theft, or burglary.
> 2　Against loss of cash in transit between our premises and the bank.
> 3　Against accident or injury to staff while engaged in taking money to the bank, or bringing it from the bank.
>
> 請求就條件做個回覆
>
> Please let us know on what terms you can provide cover for the risks mentioned.
>
> Yours faithfully

(b) 爲貨物海運投保

→ p.296

> Dear Sirs
>
> We will shortly have a consignment of tape recorders, valued at £50,000 CIF Quebec, to be shipped from Manchester by a vessel of Manchester Liners Ltd.
>
> We wish to cover the consignment against all risks from our warehouse at the above address to the port of Quebec. Will you please quote your rate for the cover.
>
> Yours faithfully

(c) 要求優惠費率

→ p.296

Dear Sirs

We regularly ship consignments of bottled sherry to Australia by both passenger and cargo liners of the Enterprise Shipping Line. We are interested to know whether you can issue an all-risks policy for these shipments and, if so, on what terms. In particular we wish to know whether you can give a special rate in return for the promise of regular monthly shipments.

I hope to hear from you soon.

Yours faithfully

30.2 投保申請

(a) 續 30.1 (c)

→ p.297

Dear Mr Johnson

We thank you for your reply to our enquiry of 6 June. The terms you quote, namely 35p%, less 5% special discount for regular shipments, are acceptable. We understand that these terms will apply to all our shipments of bottled sherry by regular liners to Australian ports and cover all risks, including breakages and pilferage.[1]

Our first shipment will be on 2 July for 20 cases of sherry valued at £6000. Please arrange open-account terms with quarterly settlements.

I look forward to receiving the policy within the next few days.

Yours sincerely

---

1. pilferage：指少量或不值錢貨物的偷竊。

(b) 倉庫庫存保險

(i) 申請

→ p.297

> Dear Mr Wilson
>
> Thank you for your letter of 15 April quoting rates for insurance cover for stock stored in our warehouse at the above address.
>
> The value of the stock held varies with the season but does not normally exceed £100,000 at any time.
>
> Please arrange cover in this sum for all the risks mentioned in your letter and on the terms quoted, namely 50p% per annum. Cover should take effect from 1 May next.
>
> Yours sincerely

(ii) 確認通知

→ p.297

> Dear Mr Smith
>
> Thank you for your recent letter. We shall be glad to provide cover in the sum of £50,000 at 50p% per annum on stock in your warehouse at 25 Topping Street, Lusaka. This will take effect from 1 May.
>
> The policy is now being prepared and it should reach you in about a week's time.
>
> Please let me know if I can provide any further help.
>
> Yours sincerely

(c) 貨物險

→ p.298

> Dear Sirs
>
> Please arrange full a.a.r.[2] cover in the sum of £5000 for shipment of 20 hi-fi music centres to Quebec by MV Merchant Shipper, scheduled to sail from Manchester on 2 July. The goods are packed in 5 cases marked AHB 1–5, now lying in our warehouse at 25 Manchester Road, Salford.
>
> Please let us have the policy, and one certified copy, not later than 30 June. The charge should be billed to our account.
>
> Yours faithfully

---

2. a.a.r：against all risks，全險。

保險經紀人

投保商業險，特別是海運（maritime）險，需要相當的專業知識。專業的保險經紀人（insurance broker）常常能夠提供極大的幫助與建議。保險經紀人會建議客戶應當投保的風險範圍，並針對客戶的特殊需求，推薦最合適的險種及保險公司。

30.3 請求經紀人安排投保

(a) 【範例 1】

→ p.298

> Dear Sir
>
> Will you please arrange to take out an all-risks insurance for us on the following consignment of cameras from our warehouse at the above address to Valletta:
>
> 6 c/s cameras due to leave Liverpool on 18 August by SS Endeavour.
>
> The invoiced value of the consignment, including freight and insurance, is £11,460.
>
> Please contact me if you have any queries.
>
> Yours faithfully

(b) 【範例 2】

→ p.298

> Dear Miss Taylor
>
> Thank you for calling me this morning. I confirm that we have decided to accept the quotation of 60p% by the Britannia Insurance Co for insurance to cover the transit by road of two $1\frac{1}{4}$ tonne boilers on 15 July. The consignment will be taken from our works in Birmingham to the Acme Engineering Co, Bristol.
>
> Please arrange the necessary cover and send us the policy as soon as possible.
>
> Yours faithfully

保費

統計資料讓保險業者可以精確評估特殊風險的範圍，幫助他們訂出一個對自己及被保險人都公平的保費等級。保費會因風險程度而異，以火險為例，在有使用火災警報器、自動灑水裝置、滅火器及防火材質等情況下，保費將相對比較便宜。

30.4 請求降低保費

提及電話內容，請求提供有關保費的詳細資料

說明請求的主要原因

條列說明，以確保資料清楚及簡單化

有技巧地請求減少保費

Dear Mr Maxwell

POLICY NO F 623104

Further to our telephone conversation I should be obliged if you would review the rate of premium charged under the above fire policy for goods in our transit shed[3] at No 4 Dock. As you know, the shed is also used as a bonded store[4] and storage warehouse.

As we discussed I feel that not enough weight may have been given to the following conditions when the present rate of premium was fixed:

1　The shed is not artificially heated.
2　No power of any kind is used.
3　All rooms are provided with automatic sprinklers, fireproof doors and fire extinguishers of the latest type.
4　A water main runs round the entire dockside and can be tapped[5] at several points within easy distance of the shed.

When these conditions are taken into account I believe the present rate of premium seems to be unreasonably high. I hope you will agree to reduce it sufficiently to bring it more into line with the extent of the risk insured under the policy.

I look forward to hearing from you soon.

Yours

3.　**transit shed** ：商品運送的庫房。
4.　**bonded store** ：保稅倉庫。
5.　**tapped** ：汲水。

居家險

大部分的火險公司均有大範圍地承保房屋本身及其內容物的「居家險」或「全險」，在一份保單裡提供除了火災險之外各式災害的保障，承保範圍還包括暴風雨、暴動、管線破裂、盜竊、發生於傭僕的意外、鏡子破裂造成的意外等等，但不包括戰爭造成的損失。承保的條件是，只涵蓋建築物及其內容物的所有價值。

30.5　投保居家險

(a) 申請

→ p.299

Dear Sirs

I have recently bought the property at the above address with possession as from 1 July and wish to take out comprehensive cover on both building and contents in the sums of £120,000 and £30,000 respectively. The former figure represents the estimated rebuilding cost of the property and the latter the full value of the contents.

Please send me particulars of your terms and conditions for the policy and a proposal form if required.

Yours faithfully

(b) 回覆

→ p.300

Dear Mrs Turner

HOUSEHOLDERS' COMPREHENSIVE INSURANCE

Thank you for your enquiry of 19 June. A copy of our prospectus containing particulars of our policies for householders is enclosed.

You will see that we offer two types of cover for buildings. Cover 'B' (premium rate 21p%) is similar to cover 'A' (premium rate 24p%) but excludes cover for accidental damage. For contents we provide only one type of cover at a rate of 70p% per annum. As you will see from the prospectus, our comprehensive policies provide a very wide range of cover.

I enclose a proposal form. Please complete and return it not later than 7 days before the date from which the policy is to run.

Please give me a call if you have any queries.

Yours sincerely

30.6　請求擴大承保範圍

→ p.300

Dear Sirs

HOUSE CONTENTS POLICY NO H 96154

On 2 June I sent you a cheque for £175.00 as the premium due for renewal of the above policy.

I now wish to increase the amount of cover from its current figure of £25,000 to £30,000 (thirty thousand pounds) with immediate effect. Please confirm that you have arranged for this and send me the customary endorsement indicating the charge for inclusion in the policy schedule.

From the conditions that apply to your householders' policies I understand that no charge for this increased cover will be made before my next renewal date.

I look forward to receiving your confirmation soon.

Yours faithfully

30.7　提高保費通知

有些保險業者會以下一年度續約時再繳多出的保費，來鼓勵居家險的保戶提高建築物及其內容物的保額，如上一封信所示。在這種情況下，被保險人最多可在新年度保單續約之前享有 12 個月的免費額外保障。

以下是保險業者寫給居家險保戶的公告信，信中提及因為通貨膨脹而出現了投保額低於實際價值（under-insurance，或稱為保額偏低）的現象。

→ p.301

Dear

Unfortunately, our efforts to encourage household policy-holders to revise the sums insured to take account of inflation have been poorly supported. In the past 5 years the monetary value of property and contents has more than doubled, but most householders have failed to provide for this and as a result are grossly[6] underinsured. The problem of underinsurance has often been made worse because the initial cover[7] was inadequate[8]. On some recent claims research shows that the amount of underinsurance has been well over 50%.

In this situation we have been reluctantly compelled[9] to introduce in all household insurance a provision automatically increasing the amount of cover at each renewal of the policy. The increase, currently 6%, will be reflected in the amount of premium payable. Allowance for this will be made in your next renewal notice.

If you have any queries please contact me.

Yours sincerely

30.8 請求提供保險承保範圍的資訊

→ p.301

Dear

POLICY NO MH 816/89068

Upon receiving your renewal notice on 21 July I sent you a cheque for £250.75 to extend cover of my premises under the above policy. Unfortunately, I have no record of the amount of cover provided by the premium paid and should be obliged if you would let me have this information as soon as possible.

Should the amount of the cover be less than £50,000 I should like to increase it to this amount with immediate effect. Please arrange for this if necessary and send me your account for the amount of additional premium payable. I will then send you a cheque in payment.

Yours sincerely

---

6. **grossly** ：非常；相當地。
7. **initial cover** ：最初投保的價值。
8. **inadequate** ：不足。
9. **reluctantly compelled** ：被迫地；不情願地。

旅遊險

出國度假，除針對行李與其他個人財產遺失投保外，將意外以及疾病納入保險是較聰明的防範之道。

假期中的醫療和住院費用，必須自行承擔，而且非常昂貴。爲此，很多保險公司會收取少額保費來承保旅遊險，通常旅行社會樂意爲客戶做好這部分的安排。

30.9 投保旅遊險

(a) 申請

→ p.302

> Dear Sirs
>
> I shall be touring Italy and Sicily in a 1996 Peugeot 405 GL for 4 weeks commencing 3 July.
>
> Please let me know the terms and conditions on which you could issue a policy to cover loss of and damage to baggage and other personal property. I should also like to consider cover against personal accident and illness, and should be glad if you would send me particulars. The car is already separately insured.
>
> I hope to hear from you soon.
>
> Yours faithfully

(b) 保險業者的回覆

→ p.302

> Dear Mr Sanderson
>
> Thank you for your letter of 8 June regarding insurance to cover your tour of Italy and Sicily.
>
> I enclose a leaflet setting out the terms and conditions of the insurance for both personal property and injury and illness, and also a proposal form. The cover for injury and illness extends to the full cost of medical and hospital treatment and of any special arrangements that may be necessary for your return home.
>
> Please complete and return the proposal form by 26 June at the latest, so that we can be sure of issuing the policy in time.
>
> Yours sincerely

員工忠誠險

雇主針對員工執行職務時的不誠實或欺騙行為而投保所謂的「員工忠誠保險」（Fidelity Guarantee，也稱為誠信及詐騙保障）。可以針對個別員工投保，也可以採團保方式，保單上註明每位員工的保額。此外，也可採流動保單，上面列出每位員工姓名，但投保的金額只有一個。

30.10 詢問員工忠誠險

→ p.302

Dear Sirs

We have recently appointed Mrs Tessa Campbell as our chief accountant. She came to us with excellent references, but as a purely precautionary measure we wish to cover her by a fidelity bond for £100,000.

Please let me know on what terms you can provide this cover and send me a proposal form if required.

Yours faithfully

暫時承保

在保險業者正式接受保單之前，任何合約都是無效的。但在評估保單期間，如果有人想立即獲得保障，保險公司通常會提供暫時性保障，並依其所請核發「暫保單」（cover note），保單上通常會載明承保期間。

在以下的書信中，保險業者未核發暫保單，後在回函中向被保險人清楚表示事實上其房產是在保險範圍內的。

30.11　請求核發保單前的承保

(a) 住戶的請求

→ p.303

Dear Sirs

1 MARGATE ROAD, ST ANNES-ON-SEA, LANCS

I have recently bought the property at the above address. A covenant in the deeds requires the property to be insured with your company against fire. In a letter to me dated 30 October the solicitors handling the transfer for me stated that you would be getting in touch with me about this.

As I have not yet heard from you, I am writing as a matter of urgency to ask you to insure the property under your usual full-cover householder's policy in the sum of £100,000 as from 7 December inclusive. This is the date fixed for the legal transfer of the property to me. This sum covers the purchase price of £80,000 and estimated rebuilding costs.

In view of the urgency I hope to receive your assurance that you will hold the property covered as from and including next Thursday 7 December. I ask this because I am in no position to accept the risks of non-insurance while the policy is being prepared.

Yours faithfully

(b) 保險業者的回覆

→ p.303

Dear Mr Brown

COMPREHENSIVE INSURANCE
1 MARGATE ROAD, ST ANNES-ON-SEA, LANCS

Thank you for your letter of 3rd November. I am pleased to inform you that we will hold this property covered for £100,000 as from 7 December on the terms and conditions of the company's comprehensive policy.

A proposal form is enclosed. Please complete it and return it to me immediately.

Yours sincerely

索賠

遺失或損害的索賠（或求償）應立即以書信提出申請，並且附上可資佐證的資料或證據。如果是和運輸貨物有關的求償，那麼必須在發現遺失或損害時提出：

1.　如果貨物是由買方投保，則向保險業者請求理賠。
2.　如果貨物是由賣方投保，則向賣方請求賠償。

30.12　房產損害索賠

申請理賠時，通常需要填寫理賠申請表，如這封書信所述。

(a) 住戶索賠

→ p.304

保單編號

告知意外細節

告知修理費

有技巧地請求進行
修理工程

Dear Sirs

POLICY NO PK 850046

I am sorry to have to report a slight accident to the work surface of the sink-unit work-table. This was burnt and cracked when an electric iron was accidentally knocked over on it.

I have made enquiries and am informed that replacement cost of the damaged work surface will be about £80 (eighty pounds). There will also be an additional charge for fixing.

I hope to receive your permission to arrange for the work to be carried out. Should you wish to inspect the damage I am at home on most days, but it would be helpful to know when to expect your representative.

Yours faithfully

(b) 保險業者的回覆

→ p.304

Dear Mrs Crowther

POLICY NO PK 850046

I refer to your letter of 14 September and our representative's recent call on you. Our claim form is enclosed. Please complete and return this to me as soon as possible with the contractor's estimate for replacement of the damaged work surface. I will then deal with the matter immediately.

Yours sincerely

30.13 **保險業者要求提供進一步資料**

有時候遭受損失者沒有提供完整、正確的資訊，希望可以藉此拿回更多的理賠金。這樣的案例頗多，保險業者的作法是要求對方提供進一步的資料，如以下的書信所示。這封信是保險業者回給因為一起卡車意外導致生意受損而提出理賠的被保險人。

遭受損失者必須儘可能地將索賠範圍限定在已損失的部分，否則可能無法獲得全額理賠。

→ p.305

Dear

I refer to your claim of 17 February for £1500 as compensation for loss of business due to damage to your lorry.

Before I can deal with your claim I shall need the following further information from you:

1   What is the actual financial loss suffered as a result of the accident, and how is it calculated?
2   What steps, if any, were taken to hire a suitable lorry until the damaged lorry could be replaced?
3   If no steps to hire were taken, please give the reason.

As soon as I receive this information I will deal with your claim immediately.

Yours sincerely

30.14 買方請求賣方提出索賠

在交易過程中，如果賣方為運送期間的貨物投保，那麼買方會向賣方報告損失或損壞的部分，並且請賣方向保險業者申請理賠，如以下的書信所示。

→ p.305

Dear

OUR ORDER NO C 541

When the SS Lancastria arrived at Famagusta on 10 November, it was noticed that one side of case number 12 containing radio receivers was split. Therefore the case was opened and the contents were examined by a local insurance surveyor in the presence of the shipping company's agents. The case was invoiced as containing 24 Hacker 'Mayflower' radio receivers, 8 of which were badly damaged.

The surveyor's report is enclosed with statement from the shipping agent.

As you hold the insurance policy I should be grateful if you would take up this matter with the insurers.

Eight replacement receivers will be required. Please arrange to supply these as soon as possible and charge them to our account.

Thank you in advance for your trouble on our behalf. If there are any queries please do not hesitate to call me.

Yours faithfully

30.15　火災損失索賠

(a) 請求理賠

→ p.306

Dear Sirs

POLICY NO AR 3854

I regret to report that a fire broke out in our factory stores last night. The cause is not yet known but we estimate the damage to stock to be about £100,000. Fortunately no records were destroyed so there should be no difficulty in assessing the value of the loss.

Please arrange for your representative to call and let me have your instructions regarding salvage[10].

Yours faithfully

(b) 保險業者的回覆

→ p.306

Dear

FIRE POLICY NO AR 3854

Thank you for your letter of 21 May. I was sorry to hear about the fire in your factory stores.

As a first step will you please make your claim on the enclosed form. Meanwhile, I am arranging for Mr John Watson, a loss adjuster, to call and assess the damage. He will be in touch with you soon.

If you need help in completing the claim form Mr Watson will be able to assist you.

Yours sincerely

---

10. salvage：保險殘餘物，可恢復的物品、可供再利用的廢物。

30.16　保險業者拒絕全額賠償（續 30.15）

有時候書信傳達的是令人失望或不受歡迎的消息，例如索賠被拒或是任何其他可能會令人失望的情形。在這類的信件中，首段就應該讓對方預先感受到接下來的結果，以緩和受打擊的程度。底下這封信示範了這種傳達不受歡迎消息的間接手法。

→ p.307

Dear

POLICY NO AR 3854

When we received your letter of 5 June we sent Mr John Watson to inspect and report on the damage caused by the fire. He has now submitted his report, which confirms your claim that the damage is extensive. He reports, however, that much of the stock damaged or destroyed was either obsolete or obsolescent.

We therefore regret that we cannot accept as a fair estimate of the loss the figure of £100,000 mentioned in your letter – a figure which we understand is based on the actual cost of the goods.

Our own estimate of the stock damaged or destroyed, based on present market values, does not exceed £60,000. We feel that this valuation is a very generous one, but are prepared to pay on the basis of it under the policy. Please let me know if you will accept this in full settlement of your claim for the value of the stock lost.

Yours sincerely

30.17　工人受傷索賠

(a) 請求給付理賠金

→ p.307

Dear Sirs

POLICY NO 56241

Our foreman, Mr James MacDonald, met with an accident on 2 March. He crushed his thumb when operating a machine. At the time we did not think the accident was serious enough to report: however, after an absence of 3 weeks Mr MacDonald has returned to his work and is still unable to carry on his normal duties.

We therefore wish to make a claim under the above policy. Please send the necessary claim form to me as soon as possible.

Yours faithfully

(b) 保險業者的回覆

→ p.308

Dear

POLICY NO 56241

收到索賠申請 —— Thank you for your letter of 27 March regarding your claim for the accident to Mr J MacDonald.

有技巧地對於所提 —— Under the terms of the policy his claim should have been submitted within 3 days of the accident. As more than 3 weeks have now passed, your claim for compensation under the policy has been forfeited.

承保人原本不必 理賠，但為表示 善意，還是予以 理賠。這裡技巧 的提出解釋 —— Nevertheless, as a gesture of goodwill we have decided to overlook this late submission. However we feel it should have been clear from Mr MacDonald's prolonged absence from work that his accident was more serious than you had thought and that there seems to be no good reason why the claim should not have been made earlier.

附上索賠申請表， 並清楚陳述未來 的立場 —— I enclose a claim form as requested but must emphasise that future claims cannot be entertained where the terms of the policy are not complied with.

Yours sincerely

30.18　疾病索賠的佐證

意外、疾病，或者其他類似案件的索賠必須要有醫師或就診機構開立的醫學證明作為佐證。

針對手術病患，保險業者會要求提具住院證明。底下這封信是一位病患請求醫生填寫保險業者所提供的表格。病患提供詳細資料，以及附上已寫好地址的信封，為繁忙的醫生提供相當體貼的協助。

→ p.308

Dear Dr Edwards

The London Life Insurance Co Ltd, of which I am a policy holder, have asked for completion of the enclosed claim form for benefits for the period I was in your hospital and later the Avala Nursing Home.

I have pencilled in the details requested on the side of the form which the company wish you to complete; this may assist you.

I have attached 4 accounts covering both hospital and nursing home accommodation for 6 weeks as follows:

> Hospital (23 April to 7 May 200—)
> Nursing Home (7 May to 2 June 200—)

The company would like you to return the completed claim form to them. I enclose an addressed envelope for this purpose.

Please give me a call if you have any queries.

Yours sincerely

海運保險

雖然還有其他重要的市場，但是大多數的國際海運保險業務是以倫敦為中心。堪稱海運保險中樞地位的是勞氏保險協會（Lloyd's），它是倫敦的一家保險公司，提供各類保險合約，但其海運保險業務特別活躍。勞氏保險協會的會員由保險公司〔或所謂的「保險業者」（underwriter）〕和保險經紀人共同組成。這些會員們以聯合承保的方式運作，專精於不同類型的風險。所有與保險協會會員合作的保險業務，都必須透過勞氏保險協會的經紀人。不願意這麼做的人，也可以雇請其他經紀人或自己直接處理。

在 1906 年海運保險法的規定下，所有的海運保險合約必須以保單形式呈現。海運保險的保單（marine policy）分為定額保單（valued policy）和不定額保單（unvalued policy），而這兩種可再細分為航程保單（voyage policy，或稱定程保單）、定期保單（time policy）、混合保單（mixed policy）、浮動保單（floating policy）或預約保單（open policy）。

所謂定額保單是依據事先同意的價值，並載明在保險單上；至於不
定額保單，其損失價值是根據損失（在投保金額的範圍內）當時的
價值而定。

航程保單就像包行程一樣，承保特定船隻的特定航程（例如倫敦至
墨爾本），而定期保險合約則像包時，承保最多 12 個月約定期間
（例如從 1997 年 4 月 5 日中午至 1998 年 4 月 5 日中午為止）的特定
船隻。混合保單則結合了航程和定期保險合約的特色。

承保範圍可以是全險，或者是包含了可以減輕保險業者部分風險的
一些條款。全險的保費會比有不承保條款的保單保費來得高。

30.19 投保全險

(a) 申請

→ p.309

Dear Sir/Madam

We wish to insure the following consignment against all risks for the sum of £10,000.

4 c/s Fancy Leather Goods, marked   AS
                                      1–4

These goods are now held at Number 2 Dock, Liverpool, waiting to be shipped by SS Rajputana due to leave for Bombay on Friday 23 June.

We require immediate cover as far as Bombay. Please let us have the policy as soon as it is ready. In the meantime please confirm that you hold the consignment covered.

Yours faithfully

(b) 回覆

→ p.309

Dear

Thank you for your letter of 16 June asking us to cover the consignment of 4 cases of fancy leather goods from Liverpool to Bombay.

The premium for this cover is at the rate of £2.30% of the declared value of £10,000. The policy is being prepared and will be sent to you within a few days. Meanwhile, I confirm that we hold the consignment covered as from today.

Yours sincerely

30.20　為碼頭上的貨物投保

→ p.310

Dear Sir

Please arrange to insure for one calendar month from today the following consignment ex SS Ansdell from Hamburg:

2 cases Cameras, marked ⟨AR⟩ value £30,000 and now held at Royal Victoria Dock.

Please confirm that you hold the consignment covered and, send the policy as soon as possible, together with your account for the premium.

Yours faithfully

浮動與預約承保合約

定期往來的國際貿易有時會用到所謂的浮動保單（floating policy），承保的是裝載於任何船隻運至任何港口（或約定的港口）的一些貨物。投保人先投保一個總保險額度，例如 100,000 英鎊，當每次運貨時，就用保險業者提供的特殊表格申報，保險業者會以保單副本記錄其價值，並且核發保險證明書（certificate of insurance，保單）代表託運貨物已獲得承保。當投保的保額全數用完時，就再投保一張新的保單。

浮動保險有時候會涉及預約（open）或通知（declaration）保單，但這些已經不常用，現在多半是使用長期保單，由預約承保合約（或稱預約承保書，open cover）所取代。預約承保合約擴大浮動保單的原則，並且承保所有於某一段期間內（通常是一年）的特定航程或交易，而不論其總價值為何，但每一筆均需在合約所載限度內。這種方式能夠保證不會有任何船期或交易因疏忽而未保險。

30.21　詢問預約承保合約的條款

(a) 詢問

→ p.310

> Dear Sirs
>
> Please quote your rate for an all-risks open policy for £100,000 to cover shipments of general merchandise by Manchester Liners Ltd, from Manchester and Liverpool to Atlantic ports in Canada and the United States.
>
> As shipments are due to begin on 30 June, please let us have your quotation by return.
>
> Yours faithfully

(b) 回覆

→ p.310

> Dear Mr Yates
>
> Thank you for your enquiry of yesterday. Our rate for a £100,000 A R open policy on general merchandise by Manchester Liners from Manchester and Liverpool to Atlantic ports in Canada and the United States is £2.10% of declared value.
>
> This is an exceptionally low rate and we trust you will give us the opportunity to handle your insurance business.
>
> Yours sincerely

(c) 接受

→ p.311

> Dear Mr Summers
>
> Thank you for your letter of 19 June quoting your rate for an open policy of £100,000 covering consignments on the routes named.
>
> The rate of £2.10% is satisfactory. Please prepare and send us the policy as soon as possible. Meanwhile please let us have your cover note and statement of charges for our first shipment under the policy, which is:
>
> 3 c/s General Merchandise (Textiles), marked ◇G◇ Value £2500.
>
> I hope to hear from you soon.
>
> Yours sincerely

30.22 申請預約承保合約

→ p.311

Dear Sirs

We will shortly be making regular shipments of fancy leather goods to South America by approved ships. I should be glad if you would issue an a/r open policy for, say, £75,000 to cover these shipments from our warehouse at the above address to port of destination.

All goods will be packed in wooden cases and despatched by road to Southampton and, less frequently, to Liverpool.

Yours faithfully

30.23 預約承保合約的出貨申報

一旦接受 30.22 的保單申請後，保險業者會寄一份原始保單給投保人，並且提供申報表格，投保人必須在每一次出貨時將表格填妥寄給保險業者。

→ p.311

Dear Sirs

POLICY NO 18752

Please note that under the above open policy, dated 18 March 200–, we have today shipped a third consignment, valued at £1620, by SS Durham Castle, due to sail from Southampton tomorrow. The necessary declaration form is enclosed.

This leaves an undeclared value on the policy of £48,380. Please confirm this figure as soon as possible.

Yours faithfully

30.24 預約承保合約續約（續 30.23）

→ p.312

Dear Sir

POLICY NO 18752

We enclose a completed form declaring a further consignment, valued £2325.

This will be the last full declaration under the above policy as the undeclared balance now stands at only £825, which will not be sufficient to cover our next consignment in December. Therefore please issue a new policy on the same terms and for the same amount, namely £75,000, as the current policy.

When we make the next shipment, we shall declare it against the present policy for £825 and against the new policy for the amount by which the value of the shipment exceeds this amount.

Yours faithfully

海損

英文的 average 用在海上保險稱爲「海損」，是指保險標的物遭遇損毀（編注：廣義包含分損及全損，狹義指分損）。至於 particular average，稱爲「單獨海損」，是指因爲意外而造成船隻或是特定貨物部分損壞，這類的損失是由遭受損壞的各財產持有人單獨負責（編注：若造成意外的原因不在投保的風險範圍內，保險公司不需理賠，即使是因所保風險造成，仍視約定條款而定）。另一個稱爲「共同海損」的 general average，則指當船隻及其貨物本身發生緊急危險時，爲共同利益而不得不或合理的進行處置所造成的損毀，例如爲了拯救暴風中的船隻，而將貨物丟入水中。這類的損失由各利害關係人按一定比例共同分擔。

根據規定，製造商或商人會爲貨物投保全險，取得一份含海損條款的水漬險（with average, WA）保單，也就是說，保險業者會承擔分損。若是不負責賠償單獨海損條款的平安險（free from particular average, FPA）保單，則保險業者只承擔全損。也因此，FPA 保單的保費比 WA 保單便宜。

車險

車主除了必須持有駕照外，根據法律規定，還必須投保造成第三人
死亡或受傷的第三人責任意外險，最高理賠金為 25 萬英鎊（英國
1988 年道路交通法）。至於為車子的損毀投保雖很常見，但不強制
規定。有一種「綜合汽車保險單」（comprehensive policy）的單一保
單，能夠涵蓋所有這類的風險。

30.25 保單續約

→ p.312

> Dear Mr Wrenshall
>
> POLICY NO M 346871
>
> Your policy and certificate of insurance as required by the Road Traffic Acts will
> expire at noon on 3 April next.
>
> To maintain the insurance in force instructions should be given to your broker not
> later than, but preferably 6 days before, the date on which the policy expires so that
> you may receive the new certificate of insurance in time. You will realise that it is an
> offence under the Road Traffic Acts to use a vehicle on the road without a current
> certificate of insurance.
>
> As a protection to you against any failure to observe the Acts I am enclosing a
> temporary cover note and certificate of insurance. However, please remember that
> this extension of cover applies only to that part of the policy which is necessary to
> comply with the requirements of the Road Traffic Acts, namely third party personal
> injury liability and damage to third party property.
>
> The temporary cover note should be kept carefully until the certificate of insurance
> reaches you.
>
> Yours sincerely

實用措詞

請求投保

【開頭】

1. Please quote your lowest All Risks rates for shipments of ... to ...
   請提供運送……到……（地點）的最低全險費率的報價。

2. Please hold us covered for the consignment referred to below (on the attached sheet).
   請替我們辦理下列（在附件）託運貨物的保險。

3. We should be glad if you would provide cover of £... on ..., in transit from ... to ...
   如果您能提供……貨物保額……（英鎊），從……（地點）到……（地點）的保險，我們會很感激。

4. We wish to renew this policy for the same amount and on the same terms as before.
   我們希望這份保單比照之前，以相同的保額與條款續約。

【結尾】

1. Please inform us on what terms this insurance can be arranged.
   請通知我們這份保險可以何種條款來投保。

2. Please send us the necessary proposal form.
   請寄給我們必要的要保書。

3. We leave the details to you, but wish to have the consignment covered against All Risks.
   我們將詳細資料留給你，但希望以全險方式來投保這批貨。

4. I shall be glad to receive your certificate of insurance as soon as possible.
   我希望能儘快收到您的保險證明。

回覆投保要求

【開頭】

1. Thank you for your letter of ... We quote below our terms for arranging cover for ...
   謝謝您……（日期）的來信，以下是我們對……保險的報價

2. Your letter regarding renewal of open policy number ... covering ...
   您來信提及有關續保編號……承保……的預約承保合約

【結尾】

1. The policy is being prepared and should reach you by ... Meanwhile I confirm that we are holding you covered.
   保單已在準備中，您應該可以在……（日期）前收到。同時已確認我們目前已經為您投保。

2. We undertake all classes of insurance and would welcome the opportunity to transact further business with you.
   我們提供所有型態的保險，也希望再有機會能與您合作。

請求理賠

【開頭】

1. I regret to report the loss of ... which is insured with you under the above policy.
   很抱歉向您報告您投保的……保單損失了……

2. I regret to report a fire in one of the bedrooms at this address.
   很抱歉報告該地址的其中一間臥室發生火災。

3. I have completed and enclose the form of claim for loss of ...
   隨函附上已填妥的……損失的索賠表格。

【結尾】

1. Please let me know any details you need from me when I submit my claim.
   在我提出索賠申請時，請讓我知道您需要的所有詳細資料。

2. If you will make out your claim on the enclosed form we will attend to it immediately.
   如果您能完成所附的申請表，我們會立刻處理您的索賠申請。

3. Your claim will be carefully considered when we receive the information requested.
   在收到要求提供的資料後，我們會謹慎考慮您的索賠申請。

附 錄

口語和書信形式的稱謂

底下的表格列出許多對官員、外交官、宗教領袖、皇室及英國貴族頭銜的正式
稱謂。這些稱謂依書寫信件的收件人及稱謂，或是非外交性的會談及正式場合
的介紹等等而有所不同。

雖然在外交或公開場合，Sir 被廣泛用在正式的書寫稱謂或口頭招呼，但它不
適合用在宗教或具特定頭銜的人士身上。另外，Madam 或 Ma'am 較少用來稱
呼女性，但可被接受，特別是針對高級官員（例如女性官員）。這種規則亦適
用於外國的高級官員。

身分	書信收件人與地址	書信稱謂	口頭招呼	正式介紹
President of the United States（美國總統）	The President The White House Washington, DC 20500	Dear Mr (or Madam) President	Mr (or Madam) President	The President or the President of the United States
Former President（前總統）	The Honorable Jack Kimball Address	Dear Mr Kimball	Mr Kimball	The Honorable Jack Kimball
Vice President（副總統）	The Vice President Executive Office Building Washington, DC 20501	Dear Mr (or Madam) Vice President	Mr (or Madam) Vice President	The Vice President or the Vice President of the United States
Cabinet members（內閣閣員）	The Honorable John (or Jane) Smith The Secretary of xxxxxxxxxx or The Attorney General Washington, DC	Dear Mr (or Madam) Secretary	Mr (or Madam) Secretary	The Secretary of xxxxxxxxx

身分	書信收件人與地址	書信稱謂	口頭招呼	正式介紹
Chief Justice（審判長；首席法官）	The Chief Justice The Supreme Court Washington, DC 20543	Dear Mr（or Madam）Justice or Dear Mr（or Madam）Chief Justice	Mr (or Madam) Chief Justice	The Chief Justice
United States Senator（參議院議員）	The Honorable John（or Jane）Smith United States Senate Washington, DC 20510	Dear Senator Smith	Senator Smith	Senator Smith from Nebraska
Ambassador（大使）	The Honorable John（or Jane）Smith Ambassador of the United States American Embassy Address	Dear Mr（or Madam）Ambassador	Mr (or Madam) Ambassador	The American Ambassador The Ambassador of The United States of America
Consul-General（總領事）	The Honorable John（or Jane）Smith American Consul General Address	Dear Mr（or Mrs, Ms）Smith	Mr (or Mrs, Ms) Smith	Mr (or Mrs, Ms) Smith
Foreign Ambassador（外國大使）	His (or Her) Excellency John (or Jane) Smith The Ambassador of xxxxxxxxxxx Address	Excellency or Dear Mr（or Madam）Ambassador	Excellency; or Mr (or Madam) Ambassador	The Ambassador of xxxxxxxxxx
Secretary-General of the United Nations（聯合國祕書長）	His (or Her) Excellency Jack (or Jane) Smith Secretary-General of the United Nations United Nations Plaza New York, NY 10017	Dear Mr（or Madam）Secretary-General	Mr (or Madam) Secretary-General	The Secretary-General of the United Nations
Governor（州長；總督）	The Honorable Jack (or Jane) Smith Governor of xxxxxxxxxxx State Capitol Address	Dear Governor Smith	Governor or Governor Smith	The Governor of Maine: Governor Smith of Washington

▶

身分	書信收件人與地址	書信稱謂	口頭招呼	正式介紹
State legislators（州議員）	The Honorable Jack (or Jane) Smith Address here	Dear Mr (or Mrs, Ms) Smith	Mr (or Mrs, Ms) Smith	Mr (or Mrs, Ms) Smith
Judges（法官）	The Honorable John Smith Justice, Appellate Division Supreme Court of the State of xxxxxxxxxxx Address	Dear Judge Smith	Justice or Judge Smith; Madam Justice or Judge Smith	The Honorable Jack (or Jane) Smith; Mr Justice Smith or Judge Smith; Madam Justice Smith or Judge Smith
Mayor（市長）	The Honorable Jack (or Jane) Smith; His (or Her) Honor the Mayor City Hall Address	Dear Mayor Smith	Mayor Smith; Mr (or Madam) Mayor; Your Honor	Mayor Smith; The Mayor
The Pope（教宗）	His Holiness, the Pope or His Holiness, Pope John XII Vatican City Rome, Italy	Your Holiness or Most Holy Father	Your Holiness or Most Holy Father	His Holiness, the Holy Father; the Pope; the Pontiff
Cardinals（樞機主教）	His Eminence, Martin Cardinal Brown, Archbishop of xxxxxxxxx Address	Your Eminence or Dear Cardinal Brown	Your Eminence or Cardinal Brown	His Eminence, Cardinal Brown
Bishops（主教）	The Most Reverend Martin Brown, Bishop (or Archbishop) of xxxxxxxxxx Address here	Your Excellency or Dear Bishop (Archbishop) Brown	Your Excellency or Bishop (Archbishop) Brown	
Monsignor〔蒙席（比神父高一級）〕	The Reverend Monsignor Nigel Frangoulis Address	Reverend Monsignor or Dear Monsignor	Monsignor Frangoulis or Monsignor	Monsignor Frangoulis
Priest〔神職者（牧師、教士、僧侶、祭司）〕	The Reverend Jack Smith Address	Reverend Father or Dear Father Smith	Father or Father Smith	Father Smith

身分	書信收件人與地址	書信稱謂	口頭招呼	正式介紹
Brother （教友）	Brother Jack or Brother Jack Smith Address	Dear Brother Jack or Dear Brother	Brother Jack or Brother	Brother Jack
Sister （修女）	Sister Linda Wright	Dear Sister Linda Wright or Dear Sister	Sister Linda Wright or Sister	Sister Linda Wright
Protestant Clergy 〔牧師（新教）〕	The Reverend John (or Jane) James*	Dear Dr (or Mr, Ms) James	Dr (or Mr, Ms) James	The Reverend (or Dr) Jack James
Bishop (Episcopal) 〔主教（聖公會）〕	The Right Reverend Jack James* Bishop of xxxxxxx Address	Dear Bishop James	Bishop James	The Right Reverend Jack James, Bishop of xxxxxxxxxxx
Rabbi 〔教士（猶太教）〕	Rabbi Arnold (or Amanda) Schwartz Address	Dear Rabbi Schwartz	Rabbi Schwartz or Rabbi	Rabbi Arnold Schwartz
King or Queen 〔國王或王后（女王）〕	His (Her) Majesty King (Queen) xxxxxxxxxxx Address (letters traditionally are normally sent via the private secretary)	Your Majesty; Sir or Madam	Varies depending on titles, holdings, etc	
Other royalty （王室）	His (Her) Royal Highness, the Prince (Princess) of xxxxxxx	Your Royal Highness	Your Royal Highness; Sir or Madam	His (Her) Royal Highness, the Duke (Duchess) of xxxxxx
Duke/Duchess （公爵／公爵夫人）	His/Her Grace, the Duke (Duchess) of xxxxxxx	My Lord Duke/ Madam or Dear Duke of xxxx/Dear Duchess	Your Grace or Duke/Duchess	His/Her Grace, the Duke/Duchess of xxxx
Marquess/ Marchioness （侯爵／侯爵夫人）	The Most Honorable the Marquess (Marchioness) of Newport	My Lord/Madam or Dear Lord/Lady Newport	Lord/Lady Newport	Lord/Lady Newport
Earl （伯爵）	The Right Honorable the Earl of Bangor	My Lord or Dear Lord Bangor	Lord Bangor	Lord Bangor

▶

身分	書信收件人與地址	書信稱謂	口頭招呼	正式介紹
Countess (wife of an Earl) 〔伯爵夫人（伯爵之妻）〕	The Right Honorable the Countess of Bangor	Madam or Dear Lady Bangor	Lady Bangor	Lady Bangor
Viscount/ Viscountess （子爵／子爵夫人）	The Right Honorable the Viscount (Viscountess) Manson	My Lord/Lady or Dear Lord/Lady Manson	Lord/Lady Manson	Lord/Lady Manson
Baron/Baroness （男爵／男爵夫人）	The Right Honourable Lord/Lady Grey	My Lord/Madam or Dear Lord/Lady Grey	Lord/Lady Grey	Lord/Lady Grey
Baronet （準男爵）	Sir Jack Smith, Bt.	Dear Sir or Dear Sir Jack	Sir Jack	Sir Jack Smith
Wife of Baronet （男爵夫人）	Lady Smith	Dear Madam or Dear Lady Smith	Lady Smith	Lady Smith
Knight （爵士；騎士）	Sir Elton John	Dear Sir or Dear Sir John	Sir John	Sir Elton John
Wife of Knight （爵士夫人）	Dear Madam or Dear Lady John	Lady John	Lady John	

國家圖書館出版品預行編目資料

英文商業書信&電子郵件寫作技巧與範例 /雪麗‧泰
勒（Shirley Taylor）著；劉秋枝, 羅明珠譯 -- 初版
--臺北市：臺灣培生教育, 2010.12
　面；　　公分
譯自: Model Business Letters, E-mails & Other
　Business Documents, 6th ed.
ISBN 978-986-280-001-0 (精裝附光碟片)

1.商業書信　2.商業英文　3.商業應用文　4.電子郵件

493.6　　　　　　　　　　　　99018502

英文商業書信&電子郵件寫作技巧與範例
Model Business Letters, E-mails & Other Business Documents (6th Edition)

作　　　　　者	雪麗‧泰勒（Shirley Taylor）
譯　　　　　者	劉秋枝、羅明珠
發　　行　　人	Isa Wong
主　　　　　編	李佩玲
責　任　編　輯	瞿中蓮
協　力　編　輯	丘慧薇、陳慧莉
封　面　設　計	黃聖文
美　編　印　務	陳君瑞
行　銷　企　畫	楊震宇
發行所／出版者	台灣培生教育出版股份有限公司
	地址／台北市重慶南路一段 147 號 5 樓
	電話／02-2370-8168　　傳真／02-2370-8169
	網址／www.pearson.com.tw
	E-mail／reader.tw@pearson.com
香　港　總　經　銷	培生教育出版亞洲股份有限公司
	地址／香港鰂魚涌英皇道 979 號(太古坊康和大廈 2 樓)
	電話／(852)3181-0000　傳真／(852)2564-0955
	E-mail／msip.hk@pearson.com
台　灣　總　經　銷	地址／237 台北縣土城市忠承路 89 號 6 樓
	電話／02-2268-3489　　傳真／02-2269-6560
學　校　訂　書　專　線	(02)2370-8168 轉 8866
版　　　　　次	2010 年 12 月初版一刷
書　　　　　號	TB011
I　S　B　N	978-986-280-001-0
定　　　　　價	新台幣 750 元

版權所有‧翻印必究

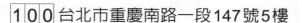

感謝您購買本書，希望您提供寶貴的意見，讓我們與您有更密切的互動。

★資料請填寫完整，才可參加抽獎哦！

讀者資料

姓名：＿＿＿＿＿＿＿＿＿＿＿＿ 性別：＿＿＿＿ 出生年月日：＿＿＿＿＿＿＿＿＿.

電話：(O)＿＿＿＿＿＿＿＿ (H)＿＿＿＿＿＿＿＿ (Mo)＿＿＿＿＿＿＿＿.

傳眞：(O)＿＿＿＿＿＿＿＿ (H)＿＿＿＿＿＿＿＿ .

E-mail：＿＿＿＿＿＿＿＿＿＿＿＿＿＿＿＿＿＿＿＿＿＿＿＿＿.

地址：＿＿＿＿＿＿＿＿＿＿＿＿＿＿＿＿＿＿＿＿＿＿＿＿＿＿＿.

教育程度：

□國小　□國中　□高中　□大專　□大學以上

職業：

1.學生　□

2.教職　□教師　□教務人員　□班主任　□經營者　□其他：＿＿＿＿＿＿

　任職單位：□學校　□補教機構　□其他：＿＿＿＿＿＿＿

　教學經歷：□幼兒英語　□兒童英語　□國小英語　□國中英語　□高中英語
　　　　　　□成人英語

3.社會人士　□工　□商　□資訊　□服務　□軍警公職　□出版媒體　□其他＿＿＿＿.

從何處得知本書：

□逛書店　□報章雜誌　□廣播電視　□親友介紹　□書訊　□廣告函　□其他＿＿＿＿.

對我們的建議：

＿＿＿＿＿＿＿＿＿＿＿＿＿＿＿＿＿＿＿＿＿＿＿＿＿＿＿

＿＿＿＿＿＿＿＿＿＿＿＿＿＿＿＿＿＿＿＿＿＿＿＿＿＿＿

＿＿＿＿＿＿＿＿＿＿＿＿＿＿＿＿＿＿＿＿＿＿＿＿＿＿＿

＿＿＿＿＿＿＿＿＿＿＿＿＿＿＿＿＿＿＿＿＿＿＿＿＿＿＿

感謝您的回函，我們每個月將抽出幸運讀者，致贈精美禮物，得獎名單可至本公司網站查詢。

讀者服務專線：02-2370-8168#8866

http://www.pearson.com.tw　　　E-mail:reader.tw@pearson.com